LUNA A ᴐ ɪHE LIE

MARIANA ZAPATA

Book Cover Design by Letitia Hasser, Romantic Book Affairs

Formatting by Indie Formatting Services

Editing by Hot Tree Editing and My Brother's Editor

❀ Created with Vellum

In memory of my Tia Evi
Love you always and forever

CHAPTER ONE

It was the "Goddamn it, Luna," that had me prying an eyelid open.

But it was the rumbled, deep voice saying it that had me aiming my eyeball in the direction of the man standing about ten feet away.

The man who had his hands on his hips as he frowned.

At me.

If I had to guess why I was the lucky winner of that mouth being turned down, it might have been because I'd had my eyes closed for... I glanced at my old but faithful G-Shock watch... the last twenty minutes.

Who was I kidding? I would have bet all of my money that was exactly why.

When I had seen him that morning bent over the opened hood of an early 1950s GMC truck, a hint of a white compression shirt showing beneath his coveralls, I'd known he was in a bad mood to begin with. Not that anyone was ever in a good mood on a Friday morning, but... the man glaring at me was always in a bad mood when he wore white. It was a fact.

It definitely didn't help that, when I had brought him his cup of coffee that morning, he'd asked me, "Did you decide?"

And like every time he had asked the same question, I had given him the same reply I always had and would. "Ah, *no.*"

You'd figure he'd have finally started to expect my reply after the seven hundred-ish times of asking the same question and getting the same answer, but it still irritated him after all this time.

And while it wasn't completely out of the norm for him —my boss, one *of* my two bosses, if you wanted to be technical—to say "Goddamn it, Luna," it wasn't common either. I didn't like to get into trouble. My friends had said more than a few times that I was allergic to having people mad or disappointed with me. It was a curse I hadn't managed to shake off, no matter how many times it worked against me.

I couldn't help but give the man with his hands on his hips and a frown on his face a smile. I thought about winking at him because I knew how much winking irritated him, but I didn't. It was a white shirt day after all, and I had to conserve my energy where I could when I still had at least eight hours left before I got to go home for the weekend.

"Yes?" I went with as a response to his *goddamn it, Luna* instead of *what did I do?* I hadn't done anything wrong by having my eyes closed for a few minutes.

...technically.

Ripley narrowed his eyes, managing to level his gaze solely on me, ignoring the other seven full-time employees seated around the break room where we had our weekly meetings every Friday. At nine in the morning, two hours after I usually clocked into work, every employee at Cooper's Collision and Customs waddled in to listen to our bosses go over things like upcoming projects, current projects, status updates, issues, grievances, arguing over who was overdoing it with the air freshener in the bathroom....

It wasn't exactly fun, and it wasn't a secret we only suffered through the meeting because we got paid to. It was hard enough to stay awake on any given morning during the work week, but on a Friday with the weekend only hours away, plus the heat of so many bodies sitting around? It was almost impossible *not* to close your eyes.

Staying up late past midnight to watch a scary movie with Lily didn't help any either, but when she had asked, I hadn't been able to find it in me to tell her no. Our time together was running out, and I knew one day I would regret not taking advantage of every opportunity we had to hang out. I'd learned that lesson with my other two sisters.

But I was pretty sure that the man glaring at me right then didn't know or care about any of that, and his next words confirmed it.

"Didn't we talk about you taking a nap during our meetings?" Ripley drawled the question in a tone that wasn't exactly nice.

Not that it ever really was.

I kept one eye on him as I stayed in the same position I'd been in when he had called me out—slumped over the table with an elbow planted on it, chin propped up on my open hand. Instead of both my eyes being closed though, I only had one open. I kept the smile on my face as I told him the answer we were both totally aware of, "Yes, we talked about it." Just in case he forgot what exactly he'd said, I reminded him. "You told me not to."

Because he had. *Luna, you've gotta quit going to sleep*

during the goddamn meetings. If you wanna take a nap, wait eight fucking hours until you get home, got it? We'd had that conversation behind closed doors and with Mr. Cooper—the man who had hired me, my original boss and owner, and as of three years ago, the now co-owner of Cooper's Collision and Customs—present.

I had got his message, and I respected it.

My boss, at least the one frowning at me, didn't physically react to my answer. He didn't even blink as he confirmed what we obviously both knew, "Yeah. That's exactly what I said."

Beside him, but hanging back verbally, Mr. Cooper coughed but didn't say a word. I didn't take it personally. I'd overheard enough of their fights to know it had taken them long enough to just get to this point in their work relationship—disagreeing with each other but not arguing over it in front of us. I was pretty sure I wasn't the only one who didn't miss that phase in our lives at CCC. For a while there, we had all mastered sitting as still as possible and staring at the wall, pretending we were somewhere else.

I had gotten that Ph.D. a long time ago.

"And nobody gets paid to be taking a nap during our meetings," Rip finished, like it wasn't common sense, hands still on his hips. That rough face, which was still shaped into the form of a scowl, somehow added a nonverbal touch of *not even you* to the end of his statement, like I expected some kind of special treatment.

I didn't and I never had, despite whatever he thought when he was in a bad mood. It... *not even you*... was just only... *me*. The employee who came in earlier than everyone else, stayed later than everyone else, and had only called out of work a handful of times in the last nine years. The person who had never said no to extra hours.

But it was and always had been my choice to do all those things, and I knew it. That's why I kept my mouth closed. I could have said no when they asked. It had been my decision to stay late and come in on the weekends each time I did.

You didn't jump off a bridge, break your legs, and then blame the friend who dared you to do it for why you were in the hospital.

Taking responsibility for my actions and not blaming other people for things I brought upon myself was one of the few positive lessons I'd learned from my family, even if it was something they hadn't tried to teach me on purpose.

I cut that train of thought off real quick. Some things and people were so acidic, even thinking about them could destroy. I was going to choose to be happy, and that meant not thinking about old crap. Today was going to be a good day, and so was tomorrow, and the day after that, and the day after that.

It was with that thought that I kept the smile on my face and let it linger on the man staring at me. It took a lot more than Rip in a white shirt to make me frown or hurt my feelings. It took a lot more than thinking of certain people for all of a second to do it either.

The point was: I was tired. I'd closed my eyes. He'd called me out on it. There was nothing to get upset about.

"Luna," Rip said my name in that ridiculously low voice that had caught me totally off-guard the first time I'd heard it. "We understand each other? No fucking naps during the meeting. It's not that hard to get, is it?"

From a couple chairs down, someone snorted, but I knew from the sound of it who it was, so I didn't bother wasting my time even looking in that direction, much less letting his amusement at me getting put on the spot bother me.

I still kept the corners of my mouth up high on my face as I nodded just once at my boss. I understood him loud and clear. I also understood the look that Mr. Cooper was giving him from his spot on Ripley's left. He wasn't supposed to be cussing at me, or any of us at the shop. That was something else the two owners of one of the most successful auto body shops in Houston, Texas had spent a lot of time talking about in the office when they didn't know I was eavesdropping....

Which was all the time.

Not that they knew that.

At least I hoped they didn't, but it wasn't like they were subtle or secretive about it either.

IT ALL STARTED three years ago.

Cooper's Collision and Customs had been a family-owned business that had been started by Mr. Cooper's father in the 1940s. The shop had been successful for a lifetime by the time I got my job almost six years before that day that set everything into motion. Every employee at CCC got paid fairly, got paid every other week, and Mr. Cooper had been—and still was—just about the best boss in the world. In my opinion, he was one of the best men in the entire world period, and I doubted anyone I worked with would argue that.

One day, everything had been normal. We'd had one boss. There had been ten of us. Everything had been fine. And the next day, I got to work, ignored the classic Ford pickup parked in the tiny customer lot upfront, and then overheard Mr. Cooper's familiar voice and a much deeper one in the office at seven in the morning, talking about how they were going to split profits and where the business would move to.

It had shocked the hell out of me. Then again, I wasn't sure how it couldn't have shocked the hell out of me. Splitting profits? Moving a business that had been in the same place for the last eighty-ish years? The shop had always been busy. Things had seemed to be fine.

Honestly, even now, I still didn't get why Mr. Cooper had decided to take someone else on to handle his business.

I had listened to them talking as long as I could before I'd taken off to pretend like nothing had happened, even though part of me was freaking out big-time at the implications of what their conversation meant. It wasn't until a couple months later, months where I'd kept my mouth closed in case I hadn't eavesdropped correctly when Mr. Cooper had dropped the bomb on everyone during a Friday morning meeting.

"I have some big news," the angel of a man had told all of us. I was probably the only person who had noticed how badly his hands had been shaking then because no one else had ever brought it up afterward. "We're moving the shop."

Everyone had started talking at once, but Mr. Cooper ignored them and kept on talking.

"We've needed more space for years now. We're too cramped. You're all aware of that. We're moving to a forty-thousand-square-foot facility...." He'd said some other things I couldn't remember as he sat there, hands tucked into the pockets of his worn jeans. Then, and only then, had he taken a great big breath and dropped the *real* bomb on everyone—everyone except me, at least. "That's not the only thing growing either. With more room, we can handle more business."

Everyone had stopped talking at that point, and I'd just sat there with my hands between my thighs, pressing my lips together as my stomach flip-flopped at the knowledge that I hadn't imagined that conversation months ago.

"Lucas Ripley will be joining the team," Mr. Cooper, a man we all loved, had breathed out, almost like he wasn't sure about the news either. Or maybe I'd just been imagining it. "He'll be a co-owner for Cooper's and will be growing and handling the restoration part of the business from here on out." He had swallowed hard, crossed his arms over his chest, and asked, "Any questions?"

Luckily for me, everyone had been too busy freaking out by the mention of the shop moving, expanding, and the new owner to notice that I hadn't asked a single question.

None of us had wondered who Lucas Ripley was or why he was joining the business.

And the next day, when I got to work and found a semi-familiar truck parked right next to Mr. Cooper's beautifully restored Mustang, I had figured out real quick who the car belonged to. Because in the years I'd worked for Mr. Cooper, no one else but he and I showed up so early.

No one.

And when I had gone into the building and walked by the office to head to the space where I spent most of my time painting, doing bodywork, or detailing, I hadn't been totally surprised to find Mr. Cooper behind his desk, talking to a man sitting on the other side of it.

The man was huge, and the long-sleeved shirt he had on in the middle of July was basically a second skin. It covered everything from his wrists up over his collarbone, only managing to show off a few inches of tattooed skin on his neck. Maybe, I had thought, it was one of those shirts that kept a person cool.

As I'd stopped right by the doorway, I'd noticed that, even in profile, the man had the grouchiest, meanest face I had ever seen in my life. I wasn't sure how to explain it, but he did. And he was straight-up gorgeous.

And I mean just freaking *masculine*. Like just testosterone and whatever the heck else was all man.

I saw gorgeous men in the wild every once in a while. I saw them online even more often. But *that one*, the one who I instinctively knew was going to be my new boss, the one sitting in the chair swallowing it whole with shoulders and an upper body that belonged on a professional wrestler, had to beat most of those men I'd seen in the past. He wasn't what my sisters would have drooled over. He didn't look like a model. His cheekbones were broad, his bone structure square, and his mouth hadn't even been exactly full. Yet packaged together it was an unforgettable face.

A stunning face.

And I'd known instantly that his face and those thigh-sized biceps and calf-sized forearms that were covered in a tight long-sleeved shirt were going to haunt me.

And *that* had surprised me.

Then it had irritated me for a second as I thought about how much I didn't *want* a new boss. Hot or not. I loved Mr. Cooper, and I knew where I stood with him. He made me feel safe. This new man was a stranger I wasn't sure what to do with. He wasn't just going to be someone I might casually work with.

Looking back on it though, there had been no way for me to know then how much Lucas Ripley would haunt me in the future. I'd had no idea as I had walked into that room to introduce myself what he would end up owing me.

And I definitely hadn't known how much that debt would end up bothering him day in and day out.

What I did know and remember was how I'd gone to stand at the doorway to the original Cooper's Collision and Customs office and waved and smiled at the two men inside.

"Luna," Mr. Cooper had greeted me immediately, grinning so wide that, if I hadn't known him so well, I would have missed how tense his shoulders were. "Good morning."

"Morning, Mr. Cooper," I had replied before turning my attention to the giant man sitting on the other side of the desk.

The huge man had looked at me, looked back at Mr. Cooper, then finally glanced back in my direction. That face, mean-looking because of the tightness along his jawline and the constant notch between his eyebrows, hadn't changed at all. He hadn't smiled back at me or even tried to look friendly. He'd just... looked.

In the blink of an eye, that look turned into a glare.

And my heart did what it always did when I met someone who didn't want to like me—it made the rest of me *want* this person to like me, this maybe-possibly new boss of mine.

That was another curse I hadn't been able to shake off even after all these years; the need to be liked. Realistically, I knew I could and would survive someone not being a Luna Allen fan, but... I had always tried. I could blame Those People I Wasn't Going to Think About for that need, if I ever let myself think about it.

But I wouldn't.

"Hi," I had said, taking a step in and immediately putting my hand out between us. "I'm Luna."

And Mr. Cooper, being Mr. Cooper, had said, "Ripley,

this is Luna Allen. She does all our paint and helps out a lot with bodywork and detailing if we need her. Luna, this is Ripley, my... business partner."

I had totally picked up on his hesitation at referring to the new man as his business partner, but I hadn't thought much of it afterward. Especially not when my new boss took his sweet time raising his hand from where it had been resting on his thigh and slipped his long fingers and broad palm against mine, giving it a squeeze for a moment before releasing it almost as quickly. His eyes had narrowed just a little, but I had noticed, and it had just triggered that need in me even more.

"It's nice to meet you," I had told him, drawing my hand back.

My newest boss had watched me carefully; his eyes— this shade somewhere between an unreal blue and green— had slid back to Mr. Cooper one more time before returning to me.

I hadn't been prepared for the question that came out of his mouth almost immediately. "You old enough to work here?" he'd asked in what I was pretty sure was the closest thing to a rumbling voice I'd ever heard in person.

I couldn't help but glance at my longtime boss, but that was because he'd asked basically the same thing right before offering me a job when I'd been seventeen. So I smiled even wider when I put my attention back on the man with dark-colored tattoos that went up to his jaw. "*Yes.*"

He didn't miss a beat, and those blue-green eyes, which seemed to pop beneath short but super curly black eyelashes, narrowed again. "How long you worked here?"

I didn't miss a beat either. "Six years."

That got me a blink before that deep, raspy voice asked, "What do you know about paint?"

What did I know about paint?

I'd almost lost my smile then, but I had managed not to. He wasn't the first person to ask me that kind of question. I was one of the few females I'd ever met who did auto body paint. As a kid, I would never have thought that painting cars and parts was what I would end up doing for a living— much less, that I would grow to love it and be pretty damn good at it, if I did say so myself—but life was crazy that way.

So I told this man, who was making the same mistake just about everyone I had ever met had made too, the truth. "I know everything about paint." And I'd smiled at him because I wasn't being cocky. I was just telling him the truth, and I didn't miss the way Mr. Cooper smiled as I did it.

The new man blinked again and his voice got even lower as he raised thick, dark brown eyebrows at me. "What do you know about bodywork?" he'd shot off next, referring to the act of fixing minor or major physical imperfections or damage to a vehicle.

I had still managed to keep my smile on my face. "Almost as much." He hadn't known it then, but Mr. Cooper had gotten me started on bodywork before moving me over to paint years ago. I'd been pretty good at it too.

But this man who had become my new boss had glanced at Mr. Cooper sitting on the other side of the desk for a moment before returning his gaze to me and asking in a tight voice I wasn't sure what to think of, "What do you know about classic cars?"

And, *shit*.

Even I glanced at Mr. Cooper, but he was busy looking over at the other man to see that I wanted his attention and support. So I had said the first thing I thought of. "Some. Not everything, but not nothing."

The man I had thought was gorgeous moments before pressed that not-thin but not-full mouth together. Then he'd asked, "Do you know how to weld?"

Did I know how to weld? I had narrowed my eyes at him. "Is this a test?"

This man I had barely met didn't hesitate to repeat his question the exact same way he had originally presented it.

And I *knew*, I knew he was testing me. So I had shrugged and told him the truth. "I know the basics."

That mouth twisted to the side as that big, bulky body leaned back in the chair he sat in. A chin covered in dark brown stubble with hints of silvery gray mixed in tipped an inch higher than it had been a moment before, and that confirmed he was still trying to test me. "If you were doing bodywork and found lead, what would you do?"

Out of the corner of my eye, I saw Mr. Cooper sigh and cover his eyes with his hand. It was the first of many, many times I would watch him do the same thing over the next three years, but that's another story.

Luckily—and I'd known right then how lucky I had been to know the answer because I was pretty sure he would have fired me if I hadn't—I told him the right answer. "You can't weld over lead. You have to burn it out."

The man had leaned back in his seat, crossed his arms over his huge chest, and said, totally seriously, totally condescendingly—the same way he would a hundred times over the next few years—"You'll do."

I'd do.

And I had.

* * *

THAT HAD BEEN YEARS AGO, and since then, I'd figured

out how to deal with Lucas Ripley, or Rip, or Ripley, as he had told us to call him way back then.

So when he asked me if I understood him or not regarding his policy on taking a nap, I said the only thing I could have. "I get it." And I said it about as happily as I could, even knowing that my response was going to irritate him even more than he already was.

But life was all about the little things, and getting a rise out of Rip without exactly pissing him off was a game I liked playing more than I should have. Every once in a while, if the situation was right and he was wearing his navy-colored compression shirt, I could get a smirk out of him. And on really rare occasions, I might sneak a quick half-smile out of him that was gone in a blink of an eye later.

And if my little heart sighed over that sneaky little smile or smirk, it was nobody else's business but mine.

And my siblings.

And my best friend.

But that was it.

I didn't let myself think too much of getting him to make an expression that wasn't a scowl, a mildly annoyed one, or an eye roll. I definitely wasn't going to think about the blank face he made that I might have kind of loved and hated at the same time. Nope.

But anyway.

It had only taken him two days of working at CCC for him to ask—with a grumpy side look—if I always smiled all the time. But it had been Mr. Cooper who had answered him that I did. Because I did.

In that moment in the break room though, I opened my other eye and full-on smiled at the man wearing a long-sleeved, almost turtleneck shirt that clung to every enormous muscle on his barrel chest. "But I wasn't sleeping. I heard everything you said," I finished explaining.

I wasn't surprised when the man who had honestly only gotten more attractive over the years, even as the crease between his eyebrows had gotten deeper and the grooves bracketing his mouth had gotten more pronounced, shifted that nearly forty-one-year-old body toward me even more. "Yeah? What'd I say?" he tried to challenge.

He could be such a pain in the butt sometimes; he really did deserve me messing with him. Someone had to.

Slightly to the side of him, Mr. Cooper looked up at the ceiling, and I swear he started mouthing the beginning of an Our Father. Two of the guys sitting around the table started muttering under their breaths. I caught a hint of "micromanaging asshole" come out of one of them, and Rip must have too because his eyes immediately swept around the room like he was looking for whoever said it.

The last time he'd done that, two people had gotten fired, and I had liked them.

"First you talked about lunch breaks taking too long," I blurted out. "Then you were talking about how the shop vac needs to be emptied after it's been used because it isn't your job."

Cutting in must have done the trick to get him to forget what he'd been doing, because I'd only gotten a few words in by the time I was back to being the focus of his mostly unwanted attention. And that was because he was wearing that white shirt, and I usually had a 40 percent success rate of getting out of conversations with him not griping at me on white days. Gray shirt days were about 70 percent. Navy shirt days were about eighty-five. On navy days, I knew I could slap him on the back and not get even a side-look. Those days were my favorites.

I made my smile widen and even raised my eyebrows at him, hoping for the best. "Is that good enough, or did you want me to try and give you a word-by-word replay of what you said? Because I probably can, boss." He could suck on those facts.

That face that I snuck glances at way more often than I had any business looking at didn't change at all. He didn't even blink. Then again, he should have known I hadn't been lying. To be fair though, I didn't think Rip trusted anyone at the shop. Not even Mr. Cooper, if the arguments I had overheard meant anything, and they had to mean something. The last time I'd been around people who argued that much, they had genuinely hated each other.

I let my lips pull back so I could show him my teeth as I forced a big fake smile at him, and beside me, my coworker snickered.

My boss—this boss—still wasn't amused.

But he didn't say "Goddamn it, Luna" again, so I was going to take it as a win.

"As I was saying," Rip finally continued on after maybe two seconds of staring at me with his expressionless face, turning his attention back to the middle of the room and banishing me from his train of thought—he had a lot of prac-tice doing that, "just because we have a cleaning crew coming in doesn't mean you got a right to leave a mess. Nobody's here to be anybody else's maid or babysitter."

Setting my hand over my mouth, I hid my yawn as I glanced over at the coworker sitting to my right, staring blankly at the wall. The forty-five-year-old was breathing hard but steadily, his mouth just loose enough for me to know he'd fallen asleep with it open. To my left, my other coworker, a thirty-year-old who had been at the shop almost as long as I had, was jiggling his foot. Noticing me looking in his direction, he slid a smirk in Rip's direction, shaking his head as he did so. *Jesus*, he mouthed.

It was moments like these that I really remembered just how lucky I was to have this job, how lucky I was that almost all the guys I worked with were nice and treated me well.

At least now they were.

It had taken a lot of the men getting fired or quitting, until CCC got to the employees it currently had, but I couldn't have been happier. This job, when I'd been seventeen, had been one of the last ones I'd tried applying for. I almost hadn't. The ad to work at what I'd assumed was a mechanic shop hadn't exactly been what I'd been hoping for. But at that point in my life, when I had met Mr. Cooper, he had given me two choices: work for him or... not.

I had taken the work, because when you're seventeen with two hundred dollars left, no idea of what you could do with your life, just knowing you couldn't go back to what you'd had before, and someone gives you a chance... the first real chance anyone has ever given you...

You can't say no.

I owed Mr. Cooper everything. I really did. He had changed my life more than anyone else ever could or would, and I had thanked him daily for years. I was sure he had no idea what to do with me back then, but he'd offered me a job, given me a home, given me a fighting chance, and everything since was history.

My phone vibrated from my pocket, and I slipped my hand inside to pull it out just as Ripley started saying something about being more time efficient. I kept an eye on him as he stood there, those brawny arms crossed over his chest, and set it on top of my thigh. I wasn't about to get caught with it out, especially not after already irritating him this early in the day. We still had the whole day left ahead of us.

I kept my gaze on my boss as I unlocked the screen from muscle memory. Rip was still going on, his attention lingering around the room like he was making sure none of us were falling asleep on him. I glanced down and saw that I had gotten a new text message from a number that wasn't saved on my contact list. I had thought for sure it would be one of my sisters, but it wasn't. I didn't let myself get disappointed over it.

One eye on Rip, I opened the message and read it as fast as I could.

210-555-1230: THIS IS JULIUS THOMAS. I NEED TO SPEAK WITH YOU AS SOON AS POSSIBLE. PLEASE GIVE ME A CALL AT YOUR EARLIEST CONVENIENCE.

Julius Thomas? I didn't know anyone with that name. The same number had called me yesterday, but I had ignored it and the voice mail they had left. It was a San Antonio number... but there shouldn't be anyone calling me from there.

I had paid all my bills. I'd forgotten to pay my electricity bill on time, but it had only been two days late. It was probably a scammer, I'd bet. Losers.

I slipped my phone back into my pocket with my attention straight on the man still talking with his butt against the counter. I slid my gaze over to Mr. Cooper who was there, listening to Rip with a funny expression on his face that I didn't recognize. It wasn't frustration for once.

They hadn't even been in the middle of an argument when I'd gotten to work that morning.

Just as I started trying to figure out what Mr. Cooper's

expression meant, a snore from my left had me sliding my foot over and kicking my coworker, Miguel. He sucked in a rough snore, his whole body tensing as he pretty much jolted awake.

"Son of a bitch," he whispered as he sat up a little straighter. "Thanks, Luna."

I wouldn't let any of them get into trouble if I could help it, and they knew that. Not even the one on the other side of the room who had gotten a kick out of Rip catching me with my eyes closed. I loved this place. Lucas Ripley picking on me every once in a while or not, I loved this place and the people who worked here. I was loved, I had a home, I had a job, and it was *Friday*. There wasn't much else I really needed.

And more than anything, today was going to be a good day. When you had so many good things and so many good people in your life, how could it not?

"Before we wrap up this morning's meeting," Mr. Cooper's sudden voice made me realize I'd completely zoned out the last couple of minutes. "There's one more announcement I need to share."

CHAPTER TWO

MAYBE I HAD SPOKEN A LITTLE TOO SOON ABOUT having a good day.

My day didn't instantly start going bad after the meeting ended, but... it went downhill soon afterward.

Things could always be worse though. Always.

When I'd gotten to work that morning, I'd started working on a smaller project that wouldn't take me long to prime; primer was kind of a preparation coat you put on things before painting. It helped paint stick to the surface better, helped increase paint durability, and helped protect the material being painted. When you were dealing with a car that might not ever get another paint job in its life, primer was one of the most important steps before changing its color.

By the time the meeting rolled around, I had finished my project and gone to the break room, already knowing the other jobs I had on the schedule. Usually, I had a pretty decent idea at least a week or two in advance of what work I would be doing on a specific date. Everyone at the shop did. We were a well-oiled machine because we passed around projects in different stages. Proper scheduling was something that Mr. Cooper excelled at to get cars back to their owners as quickly as possible.

That was part of the reason why the shop hadn't just survived but thrived despite recessions. We worked hard, worked as fast as possible without compromising quality, and Mr. Cooper charged fair prices for everything. Cooper's wasn't the cheapest, but it wasn't the most expensive either. I'd heard from more than enough friends over the years about how they were overcharged or how a mechanic had taken too long to work on something.

Mr. Cooper didn't play those kinds of games. We were all supposed to work together. And we usually did.

Usually.

The issue was that the car I needed to work on next had been added onto my schedule as an emergency job that the owner had requested, and was paying out of his butthole for, for us to have done by next week. But the instant I went to look for the car, I found it in the same condition it had been in the last time I had seen it.

Not freaking ready. Not anywhere close to being ready.

And that was why, two hours after our meeting had ended, I found myself going to lunch, just a little irritated.

Just a little. Because I wasn't about to really get mad. It wasn't a big deal in the grand scheme of life. If something didn't kill or injure me or anyone I loved, I didn't let it linger in me for too long. The body guys—the employees whose only job it was to fix the imperfections before sending a car over to me—hadn't finished. There was no point in getting *all* bent out of shape, but a little bent out of shape was all right.

I had better ways to spend my energy; on that day it was finishing the freaking bodywork.

My frustration had to be apparent on my face, because I'd barely walked inside the break room when Mr. Cooper asked, "What's wrong, little moon?"

I couldn't help but smile at the term of affection the older man called me when we were out of the shop or when no one else was around while we were working. We had never talked about it, but I knew he did it so that no one would assume he had favorites. I was pretty sure everyone knew I was his favorite anyway.

It wasn't just anyone he took into his home and into his life and family.

We didn't hide that we spent birthdays, Thanksgivings, and Christmas Days together, and in years past, New Year's Eve too. Now he claimed he was too old to stay awake until midnight. He was part of my family and had been for going on a decade. Just like his wife was. Just like my siblings were too.

Because he was my family, because he had gotten to know me so well, I couldn't hide the fact that something *was* bothering me—specifically, a person who worked for him.

The same person I had never totally been honest with him about.

"It's no big deal," I lied, trying to give him a genuine smile, but I must have failed because the worried expression on his face didn't change.

The seventy-one-year-old man, in a brand-new olive green collared shirt with COOPER'S COLLISION AND CUSTOMS stitched onto the breast, who stood right around six foot three, just kept on frowning. "Luna," he said as I walked behind him, setting my hand on his shoulder for a moment before heading to the fridge. "Even if it's a little deal, what's wrong? Is it the girls?"

"No, the girls are fine," I replied, knowing he was referring to my younger sisters.

"Something wrong at the house?"

"No, everything is fine, Mr. C, I promise," I partially lied, grabbing my lunch bag from inside the fridge, finally wondering for a moment what my little sister had made. I'd worked late the night before, and by the time I made it home and showered, she had already loaded my bag up and set it back in the fridge for the next day.

That was definitely something I could be grateful for today. *Thank God my little sister makes me lunch every day.* She was the best cook in the family and wasn't stingy about it. And I wasn't going to let myself be sad that I had less than two months left of having my own personal chef in the house before she left me.

"Tell me what that face is for." Mr. Cooper's quiet, careful voice brought me back from the brink of being sad over something I had promised myself I wouldn't be upset about. My baby sister was growing up and going to college. I had always known it was going to happen. It was what I had hoped for. I had already gone through it with my other two sisters, and I was proud of her—them—and happy. I was.

But I was never going to tell anyone that I'd cried twice already just thinking about Lily leaving.

And I was definitely not going to get upset about it at work. No, siree.

"Are you sad or mad, Luna? I can't tell."

Setting my bag on the table beside the seat Mr. Cooper was in, I started pulling containers out of it, eyeing the plastic Rubbermaids. There were three. One was full of chopped greens. The second one had what looked like rice, beans, and ground beef, and the smallest looked like it was full of pico de gallo. Yum.

"I'm not sad. I promise." Liar. "The car I needed to start today wasn't ready is all," I told him, prying open the lids to take a peek inside of them, trying to ignore feeling like a snitch for even saying that much.

"That looks good," the much older man commented as I turned around to stick the bean mix into the microwave. His voice was almost a whisper as he asked, "Who was supposed to be working on it first?"

I bit my lip as I pushed buttons on the screen. *I wasn't going to get mad. I wasn't going to assume the worst.* "You know who," I told him in my normal voice, because I wasn't doing anything wrong telling him, so I wasn't going to be secretive.

And he did know. Mr. Cooper might be the boss—*one of* the bosses—but I rarely complained to him about anything, mostly because there were rarely things *to* complain about. I wasn't going to tattle on anyone and get them into trouble. I was never going to abuse my relationship with Mr. Cooper, which was why I was totally fine with us usually being mostly professional at the shop.

But...

I *had* told him a couple times in the past about a certain coworker that I swear went out of his way to not just be a jerk, but a pain in the ass. But only to me. Because that was my luck.

I didn't say anything to get the guy into trouble but just to vent. Mr. Cooper was mature enough and professional enough to take my words one day at his house for what they were: his daughter-like figure complaining to her father-like figure about someone who had cheated on someone she loved. Except I had never told him that part.

That "someone" being the middle of my younger sisters. So, of course that was already going to be a strike against the jerk who had made my sister cry. The fact that he wasn't very nice to me even now didn't help our relationship.

But in this case, Mr. Cooper, the owner of the business, peeked into our conversation, and I saw his head swing toward me, a frown on his well-loved face. "Again? Didn't he do something like that a couple weeks ago?"

He had. Two weeks ago exactly. And a month before that, he'd done it too, but on a smaller scale.

But I did the same thing I had done every other time; I sucked it up and did what I needed to do. It was my job, and I wasn't going to get in trouble because someone didn't do theirs. The only reason Mr. Cooper had found out about two weeks ago was because he'd walked in to find me putting filler on a car and hadn't understood why I'd been the one doing it when he knew I had other things on the schedule.

I watched the seconds count down on the microwave screen. "I've worked on it for two hours, Mr. C. I still have another two before I can even start priming it. I'm supposed to work on another one after that too."

Goodbye, my plans tonight.

I was getting aggravated again. Not because I was going to have to stay late, but because I had to stay late because my gut said my coworker hadn't finished the job on purpose. He would deny it for the rest of my life, but I knew the truth. I'd heard him snickering that morning when Rip had gotten on my case.

"Did he explain why he didn't finish?" he asked, sounding genuinely baffled.

I didn't blame him. At the same time, it warmed my heart that he didn't expect the worst out of people... even if I had a feeling that he should expect the worst out of the person we were talking about. I doubted Jason ever messed up things Mr. Cooper asked him to do.

I bit the inside of my cheek again and kept my voice low as I glanced toward the door to make sure a certain someone wasn't standing there, listening. "He said something came up with another car and he didn't get a chance to finish it."

I wasn't sure he knew that I'd had the same job as he did at one point. Cars that were on the schedule to go to paint took priority over everything else. There was no reason why Jason, the pain in my ass in question, would have just not gotten to it when he knew damn well I needed him to.

That punk that Mr. Cooper had hired six months ago— without me knowing it was him that had gotten hired until it was too late—*would* try and give me more work to do. Jason wasn't technically a body guy. He got stuck covering for whoever was on vacation or had a personal day; he was basically me when I'd been his age, doing whatever anyone asked me to do.

"It's all right," I trailed off, reminding myself again of everything I had. *I was loved, I had a good job, I had a home. I was happy, and I was safe.* Most importantly, so were my sisters. So this was no big deal. "I'll still get to everything."

But Mr. Cooper seemed to be hesitating, probably still trying to work out a reason why something like that would have happened that wasn't malicious. "Do you want me to talk to him?" he asked after a moment.

I blew out a breath as I dumped one container into the other before grabbing the container of pico and putting it in with the rest of my food.

I was a little pissed, but was I pissed enough to get the human yeast infection in trouble?

I hated how guilty just thinking about it made me feel.

"No," I found myself muttering to him. "I'll give him the benefit of the doubt."

There I went lying again. I definitely wasn't going to give him that. I knew he was lying. I just knew it.

But the idea of him getting into trouble because I complained to one of the bosses—a boss that would do just about anything for me if I asked—made me feel bad. He was a lying turd, *but* you never knew what someone had going on in their life to get them to act like a jerk. Even if the acting like a jerk part had lasted for the last six months—and the six months he'd dated my sister before sleeping with some other girl. Maybe he needed money. Maybe I looked like his mom and he had mommy issues. Maybe he was stressed and I happened to be the easiest person to be mean to.

...but probably not.

"You sure?"

I slid him a look. Then I nodded.

Mr. Cooper raised those super thick, gray-white eyebrows at me, blinking bright blue eyes, his face deeply wrinkled and pretty freaking serious.

"I'm sure," I confirmed as I started shoveling at the food with the fork my little sister had packed for me from home. I didn't trust the other guys' cleaning more than mugs at the shop, and she knew that.

My phone decided to ping from the front pocket of my jeans in that moment. "One sec," I said to him as I pulled it out and glanced at the screen.

Thea: I'm going to stay in Dallas this weekend after all, but I'll come down for Lily's graduation for sure. Need to make some $$$.

I typed up my reply to my sister instantly, ignoring the pinch of disappointment I realistically knew I had no reason to feel when I understood why she wasn't coming down to visit again. It was just that I hadn't seen her in almost three months.

Me: Okay. Good luck.

A second passed before I got a response.

Thea: xx

"Kyra?" he asked, referring to the middle of my three younger sisters. The same one that Jason, the jerk, had dated.

"No, Thea," I corrected him. Thea was the oldest after me at twenty-one. I pressed the home button on my phone to clear the app and then set my phone face down on the table between our food. "She's not coming down this weekend after all," I told him as I picked my fork back up.

He knew all about the last time she had promised to come and ended up bailing. Just like on this failed visit, I had marked myself off on the schedule so that everyone knew there was no way I was coming in over the weekend. It wasn't unheard of for me to work on Saturdays. I had bills, no money tree and no sugar daddy; I was all about that overtime life. But I could be honest and say I'd been looking forward to having the time off to spend it with my sisters. Oh well. "I guess they offered her some more hours at the school or something."

The way he said "Oh" told me he could see right through me. Mr. Cooper knew my sisters almost as well as I did. And because he did, and because I talked to him about them pretty often, he had a decent idea just how often Thea and Kyra cancelled on me.

Even though it was always for a good reason.

I gave him another tight smile before giving my food a poke. "She said she's for sure coming down for Lily's graduation next week though, so that's good."

"That is good," he agreed... a lot more softly than he needed to because it really wasn't a big deal that she wasn't coming to visit after all.

It wasn't.

"I can't believe that girl is finally graduating. I'd swear she's still eleven."

That made me smile. "Me too, Mr. C, me too." Just a few weeks ago, we had gone to scope out apartments for her in Lubbock.

Either Mr. Cooper realized that I didn't want to think about it anymore, or he understood that there wasn't anything more to say, because he took another bite of his tuna sandwich before mumbling, "I meant to tell you someone called this morning asking for you."

I scrunched up my face as I looked down at my food.

"It was a man."

I blinked.

"I asked a few times for a name, but he wouldn't give me one," he went on.

There was no way it was a customer, because I rarely ever met any of them. I might walk through the shop while one or two were inside talking to Mr. Cooper or Rip about a car we were working on for them or a car they wanted to buy from them, but it was rare that they let customers onto the main floor during work hours. But me personally speaking to any of them? No way. The only people I had to listen to were Mr. Cooper and Ripley.

"I wasn't sure if maybe you were trying to pull a line of credit or if someone was trying to verify your employment —" He let out this adorable chuff like he couldn't imagine me applying to work anywhere else. "—but I also didn't want to confirm that you work here. You know, *just in case.*" We both knew what he meant by a *just in case* situation.

Just in case it was someone I didn't want to speak to. Just in case it was someone who I wouldn't mind assuming I was dead. "I asked him who I was speaking to, then he asked again if he could speak to you. We went back and forth before he thanked me, then hung up, but something about it sounded professional."

Hmm.

There was no logical reason why anyone would be calling looking for me.

At least not anyone that I wanted.

"I'll let you know if they call again," he told me. "I'll do the same thing. I won't say you don't work here, but I won't say you do either."

"Thanks, Mr. C," I muttered, trying to think, but also taking a bite of the food my little sister had prepared for lunch. I let my gaze slide over to him, picking up on the tension in his own shoulders. I had an idea what the cause was. "You okay? I was pretty surprised when you announced that Rogelio is leaving."

The older man grunted as he chewed. The last thing he'd said during our meeting had been that one of the shop's longtime employees was leaving to start his own mechanic shop. "I'm happy for him," he finally said, and I knew he was telling the truth. "But you know how hard good workers are to find, and now I need to get someone else before he leaves. We'll be hurting if we end up short-staffed."

We were always almost hurting, and with one person less?

He shrugged the shoulder closest to me. "I'll find someone. I get resumes all the time from kids straight out of school."

I smiled at him. "If there's anything I can do, let me know."

Mr. Cooper put his arm around my shoulders and hugged me to his side.

He rarely ever did that, and it caught me by surprise so much I barely had time to smile over at him.

His quiet laugh had me glancing down at where his eyes were focused: on my wrist. On the bracelet of linked, tiny plastic donuts with colorful icing on my left hand to be specific. "I was wondering what your fun thing of the day was."

I gave my hand a shake. "Lily bought it for me," I explained.

"That's pretty fun, little moon," the older man confirmed with a warm smile.

"Luna," came a familiar male voice that had me looking toward the door just as Mr. C's arm started to retreat.

Sure enough, Rip's massive body took up the width of the doorframe as he stood there, a piece of grease-stained paper in his hand, his gaze intent on me. Totally ignoring Mr. Cooper sitting beside me, pulling his arm back toward his side. He wasn't frowning, but there was something about his expression....

"Hey, Rip," I said, giving him a smile as I straightened.

He tipped his chin up, making my eyes flick to the lines alongside his mouth from all the scowling he did. His voice was gruff *and* irritated. "You get started on that Thunderbird yet?"

"Not yet." Should I tell him about what happened? I eyed his shirt once more and thought about how grumpy he'd been at the meeting that morning. Because of Jason's screw up, it pushed back me getting to the car he was asking about.

"Do me a solid." His eyes stayed on me so intently it made me feel like I'd done something wrong by letting Mr.

Cooper give me a hug. But I hadn't, and Rip was well aware of the father-daughter relationship I had with the older man. I had invited him to my house twice for Thanksgiving, making it clear that Mr. Cooper and his wife would be there too so that he wouldn't think I was trying to flirt with him. He didn't show up either time. "I changed my mind about it and left a new work order for it on your desk. Take a look at it. I know we've got the color in the back, so use that one instead, got me?"

I nodded. New work order. New color. He was using that barking, something-up-his-butt voice. All right.

Ripley's blue-green eyes narrowed as he watched me from the doorway, pointedly still not looking at the man beside me. "Do you need to write it down?" he asked, dipping into that condescending tone just a little.

I let it slide right off me. "No, I'll remember."

From the doorway, Rip gave me a nod before walking off. I didn't need to watch him leave to know what his butt looked like in those coveralls. It was perfectly proportionate in comparison to the rest of his six-foot-four built-like-a-tank body. Big and thick.

Beside me, Mr. Cooper let out a sigh that I'd heard a hundred or two times before. I couldn't blame him. The less they communicated, the better everyone's day was.

Especially his.

But at that moment, I couldn't focus on Rip's butt, or relish in the fact that I'd gotten to see his face not completely scowling in my direction, even if it was only for a second. Sometimes he'd come up for lunch at the same time I did. Sometimes he'd sit next to me and eat. His elbow would brush mine. Maybe his forearm would touch mine. If it was a good day, he'd give me an eyebrow raise that I would take like it was a smile. If it was a really good day, I could talk to him about the car he was restoring, and we might talk about it for a few minutes.

I had given up trying to ask him personal questions about two months into him arriving at CCC.

But on days when Mr. Cooper and I happened to eat at the same time, none of that ever happened. I'd watched Rip turn around and walk out, noticing how Mr. Cooper sat there and tried not to let it bother him.

On this day, it was impossible not to notice that getting ignored was eating up the kindest man I had ever met.

So I turned my head to my favorite boss and gave him a smile he probably saw right through. "Have I told you that color shirt looks really nice on you? You don't look a day over sixty-five in it, Mr. C."

It was hours later when I realized how bad I'd screwed up.

I wasn't sure what exactly had snapped together for me at the last second just as I had started to crouch down to keep moving the gun across the surface of the quarter panel I was in the middle of painting. But something had just clicked as I stood in front of the section of the car between the rear door and the trunk. That click had said *Luna, wait a minute*.

Wait a minute.

"Shit." I pulled the hood of my coveralls down, raised my goggles to rest at the top of my head, and tugged my respirator to my chin, trying to think as I stared at the panel in front of me.

But the color on the car didn't change without the goggles.

It was still a silvery blue.

It was still Silver Mink.

I left the work order for you at the top of your desk, Rip had said during lunch.

I had picked up the work order on the desk. I knew it. Silver Mink, it had said. I knew it. I wouldn't have screwed up reading it.

But... Silver Mink.... Something about the color, about the name, didn't sit well.

Silver Mink, Silver Mink, Silver Mink....

Wasn't Silver Mink the original color he had requested?

Had I read the wrong order?

Heart freaking instantly pounding, I swallowed and tried to think about what I'd done. I had picked up the invoice, read through it three times, and gone to get the paint. I knew that for sure. I *knew* it.

But...

I ran back to my desk and went through the invoices sitting on it. About a minute into looking, I found it—*them* more like it. I freaking found *them*.

It only took a second to look up the work order on my computer to confirm my suspicions.

I had started painting the car *a different freaking color*.

Holy crap.

Not Brittany Blue.

Not Brittany Blue like one of the invoices requested. The *right* invoice.

Why hadn't I double-checked? I always did. *Always.*

"Shit." I blinked down at the sheet, the urge to throw up getting strong and stronger. "Shit, shit, *shit!*"

I wanted to punch the wall. *Punch myself* more like it. But the fact was, I remembered that I'd been thinking about the phone call Mr. Cooper had mentioned and my sister bailing on me, and being frustrated with my coworker for screwing me over. I'd gone back downstairs after lunch, still thinking about things that I couldn't change even if I wanted to, gone to my room, spent another four hours sanding down the car then priming it. I let it bake while I picked up the first file I found for the Thunderbird, read it, and finally pulled the paint from the locker where we kept all the extra unused supplies.

The rest was history. I grabbed the paint, prepared everything, Miguel helped me move the cars around. Then I got in the booth and started spraying, my head going back to the text and the phone call despite the headphones I had on blasting the *Wicked* soundtrack into my ears. Then, *then*, it had clicked.

Holy freaking shit, I had read the wrong work order.

Oh no. Oh no, oh no, *oh no*.

"Fucking shit," I whispered to myself, panic filling up my stomach, making me nauseous instantly. *Instantly.*

For one microsecond, I asked myself how I could fix this without involving anyone. But just as quickly as I wondered that, I reminded myself that there was no way. What was I going to do? Hide the car and do everything all over again? The primer alone needed a day to dry.

I wasn't sure I believed in miracles, and I wasn't about to start now.

My hands went up to my hair on their own, smoothing over the chin-length hair I had bobby-pinned back behind my ears to keep it out of my face. I tugged on the ends, hard. But the color didn't change and the words on the work order didn't magically disappear, and I was still in deep shit.

There was only one thing I could do.

Suck it up, sugar tits, my sister would say.

What if you get fired? My brain tried to ask the rest of me.

I had messed up once before, but it had been wheels I had screwed up, and only two of them.

I rarely called out. I was never late. I couldn't remember ever complaining. Sure, Mr. Cooper was the closest thing I'd ever had to what a real dad was supposed to be like. But this was going to be hundreds of dollars' worth of work that was going to need to be redone because of me. That money being mostly what they paid me hourly for labor and the paint I'd just wasted. All because I hadn't taken the time to find both orders and look at the stupid freaking *dates*.

I was going to be sick.

What if I got fired? It could happen. It was a white day for Rip.

And he'd fired people for less on white days.

Shit. *Shit, shit, shit.*

There's only one thing to do, Luna, the voice of reason in my head told me.

Letting go of my hair, I took a deep breath that wasn't deep at all and sounded more like I had asthma. I wasn't going to be even more of an asshole and pretend like nothing had happened.

I had messed up.

I took ownership of my actions.

I didn't run away from my problems, even if I some-times ignored them.

I was better than that. *I was better than that.* I wouldn't be that person.

I might have prayed a couple of Hail Marys I had learned from the Coopers under my breath as I headed toward the main floor. I considered calling Mr. Cooper to tell him because I didn't think he was capable of yelling at me.

I couldn't though.

It was a white day, and Rip had already blatantly ignored him. He'd be at home by now, and Mr. Cooper didn't deserve to get chewed out for something I did, because that would be what inevitably happened if I used him as a buffer between me and the person who had actually given me the orders for the project I had screwed up.

I tried to tell myself that there was nothing to be worried about. What was Rip going to do? Yell at me? It wouldn't be the first time someone had done it. I'd mastered getting yelled at as a kid. It wasn't like he would hit me or call me stupid or hint that my entire existence was a mistake. He would make a face, use that condescending tone he used on everyone regularly, maybe he'd be grumpy for a few days, and then...

He'd decide to fire me.

No big deal.

I could find another job. I had job offers pop up every few months. Sure, none of them were in Houston, and sure I didn't *want* to change jobs and start over again around people who didn't know me and didn't care about me, but....

Don't you dare get upset, Luna, my brain warned me. *Don't you even think about it.*

I took another deep breath, but it went in jagged and crooked. I'd own up to my mistakes, I had sworn to myself a long time ago. I'd take responsibility for my actions.

Don't overreact, I told myself as I placed one foot in front of the other, heading to the main floor of the shop and looking around at the eight different cars parked inside at the moment. There were four "lanes." Each lane had two cars on it. Three lanes were usually reserved for cars that were getting mechanical work done, usually a car involved in a collision. One lane was always set aside for whatever car or cars Ripley happened to be restoring.

Sure enough, most of the mechanics for CCC had left for the day, but I still spotted two heads on the floor that weren't Rip's brown and silver mix.

At the lane furthest from where I stood, I could see him taking the seats out of a GTO that I hadn't seen before lunch.

Why? Why had I screwed up today? Crap, crap, *crap.*

I had done it. There was no hiding it. I couldn't go back in time and change my mistake, as much as I would have wanted to.

Own it. I had to own it. *Lying was bad—most of the time. Pretending to be stupid was worse.*

I repeated all those things to myself as I crossed between the cars, purposely ignoring the glances I got from the two guys still working as I made my way toward Rip. It wasn't unusual for me to come out on the floor, but it wasn't that normal either.

Maybe I could get him to talk to me in his office or in my room.

How could I have screwed up like this? Realistically, I knew that people made mistakes. The man who had taught me everything he knew had messed up all the time.

Okay, it had never happened while Rip had been at CCC, and it had never been a mistake of this size. When the old lead painter had messed up, it was picking out the wrong color tone or not noticing that something had needed an extra coat of clear. It wasn't a chunk of a car being the wrong color.

You will not cry, Luna. You will not cry. He's not going to hit you, and if he yells at you, you can take it better than anyone else here. If you get fired, it's your own fault. You can't blame anyone else but yourself. You'll be fine. Thea, Kyra, and Lily are almost all self-supportive. One day you'll be able to laugh about the day you screwed up big-time. It might just take a decade to get there. You're a decent person and you try to do what's right, even if it sucks.

It was with that thought that I marched my butt toward the man who had ducked back into the car. I couldn't see his head or his body as I got closer. I could handle it, I promised myself.

Then I made it.

Rip was taking the bolts off the driver side seat like I had expected, so I walked around to that side and stood there, watching him on his knees, half of his upper body inside the car, the other half kneeling on a dirty towel on the concrete floor.

He didn't see or hear me.

Knowing him, he might just be pretending he didn't.

So I said, loud, "*Hey*, Rip." He was going to know something was wrong, I just knew it.

He didn't stop working, and if he rolled his eyes, I had no idea, but I caught his reply of "What?"

What? Not *what do you want* or *what do you need*. It was a white day. What did I expect?

"Can I talk to you?"

"Talk," was his simple reply.

I could do it.

"Can we talk in the office or in my room?" I practically croaked, wincing and hoping he'd miss it.

Only then did I see his arm stop moving, but I heard his voice clearly as he rasped, "Busy, Luna. What's up?"

What's up? Okay. That was a decent sign.

But I still couldn't manage to say anything more than, "Did I tell you that your hair looks nice today?" The way he had it parted *did* look extra nice today. I wasn't lying.

Just stalling.

"Talk, Luna," he clearly grumbled, aware I was full of it. "I don't got all day. I need to get this car stripped. What's up?" my boss, the same boss I had been planning on baking a cake for this weekend, the same boss who had already lost this patience with me when I didn't give him an answer at seven in the morning when he asked what favor I wanted from him, and then again when he'd caught me with my eyes closed during a meeting, asked, not giving me a second to think of what I could say to get out of this.

Why? Why couldn't have I screwed up with something Mr. Cooper had ordered me to do? He'd be disappointed in me, but at least he wouldn't give me the death glare. He wouldn't get rid of me.

On the other side of the Eclipse parked next to me, I spotted my two coworkers looking over at me, being nosey as shit. Owen and Miguel weren't even trying to hide that they were eavesdropping. I wasn't even sure what Miguel was doing here so late, much less why he was helping Owen, but oh well.

I forced myself not to curse Jason's name. It was kind of his fault that this was even happening. If he had done his job, I would have already started painting the car by the time Rip had come to find me in the break room.

But at the end of the day, I could still only blame myself for not double-checking the work order.

I waved at my coworkers. "Owen, tell your daughter I said happy birthday!" I called out.

They both grinned, but it was Owen who gave me a thumbs-up. But they didn't look away. Whoever had spread the rumor that women were worst gossips than men had never worked with a group of men on a regular basis before.

"Luna, what the fuck is up?" Rip asked, his tone finally genuinely taking on an impatient streak to it.

Now or never.

"Umm," I trailed off some more, forcing myself to look away from Miguel and Owen and look down at the hint of an elbow that had started moving again inside the GTO.

"You gonna say something or not? This needs to get done," he kept going, sounding even more aggravated and impatient.

I could do it. I had to.

"Luna," Rip drew out my name, any and all ease finally gone from his voice.

"Rip," I started, closing both my eyes for a moment. "I screwed up."

There was a pause, and then he asked, slowly, so, so slowly I wasn't a fool enough to assume he hadn't heard me. "What's that?"

He was going to make me do this. Of course he was. "I screwed up," I repeated. I didn't deserve to wince. This really was my fault. And Jason's. "I picked up the wrong work order for the Thunderbird. Instead of the Brittany Blue, I did the Silver Mink that had been on the original form, and I already started before it hit me." I did it. I had freaking done it. I knew it was pointless and didn't mean a thing, but I still threw in, "I'm really, really sorry."

At some point, his elbow stopped moving. Hell, I was pretty sure he even stopped breathing because the two inches of his upper half that weren't hidden inside the car weren't moving either. Oh, hell.

"It's my fault. I just... I spaced. I should have double-checked the system and I didn't. I'm so sorry."

Still, he said nothing.

Crap.

"I can stay late tonight to start fixing it. Monday I can

do the primer, and if I stay late, I can get all caught up again...."

He'd stopped listening. I could tell. So I stopped talking.

His body had started to move as I had blabbed on. First I noticed more of his abs, then his upper chest, followed by his neck, and finally his head came out from inside the car he was gutting. Those intense eyes zeroed in on me from a carefully blank face I had seen before, usually from a distance. Usually as an observer and not the focus of it.

And I knew. I freaking knew...

He was going to ream me.

Lucas Ripley didn't let me down. His voice was calm and almost cold as he said, "I specifically asked you if you needed to write that shit down. 'Member that?"

Oh, man. It was going to go bad.

What else could I do but nod?

Those almost green-blue eyes didn't even *flicker*. "I *asked you* if you needed me to write it down and you said no," he kept going, staring at me with that furious face that was so roughly handsome, I didn't want to look at it, not then. His voice got even cooler, if that was even possible, and I swear I could feel the skin on my back prickling. "And I'm gonna have to pay you overtime for work that was already done?" He narrowed those intense eyes. "I have to pay *you* to fix a mistake *you* did?"

All I could do was stand there.

I had messed up. There was no escaping that. "Rip, I'm sorry. I've never made a mistake like this before—"

That giant hand speckled in some kind of oil or grease sliced across the center of his body. "That's not the fucking point, Luna," he snapped, looking up at me. "It's a waste of time. It's a waste of money. It's a waste of fucking paint." Rip shook that dark brown head of hair that had just a few lines of silver through it, just in time for his birthday that upcoming Monday.

He was laying it on real thick, and I was taking it all in, feeling worse and worse by the second. He was right. He would have gotten mad at anyone who made the same mistake; that only microscopically made me feel better. "I'm sorry. I'll stay late, and you don't have to pay me. I know it's my fault," I replied, hoping Owen and Miguel couldn't hear how pitchy my voice had gotten. I had to clench my fists when the urge to crack my knuckles got bad.

My boss raised his thick, dark eyebrows in a way that confirmed I wasn't going to get out of anything, and I definitely wasn't going to get absolved of a freaking thing. "Now you're gonna try and give me a goddamn guilt trip for telling you shit any boss would?" His eyebrows lowered, and that mouth I thought was pretty sexy on good days stayed in a scowl. "You're not gonna make me feel bad, Luna. You fucked up and that's the end of the story."

I had fucked up. I wasn't trying to make it seem any other way. I nodded at him, making sure to avoid glancing over at where I had last seen my coworkers standing. "I know, Rip. I'm not trying to. I'm sorry," I told him.

He shook his head. Shook me off. The man pulled out a clean-ish rag from inside his coveralls and swept it over his face as he muttered, "Sorry doesn't fix shit."

Of course it didn't. I'd learned that lesson long before he'd come into my life.

"I know that. I'll do everything myself. I'll get started on it—"

His face was still covered as he breathed out, "Don't bother."

What did that mean?

"But I can do it. I know it's my fault—"

"No." He moved the cloth away from his face and zeroed in on mine instantly. His jaw was set, and if I'd had any doubts he was pissed, I would have gotten a confirmation then. There were more lines at his forehead than I had ever seen before. "Keep the paint the same goddamn color you already did," he grumbled, dragging the rag roughly over his hands as his eyes pretty much burned a hateful hole straight into the middle of my features. "For the record, it's fucking bullshit."

"I'm sorry," I murmured, ignoring the fact that I was pretty sure my coworkers had started creeping closer to us to hear better.

Rip shook his head again. "Sorry doesn't fix your mistake. Go paint the car the color you already started."

"But—"

"I don't want to talk about this shit anymore, Luna." He glanced up at the ceiling before saying in a crystal-clear voice, "And this is going down in your file."

In my file? As in strike one? Strike one of three that would get me fired? Was that how these things worked? I hadn't even known that was a thing.

I stared at him, pressed my lips together, and then I sucked in a breath through my nose. I wasn't going to get upset over getting in trouble. *I wasn't.*

Rip, on the other hand, watched me with that quietly furious freaking face that said he didn't even want to look at me in the first place. He didn't want to look at my face that was usually makeup-less minus the pink lipstick I wore every day. He didn't want to look at the cotton-candy blue hair I had kept over the last year. He didn't want to look at *me.*

He wouldn't be the first person.

"I am sorry," I said to him, trying to cling onto whatever was left of my pride while feeling all of about an inch tall.

He just stared at me, and I knew he wasn't going to say anything else.

I'd apologized and I'd meant it. That was all I could do. I turned around and slowly headed the way I'd come, purposely avoiding making eye contact with the guys watching because I didn't want to see pity on their faces. I'd probably only gotten about two lanes away when I heard Rip call out, "You all gonna get back to work or what?"

I pressed my lips together and glanced down at my donut bracelet, rubbing my thumb over one of them. It could have been worse.

He could have fired me, and maybe then he could have gotten himself out of repaying the favor that he had felt like he'd owed me for the last going-on three years. I bet that would have made him happy.

Everything was fine, even if it didn't feel that way.

Things could always be worse.

CHAPTER THREE

EVERY SINGLE LIGHT WAS ON INSIDE THE HOUSE WHEN I pulled into the driveway at ten that night.

Literally every one.

I sighed as I turned the ignition off and told myself that soon there wasn't going to be anyone at the house to turn on a single light. Or make my lunch. Or give me a hug when I needed it. Or talk me into staying up late to watch a scary movie.

That reminder just made me sigh again, but for a totally different reason.

Then I remembered how high my electricity bill was going to be this summer if my little sister didn't calm down, and I opened the door and got out.

In the dark, it was too hard to see the old house except for the squares and rectangles of light behind the curtains that Thea, my slightly younger sister, had bought as my birthday present a year ago.

Up the two steps, I swung my keys around my index finger and then slipped the right one into the lock and turned it. The television blared, but somehow my baby sister, Lily, heard me open the door because she called out, "Luna? Is that you?"

"No, it's the ax murderer." I dropped my keys into the bowl my other sister had bought for my birthday the same year. "Did you make something for dinner?" *Please, please, please....*

"No, I ordered pizza!" my little sister replied from where she usually was stationed on a rare Friday she wasn't working—in front of the TV because senior year of high school was *exhausting* apparently. Not that I would have known that.

I'd always been able to see right through my sister's BS. She stayed home on no-work-Fridays so that she wouldn't spend money. She was always saving for something. For the last year, she'd been saving for college expenses. The year before that, she'd been saving for a car—a car I had ended up splitting with her.

At the thought of pizza, my stomach grumbled, reminding me I hadn't finished my lunch, and since then, I had only stuffed down a banana and a handful of Skittles from my not-so-secret stash after my incident with Rip. I thought it was some kind of miracle I hadn't ended up with a headache, but the Coke I'd had with the Skittles had probably helped.

I was *tired.* Inside and out. No matter how much I had tried not to wallow in the guilt I felt for screwing up—and how much I tried not to think about how unforgiving Rip had been about it—it had happened. His facial expression, tone, and the guilt in my gut just kept running on a loop in my head. The tightness in my chest hadn't gone anywhere in hours.

It was *still* hanging around the general vicinity of my heart. I was embarrassed and disappointed in myself.

Sorry doesn't fix your fucking mistake.

I sighed once more as I untied my boots and then toed them off, leaving them right next to Lily's black Converse, eyeing the pair of checkered yellow Vans and pink New Balances there too.

Rubbing my brow bone with the back of my hand, I dragged my feet in the direction of the living room down the hall. Passing through, there were still so many things I wanted to redo to the house, and tearing down some of these walls were next on my list. Hopefully I could get Lily to help me before she left, and if my other sisters came to visit, I could get them to help too. There weren't enough hours in the day or days in the year.

In the living room, I found her sitting in between a girl and a boy her age that I had met before. I lifted my hand at them but blew a kiss at the dark blonde in the middle.

"Hey," I said to the three of them, watching as my little sister raised her arms up to the ceiling as her way to get me to come toward her.

She was the most affectionate one in the family, which was just one more reason I was going to miss her when she left for college. That thought pierced me straight in the gut.

She was graduating high school next week. *Next week.* She'd be eighteen in a couple of weeks. Legally an adult but forever my baby sister who had grown up way too fast, no matter how hard I had tried to prevent that from happening.

Bending over the back of the couch, Lily's arms went around my neck as she pressed my cheek to the side of her face. "Tough day, sugar tits?"

My "It wasn't the best, but it wasn't the worst, sugar lumps" went right into her cheek as I dropped a quick kiss on it.

"Sorry, boo." She pecked me right back. Her green eyes

—the same shade as mine and both of our sisters too—were extra watchful. She had told me enough times how I worked too much and was going to wear myself out too quick. "Want us to go to my room?" Her gaze flicked to my wrist and she smiled. "Oh, look, you're wearing it."

I gave her another kiss on the cheek before straightening. "Of course I am, and not unless you care if I sit here for a little while with your leftover pizza."

She made a face. "You've been snorting too many paint fumes today."

I made a face back at her before turning around and heading into the kitchen down another short hallway. I really needed to open up the house more and make the layout better. I'd gotten the plans for it right after I'd bought the place, and I'd bet I could find an engineer or an architect who could tell me just how many of the walls I could take down. I worked too much to really get a lot of the Home Remodeling Network shows in, but I had a general idea of what I wanted this place to look like eventually.

I took in what I had currently—a closed-off kitchen that had been popular in a different century, solid cabinets, a countertop that had been replaced at some point in the last twenty years, and a stove and refrigerator that got the job done... There were glass and ceramic containers on the countertops, a fancy blender that Lily had talked me into, a countertop mixer that I had splurged on during a Black Friday sale, and a wire basket half-filled with apples and oranges.

I had so much, and I was so lucky. Even in its current state of needing a serious uplift, even the kitchen could make me happy. Because it was mine, and no one could take it away... unless I stopped paying the mortgage, but I hadn't gotten fired yet, so that would be a worry for another day.

I could still easily remember the days of looking through a pantry and refrigerator with no food in it. I had made myself a promise that I would someday open a cabinet and always find something in there to eat and my sisters could have the same. I had sworn to myself that if I ever became a parent, I would give my kids what my parents had been too selfish and negligent and careless to give us.

And right then I remembered that I had managed that. Maybe it took working sixty hours a week and getting scolded by a boss who usually blatantly ignored me when I tried to put him in a good mood, but I had done it. *I* had done it.

As tired as I felt then, as much as my shoulders ached from holding the spray gun, and my arms and hands and back and feet hurt from the hours of bodywork I had done that day, it was all worth it.

There was a laugh from the living room that I knew was my little sister's and that too just cemented how worth it busting my ass was.

So, as I made my way toward the pizza box sitting on the counter beside the refrigerator, I felt lighter again.

Maybe I had gotten in trouble. Maybe it hadn't been the best day ever. Maybe everything hurt. But I was home. I had gotten a kiss from someone who loved me. I had a bed to sleep in.

For all intents and purposes, it was a good day despite a couple things.

Then I opened the pizza box, saw there was only one single slice left, and I told myself again it was still a pretty good day.

I had enough in the budget to call and order another pizza if I really wanted to, and that was pretty damn good if I said so myself.

CHAPTER FOUR

I KNEW I SHOULD HAVE TURNED AROUND AND WAITED to get my coffee the moment I walked into the break room and heard my bosses arguing the following week.

Again. For maybe the thousandth time or pretty close to it.

In my defense, if I walked out every time I heard them fighting over something, I would rarely get to drink a single cup of coffee. Or eat my lunch. Or refill my water bottle. Or find out if I'd read their chicken scratch on Post-It notes correctly.

That morning, more than normal, I needed caffeine. I'd had a dream about my dad for the first time in months. It had felt so real I'd woken up with tears rolling down my cheeks. It had been years since the last time I'd cried so hard... and that had only made me cry even more. It had felt like I was back living with them, back to those nights when my dad would get drunk and go from being unbearable to being a nightmare; back to the days where, if I was lucky, the woman my sisters had known as their mom would be on the couch, high out of her mind, doing nothing other than letting me know how much she hated me. I'd ended up staying awake, lying in bed, telling myself things I had told myself a thousand times.

I was loved. I had a roof over my head. Food to eat. A bed to sleep in. Money in my bank account.

I reminded myself that life was a gift—sometimes one you wanted to return, and other times one you'd want to keep forever, but it was still a gift. The grass might look greener on the other side, but at least you still had grass. There were places in the world that didn't have any to begin with.

I was fine.

I had more than I ever would have let myself hope for.

I was *fine*.

I was really glad my little sister could sleep through anything. Otherwise telling her why I'd woken up crying my guts out would have been a real pain. While I went long periods of time between thinking about them, about those times in my life, my youngest sister had decided just never to think about them at all in the first place—at least not that I knew of. I had tried before to get her to discuss it, just to make sure she was fine, but she'd refused.

Knowing all that I had and reminding myself of it hadn't helped much, but it had done enough. It got me to take a deep breath, climb out of the bed I'd had to save six months for, and shower in my own bathroom in a house I had a mortgage on—a mortgage I paid every month and even managed to put in a little extra for the principal. I grabbed my lunch bag from the refrigerator, filled with food Lily had bought that weekend, and somehow managed to remember to grab the cake I'd made the night before while Lily had made our lunch. I had fought her for so long about how she should just buy food at the school, but she'd insisted it tasted like crap and she could make something ten times better herself. After all that, I drove to work in a car that I had bought with my own money and headed to a job that I loved most of the time.

I was loved. I had a roof over my head. Food to eat. A bed to sleep in. I had an enormous bag of Skittles in my desk at work. Had an oven to bake cakes in and money to actually buy the ingredients to make them. All on my own. All because someone had given me a chance, a little love, and let me work hard to have all the things I did.

And *that* made me feel better more than anything else— the knowledge that I wasn't vulnerable and didn't have to rely on someone else for basic things.

So, more than on any other day, hearing my two bosses argue weighed me down like a hundred-pound sack of flour on my shoulders. I needed to make some coffee to wake up and get to the booth where I worked so I could pretend like I hadn't woken up upset. I didn't feel like trying to be subtle and break up an argument between anyone.

But I knew I would. I hated people arguing, especially when I loved one of them and cared too much about the other.

"When were you going to tell me?" came the voice that was all gruff, hoarse, round edges dipped in chocolate. It was such a nice voice, even if he did wield it like a freaking sword to chop people and their feelings in half. But at least he did it with everyone. He had high expectations and didn't let anyone at the shop get away with things. Me—and my screwup—included.

Regardless of how he'd been with me on Friday, I had still made a nice, big birthday cake for him yesterday. I made one for everyone, even the ones I couldn't stand at CCC. I didn't have it in me to be mean and single them out by not bringing something for them too. But my favorite people at the shop got their favorite cakes. Everyone else got whatever box mix was on sale.

"Ripley, give me a break. I didn't think you would care," the other voice, the one I'd been listening to for nearly the last ten years of my life, responded. It was softer, lighter, *patient.*

The exact opposite of Ripley's in more ways than one.

"You think I wouldn't care about who you hire to work with me?"

"Of course you'd care about that, but all I did was post an ad for the job opening. I didn't think I needed to check with you about posting one. Come on, son," Mr. Cooper said.

"Don't fucking call me that. I'm not your son."

If I had a dollar for every morning that I'd come into the break room and overheard them disagreeing over something in one of the two offices, I would have had enough money to go on that vacation to Greece I'd been promising myself for forever.

The first time I'd heard them fighting, it had worried me. It had been an argument over payroll and how the shop had too many employees the day after he had put me through his random test over how much I knew. I'd been worried for days that a lot of us at the shop were going to get fired. I was one of the youngest employees. If anyone was going to get the boot, I'd figured it would have been me. They could always contract out to a business that only did paint. I was fully aware of that.

Luckily, no one had gotten fired. It had taken two months of waiting around and eavesdropping almost daily to figure out that Mr. Cooper had put his foot down and wasn't letting anyone get axed.

At least, no one got fired unless they deserved it.

Now, I just accepted that the man with the voice I liked listening to—and the face I liked looking at—picked arguments with Mr. Cooper for no reason at all. The sky was too blue? He'd blame him. There was some part that he needed that hadn't been ordered? He'd blame him.

I didn't get it, and I doubted I ever would; Mr. Cooper was great. Greater than great. I would give him any organ in my body if he needed it.

As much as I eavesdropped, I hadn't been able to figure out what had happened to make them the way they were. If I really thought about it, there were a lot of things about them I hadn't been able to figure out. None of us had, and we had tried. I had spent a lot of time listening to Mr. Cooper and Rip because something about their arguments felt... weird.

I was pretty sure there was some serious resentment, at least on Ripley's part, but I couldn't figure out why. Why Mr. Cooper would bring someone into the company—*his* company—who he didn't get along with?

There had to be a reason why a man had shown up one day and become our newest boss, almost without warning, without anything more than a strained smile from the owner of the business and a "I'd like you all to meet Ripley" in the break room.

Ripley, this man who constantly kept his skin covered with long-sleeved shirts. I had *never*, ever seen him wearing anything else. Not when we worked until midnight. Not when we worked until two o'clock in the morning. Not at seven in the morning. Not even on a Saturday. He constantly hid whatever tattoos he had.

At first, I had wondered if they were ugly or old, but he didn't strike me as the type to care what other people thought. Plus, wouldn't he have just gotten them redone if that was the case? Mr. Cooper had never been slumming it financially, and the business had only boomed in the years since it had expanded into the restoration business—specifically with the cars Rip bought, restored, and then sold. I couldn't think of a single car he'd worked on that hadn't been flipped in a matter of weeks for a lot more than he had invested in them. He could have easily afforded getting tattoos redone if he didn't like them. The only reasonable explanation I could think of was that some tattoos were intensely personal to people. I didn't walk around flashing the one I had around.

A part of me was holding out hope that one day he'd slip up and tug his shirt up his forearm or something. He could accidentally pull up his shirt too if he wanted, and I wouldn't complain. Knowing him, that day was never going to come. If he hadn't shown them off already, I really doubted he ever would.

Then again it wasn't my business what they were. If I wanted to know bad enough, I guess I could have used the favor he owed me to get him to tell me, but I didn't. I wouldn't, either.

Focusing on that moment though, I decided to do the same thing I always had when I overheard them. While I was at it, I could drop off the cake that I had made for Rip. Up until last year, I hadn't even known what day his birthday was; the only reason I found out was because he'd tossed his wallet at me one day so I could grab his credit card and buy his lunch, and his driver's license had been right there.

Last year, he had looked like he didn't know whether he wanted to throw his cake away or eat it, but he had still thanked me.

I was expecting pretty much the exact same thing this year, but that was good enough for me.

After filling the coffee pot with water and a brand-new filter, I pulled out the secret container of decaf I hid in one of the cabinets and scooped some into the basket. Then, turning around to make sure no one was hiding in a corner and watching what I did, I filled up the rest with regular caffeinated grounds. So far, in the years since I'd taken over making the first pot of coffee, no one had caught onto my blend. Otherwise, there would be a whole lot of crying over drinking decaf.

The fact was, I didn't need my hands shaking from too much caffeine when I had to deal with paint, and the last thing most of the people I worked with needed was anything else to get them even more wired than they were on a normal basis.

I watched the pot and waited.

I also kept listening to the two men in the room next door because there was nothing else to do. At least that's what I told myself to justify eavesdropping. I wasn't standing outside the office door with my ear pressed to it or anything. It wasn't my fault the building wasn't sound-proofed that well.

"Last time I checked, this is our business and we make decisions together," the deeper voice grumbled.

"You're getting mad over an ad?"

"I'm getting mad over you not including me in decisions that affect me," the younger man replied.

I had to give it to Mr. Cooper. I wasn't sure why Rip was picking an argument with him over an ad for a job opening. I mean, really?

"Ripley, I didn't hire anyone. All I did was place an ad."

"It's not that you placed an ad. It's that you didn't tell me

about it. I'm sick and fucking tired of you doing things without telling me. You don't listen."

"What haven't I listened to you about?" Mr. Cooper asked, finally sounding a little impatient.

"Where do you want me to start? You want me to work my way back or work my way in order to this?"

I winced.

This wasn't going to get any better. I didn't need a crystal ball to know that, if anything, this was going to go downhill real quick. Crap.

So I did what I'd been doing when I thought their arguments were on the verge of spiraling out of control—like that one time I'd heard something break from inside the office and then hadn't seen Mr. Cooper at the shop for days afterward. He had finally told me, weeks later, that he wasn't used to having someone else to answer to and had needed time to get away because his blood pressure had gone up so much his chest had ached.

I didn't want Mr. Cooper, who had been taking blood pressure medicine for as long as I'd known him, to have an achy chest. So I was going to have to be the one to do something. No one else would.

A memory of my dad calling me a nosey-ass slipped into my thoughts for a second, but I forced the memories down and snagged two mugs from the drying rack beside the sink and poured identical amounts of sugar into each.

The light on the coffee maker came on just as I finished pouring the last of the creamer into one of the mugs. At the same time, I heard Mr. Cooper raise his voice on the other side of the wall, sounding more frustrated than I had heard him in a long time. *"What have I honestly done lately to make you be like this with me?"*

Part of me wished that wasn't about the tenth time I'd heard those exact words said out loud.

It only made me wonder even more what the hell that even meant.

What have I honestly done lately to make you be like this with me? I mean those were some harsh words. Resentful words. But it was as far as they went.

Filling the cups with the hot coffee, I stirred both of them with the same spoon and slipped the loops of the shopping bag carrying the cake container around my wrist. Then I picked up the mugs by their handles, ignoring how many times I had done this exact same thing for other people in my life—except in those cases, the coffee never did anything, no matter how much I would have wanted it to. It had always come back around to bite me in the ass.

But anyway.

"Mr. Cooper?" I called out as I walked out of the break room and turned to the left. Making sure I didn't spill coffee on myself, I tapped my elbow against the closed door directly next to the one I'd just come out of. The only thing that told anyone what was behind the door was a small faded green plaque that said OFFICE. We had brought it with us during the move from the original CCC building.

There was a pause before Mr. Cooper's familiar voice called out, "Morning, Luna. Come in," like he had every time I knocked on his door.

I made myself smile as I pushed the door open and found Mr. Cooper behind his desk, looking pretty worn out for how early it was. His hair had already been a mix of silver and white by the time I'd met him, but it was hard not to notice how much more there was now. The lines at his eyes were deeper than I remembered, and his thin lips were pressed tight so often now it was hard to remember what they looked like when they weren't.

The man needed a vacation, and not just a quick weekend getaway but a nice long one. I should mention it to Lydia. He needed to start cutting back on his hours too, while he was at it, but that was another battle.

"Good morning, Mr. Cooper," I replied as I took a step inside the tiny room he called his office. "I heard you both in here and wanted to bring you some coffee before I head to the booth and get started." I walked toward his desk and handed over the chipped white mug that said COOPER'S COLLISION AND CUSTOMS that was more than likely about as old as I was.

Mr. Cooper smiled at me, but I could see the tension along his eyes. "You didn't have to," he said, like he had every morning we did this routine of me pretending to come in here to be nice, but all of us knowing that wasn't exactly the truth. Maybe they didn't know how much I eavesdropped when they spoke in normal voices, but we all knew there was no ignoring them when they raised their voices or yelled.

"It's no problem," I told him as his hands clasped the bottom of the mug and he took it from me. I eyed him and raised my eyebrows. "Nice haircut."

"Thank you," he replied, a wary expression dusting his cheeks as he kept on smiling.

I flashed him one back, except it wasn't forced or strained at all before I turned with my other hand outstretched, holding the second mug of coffee—a vintage one that Lenny had given me that said Cats The Musical on the side—and faced the other man in the room. I didn't let my expression change. I kept the big smile on my face. "I brought yours too, Rip," I said, calmly holding the coffee cup out, my eyes gluing themselves to the hint of a tattoo on his throat that he always had mostly concealed by the high-necked gray layer he had on.

I hid my surprise that he was arguing with Mr. Cooper on a day he wore gray and let my smile grow even bigger instead, just to be a pest. Maybe Friday hadn't exactly gone great, but from experience, he didn't hold grudges for too long. Also, he wasn't going to ask if I'd decided what favor I wanted because we weren't alone. He'd find me later on and do it.

I watched as a hand that seemed to be twice the size of mine lifted from beside where it had been hanging loosely at his side. Then I watched as his fingers and the back of his hand—covered in a miniature grim reaper with a sickle and other random thick black lines and a letter that I was fairly certain was an M on the ring finger—took the cup from me. Then, and only then, did I let myself glance up and take in the face that I thought about way too much for my own good, even when he wasn't being his nicest.

Because even if I only thought about him once a day, it was one time too many. I knew where we stood. I also had an internal radar for pointless things, and he was one of those.

I wasn't in love or anything, but I liked a lot of things about him. What I honestly probably liked the most was that he didn't take anyone's BS, even if he did take that a little far sometimes. I admired Lucas Ripley. I admired a lot about him. Maybe he wasn't the kindest or the sweetest man in the world, but he wasn't mean or unnecessarily rude... the majority of the time. The other guys at the shop called him a hard-ass, but I thought he was a decent man.

I liked Rip the same way I liked Louis Vuitton purses that I realistically knew I would never own because there was always something else I had to spend money on. Just because they would never be mine didn't mean I couldn't appreciate them. So...

What I didn't like was how grouchy he was with Mr. Cooper, but Mr. Cooper had told me three years ago, not to let it bother me after I had brought it up. *I've known him forever, little moon. He's a good kid beneath it all. Don't think twice about it. I can take it.*

"Thank you, Luna," the huge man replied.

"You're welcome," I said, like I had every morning that we had the same exchange.

Because this was what we did every morning, even if he wasn't fighting with Mr. Cooper when I showed up. I made coffee, prepared a cup how he preferred it—I'd learned how he liked it by watching him a couple of times when we were in the break room at the same time—and took it to whatever car he happened to be working on in the massive open floor space. I would set the mug on the nearest flat surface and say, "Good morning." Then, depending on what color shirt he was wearing, he would tell me "thank you" either clearly or in a grumble. I would say, "You're welcome." He would ask me "Did you decide?" I would tell him I hadn't, and also depending on his mood, I'd ask if he'd had a good night or a good weekend, or whatever. I would either get a one-word answer or two-word, if I was lucky, and that was that. That was it.

I pulled the handles of the bag off my wrist and opened it. "Happy birthday." I pulled the metal pan with the plastic cover over it out and then held it in his direction, still smiling. "It's chocolate with vanilla frosting," I explained, still holding it out toward him.

Those blue-green eyes widened.

Then those eyes—those freaking eyes that were a shade

of color that didn't seem natural—flicked down toward the cake then back toward my face.

His eyes widened just a little more.

Then he did it.

For the first time in months, his mouth tipped up maybe a millimeter. At the most a millimeter. But it was a smile. A tiny smile that might have been interpreted a dozen other ways by people who hadn't spent a whole lot of time looking at this man's face... but I had, and I knew what it was. A little smile.

All because of a birthday cake.

Like a hopeless dummy, my heart thumped.

"No shit?" he asked, sounding like he hadn't just been arguing two minutes ago. Like he was still surprised I had made it for him even though I had done the same last year. His mouth was still formed into that microscopic smile, and I could see his eyes stray to my earrings of the day. They were cupcakes. I'd put them on for his birthday.

So I nodded, still grinning. "I didn't want to leave it in the fridge in case you didn't want to share."

That and he wouldn't want anyone to make a big deal about his forty-first.

Those huge hands came up and took the container from me, moving it up and down like he was testing the weight. It was just a sheet cake in a normal pan with a lid on it. It wasn't a big deal. The whole thing took maybe thirty minutes total to mix ingredients and then decorate. It was nothing. Really. I just remembered what it was like to want a birthday cake and not have anyone around to buy one or make one for me. The girls had been too young then.

"Thanks, Luna."

I tried not to beam at him, but I was pretty sure I failed. "You're welcome." I wasn't going to warn him it said Happy

Birthday Boss-Man on the inside. Hopefully it would make him smile when he was alone in a dark room. "You don't look a day over forty."

He didn't react to my joke. Those almost teal-colored eyes were still on the red lid when he basically muttered, "You coming to Mickey's tonight?"

Mickey's was the bar a few blocks down where everyone at the shop celebrated birthdays or just randomly met up for drinks sometimes after work. He had never made it a point before to spend time with any of us though. Not even on his last birthday or anyone else's. So....

"Sure," I told him, just barely holding on to my smile. I'd have to tell my sister I was going out, but according to her work schedule on the fridge, she'd be waiting tables until ten anyway.

Rip nodded, that tiny smile melting off until his facial expression was just... more easygoing than usual. "All right."

That was the level of excitement I was expecting, and it made me smile.

It was fine. I was ready to get the hell out of there and get to work, forget my nightmare and this morning, and just... be fine.

"I hope you like your cake, but I should get to the booth," I told him, taking a step back and keeping the smile on my face.

"Busy day?" Mr. Cooper asked, sounding about as professional as he ever did with me because we were in front of Rip.

I turned to look at him and nodded, giving him a rundown of what I had on the schedule. "It's been so humid, the paint is being a pain drying, but I'll figure it out."

Mr. Cooper nodded. "Miguel called in today."

Miguel was one of the shop's body guys, and one of my favorite people at CCC. He called out every other month, usually always on a Friday, but when he did, it was to take his kids out of school early so they could go do things. I thought it was sweet. For him to take a Monday off, especially on a day that wasn't a school holiday, was weird. I'd have to text him and see if he was all right.

Rip was the one who kept talking though. "I needed his help." I already knew where this was headed. "Think you can squeeze in some time to help me finish up some bodywork and do at least a coat of primer before you go today?"

Well, the only plan I'd had for the evening was going to his birthday get-together thing that evening... and even if that hadn't been my only plan as of two minutes ago, I already knew I would have said yes.

Even though I would have rather *not* added more items to my list of things to do. I guess I could skip taking a real lunch break and eat in my room instead? That would clear up some time.

It wasn't like I needed to go to his birthday thing in the first place.

Or needed to get there at a certain time.

"You don't have to," Mr. Cooper added a moment later.

I watched Ripley open his mouth—to argue? To tell him that I did have to? I had no idea—but he closed it almost immediately. They weren't supposed to argue in front of employees.

Even me.

But I didn't miss the aggravated look he shot Mr. Cooper for giving me an out.

"It's okay, Mr. Cooper." I had my eye on a granite countertop that was way out of my budget, and more overtime meant I was closer and closer to affording it. I nodded at

Rip, still giving him a smile. "Let me look at my list for the day and rearrange some things, but I think I can make it work."

It was Mr. Cooper who asked, "You're sure?"

Not really but, "Yeah."

Rip nodded, but I could see the look my original boss shot the man who was sharing his responsibilities with him now. He wasn't pleased. It was nice at least that he wasn't.

"If you need help, let us know. I've been thinking Jason should get some time in the booth," Mr. Cooper offered after a moment, watching me carefully. The booth was what we called the large, isolated, illuminated room where the painting went on for the shop. It was where I spent most of my time, unless I was helping out doing bodywork or detailing, if things were slow.

The idea of spending time with Jason sounded worse than flicking bleach into my eyes, but I nodded and kept the grimace off my face. At least I hoped I did. Mr. C knew better than anyone how I felt about him. If he was trying to get me to work with him... maybe he knew something I didn't. Then again, maybe he didn't and he figured the only way to fix things between us was to stick us together. I wasn't a fan of that plan though. "Thanks."

Mr. Cooper's mouth shaped into a smile that eased my horror over Jason a little. I guessed he was pleased I wasn't automatically telling him not to send that pain in the butt over to me. "We'll chat later?"

Not thinking anything of it, I said, "Sure. I'll see you later. I'm going to get started." I glanced in Ripley's direction, briefly taking in his long-sleeved shirt and the jeans that had so many stains on them there was hardly any hint of blue still on them, and gave him one last little smile. "Have a nice day, Rip. Happy birthday again."

In the same way he always had and probably always would, he grunted his response. "Thanks, Luna."

"See you later," I said to Mr. Cooper.

"Let us know if you need help," the older man called out to me as I backed out of the room. "I can get Jason to go back there, if need be."

I raised my hand and waved in acknowledgment.

Swallowing at the pulse in my chest from that smile Rip had shared, I made my way toward the break room and tried to prepare my coffee as fast as possible. I was going to need every minute I could get if I wanted to try and make it to the bar for Rip's birthday.

I wondered why he'd made that decision but then decided it didn't really matter, did it?

I'd barely managed to scoop one teaspoon of my stash of coconut sugar into my travel mug when I heard the men on the other side of the wall begin talking again.

But this time in almost whispers. I guess they either didn't realize how good my hearing was or how thin the walls were, because I could hear everything.

It was Mr. Cooper who spoke first. *"She's such a nice girl."*

There was a pause that I wasn't sure what to do with and then a response of, *"Yeah."*

That was probably the nicest thing he'd ever said, other than the occasional compliments he gave one of my paint jobs.

Then Mr. Cooper kept talking, *"You should—"*

The response came in the form of one word. *"No."*

No.

No what?

What the hell was Mr. Cooper trying to say before Rip had cut him off? He should what? Tell me thank you? Buy me a card? Be a little friendlier? Not be so abrupt with someone who was slightly fonder of him than he probably deserved? I had never said anything to Mr. Cooper, or anyone at the shop, about finding Rip attractive or anything like that. I couldn't see him making such a forceful "no" to Mr. Cooper suggesting he tell me thanks or buy me a card being worth that, but...

There was no way it would be anything else. Like Mr. Cooper would tell him to be interested in me. And like Rip would even put thoughts into his head like that. *Yeah, right.*

I couldn't even—

What was I doing? Was I really going to let a dumb dream about my dad get me down? Was I trying to feel sorry for myself? Was I going to get flustered because Rip didn't *like me*? I knew damn well that had never even been a possibility in the first place. He could barely talk to me without huffing and puffing half the time. He'd agreed I was a nice girl, not that I was pretty or that he should ask me on a date or anything like that.

I needed to get to work and forget all of this. I was going to ball all this up and just... throw it away. I'd done it enough over the years. I could do it again.

And I did. I wrapped up the tiny bit of hurt I felt at the idea that Rip would never be interested in me, my dream about two people who didn't know what kindness was if it kicked them in the face... and I dropped it into the imaginary trash can that was full of other things I didn't let hurt me anymore.

I was fine. The heart is more resilient than anyone ever gave it credit for, and I liked to think mine was a bad bish.

I rushed through pouring way too much milk into my cup, mixing in the coffee, giving it all a stir, and then hauled my ass downstairs so I could get to work.

I was fine. I was loved. I had everything I really needed. And my sister had made cherry pie, and I was pretty sure she'd put some into my lunch bag. That was definitely something great about today.

I'd been at Cooper's for so long I could have gotten around with a blindfold, luckily. Down the stairs and straight forward was the main floor where the repairs and remodels happened. Down the stairs and to the left, then straight, I could take the hall that would lead to the part of the building where I worked. It wasn't anything fancy, but there were two big bay doors. One that led into the hallway connected to the main floor and another that opened to the parking lot surrounding the building. The rest of the room was pretty sparse, containing a desk with a computer and printer on it, three different machines used to agitate the paint, a big industrial sink with soaps and products beside it, and a couple of chairs. The big, white booth set up against a corner took up a third of the room.

I'd already dropped off my things when I'd first showed up. I set my tumbler on the desk and went to unlock the drawer to get the folders for the projects I'd be working on. I opened the first one and had just started reading through what needed to be done, when my ringtone went off.

With my eyes still on the folder, I opened the drawer my purse was in and pulled my phone out.

I only hesitated for a second. It was the same number that had called and texted me last week. The one I had ignored.

Screw it.

I answered it. "Hello?"

There was a sound on the other end of the line before a voice I didn't recognize answered, "Hello, can I please speak with Miss Luna Allen?"

Miss Luna Allen? That was formal. I couldn't remember the last time anyone had used the m-word on me. "Hi, this is me."

"Oh," the unfamiliar male voice answered. "Hello, Miss Allen. How are you today?"

"I'm doing great," I lied a little. "How are you?"

"I'm well. Thank you for asking," the man replied. "My name is Julius Randall, and I'm calling on behalf of Miss Eugenia Miller."

At the mention of my grandmother's name, my chest went tight. I hadn't heard her name in... years. Not since I had gone to pick up Thea, Kyra, and Lily from her house.

Don't come back here, Luna, she had told me the last time I'd seen her. *Take them and none of y'all come back.*

And I hadn't. None of us had.

"Is everything... okay?" I asked, ignoring how quiet my voice had gotten.

"Unfortunately, Miss Miller passed away Saturday evening."

I swallowed and blinked at the timeframe.

"I attempted to contact you when she first went into the hospice..." He trailed off before clearing his throat. "She specifically requested that I reach out to you."

She had wanted me to know that she was sick?

I hadn't....

Something heavy—guilt, it was freaking guilt—settled right onto my chest. Had he called me before because she'd been asking for... maybe not *me* specifically, but my sisters? To see them one last time? To make sure we got to say good-bye, even if she wasn't aware of it?

"I'm so sorry," I muttered, trying to process his words. "I haven't spoken to my grandmother in years."

There was a pause on the other end. "I apologize for

being the bearer of bad news, Miss Allen, but she made it very clear that when the time came, that she wanted you to be informed."

It seemed like the words got sucked straight out of my mouth. I didn't wonder *why* she wanted that. I knew she had cared for my sisters. She had taken them in for three years before she had decided they would be better off far, far away from the rest of the family. She had told us not to come back.

We had never been that close in the first place, and... because life had gotten so crazy after that, I hadn't kept in touch. I hadn't realized that my siblings wouldn't have either. We rarely ever talked about life before they had come to Houston.

"Can you tell me what happened?" I asked, heaviness still weighing down on my chest.

"She suffered complications from pneumonia," the man on the line explained in a gentle but professional voice. "She had been diagnosed with dementia a few years ago. The funeral arrangements have been settled. There was an announcement in the paper. The funeral will be this upcoming Thursday."

"This Thursday?"

"I apologize if this seems last minute," the man apologized, too polite to say that he'd tried to warn me she wasn't doing well. "I can provide you with the service information if you're interested in attending."

Interested in attending her funeral?

The reality of what that meant suddenly clicked but...

My grandmother had *wanted* me to go. Or at least one of my sisters. Otherwise she wouldn't have asked her lawyer to contact me. She had wanted us to know.

I didn't want to go.

I felt terrible for thinking that but...

I didn't want to go. I didn't want Kyra or Thea or Lily to go either. No. Way.

She had known there was a reason why we hadn't physically seen each other since I was twenty. Yet she had still asked at some point when she had been well enough to make that kind of request. After everything Grandma Genie had done... taking in three kids while I'd been off in Houston, hundreds of miles away, working and trying to piece my life together, I could do it. For her.

Oh, God, but I didn't want to. I didn't freaking want to. I didn't, I didn't, I didn't.

The idea of my little sisters going was even more unbearable.

Memories of my life before I'd been seventeen, before I'd gotten the hell out of that house, ripped right through me and one of my knees instantly went numb.

I didn't want to go.

"Miss Allen?" the man spoke up.

I swallowed and clenched the muscles in my quads to wake my leg back up. I remembered everything good in my life.

And I still didn't want to fucking go.

I didn't want to see anyone, not in this lifetime or the next, if I was going to be totally honest.

"Miss Allen, are you there?"

I didn't want to see any of them. I had told myself that when I left, I never would ever again. I had promised myself that I wouldn't.

But Grandma Genie asked. Grandma Genie who had taken care of the girls when you couldn't. Who had called you to come for them.

I fisted my free hand and felt this horrible sense of

anxiety wrap around my heart, stealing the breath right out of me.

She had asked for me specifically.

It was the least I could do.

I don't want to go.

I didn't want to see the biggest assholes on the planet.

But Grandma Genie....

"I'm here," I muttered, flexing my quad muscles again. I couldn't even stand the sound of my own voice as I replied, and I sure didn't like the sound of it as I said, "Can you give me a second to get a piece of paper so I can write down the information?"

"Of course, Miss Allen. While you do that, I would like to inform you about a matter of an inheritance that Miss Miller endowed on you in her will. There are some forms you'll need to fill out and return to me—"

I hated how much my hand shook as I wrote down the name and the address of the funeral home, memorizing the time for it. I let the information about inheritance go in one ear and out the other. None of that mattered to me even a little bit, especially not when I was too focused on all the rest of the news that came with Grandma Genie passing away in the first place. On what going to her funeral might mean.

I thought I was better than this. I thought I had gotten over it. I had grown up. Gotten stronger.

I didn't want to go. I didn't want to go. *I didn't want to fucking go. Not to San Antonio. Not to anywhere near San Antonio.*

Part of me wanted to believe they wouldn't be there. Or maybe if they were, they wouldn't have the balls to say anything to me. They picked on people they thought were weaker than them. I was older. Not tougher, but I was older and stronger.

Lily and them might be mad when I told them that I didn't want them to go, but they'd get over it.

We had made a pact when I had picked them up and taken them back to Mr. Cooper's house. We weren't going back *there*. We were going to start over again, together. We were going to do great.

I stared at the notes written on the work order I needed to get started on, but not remembering a single word of it because...

I didn't want to go.

Just as quickly as that thought entered my head, another one did too.

Hell.

I had something to think about.

CHAPTER FIVE

I HAD MADE A LOT OF DUMB DECISIONS IN MY LIFE.

A lot.

I could be honest about it, mostly because I had learned valuable lessons from each screwup in my life.

Don't waste your time expecting people to change, and if you think you might be starting your period, don't risk it and leave your house without a tampon.

Honestly, the list was pretty freaking long, but those were my favorite lessons.

But as I sat there at the bar, at an empty table, all by myself, I accepted the fact that coming here tonight could easily go down as one of those dumb decisions. Dumber than when I'd bought clothes a size smaller than what I usually wore to "motivate me to lose weight." They were still in my closet with the tags on. The problem with this dumb decision was that I doubted there was some lesson to be learned from it.

Nobody had forced me to come to the bar. No one had whispered into my ear, *"Luna, ruin your entire day by contemplating the idea of asking Rip to cash in your favor.*

Rush through work, head to the bar to sort-of celebrate his birthday, and then act like everything was fine."

I was going to ask Rip for a favor.

A favor he technically did owe. A favor he usually asked me about every single day we worked together, unless it was one of those mornings that had me breaking up an argument between him and Mr. Cooper and then we didn't see each other the rest of the day.

I didn't want to ask though.

I didn't want to ask him for anything.

The problem was, I didn't want to go to my grandmother's funeral alone. Just the idea of going by myself made me more nauseous than asking Rip for something. But the near panic I got at the idea of having my siblings go with me trumped everything else by far, and asking Mr. Cooper or one of my friends to go with me and possibly *see* up close who I was related to...

No. Just, no.

It was just a trip to San Antonio. Nine hours total. He would just have to sit there and possibly give people that death glare he'd perfected before he had started working at CCC.

It was nothing to worry about. If anything, Rip should be happy this was all I was going to ask of him. Shouldn't he? Maybe he'd be in a better mood, not having to ask me the same question only to get the same answer all the time.

He'd wanted to get rid of this loose end between us from the very beginning. He had never hidden that. Not once. So I was going to do him a favor and get it over with after so freaking long.

Maybe he'd even thank me.

Yeah, right. I'd lost my mind. I was seriously going to ask *Rip* for a favor? Ripley the same man who, based on the scarring on his knuckles that marred the letters he had tattooed on them, had more than likely gotten into more fights in his life than a professional MMA fighter? I was going to ask him to go with me to my grandmother's funeral so that he'd hopefully stop my family from trying to talk to me?

I was pathetic. I really was. Just like my dad had said for so much of my childhood.

Sad, stupid-ass.

That memory came out of freaking nowhere.

I stomped it back down into its little box.

I was having a good day. My sister *had* put a piece of cherry pie into my lunch, and that was something great about today. I had gotten all of my work done and then some.

I was happy. I was loved. I had everything and more I could have wanted.

I could do it. I had done scarier things than asking for something. I was past all this crap.

That's exactly what I was going to think to myself as I sat there, alone, watching Rip at the bar as he got a drink, and waiting for more of my coworkers to show up because so far no one else had gotten there yet even though I'd been the second to last one to leave. Knowing most of my coworkers, they either wouldn't come or they were at home pre-gaming, aka having beers so they wouldn't spend as much drinking at the bar. It wouldn't be the first time they did that.

The good thing with me was, I didn't drink that much in the first place. I didn't like the idea of being in a car with a stranger drunk or even slightly out of it. Plus, there was also that worry that I had always carried inside of me about how I would act if I was under the influence of anything.

Was I really going to ask him?

My phone buzzed from inside my purse. I took it out and saw my best friend's name on the screen, and an idea came to me. If Rip told me to fuck off, I could always tell her to ask one of her friends to go with me. One of them would say yes. I wouldn't care what someone I didn't know thought.

There was always a plan B.

Lenny: What are you doing tonight?

I didn't hesitate texting her back. It wasn't like there was anything else to do but look around and stress.

Me: It's my boss's birthday and I'm at the bar.

Lenny: Rip?

Me: Yeah.

I realized right then that I had been so busy I hadn't texted her all day.

Me: My grandma died a few days ago. Her lawyer called to tell me about the funeral arrangements. She had asked that he let me know....

A wave of sadness and guilt had me holding my breath before I kept typing.

Me: The funeral is next week in San Antonio. I don't want to go, but I kinda owe it to her to have one of us go. Better me than Lily, Kyra, or Thea.

Was my head starting to hurt or was I imagining it?

Gripping my phone in my hand, I glanced up and took in the man ten feet away. I studied his wide back, no longer covered by a gray shirt but instead by a deep green Henley that hugged the flat expanse of his stomach, every notch of his spine, and curve of his lateral muscles, yet managed to still cling to his waist. He was plain big all over. Everywhere. I'd watched him enough to know. I could live the rest of my life and not forget any part of what he looked like.

I sighed, but I still didn't look away. He'd already been standing at the bar for at least five minutes, either still waiting for his drink or pretending like I wasn't the only person from work here.

My phone buzzed again.

Lenny: That blows. I'm sorry.

Lenny: I'll go with you. I ain't scared.

I bit the inside of my cheek and typed my response.

Me: I know you would, Len, but you're still healing from your surgery and can't choke anybody out.

I knew I should tell her that I was thinking about asking Rip, but she didn't know about the favor. She had heard, better than anyone, just what I thought about him. It wouldn't make sense to her why a man who barely spoke to me would go with me back home.

I had buried myself in a lie by not telling the truth, and now there was no way to get out of it without having to explain the whole thing, and as much as I loved and cared for Lenny DeMaio, it wasn't my business to tell her what had happened.

Rip and I were the only two people in the world who needed to know the truth.

Me: Next family funeral.

Next family funeral. Like there was someone else in my biological family other than my sisters who I would miss or go visit when they were gone. How sad was that?

When I'd been growing up, I would have done freaking

anything for a dad to tuck me in. For a mom who would hug me and put Band-Aids on my boo-boos. For an older brother to protect me when people were mean. For my dad to play with me. For the person I had called my mom for years to hug me. For my older brother to just pay attention to me.

I had a faint memory of writing a letter to Santa when I'd still been holding out hope that he would finally be able to find my house so I could ask for things. But Santa never took my letters. He never answered any of my requests.

Christmas as a kid had included my uncle's family coming over for whatever fast food whoever was sober enough to realize we needed to eat, brought over, and so much beer and alcohol, everyone over the age of fifteen got drunk and started arguing. There was always at least one fistfight or two and at least one drug. There were never any gifts. A single tree or ornament. Or any love. Christmas hadn't been anything like what movies showed.

For a long, long time, I would have done anything if the family I had at that point would have just been... a fraction of the people I wanted them to be.

But they hadn't been.

A lot of people didn't have that. I wasn't alone, and that knowledge had helped the older I'd gotten. It still hurt, and part of me still couldn't help but wish...

I sighed.

Then one little sister had come, and another, and then Lily... and they had been everything I could have hoped for. It probably helped that their mom didn't have a nurturing bone in her body, but they had been my little people. They had given me their love, and I had taken it all.

I had done my best to make sure at least my sisters had a tiny little something on Christmas Day from money I stole from whoever was dumb enough to leave their purse or wallet lying around. A hairbrush from the dollar store. Some barrettes. Maybe it wasn't anything flashy, but it was something, and none of them had ever complained.

That's why I was going to go to San Antonio. So they wouldn't. So even Grandma Genie wouldn't be alone with people she hadn't been able to stand either while she'd been alive.

My best friend wrote me back immediately, saving me from going down that path of useless wishes that were never going to come true.

Lenny: I have another arm, bish, and two good legs.

Lenny: I know at least 3 guys at the gym that would pretend to be your bodyguard if you just fed them.

That solidified plan B, even if I hated asking for favors almost as much as I hated relying on people.

My only consolation with Rip was that he owed me in the first place. At least he thought he owed me. It also helped that I couldn't think of a single person, a big MMA fighter or not, who was as scary or intimidating as Lucas Ripley was. That was the truth.

The fact that I didn't mind looking at him, and that I enjoyed him when he wasn't grumbling at me, was only a tiny factor. Tiny, tiny.

Only idiots liked men who they had no chance with.

But this was my curse—to love and care for people who didn't love or care for me back. At least not the way I wanted them to.

With Rip, I'd accepted what our relationship was from the beginning.

Out of all the men in the world that my heart could go

whoosh, whoosh, whoosh over from time to time when I didn't have it reined in, out of all of the men who could have the ability to make me master looking out of the corner of my eye, it had to be one of my bosses who had that effect on me.

Of course it had to be.

My not-so-very nice boss.

Because it was my curse.

I was so dumb.

Holding my phone on my lap, I glanced up, even though a giant part of me didn't want to, but all I saw was the same thing I'd seen moments before. A man, who I knew was six foot four, wedged onto a tall stool. A man with deep brown hair with a hint of silvery gray threaded through it. A man with a face that was usually set into an aggravated expression or an angry one... except when there was good news that was work-related. Well over two hundred pounds poured over a frame that was *all* solid Huge thighs, big butt, forearms the size of my biceps if not bigger, a chest that could double as a bed for a medium-sized dog....

Buck up, Luna, just ask him, my conscience told me. *He owes you. He owes you big time. Sort of.*

Squeezing my eyes shut, I tried to tell my dumb heart to calm down. I tried to tell my eyes to go somewhere else. Anywhere else. Anyone else.

But the heart wants what it wants. And it's scared of what it wants to be scared of, no matter how reasonable you try to be about it.

Like a fearless but total moron.

The vibrating from my lap had me glancing down at the screen to see the last message that had come through.

Lenny: Don't go to the funeral if you don't want to. Your grandma would understand.

That icky, thick feeling flooded my stomach again, covering over the frustration I felt with myself for being attracted to Rip in the first place. But if there was something that could make me forget about that, it was the guilt I felt for walking out of my grandmother's life so many years ago and never seeing her again.

We had both known it was the only way things could be between us, but it still didn't help me feel any better.

Me: I have to, even though I would rather get stuck behind someone driving ten miles under the speed limit for an hour. You know what she did for us. It's the least I can do.

That much, Lenny did know. She and her family had been there for me when I had taken my siblings. She knew almost as much as I let anyone know, minus the Coopers. It wasn't everything. No one knew about all the little pieces, but it was a lot.

Two seconds went by before I got a response.

Lenny: The offer stands, bish.

Lenny: You're the best person I know, fyi.

I smiled down at my phone.

Me: I love you too

Lenny: [eye rolling emoji]

Lenny: I was texting you because Grandpa G is making margaritas and he was asking where you were.

Me: Tell him I love him.

Lenny: I will. You find Rip?

Me: I'm watching him.

Lenny: Stalker

Me: He's standing in front of me, I can't help it.

Lenny: Pretty sure that's what every stalker thinks.

I chanced another glance at the man and held back a sigh.

Me: Sometimes I don't understand why him.

Lenny: Because he looks like he's been in jail and that's about as far away from what every jackass you've ever dated looks like?

Lenny: Grandpa G says he loves you too and to come over and bring the girl with you if she's around. I didn't tell him you're at the bar, otherwise he'd want to invite himself. You know how that man gets in public.

I almost laughed at the first comment and definitely laughed at the second one. Rip did look like he'd done time. That was unfair, but it was the truth.

For all I knew, he probably had.

Then again, I was probably judging him by a face he had no say in. For all I knew, he had a marshmallow heart and rescued and rehabilitated small animals when he wasn't at work. Deep down, he might have a caring and loving disposition that he only shared around very few people—people who had won his trust.

You never knew.

The idea of that put a small smile on my face and kept it there as I typed a message back, leaving the first comment alone.

Me: I don't know how much longer I'll be here, but if I leave soon, I'll drop by. Tell

Grandpa G that the girl is working tonight. You're all coming for the graduation, right?

Lenny: Yes. I'm legit ready to cry this Saturday.

Lenny: I've got the blow horn ready by the way. TOOT TOOT, bish.

She wasn't the only one preparing herself to cry this weekend, and that made me happy for some reason.

I was still smiling over Lenny's text when Rip turned from where he was at the bar, holding a glass with some dark liquid inside, and instantly locked his gaze on me.

I didn't hesitate smiling wider before setting my phone back on the table, even as my heart started thumping at the fact that I was about to ask him for something.

I didn't want to. I had never wanted to. I had planned on never asking him for anything.

But...

Well...

I would ask him for this.

I had to. For my sisters. For me, because I really was nervous going alone back to the place I'd grown up.

Almost like he could sense what was going on inside of me, his eyes narrowed just a little, just barely enough for me to be able to tell that he had. And because of that, I made my smile go as big as possible, even flashing him teeth. He already had a feeling that something was going on. There was no hiding it, unfortunately. I was a decent liar until people got to know me.

Rip stood there for a second watching me with those heavy, dark brown eyebrows low over his blue-green eyes. By the time another second had passed, he had taken a step forward. Then another foot went ahead. And another.

He was coming toward me in his tight long-sleeved green shirt, showing off more tattoos on his neck than I had ever, *ever* seen in the years we had known each other. There was a skull—an actual skull—tattooed over his Adam's apple with lines and shapes spread out along the sides of it. And I was thinking to myself that I wanted to change my freaking mind about the favor... but I couldn't.

I wouldn't.

I had done scarier things than this. I would do scarier things than this. Fear, I thought, was more like a hallucinogenic. It was all in your mind, and there was nothing to really be scared of as long as you knew and expected the worst and the best.

"Hi, Birthday Man," I managed to get out, still grinning at him with my stupid heart beating in my throat even though I told it not to, trying my best not to look too hard at the very dark ink permanently etched into his skin.

Rip slid me a look out of the corner of his eye as he pulled the chair in front of mine out. He took the seat. Right *there*. Right by me.

Okay. I could play it cool. I could take it easy.

"You been here long?" he asked in that grumbled, deep voice that constantly sounded irritated... even now.

I shook my head. "Just about twenty minutes," I replied. "You?"

He made a noise that sounded like a grunt as he raised the glass of whatever he was drinking to his lips and took a sip.

Well, it wasn't like it really mattered how long he'd been around.

"Is anyone else coming?" I asked him when he didn't say anything after setting his glass back down on the table. I'd overheard a couple of the guys talking about Rip's half-hearted invitation when I had taken a bathroom break, but I hadn't heard more than that.

His gaze hadn't left mine from the moment he had spotted me, and it didn't go anywhere as he shrugged and said, "Doubt it."

I must have made a face because he added, casually, "I'm not exactly anybody's favorite, Luna."

The smile fell right off my mouth, and I couldn't help but frown at him. At the harshness of his words. At the... fact-like nature of them. That wasn't very nice for him to assume. That wasn't very nice to assume at all, and it bothered me... even if it was true that Mr. Cooper was my favorite person at the shop. And I was his. And Miguel's—

Crap.

"I'm sure—" I started before getting cut off.

"I'm not," he told me, tapping his short fingernails against the glass. Rip tipped his chin up a millimeter, giving me a slightly better view of the shading tucked up against his jawline. He swallowed, everything about his body language saying that he was telling me these words in this way because it wasn't a big deal to him. He didn't care. Why should he? His body said.

His next words confirmed it. "I'm not around to be anybody's friend."

All righty then.

I wanted to tell him something that would make it seem that it wasn't like anyone hated him or disliked him.

Most of the guys were just... wary.

Even I was wary, and he didn't scare or intimidate me... unless I screwed up.

But I didn't know what to say to that comment. I hated liars as much as I hated aggressive drunk people and cooked carrots. So I did the only thing I could think of: I smiled at him and shrugged. He didn't look even a little put out or hurt by what he'd been saying. Who was I to make it a big deal if he claimed he didn't care? "Did you like your cake?"

All he did was tip his chin down as he nailed me with that intense, bright gaze, his fingers still wrapped around the nearly full glass.

And something told me *"Do it now, Luna."*

It was now or never.

I gave him a big smile. "Hey, Rip?"

He watched me as he lifted his drink and took another sip of it.

I guess that was going to be his version of saying yes.

Screw it. *Do it.*

I kept the smile on my face as I rushed out, "Iwantto-cashinmyfavor."

He didn't say anything for so long, I thought for sure he would end up telling me to fuck off, that he'd only been joking all along.

And it was right then, with the j-word at the front of my brain that I realized how stupid that thought was.

Rip joking? In my dreams.

If he was going to tell me no, he was going to need to say it. It wouldn't bother me. It wouldn't offend me. I'd move on and find someone else to go with me.

But what he said instead was "You wanna cash in your favor?"

The "yes" out of me was croaked and dumb-sounding, but if he didn't understand it, my nod would have to be enough.

Rip... Rip just sat there, lowering his glass to the table. He let out a deep breath that I barely managed to hear. A muscle in his cheek twitched. Then he just said one word, and it wasn't the one I'd been expecting. The one I wanted, but not anticipated. "Okay."

Okay?

That was it?

I'd learned as a kid never to give someone a reason to second-guess their answer if you had already gotten the one you wanted. So, all right. Maybe I didn't trust how easily the answer had come, but I was going to work with it. "I need you to go with me to a funeral."

The only sign I had that he'd heard me was his nostrils flaring. Then, he blinked. Lucas Ripley sat back in the stool, that tight shirt curving over his impressive chest, and pressed his lips together. His sentence was slow. "You want me to pretend we're getting married or something?"

Yeah. My mouth opened. Then it closed.

It was my turn to stare at him. My turn to press my lips together.

Then, and only then, did I tip my face up to the ceiling and freaking *laugh*.

I slapped my palm over my eyes, leaned back in my stool just like he had done, and I laughed even more.

I was so caught up in it that I almost missed out on the way he barked, "What?"

Did he think I wanted us to pretend we were engaged?

I laughed even more, dropping my palm but only to drag the back of my hand across my eyes.

"What the fuck is so funny?" he growled.

I couldn't help but grin at him, at this moment, at myself, at everything, and I couldn't help but keep laughing as I said, "No, I don't want you to pretend we're engaged."

I burst out laughing again, looking up at the ceiling as I did, before somehow managing to get out, "Why... why would I want that?"

I would swear on my future children that his face instantly went red. If someone had asked me if I thought he was physically capable of blushing, I would have thought they were nuts. But there it was: red on his cheeks. Even on his nose.

On anyone else, it would have been kind of adorable because he was scowling at the same time.

"No, that's not what I'm asking." I laughed again, genuinely trying to stop but not capable of it because his face was still red, and I was eating it up. "I wasn't expecting you to say that. It was straight out of a rom-com," I pretty much cackled, imagining him watching one at home, smiling to himself.

My boss full-on frowned. "What's a rom-com?"

Like he didn't know what a rom-com was. *Sure*. I could let it go. For now.

I took one look at his pink-red face and lost it all over again. *Pretend we're getting married.* Who would have known that Rip would make me laugh when I'd been so stressed about asking him for my favor all freaking day?

He didn't even let me enjoy it because his expression went *I'm gonna kill you*-like as I cracked up at his expense. "All you want is me to go to a funeral with you then?"

And there was the reminder of what I was asking of him. *Why* I was asking.

The smile and the laughter instantly left my face and my heart when I nodded, the severity of it stripping all that joy away. "Yes, please."

His eyes didn't narrow. He even lost the serial killer face. He just watched me. I wasn't sure if he didn't trust me or didn't believe this was what I was asking him, but I didn't really care.

I just stared right back at him, one single memory flipping out of me as I thought about why I had never planned on going back home.

I'm gonna fucking kill you, Luna! You ever come back, and I will literally fucking kill you, you little piece of shit! I can't fucking believe you!

It was enough to make me swallow. Enough to feel guilt for all of a split second before I squashed it with the heel of my work boots. I had no reason to feel bad.

Rip waited, thinking who knows what before he gave me a brisk nod, like it was a business transaction we had finally come to an agreement to after a lot of haggling.

Which I guess it was.

I had done something for him, and now he was doing something right back for me. It was what he had offered. It had been his idea.

But then he asked *me* something surprising. "You sure? That's what you want your favor to be?"

I nodded gravely. "I didn't want to ask you for anything, but, yeah, that's what I want." I gave him a smile that made my teeth hurt from how hard they were pressing down on each other at the memory I had just pushed right back out of my brain. "Please."

I was doing this for Grandma Genie. I was doing this for Thea and Kyra and Lily. I was going through with it because doing the right thing was hardly ever the easiest thing to do.

This handsome, hard-faced man, who I barely knew anything about after three years, kept watching me carefully. He sipped on his drink for a moment and then two. He slid me another narrow-eyed gaze as he did it, but it wasn't a *mean* one, or even an annoyed one.

"Okay," was Rip's reply.

Oh.

"Okay," I breathed out, relief like I couldn't put into words sliding right over my entire body. Just. Like. That.

Okay.

"Great," I told him, jumping on it before he could change his mind. "Thank you."

Those colorful eyes strayed to one of my ears and lingered there for a moment as he leaned back in his seat. "When?"

"Thursday," I answered, tempted to reach up and touch my earring, but I didn't. "I'm going to need the day off. *We're* going to need the day off."

He nodded again, looking so at ease it was like I hadn't asked him for anything.

"It's in San Antonio."

That had him grimacing, and I wondered why. But when he didn't complain or change his mind, I kept my mouth shut. If he didn't want to do it now for whatever reason, I wasn't going to rub it in and make him change his mind. There was always plan B and plan C.

"One day?" he asked, his voice sounding off after that initial grimace.

"Yes." There was no way in hell I wanted to stay in San Antonio longer than I needed to. Even one night would be way too much. One day felt like too much.

I didn't admit any of that though.

He only tipped his chin down, moved his gaze to the empty spot at the table, and then glanced back at my face. I almost missed the way his nostrils flared again. "Thursday then."

This Thursday. It hadn't hit me just how soon that was until right then.

"Yeah," I agreed, hoping he couldn't hear how much I was dreading it already.

Before I could say another word, or he could, a hand landed on my shoulder and gave it a squeeze.

I didn't need to look over to know it was one of my coworkers.

I was a little surprised when I heard, "Happy birthday," in Mr. Cooper's deep voice.

With the exception of maybe two or three times, Mr. C had never come out with us before. The only times he had were for Owen's bachelor party, which wasn't a party at all because he hadn't wanted to piss off his lady, and to celebrate when another coworker had quit after finishing college and getting a job as an engineer.

Besides that... never.

And then another voice came.

"Happy birthday, Ripley," came the feminine voice that I knew belonged to Mr. Cooper's wife.

If I wouldn't have moved my gaze back over to Rip, I would have missed the way that, with each word that came out of Mrs. Cooper's mouth—Lydia was her name—the harder Rip's face became. It had gone from pleasantly blank while we had been making arrangements to an instantly guarded expression when Mr. Cooper had spoken... and then with Mrs. Cooper's words, his jaw became more defined. The tendons at his neck became more pronounced. Then he slowly sat up in the chair he had just begun relaxing into.

Ripley had never been a comfortable, easygoing person.

But he had never looked the way he did right then either. At least never in front of me, and I had seen him pissed off and angry with the other shop guys before.

Not even when I had made him mad about screwing up the color on that Thunderbird had he made a face so cold.

But this... this wasn't anger. It wasn't fury or disappointment. At least not exactly. I was familiar with those expressions.

It looked like a million different emotions wrapped inside a body ready to burst at the seams.

He had never looked at Mr. Cooper like that before, even when he didn't know I was watching.

There was no way Mrs. Cooper had ever done anything to him. She was one of the nicest women I had ever met. She was loving and caring and warm. She had given me countless hugs and made *me* a birthday cake every year we had known each other.

Mr. Cooper had called her a saint before, and I believed it. I had lived with her for years. I'd spent almost every holiday together with her since I'd started working for CCC.

If he was wonderful, she was just as wonderful, and I loved them both.

So when I heard the deep breath that Rip let out, I didn't know what to think. He sounded... he sounded like he'd seen a storm and decided to put down shutters all over himself. From us.

I watched as his eyes went from Mr. Cooper to Mrs. Cooper and then back to the older man, his Adam's apple bulging more than I had ever seen. Then he said, "Thank you" like someone was torturing him to get the words out.

I didn't need to glance at the Coopers to feel the tension on their end.

It became even stronger as Ripley grabbed his drink from the table, put it up to his mouth, and tossed it back, not even wincing as he did.

In one swift move, he shoved his stool back and muttered, "Thanks for the birthday cake, Luna. I'll see you at work," talking to me and Mr. Cooper, obviously.

But he didn't look at either one of us.
He didn't look at Mrs. Cooper either.
One exhale later, he was gone.
Well.
That was freaking weird.

CHAPTER SIX

I couldn't say I wasn't relieved when I got to work the next day and only found Rip's truck in the lot. Without Mr. Cooper's car, I knew I wasn't going to head inside and overhear them arguing after what happened the night before. *Awkward.* I wasn't sure what was going on with him and Mr. Cooper lately, but things had seemed more tense than normal, and they hadn't been *that* great to start with.

On the way over to CCC, I had considered trying to avoid Rip so that I wouldn't give him a chance to tell me he'd changed his mind about going to San Antonio. Then I decided I wasn't going to be that much of a chicken. Because if I was nervous, then he'd begin wondering why that was the case.

I made my way inside, dropped off my things like normal, then headed upstairs to start making coffee. I hadn't spotted my boss slash future bodyguard on the way in, but I didn't think anything of it. I couldn't hear him in his office either, but there were a half-dozen places he could have been. I made both of our coffees then made my way down, finding him bent over the opened hood of the GMC truck he'd been working on. From what I could see, he wasn't wearing a white shirt under the navy blue coveralls he had on. I was pretty sure it was... a gray one. Gray wasn't a great color for his mood, but it wasn't white.

So.

Act normal.

Don't give him a reason to think twice about it.

"Morning, boss," I called out, hopefully sounding normal.

He didn't peek out while under the hood, but I did hear his low, nearly grumbled, "Morning."

At least he'd replied. I'd take it.

"Leaving your coffee on the blue bench," I told him as I was setting it down on one of the many tool chests along the wall.

There was a pause and then a "Thanks, Luna," that didn't sound *as* grumbled as his "morning" had come out. Maybe because it was the first time in forever that he hadn't needed to ask if I had decided on a favor I wanted from him.

Maybe.

I took a step back and eyed the butt partially outlined beneath the baggy material of the coveralls he already had on. Just for a second. His shoulders and arms were so wide he had to squeeze into an extra-large that was baggy around the middle. I let myself look once more before basically yelling, "You're welcome!" Asking him how the rest of his night had gone seemed like a terrible idea, so I didn't ask. You didn't storm out of the bar on your birthday and have a good rest of the night.

I managed to take maybe three steps backward and hadn't even turned around to head back, when I heard, "Hold up a sec."

I stopped in place. "Need something?"

Halfway hidden inside the car, he didn't raise his voice as he said, "I want to talk to you about that Mustang you've got on the schedule. Hold off on it until I think through it some more. I'll come down and tell you what to change later. All right?"

I hadn't looked through the paperwork yet, but okay. "Okay. I'll work around it."

"'Kay," he echoed from under the hood.

I made my way toward my room, holding my coffee and trying to remember what exactly I had to do. I was trying my best not to think about my grandmother. Or the funeral. Or going to San Antonio period. Or my sister's graduation and how it meant the beginning of the end. Instead, I thought about how nice the evening had been after Rip had left. I'd had a good time with the Coopers and the two CCC employees that had eventually shown up.

So that was what I was going to try and do, and if it required me to zone out everything else going on in my life, well, I could do it.

I managed to make it into my room and open my drawer to pull out my files, finding the one I was looking for. It was a Mustang that I had put primer down on last week, but they had held off on me finishing it. That kind of thing happened often enough, I didn't think anything of it.

Luckily, there was always something for me to work on. I went through the albums on my phone, picked out the *Grease* soundtrack and started my day.

* * *

I HAD JUST FINISHED what I could for the day when I went looking for Rip.

"He left," Miguel, one of my favorite coworkers, told me.

I blinked at one of the only two men at CCC who had been there almost as long as I had. "Where did he go?"

My coworker squinted an eye. "I think he went to the yard to look for some parts he couldn't find."

Figures.

His light brown eyes slid to the side before coming back to me, and he couldn't hide the hesitation in his tone as he asked, trying not to make a face as he probably silently begged me not to take him up on his offer. "Want me to call him?"

I shook my head. Even if it wasn't a huge difference, he was a little nicer to me than he was to the rest of the guys at the shop. Rip rarely cussed at me at least. But I still appreciated Miguel offering to take one for me. "It's okay. I can call him."

He didn't even bother trying to hide his relieved sigh. "Let me know if you need help."

"I will. Thanks, Miguelito."

He grinned at the nickname I had taken from his wife one day a long time ago. With another smile aimed right at him, I headed back to my room and dialed Rip's number from memory.

He answered immediately. "This is Rip."

"Hi, boss-man, it's Luna—"

"Yeah?"

"Hey, I need to get started on that Mustang. What did you want to talk to me about?"

There was a male voice in the background on the other end of the line and it sounded like he was asking him something... "What?" Rip asked, aiming the question at me, after a moment.

"The Mustang. I'm calling about the Mustang."

There was definitely some more irritation in his tone. "What about it?"

I tapped my fingernails on the counter of the one and only desk in my room. "You told me you wanted to talk about the Mustang this morning."

There was more noise in the background, voices talking over other voices, and finally, "I don't know what you're talking about."

I bit the inside of my cheek. "So you *don't* want to talk about it?"

There were more voices in the background, but after a moment he came back on the line. "I'm busy, Luna. Don't you have enough to do?" he snapped, making me pull the phone away from my face to look at it.

Good grief. Somebody was extra grumpy. This was exactly what I'd been anticipating from him after the night before. Sheesh.

"I guess not, boss," I mumbled, still making a face at the phone before I brought it back to my ear. "I just wanted to make sure we were on the same page—"

He made one of those grunting sounds.

And then he hung up on me.

Dropping the headset into the cradle, I shook my head and picked up the dumb file again. He made it seem like I'd been calling him for no freaking reason.

The sooner I got started, the sooner I could get it over with.

Maybe I could actually leave on time and get home early enough to call my sisters and tell them about Grandma Genie and the funeral. But part of me hoped I could put that phone call off a little longer too.

* * *

I HAD JUST CLOSED the doors of the booth after putting on a second coat of color on the Mustang when the door to my room swung open. My hand went to the top of my protective suit so I could drag down the zipper when Rip's big body appeared, covered from collarbones to toes in his coveralls and work boots, which all should have been fine and normal but...

He had this expression on his face I had only seen maybe a few times before.

The last time had been the day of the Silver Mink color episode, aka way too recently.

"Hey," I said to him, hearing the caution in my own voice. I even stopped dragging the zipper down right around my belly button.

His tone matched the death glare he was giving me. *What color did you paint the fucking car?*

I completely stopped trying to pull my suit off and watched as he stopped maybe five feet away, his jaw as hard as it usually was. "I think it said something Mist, but I can't remember exactly. I ordered it two weeks ago...." I almost narrowed my eyes, trying to think over why he was standing there, looking at me like I'd just lost his lucky wrench.

His jaw moved to the side then the other side and his Adam's apple bobbed. That deep line formed between his eyebrows and something that was pretty close to hesitation made me totally quit moving and focus instead on the man standing a few feet away from me.

"Luna."

Did it sound like he growled my name or was I imagining it?

Of course I wasn't imagining it.

When his fisted hand came up to his forehead, I knew he was definitely pissed over something. I just didn't know what. I'd done exactly what he had asked for, hadn't I?

"What color did you paint the fucking car?" he repeated slowly.

I pressed my lips together for a moment before answering, carefully, watching him the entire time, "The color that was on the order."

Rip tipped his head back, showing me the long line of thick, muscular neck and perfectly proportionate Adam's apple as he blew out a breath so rough it was impossible for me not to hear it. "Didn't I—" he started to say before cutting himself off with a harsh grunt.

Didn't he... what?

His voice got even lower. "Didn't I tell you not to do anything to it until we talked?"

"Yes." I narrowed my eyes, wondering what had gotten his panties in a bunch. I had reread that order *three times* to make sure I had it right. I'd even looked at the dates and checked on the computer system to make sure there hadn't been any other orders written up for it since.

There hadn't been.

So... "And I called you..." I trailed off, more confused by the second on why he was looking at me like he wanted to kill me again so soon.

Rip's eyeballs didn't move in my direction. His fist was still at his face. "Luna."

Part of me knew it wasn't time to joke, but... I still said it. "Ripley."

Yeah, that had him moving his eyes back down to me somehow, that gaze shooting straight down his nose as his jaw got even tighter. Gritted. Pissed. "I'm not fucking playing right now," he hissed down at me.

It was my turn to swallow. Even my poor little heart got tight at the pretty freaking uncalled-for expression he was aiming my way.

Rip was mad. At me.

So I blinked and wondered what the hell I had done to deserve it.

He must have been able to read my mind because he went off. "I asked you to talk to me about the car, didn't I?" he snapped, his voice almost quiet but still so mad it caught me totally off guard.

I held my breath, and then I nodded because… well, he had.

But the thing was, I had tried to talk to him about it. I *had* called him. I just didn't think it was the right time to argue that. From the way he was still looking down at me, I didn't think that time was going to change anytime soon.

"Why would you paint the goddamn car after I told you I wanted to talk to you about it?" he griped, honestly, truly angry.

Still, I stood there.

He wasn't going to hurt me or say anything I hadn't heard before from a mouth I had loved.

So, I didn't lie. Or bother trying to explain myself. I'd learned a long time ago that when certain people were mad, there was no reasoning with them. And Rip… he was being a jerk—a real jerk if I was going to be totally honest, because I *had called him*—but I wasn't scared. I wasn't worried. Not truly.

I stood there, my heart beating a little faster than it had been before, and told him the truth that wasn't going to win me any more points. "I painted it because I called you to talk about the car, and you said you had no idea what I was referring to." I kept my voice steady. "I did my job."

I had.

His fingers went loose, and he swallowed again. "But I specifically fucking told you to wait for me to talk to you about it."

I held my breath and didn't move my gaze away from his face, not even for a second as I told him the same thing I already had. "I know, but I called you about it."

Those white, white teeth flashed suddenly, and he hissed in that ugly, mean tone, "I didn't want you to paint the fucking car that color, Luna!"

All right.

Everything was fine. Everything was fine. Everything was fine.

I finally let myself take a breath in through my nose and tried to keep my voice calm as I told him, *again*, like a dummy that didn't know firsthand that you couldn't get through to someone who was already mad, "But I called you—"

"I was fucking busy!"

I just... I just stood there, honestly, seriously, totally confused. What the hell was happening to him? It was one thing for him to be in a grumpy mood and gripe and be all condescending, but this?

Ripley looked at me and shook his head, his breathing choppy, going in and out of his nostrils. He dropped his hand then lifted it back up to the top of his head.

I didn't move.

Rip shook his head, shook his hand out at his side and muttered in this crazy calm voice that I didn't know what to do with. "Do it all over again."

Do it all over again?

Was this a joke?

I wasn't a drama queen, and I didn't get offended easily either, but all I could do was literally stand there.

What he was asking me to do...

I squeezed my eyes closed, squeezed my hands closed, and told myself that there was nothing to be upset about. It wasn't like I wouldn't get paid hourly. It wasn't like this was going to hurt me.

Besides internally for getting blamed for something that wasn't technically my fault.

At least I thought so.

And you screwed up not that long ago, my brain reminded me.

"Start on it now. I'll find the paint sample and call in the order. I'll get somebody to pick it up," he said in that low, icy voice that I had zero affection for.

I didn't say anything as I opened my eyes and just stared at him, indignation and I don't know what else taking the breath and the fight right out of me.

He wanted me to start over again. He wanted me to repaint a project I had already been working on. And if that wasn't bad enough, he was blaming *me*.

We both knew I was right. Deep down he had to know I hadn't been in the wrong. Because we both knew that I had called. It wasn't my fault he hadn't been paying attention or he'd been too distracted to tell me what he wanted.

It definitely wasn't my fault that he'd been on a roll with his triggers and short temper.

But I didn't call him out on that or say any of that to his face.

He was my boss.

This was a job I didn't want to lose, especially not over something that some subconscious part of me realized wasn't worth being right over.

But that little part of me... that little Luna who'd gotten blamed for things she had nothing to do with... she wasn't a fan of getting blamed for something that wasn't anywhere near being her fault. I was tired of that.

But he was my boss.

My boss that was staring down at me, as I stared right back at him.

There *was* something going on with him. I knew it. This wasn't like him. He couldn't have hidden this kind of crazy for three years, and I had to understand it.

I bit the inside of my cheek and just went for it. What was he going to do? Yell at me some more? So I asked him, even though I wasn't sure if this would just come back and bite me in the butt even more. "Rip, what's wrong?"

Those teal eyes stayed zeroed in on me. His body almost too still, but he said, "You fucked up the car, Luna. What do you think?"

"That's not what I meant."

His response was a glare.

So, we were back to that. Okay.

I wasn't going to say anything about the dumb car. I knew he was wrong, he knew he was wrong, and something in my gut said that this, to a certain point, had nothing to do with the damn car he claimed to be so riled up about. But I had always struggled with leaving people alone, even though they might take their anger out on me, yet I still couldn't keep my mouth closed.

I stood my ground. "I know you hate how much I try and joke with you, but if you wanted to talk about something, I would never tell anyone. Honest." I blinked at him, lifting a shoulder. "I'm really good with secrets. No foolin'."

He watched me, but he still didn't respond. Those wide shoulders stayed tight. That mean expression stayed on his face, and this handsome, handsome man gave me nothing at all. Not a single thing.

I should have been used to it.

After a moment, he started to shake his head. "Start all over again" was all he said.

Then he turned around and walked out.

Life was a choice.

You get to choose how you handle things. You get to choose how you deal with those things. You get to choose if a rose is beautiful or if its thorns are a menace to your fingers.

What I chose was to not let Rip ruin my day. I was going to choose to not stay mad or hurt over this.

So, I balled up my anger toward Rip and I threw it in the trash.

He was my boss.

He was going with me to San Antonio, I was going to assume, and that was all that was going to matter to me. Something was wrong with him, and I'd just had the misfortune of being in the wrong place at the wrong time. Or something like that.

Whatever had just happened hadn't been my fault.

But he'd still been a jerk. An unfair jerk to be specific.

I had a job to do though. I had money that needed to be made. That's what I had to do. Ripley wasn't my friend and wasn't trying to ever be my friend. He was my boss.

I accepted that with a sigh, and then I got to work.

CHAPTER SEVEN

WHEN I GOT TO THE SHOP THE NEXT DAY THIRTY minutes earlier than usual, I told myself I was doing it because I had a lot of work to do.

Not because I was holding a grudge toward Rip.

And most definitely not because I'd had another bad dream including my dad that had me waking up sweating. I couldn't remember exactly what had happened in it, only bits and pieces, but the dread and the nausea had been there. Live and present even after so long.

I had tossed and turned the rest of the night, trying to avoid the tiny bit of heartache I had felt because of it. Of how real it felt. Maybe because what I did recall was so similar to things that had really happened. The stupid-ass. Being called the wrong name. The drunkenness... That fear.

What the dream didn't continue reminding me of was how I had grown up. Of how I'd gotten the hell out of there and gotten my sisters out too, the only way I'd known how.

Since that moment, that decision, I had clung onto every moment of happiness that I could.

So just like I had for the last going-on ten years, when I had felt more helpless than ever, I went to the one place that always took my mind off things I didn't want to think about. I went to the shop.

I told myself that it worked in my favor because I hadn't exactly had the most productive afternoon the day before thanks to the hours I'd spent fixing "my mistake." Miguel had come over and helped me for about an hour, telling me all about how Rip had chewed him out for standing in his way.

But even with his help, I still hadn't gotten enough done. It didn't help that I had left work right at five o'clock. Rip hadn't looked at me when I had walked by him with all of my things, but I had been ready.

Ready to pretend like I hadn't heard a single word he might have said since he was going to pretend like I hadn't called him to ask about the one thing he'd blown up at me over.

Ugh.

I couldn't say my day had gotten better once I made it home.

My sister had been home, and that had been great, but the second I told her about the phone call I had gotten days ago—not that I admitted that part—it had gone downhill real quick. Specifically the part that involved me going to San Antonio had been like pouring gasoline on a small fire.

"Why are you doing this?" Lily had wailed. She had stood up the second I had mentioned the name of the city I'd be visiting for the first time in six years. "You know what they're like!"

Of course I knew what they were like. How could I forget?

That conversation had spread wide and far to include a

three-way call on speakerphone with our other two sisters, who had gotten tense and quiet as Lily ranted for fifteen minutes about how dumb it was for me to go.

I had a feeling they were all going to give me the cold shoulder for a while, even during the weekend when everyone came down for Lily's graduation, but they weren't going to change my mind. I knew the best thing I could do for my sanity was not to think about going in the first place so that I wouldn't get more nervous or start second-guessing myself more than I already had. I needed to go. It was the right thing to do.

So, I knew going in that morning that I needed to zone out everything else and spend the day preparing the car for the Tropical Turquoise that was going to cover the pale grayish-blue it had been the day before. Then, eventually, I'd be spraying more color before topping it off with two coats of clear.

Hooray.

I hated making mistakes, even if what had happened hadn't technically been one. I remembered Mack, the man who had taught me everything I knew, telling me once that I was too hard on myself when I didn't do something right. *Everyone makes mistakes*, he had said, giving me a slap on the back. *It isn't the end of the world, Luna-girl.*

And part of me was well aware of that. But the majority of me couldn't let go of that mentality, no matter how old I got. Probably because I thought the whole thing was mostly Rip's fault. I had called him. He hadn't been paying attention, but it was still my fault.

Like it was always.

If I stopped at the drive-thru and bought a cup of coffee instead of making my own, it was only because I was in the mood for a white chocolate mocha instead of the same old thing I had every other morning. If my hands weren't going to be as steady as they usually were... Oh well.

I was in the middle of working on the freaking Mustang in the big room right beside mine when I happened to look up and see a familiar face on the other side of the window of the door.

Rip.

Not wanting to mess up my flow so I could get to priming sooner than later, I turned my attention back and moved my arm along. I kept moving, finishing up the last section before I stopped.

If he needed something and didn't want to wait, he could leave a note.

He knew better than to try and get me to stop in the middle of what I was doing. I didn't want to screw up again, especially not in front of him.

When I was finally done, I left the sanding pad on the floor and pulled my hood down, my fingers snagging for a second on my headband as I made my way toward the door to open it.

"Morning," I said, trying not to make it sound like a mutter as I peeled my goggles off and then tugged my respirator over my head. Most of the guys just wore masks, but I didn't mess around with inhaling things that would come back and kill me later.

He blinked, and it was right then that I noticed he didn't have his coveralls on. He had his gray compression shirt on, except this time it was underneath a tight black T-shirt that said COOPER'S COLLISION AND CUSTOMS in marigold yellow lettering. I'd forgotten today was an auction day. And even though I didn't want or mean to, I flicked my gaze down to see he had on a pair of faded jeans that didn't have any stains on them and boots that weren't the same boots he wore to the shop all the time.

A small white paper bag hung from where it was being pinched at his side by his index finger and thumb.

I bit the inside of my cheek, remembering just how unfair he'd been yesterday.

Then I reminded myself he was my boss and even if he was wrong—and he was—I would have to be the one to eat shit unless I wanted to trade jobs.

And I didn't want to do that.

"Luna," he said in that deep voice that normally felt like a cold finger up my spine but today did nothing.

Okay, mostly nothing.

"Morning, boss," I greeted him, my face straight.

Rip thrust the small white bag at me. "I'm not mad at you," he said first thing, his voice calm, those teal-colored eyes locked on my face.

He wasn't mad at me?

Like I had done something in the first place to get him angry?

I pressed my lips together and eyed the bag he was still holding between us.

Those eyes moved over my face, and something small moved across Ripley's, almost... softening? Nicer? ...Guilt? "It's not the end of the fucking world, Luna."

Of all the words....

"I can't let you get away with things that I wouldn't let the rest of the guys get away with," he kept going, watching me closely with that face I wasn't sure how to take from how serious it was. "Making me a birthday cake doesn't get you a Get Out of Jail Free card."

All I could do was stare at him and swallow his Monopoly reference.

He gave the white bag a light shake, inching it even closer to me. "I brought you that donut shit you like. Take it. It's the twist one," he went on, like I had no idea what my favorite donut was.

But the only person who didn't have an idea of what was going on was him.

He'd brought me a donut?

Was this his way of apologizing for blaming me for something that wasn't my fault?

Yeah. It was. It had to be.

It really was his way of apologizing.

A tiny little part of me wanted to hold a grudge....

But most grudges were a waste of time. They were a vortex where you lost time, energy, and happiness. Time, energy, and happiness you could apply toward something that was good, something that your whole life benefited from. Something that could actually make you happy.

And I wanted to be happy more than I wanted to be right.

Which was why I only really held onto big grudges, and I rarely let myself think of them. Usually.

I eyed Rip one more time then glanced down at the bag... and then I sighed.

I was going to choose, maybe not necessarily being happy, but not being mad. Ripley wouldn't be the first person to blame me for things they had caused. If anything, he might be one of many, but he was one of the few to ever apologize... in his own way.

That was worth something. More than something really. And if I really thought about it, I might have appreciated the effort it took to even do as much as he just had. Hadn't I just avoided telling my sisters that I'd known something for days because I didn't want them to get madder at me than they already were?

I didn't want to be a hypocrite.

I bit the inside of my cheek and said, "Thank you," even though it sounded like more of a question.

He tipped his chin down once and only once, his eyes narrowing like he could read my mind.

He didn't say he was sorry for bitching me out—*for no reason*—but he'd brought me a donut. My favorite. I hadn't figured he'd paid enough attention to know something like that.

I reached over slowly, like he was going to change his mind and jerk it away at the last minute as I took the bag from him, watching his face as he did the same in return to me, looking for who knows what. To make sure I didn't quit? To make sure I didn't cry?

I'd barely taken it when he asked, "How busy are you today?"

It was hard not to think that was a trick question; he knew I had an entire car to prime and paint on top of trying to catch up on things so that I wouldn't fall behind since I was taking a day off to go to San Antonio. "Pretty busy."

His eyes slid around the room for a moment before he dipped his chin down in a way that seemed like it was more for himself than me. "Finish what you're working on and meet me outside."

"Why?"

He still didn't look at me. "There's an auction going on. You're coming with me."

What? "But—"

"Hurry up. It starts in an hour," he stated, taking a step back and finally making direct eye contact again. His face was smooth. No hint of frustration or tightness on it at all, and I wasn't sure what to think of that.

"I have to do the car that you—"

Those bright eyes landed on me, and his eyebrows went up a quarter of an inch. "It can wait."

Now it could wait?

"But"—*why did he want me to go in the first place?* —"Mr. Cooper goes with you."

On the rare occasion that I did go, it had been with Mr. Cooper, but the last time I'd gone with him had been... three years ago? Four years ago? Maybe longer? When I'd first started trying to learn things about cars, he would take me all the time and point at things, explaining everything he could think of and everything I was curious about. I'd enjoyed it a lot. I would have never guessed just how much it would have interested me.

But since taking over the lead painter position, I had other things to do instead.

"He's not coming in today. You're up."

I reached up to flick at one of the heart-shaped fake ruby earrings I'd put on that morning with the tip of my index finger. "But—"

Rip's eyes strayed to the side of my face for a moment before focusing again. "Everything can wait. I'll meet you by my truck."

He was being serious about me going with him. "But...," I mumbled, trailing off, because I wasn't sure what other argument to give him for why I should stay.

Other than him taking his crap out on me the day before, there was no reason I should *want* to stay and work. Who would say no to taking a few hours off? Me, apparently, and I wasn't even sure I knew why I was totally fighting it other than just being a tiny bit resentful over how he'd been. Sure, I was going to forgive him and get over it, but I wasn't a robot. I couldn't just turn my feelings on and off. I needed at least ten minutes.

"I'll deal with it if you fall behind. Let's go," he stated in that voice that was somewhere between patient and not.

He took another step back and then turned around to head toward the door, calling out over his shoulder, "You can eat that in my truck. Let's go."

Eat—

He was really being serious. He wanted me to go with him.

The door shut just as I stood there and glanced at the bag in my hand.

I sighed again.

It didn't take me long at all to walk back to my room, strip out of my protective suit and grab my purse. I doubted I'd need it, but I'd watched an episode of a show once of someone who was in a wreck, died and couldn't be identified, so now I didn't like not having my ID with me at all times. That and my paint-specked leggings didn't have pockets to put my cell phone in. Then I headed out of the room and made my way toward the parking lot, kicking the door to the shop closed behind me.

Rip was already waiting inside his truck, chin high while he relaxed against the headrest. His lips were moving just enough so that I knew he was either talking to himself... or lip-synching along to whatever was playing on the radio.

Some part of me knew he was singing along.

I wasn't going to think it was adorable. Nope. Not when he'd been so strange and on edge the last few days. Not when he'd been unfair over something that hadn't been all my fault. It wasn't going to happen.

...but it was happening.

I managed to keep the smile on my face, one hand holding my purse, the other holding my donut, and watched as Rip's head turned to look at me as I walked toward his truck. Before I was there, he reached over and opened it for me from the inside, pushing the door open. I climbed in, careful not to scratch the leather or do anything else that would screw up the completely restored interior.

"I tried to go as fast as I could," I told him as I set my purse on the floor and reached for the seat belt.

He put the truck into drive. "I've only been out here a minute."

I shot him a look out of the corner of my eye as I closed the door and finally set the small white bag on my lap, wondering once again why he wanted me to go with him.

And where was Mr. Cooper?

I waited until he'd pulled the truck through the gate that was connected to the fence that went the entire way around the building before I asked, "Do you mind if I make a quick call?"

The only answer I got was a shake of his head.

I bent over and pulled my phone out of my purse, going straight to my favorites and looking for one of the only two men's names I had saved under my favorites.

The line only rang twice before a familiar voice picked up. "Little moon," Mr. Cooper answered, sounding totally normal, totally fine.

"Hey, Mister C," I replied.

"I meant to call you last night. Miguel texted me over what happened with Rip"—I shifted my eyes to the side to make sure that someone wasn't listening. If he was, his face didn't register any signs that he'd overheard Mr. Cooper talking about him—"but Lydia came home and it slipped my mind."

"It's okay," I said before he could keep going. "Everything is all right."

The sigh he let out told me he didn't agree with me, and that warmed my heart.

"I was calling to tell you that I'm going with Rip to the auction today."

Silence.

I slid my gaze back to Rip and found the cheek closest to me doing this weird twitch thing.

"I don't know how long we'll be gone, but I just wanted to let you know in case anyone calls to ask you where I'm at. He said you weren't coming to the shop today."

There was another beat of silence. Then, "Okay. Sure." Another moment of silence. "That's good, Luna."

"Are you okay?"

More quiet, then, "I have a doctor's appointment. I'll be in tomorrow."

A doctor's appointment? "Are you having problems with your blood pressure again?"

The hum he made in response was 1000 percent fake. It was his way of not wanting to lie but not wanting to say the truth either.

"That's what I thought," I mumbled. "Good luck with your appointment then and let me know how it goes." I paused. "Don't forget to tell the doctor about how you've been sneaking sandwich meat and frozen pizza at work when you think no one is looking."

I hung up after Mr. Cooper started chuckling and eventually got out that he'd see me on Friday.

But seriously, I hoped he'd tell his doctor about the snacks we both knew he had no business eating. I had done what I could by throwing stuff away when I found it. Slipping my phone back inside my purse, I sat back up and settled my hands on my thighs, glancing at Rip out of the corner of my eye.

"I could've told you he had a doctor's appointment," he claimed, steering the truck into a left-hand lane.

I couldn't help but bite the inside of my cheek and make a face. He could've told me? "I wasn't sure you knew." Honestly, I wasn't sure he would have cared enough to know or ask. Then again, based on the things I had over-heard, Rip would probably ask Mr. Cooper to bring in a doctor's note to prove he'd actually done what he'd said he would.

But that wasn't supposed to be any of my business.

Neither one of us said anything for a while. I looked out my window and sometimes glanced at Rip but really spent the whole time telling my body to relax. I wasn't going to hold this grudge against him when he had sort-of, kind-of apologized, at least apologized more than anyone else in my life usually had or did. I'd forgiven people for doing worse. There was something going on with him that I didn't entirely understand, but I could be patient. I could be understanding. Some people just had to work things out on their own.

Most importantly, I needed to remember—and accept—that he was my boss. As much as I might try, as much as I might sometimes wish in the back of my mind, in the deep-est, most secretive corner of my soul, that was all there was ever going to be. We weren't friends, and he had no interest in being nice or polite or being kind.

He was fine not being anyone's favorite. It wasn't what he wanted. It wasn't what he was ever going to want.

My heart ached for a moment as I sat there, thinking for a second about *that* thought. About how I'd spent the last three years eyeballing and thinking a little too much about someone who I had no chance with. It was just... admiration. Serious admiration.

But maybe instead of daydreaming about that Louie Vuitton purse I would realistically never save up to buy, I could go to the outlet and get a beautiful purse for a tenth of the price. It would do everything the other one did. The only difference was, it would be within my reach. I could afford it.

It wouldn't need to be a dream. It wasn't like I believed in them in the first place.

"You gonna eat that donut today?" Rip asked out of nowhere.

I glanced over at him. Was he trying to make a joke? Nothing about his face looked particularly amused or playful but... "Yes."

"You're not on a diet, right?" he asked as he steered us onto the freeway. I didn't even know where the hell we were going.

If he would have been anyone else—and if my previous thoughts hadn't been about Rip and his lack of friendships—I would have laughed. Instead, I barely managed not to smirk. "*No.*"

I mean, I wasn't as thin as I used to be back when I'd been a teenager. I also worked too much—and was too lazy —to hit the gym five days a week... but I tried my best. I ate decent, some days I ate better than decent, but mostly, I was never going to say no to a donut. Or a slice of cherry pie.

But especially not my favorite donut.

"There a reason you haven't eaten it then?"

I touched the tips of my fingers along the top of the bag, which had been rolled down. "I figure I could eat it at the auction. I didn't want to make a mess in your car."

Those eyes flicked in my direction. "You won't."

"But I don't want to take a chance." I didn't need to look around to see that the inside was immaculately clean. He kept the outside beautifully detailed constantly. Even his office was pretty spotless.

"It's just a truck. If there are crumbs, we have vacuums," was his argument in that cool, laidback voice.

That wasn't at all what I was expecting him to come back with. "Are you sure?"

"Yeah, I'm sure, Luna. Eat your fucking donut. I didn't buy it for you to look at."

I mean, if he was going to insist.

I unrolled the top of the bag and stuck my hand in to pull out my treat. My treat that my boss had bought me. Because he might have felt a little bad. I thought. Maybe.

Which he should.

Leaning forward, I grabbed my phone out of my purse and hit the camera icon. Glancing at Rip, I noticed he was still looking forward. I took a picture of the donut, attached it to a text message then shoved my phone under my thigh.

"Didn't know you were one of those people that took pictures of their food," he said quietly.

Those people. I pressed my lips together to keep from smiling.

"My little sister really likes these," I found myself explaining, still trying not to smile. "I'm just rubbing it in her face."

He took so long responding, I didn't expect it when the question out of his mouth was, "All three of them are younger than you, yeah?"

I wasn't even sure how he knew I had three in the first place.

"Yeah, three. My baby sister, the one I sent the picture to, will be eighteen in a few weeks. She's a senior in high school," I told him, bringing the donut up to my face and taking a bite, just barely holding back a moan at how good it was. "The other two are nineteen and twenty-one, but they don't live with me anymore."

The only thing he did to acknowledge that he'd been listening was nod, and I didn't feel like offering up any more information that he probably didn't care much about.

He still didn't say a word as I ate the rest of it, ignoring how that much sugar made my stomach hurt, but too freaking bad.

Just as I was about to take the second to last bite, I paused. "You want a piece?"

There was a huff that had me turning my neck to look at him. The only side of his face I could see was tilted up. "I'm good."

I finished off the rest of it before he could change his mind. I was in the middle of licking my fingers clean when Rip spoke up again.

"What time you want to leave tomorrow?"

I almost gulped, but doing that would have been a hint of how much I was dreading the trip, and I didn't want to give him a reason not to go with me. "The service is at eleven. Is seven-thirty fine?"

There was no hesitation at least verbally, but from where I was sitting I could see the way his cheek flexed, and it only confirmed that I didn't want to make him think twice about agreeing. "Works for me. I'll pick you up," he offered.

"Okay."

Perfect. Just perfect.

I didn't want to go. God, I didn't want to go.

But I was and that wasn't going to change, so I needed to live with it and accept it. There was no point in ruining the day dreading the inevitable. So, I changed the subject and kept my voice bright. "So, is there anything specific you're looking to buy today?"

It was the right question to ask.

And if listening to him talk wasn't a hardship, it was only because he had a nice voice.

* * *

I'D LOST HIM.

Crap!

Rip and I had split up half an hour ago. We'd gotten to the auction early enough to really get a good look around at all the cars that were parked in the junkyard's lot. I'd never been to this particular one before, but I'd heard all about Rip and Mr. Cooper sometimes scoring some really great deals here. This auction only happened once every other month; on some visits, they didn't buy anything. It was one of the smallest auctions on this side of the state. A couple times a year, one of the two men would go to the bigger sales that took place in other cities along the southwest.

Fortunately, I'd found two cars that hit almost all the criteria Rip had given me on the way over. One of them had a little more rust on it than I would have liked, but it was still in better shape than a few of the cars that he'd bought in the past. The other one was great though, but I'd spotted a couple other guys from restoration shops I was familiar with eyeing it too. We all made a point not to make eye contact with each other, so I knew they were serious about it. It wasn't exactly going to be a steal, but it would have been worth it.

And now the auction was set to start in... a few minutes, and I had no clue where he was. I had tried calling his cell, but he hadn't answered. I remembered seeing him leave his phone in the pickup. Reaching up to the tips of my toes, I looked over the lot, trying to ignore all the blonds and the men with black hair, looking for the one with the perfect shade of mostly mahogany brown.

I'd already had one man stop and ask if there was something he could help me with. I really doubted he believed me when I told him I was looking for my boss. Turning around to face the end of the lot that I'd walked around for the last almost hour, I stretched my chin up as high as I could. Looking, looking, looking...

Bingo.

Taller than everyone else, bigger than everyone else, and wearing that tight shirt that should have been too hot to wear in Houston, but I'd bet it was one meant for the heat, I spotted Rip.

He had his hands on his hips while he talked to another man two or three inches shorter than him.

I wasn't sure why it surprised me that he knew people, much less that he seemed to be having a conversation with someone, but it did. It wasn't like he didn't talk, but usually he was talking at people rather than with them. Keeping my gaze on him so I wouldn't lose him again, I started making my way over.

I took in the other man. He looked about Rip's age, if not a little older and leaner. But it was the tattoo he had on one side of his neck that had me focusing.

I glanced at Rip, then back at his friend, and kept my gaze there. Tattoos poured down the man's arms in thick, black marks that were really hard to distinguish, but something about them....

The man shook his head at Rip, but his body stayed relaxed.

But Rip... Rip was looking around by that point. For me?

"Ladies and gentlemen, the auction will begin in five minutes. I repeat in fiveee minutes," a voice crackled over the speakers that the auction had set up right by a makeshift podium.

Shit.

I raised my hand over my head and waved it. "Rip!" I yelled.

His head snapped to the left before slowly moving to the side more, like he was looking for me.

I waved some more, feeling bad for interrupting him but knowing I needed to show him what I thought he would want to see before time ran out. That was why he'd brought me over, wasn't it? Screw it. I headed over, weaving through the small crowd as fast as I could. It didn't take me long at all to make it a few feet away from where Rip and the other man were still standing. I waved my hand as far over my head as possible. "Boss-man!"

He must have seen me because he dipped his chin, his eyes covered with sunglasses, in my direction. But his mouth began moving. Fast.

But not quickly enough before I was at his side, sharing a smile between him and his friend. His friend who was looking at me with a surprised but curious expression on his face while Rip ended what he'd been saying with a "see you later" that was all clipped.

And before I could get out a word, my boss slapped his palm against the other man's and turned toward me.

Okay.

He didn't want me to meet his friend. That was fine. Sure.

He was my boss. There was no reason for me to meet his friend.

The other man let out a snort before shrugging and turning on his heel to go who knows where.

The smile I gave Rip was genuine. He was my boss and he owed me nothing but a paycheck for the hours I worked. "I'm sorry I yelled and came over, but I wanted you to see these two cars before the auction started," I told him, not letting curiosity get the better of me.

There was something off about his facial expression. "What'd you find?" he asked, sounding totally normal, or as normal as ever. Not giving me a single hint who the other man had been, but why would he?

I hooked my thumb over my shoulder to aim it in the direction of where I'd found the goods. "There's rust on both of them, but nothing worse than what you've gotten before. Let me show you, boss man. I think with a little TLC, they'd look really nice."

His eyes seemed to sweep over my face and head, and I didn't miss the way he positioned his body to block me from seeing the man he had been talking to. He said, "Show me."

I did, and I was pretty proud of myself when he ended up winning both.

CHAPTER EIGHT

When my alarm went off the next day, dread like I hadn't felt in years instantly made me want to vomit.

It had been a long, *long* time since I'd been so nervous or overwhelmed that I wanted to puke.

But I still dragged myself out of bed. I had to get up. I didn't want to, but I had to.

I showered even though I had the night before, put on makeup, got dressed, and headed to the kitchen, ignoring the way my knees wanted to shake and my stomach wanted to revolt. I heard pots clanking from the kitchen area. I was usually on my way to work by this time, and my sister Lily was usually in the shower, so it surprised me to hear her banging away.

If the clangs meant anything, it was that she was still mad at me. I hadn't seen her at all the last two days. She'd been in her room by the time I got home and hadn't bothered coming out to say hi.

Sure enough, the second I entered the kitchen and found her, violently scooping what looked like oatmeal into two bowls on the counter, it confirmed she was in a bad mood. Lily was like me: she was a morning person. Unlike our other two sisters, I had never had to be on her case about waking up on time for school. I was usually in a good mood, but Lily was always in a better mood than me.

Today being the exception from the look and sound of it.

"Morning," I told her pretty softly, hating that we were in this position in the first place.

She didn't look at me, and it gave me the chance to see she hadn't showered or anything yet. She was still in her pajamas. "Morning," she pretty much grunted, almost making me smile.

Eyeing her, I went to the cabinets beside her, watching as she scraped cut-up berries from a small cutting board into the bowls and then shook some walnuts out too. Filling up my glass with water, I tried my best to ignore how much my stomach ached. *I didn't want to go.*

"You have time to eat, don't you?" my beloved little sister grumbled, sounding grumpier than I had ever heard her.

"Yes," I answered before gulping down the entire glass of water just as she slid one of the bowls across the counter.

She grunted before turning back toward the stove and picking up the saucepan she'd cooked with. "Eat it. Who knows when you'll have lunch."

I didn't feel like smiling, I really didn't, but affection for this not-so-little girl made my chest ache... with love, of course. With so much love it reminded me of why I was going today. So she wouldn't have to. "Thank you, Lily," I told her as I opened one of the drawers and pulled a spoon out.

Lily grunted again as she turned on the tap at the sink and waited, then put the pot under the stream of water.

I didn't say a word as I scooped up one spoonful after the other of steel cut oats as she finished washing everything. I ate so fast that by the time she was done, more than half of it was in my stomach, and I honestly wasn't sure if I had tasted more than the first bite.

I didn't want to go.

"What time will you be back?"

I blinked at her back as she stood in front of the sink, hunched over it. "I don't know for sure. I'm guessing maybe around three." I tapped the tip of the spoon against my nose, seeing her spine curl further into the sink area. "I'm not going to be there longer than I need to, sugar lumps, I promise."

The deep breath she took made her shoulders go up a few inches; I could even see her ribcage expand too. But she didn't make a sound. She didn't turn around either.

I wanted to go and give her a hug, but my feet wouldn't move. I wanted to tell her it was going to be fine. That I didn't want to go in the first place but that I owed Grandma Genie for taking care of her for years.

But...

I wasn't sure I could handle it if she pulled away from me or told me not to touch her. It wouldn't be the first time one of my sisters had done that. So like a coward, I stayed there, fisting my hands at my sides and just watching my little sister struggle with whatever she was thinking. She was the last person in the world I would want to hurt or have mad at me.

"Lily, I love you. I don't want to go, but one of us has to, and if Dad and your mom are there... I don't want them to see you. I don't want them to see any of you. Nothing good would come of it, and somewhere deep down inside, you know that," I told her quietly. "It'll be fine. I promise. Your mom will probably be too high and Dad.... Don't worry about me, okay? I showed you that picture of Ripley. No one's going to want to mess with him, and I can take care of myself."

She sniffed.

And still I just stood there, really wanting to go to her but just... not able to. My eyes caught onto the clock on the stove, seeing the 7:25 and sighing. "I'm not going to work afterward. If you don't have plans, we can go do something."

My little sister sighed right back. "Okay."

"Okay?" I asked her to be sure.

She nodded. "Yeah, okay."

Pressing my lips together, I scooped the rest of the oatmeal into my mouth as I grabbed a bottled iced coffee from the fridge. Next, I filled up a water bottle from the filter and had just picked up my purse when Lily muttered, "Do you have your pepper spray?"

I froze. Then I glanced inside my bag to make sure it was in there. "I've got it," I told her, looking down at the gift she had bought me for my birthday last year.

I turned toward her, holding my things in my hand, and found her still facing the sink. I wanted to give her a hug. I really wanted to give her a hug, or get one in return, but I was going to need all my bravery for later.

"I need to go, but have a good day at school, okay? Thank you for breakfast."

"Good luck."

I smiled at the back of her head and held my things to my chest, then turned around. I had barely made it down the hall when my little sister called out, "I love you, Luna! I'm not mad at you! I just want you to be okay!"

I bit my lip and shook my head, relief flooding through me. "I know. I love you too! Don't worry about me and have a good day at school!" I called back, making sure not to let my voice betray me.

I got my keys and headed outside, trying my best to ignore the way my heart beat steadily but a little faster than normal. I had barely locked the front door and sat on the top step when a familiar yellow pickup pulled up in front of my house. According to my G-Shock, right on time.

I didn't wonder how Ripley had known my address, but I had figured he would have asked for it if he needed it. A few of my coworkers had visited since I'd bought my place, and the Coopers of course knew where I lived. At just around fifteen hundred square feet—and with the price tag that had come from it being a foreclosure—it was perfect for me... and the one sibling I still had. It had needed a stupid amount of cosmetic work when I bought it, and even after so long, it still did. What had been worked on, I had done mostly by myself and with a little help from my sisters, friends, and their families. It was getting to where I wanted it.

At the rate I was going, it was more than likely going to be a couple more years before it was the house that I'd envisioned, and only for a second did I wonder what Ripley thought of the old bungalow.

Then I decided that he probably didn't care and might have not even really looked at it in the first place, even if it was possible to ignore the dark purple house with medium gray and white accents and trim.

It had taken me months to change the color from the faded white and blue it had originally been, but every time I pulled into my driveway, seeing it... it just made me happy. And if something made you happy, it was worth the cost and effort every single time.

As I walked down the steps of my stoop and then the

pathway that my best friend's grandpa had helped me redo before starting on the painting, I couldn't help but look over my shoulder at my house.

And I smiled.

I was so lucky.

I was so damn lucky I forgot how lucky I was.

Rip was looking at me through the passenger window as I walked up to his truck door and opened it.

"Morning," I greeted him as I got inside and shut it behind me.

He was still watching me as I pulled the seat belt across my body and clipped it in, noticing the black jacket on the seat between us. Only then did he say, "Morning."

Setting my purse and drinks on the floor, I slid my hands down my thighs to smooth my black skirt down and then shot him a smile. I had to play it easy and cool and not at all like I'd woken up that morning on the verge of praying for a natural disaster that wouldn't let us make it to San Antonio. "Want me to navigate us or do you know how to get there?" I asked as I finally got a chance to look my boss over.

And look him over I did.

The first thing I noticed was the thin black and white scarf he had on.

In June.

Then the second thing I noticed was the freaking rest of him.

I had warned him we were going to a funeral, but I hadn't been ready for... this. Ripley dressed up like I had never, ever seen him before. In a charcoal gray button-up shirt beneath the scarf wrapped around his neck, his eyes seemed even brighter than usual. I glanced at his shiny black dress shoes—shoes that looked brand new. Black dress pants that looked brand new. I looked down at the black jacket between us and thought it looked like it had never been worn either.

Forcing my gaze back to his face, I took in his close shave, and the way his short hair was styled gave me the idea that he'd slicked something through it that made it look more controlled than normal.

Lucas Ripley had dressed up.

And if they were there, I was taking him to see the most awful people I had ever met in my life.

Probably.

More than likely.

Who was I kidding. This was me. It would be my luck ten times over that all of them would be there. Even my older brother. Why not.

I didn't have the same hair color or length anymore, but they would know who I was.

I could do this. I would do it. It was only a couple of hours.

I needed to get it together before he figured out just how much I didn't want this to happen. So I said the first words that came to mind as I sat there. "You look dapper." Which was an understatement, but I didn't need to cake it on.

How did he respond? By reaching up to pull at the collar of his shirt, digging beneath the scarf he had on, tugging at it and muttering, "I feel like a dumbass."

I surprised myself when I laughed. "You don't look like one." My smile wasn't forced or fake either. "You look great," I told him.

What did he do? He rolled his eyes, but I didn't miss the way his cheeks seemed to get a little pink. I didn't know somebody was bashful.

"So, GQ? Need me to navigate us or do you know how to get into the city?"

He rolled his eyes again as he put the truck into drive. "I know how to get there." And if I thought he muttered, "Unfortunately," then I would have been right.

NEITHER ONE OF us talked much over the next three hours.

Rip had put the radio on the oldies station, which had made me smile while I looked out the window because that was the last thing I would have figured he'd listen to. I'd caught him humming along to a few songs, and that had made me smile even more. He wasn't exactly trying to hide it. I played solitaire on my phone until I got nauseous, then played it again once the worst of it had passed.

But as the minutes went by, and then an hour, then another hour and another hour...

My nausea got worse for reasons that had nothing to do with looking at a tiny screen in a moving car; all the breathing exercises in the world didn't do anything. Neither did closing my eyes and telling myself that I needed to buck up and that I could handle whatever happened. All the optimism I'd felt that morning had slowly melted away as the reality of where I was going became more and more present.

The truck wasn't going to break down and end up making me miss the funeral.

I was going and it was happening.

But I was going to survive it, and that was the most important part.

We drove further along into the city and slowly I took in a lot of things that were familiar from when I had lived in

San Antonio. The city had changed a lot over the last almost ten years but not enough to be completely different from where I had grown up.

I hadn't planned on ever coming back.

I turned on the navigation app on my phone and put in the address that the lawyer had sent me. The app said we had twelve minutes left to travel. The service was supposed to start in twenty, so the arrival couldn't have been any better.

I laced my fingers together and stuck them in between my thighs. I kind of wished I had paid more attention to Mr. Cooper when he recited an Our Father when he was riled up and needed to calm down.

"You gonna be all right?" Rip finally spoke up after hours of near silence.

I glanced at his profile for what might have been the twentieth time—maybe the fiftieth time—since we'd gotten into the car. The tightness at his jaw had only gotten more pronounced mile after mile. The lines at his eyes had deepened. His coloring was different. More flushed.

I wasn't imagining the fact that he honestly looked like he was dreading this as much as I was.

But was it because he was with me and he didn't want to be?

"Yeah, sure," I told him honestly but watched him even closer. "Are you?"

His fingers flexed on the steering wheel and his voice was rough when he answered simply, "Yeah."

He was full of it. He really was dreading this.

Just like that, guilt made my stomach feel off all over again, for a reason that had nothing to do with me and what I wanted.

Maybe he didn't handle funerals well. Maybe they

made him feel terrible. How was I supposed to know? I'd worked surrounded by men for almost the last decade, and over that time, I'd learned that even if they didn't want to do something—and I mean they *really* didn't want to do something—they would if it involved or compromised their pride.

I wouldn't force someone to do something they didn't want to for my sake.

"You can just drop me off and go back. I can get myself back to Houston," I offered, watching the lines along his mouth tell me just how uncomfortable he was.

Because I had put him into this situation.

The man beside me slid me a look so slow that a sloth would have managed to catch it. His eyebrows went up at about the same pace, and he locked those blazing blue-green eyes on my face and said in that hoarse voice of his, "Not doing that."

Pride was a bitch.

"I'm being serious, Rip." I gave him a smile that was tight and probably totally fake. "I can go by myself. It isn't a big deal. You've done enough."

I'd swear he rolled his eyes. "Shut it, Luna."

He was such a liar. "You look like you've got the flu, boss."

"I'm all right," he tried to insist.

I pressed my lips together and looked at the coloring on his face. "Is that why you've been squeezing the steering wheel so hard your knuckles have been turning white for the last hour?" I asked him, pressing my lips together again immediately afterward because... well, it was the truth.

That hard jaw jerked from side to side, and he even shook his head a little. "Luna, I'm good," he tried to tell me.

"I don't want you to do something you don't want to do."

He didn't say a word for a moment, but I watched as his shoulders lost some of their tension and lowered unexpectedly. His voice was calm as he said, "I got no problem going to the funeral or the service. You can drop it."

I bit my lip and watched him, trying to decide whether I needed to keep arguing with him. It was obvious he didn't want to be here. I wasn't that blind or dumb. I also believed him when he said it wasn't the funeral he had an issue with.

But then what else could bother Rip... that wasn't Mr. Cooper or Lydia? Or screwups at work?

Just as I opened my mouth to tell him to wait in the car, his fingers flexed on the steering wheel again, and he told me, "I'm doing this with you. I owe you. It's fine."

He owed me.

That was the only reason he was here. It wasn't like I didn't know that, and it wasn't like that should hurt my feelings. Because it didn't. What it did was make my heart clench up a little at the reminder that it was only a favor... a favor I had earned through a lie... for why he was with me right then, sitting not even two feet away in a dress shirt, pants, and a scarf with a coat between us. Looking more handsome than I ever could have imagined, if I did that kind of thing.

I kept my mouth shut and nodded, even if chances were he didn't see me do it.

The navigation gave an instruction for an upcoming turn a quarter of a mile away, and he got into the lane a second before asking, "Whose funeral are we going to?"

I squeezed my fingers together tighter. I owed him that much information, didn't I? "My grandmother."

His "Oh" was just about what I was expecting. What I didn't expect was the way his question came out. Maybe it was the fact that he even asked the question in the first place. The last time I'd been sick, he hadn't asked if I was feeling better, he'd asked *you contagious still?* So the "You good?" right then, caught me totally off guard, especially when it came out soft.

But I still lied. "I'm good."

I didn't miss the way his eyes slid in my direction, his expression mirroring the tone of his voice—thoughtful, different. "You don't look good."

He didn't need to know that I didn't feel good about this whole thing. So, I made a face. Then I shrugged the shoulder closest to him. "I'm just..."

Should I tell him?

Nah. I was greedy and enough of a liar to keep the bad to myself since we were so close already. Plus, he was being a liar about being fine coming with me, when it was clear he wasn't.

"I haven't been home... to San Antonio," I corrected myself, hating that I called this city home, "in a long time."

His hands flexed on the steering wheel once more, and I wasn't sure I imagined that his voice seemed to get deeper, losing that almost sweet edge to it. "You used to live here?"

"Yeah," I told him vaguely. "I grew up here."

Those teal-colored eyes came my way again, and a muscle in his cheek tensed. "When'd you move away?" he grumbled the question. These were more personal questions than he'd asked me in the three years we had known each other.

I squeezed my fingers together. "A few months before my eighteenth birthday. So that's nine years."

He made another thoughtful face that had his eyebrows knitting together and that little dash between his eyebrows indenting, probably wondering why I would have moved away at that age. So when he asked, "You got family here?" I figured he was trying to figure out just that.

While I might have told him everything a week ago... I didn't want to do it then.

I looked forward and stopped myself from frowning. "My grandmother's the only person I would still call family here, and I haven't seen her in years. I just found out about the funeral on Monday right before I asked you to come with me."

His eyebrows did that thoughtful thing again, and some more guilt filled my stomach.

Should I tell him? At least warn him? If I was in his position....

I should tell him. I had never been good at playing games. I had never liked other people playing games with me either. It was the right thing to do.

"Rip?"

"Hmm?"

I could do it.

"Look, I want you to know that I have people I'm related to that might be at the funeral and... things are complicated with them... and I asked you to come with me because you're the biggest person I know, and I don't think anybody would willingly mess with you, and I don't think you'd let anyone mess with me too much if you were around, even if... you know... you didn't think you owed me one...," I rambled, trying to think of my words and not sure what the hell else to say that wouldn't be me admitting just how much my family sucked.

I squeezed my fingers again. "My plan is to mind my own business, go to the funeral, and head back home. I just want you to know why we're sitting by ourselves. I don't want to talk to any of them if they are there," I told him, leaving out the part that warned him that half the people in the room might end up looking at us like they wanted to kill me.

There. He couldn't say I hadn't warned him. That's what I was going to tell myself at least.

The last thing I expected was the smirk-like quirking way the corner of his mouth went to the side.

Then I waited until he let out a sigh that wasn't unhappy exactly because... because he was still doing that smirk thing.

"What?" I asked him slowly.

He was still making that facial expression when he said, "I didn't think you invited me to go somewhere because you didn't want to go alone."

I pressed my lips together before grumbling in an almost-whisper, "But you thought I wanted you to pretend to be my boyfriend."

That had that smirk of his going away real quick, and I definitely didn't imagine the harshness in his voice when he replied, "No, I didn't."

I burst out freaking laughing, remembering, *remembering* him asking if we were going to pretend we were getting married.

Married. Me and Rip. Pssh.

Rip, on the other hand, decided to ignore me there in the seat beside him cracking up as he went back to the original topic. But nothing could hide the color on his cheeks or the way his spine went straighter after I'd started laughing. "I figured there was something else you wanted, all right? If it was something important, I figured you would've said something."

And *that* had me shutting my mouth. Then it had me biting my cheek.

The sigh out of his mouth went straight to my heart. "I didn't, and I don't give a fuck what you want, Luna. If I could do it, I would."

Because of the favor.

"I'm sorry—" I started, feeling guilty all over again, because no matter how much he might deny it, I could still sense he was put off about something with this entire situation. He was here because of his pride and that white elephant wasn't going to let him admit anything.

"Don't," he cut me off. "It's not a big fucking deal. It ain't even a little fucking deal."

Somehow I managed to hold back a sigh. I hoped he still thought that when we were heading back to Houston. I hoped he thought that when we were sitting in the funeral home to begin with.

"Okay." I still felt bad regardless of what he said.

Maybe to him, this wasn't a big deal, but to me, it was, and regardless of why he was here, I really was grateful this was the case.

In no time at all, Rip was pulling his truck into a funeral home that looked faintly familiar. From what I could remember, my grandmother hadn't lived too far from this side of town. Twice, I had ridden my bike—something I had bought by slowly stealing small bills from my dad's wallet over the course of six months when he'd pass out around the house—to her house when I couldn't stay at my house a minute longer. While she hadn't lived on a nice side of town, it had still been way better than where we had lived.

Then again, at a lot of moments, Hell would have been a better place than where I had lived.

I swallowed down that memory and did the sign of the cross inside of myself. The lot was only about halfway filled, mostly with late-model cars. I didn't see the beat-up

Voyager my nightmares had memorized, but then again, I wasn't expecting to.

Rip pulled the truck into a spot and parked it, his body shifting toward mine, all broad shoulders and huge chest contained within that beautiful dress shirt, before he asked the same question as before. "You good?"

No. "Yeah," I lied, hearing it sound weak and full of shit even to me, but you had to fake it till you made it, or something like that.

He blinked, and at that point, he definitely knew I was full of it. But he watched me with those eyes for a moment longer before he turned off the ignition. "Ready then?" he asked, calling my bluff.

Now or never, Luna.

"Ready," I agreed, giving him a cheerful smile that inside felt way more like a grimace.

I opened the door a second before he opened his and we both slammed them shut at about the same time.

I was fine. I was loved. I had everything and more than I had ever wanted. I was choosing to be happy for the rest of my life.

None of this was going home with me. I wouldn't let it.

I swallowed as I made my feet take me one step closer and then another step closer toward the brick building.

My heart pounded in my chest, and honestly, part of me felt like if I would have really wanted to, I could have passed out. Passing out would have been a perfectly acceptable excuse for not going into the building.

But that wasn't going to happen.

When Rip's tall, beefy body caught up to walk beside me, closer and closer to the building, I forced myself to let out a deep breath I hadn't realized I'd been holding.

I could do this. There was nothing to be scared of. I had

survived living in a house with these people for seventeen years.

Nothing was going to happen.

I didn't have a single word to share with Rip as we approached the doors. He opened one and motioned me forward, his face grave but focused on mine when we made eye contact. I managed to give him a tight smile as I stepped inside.

The foyer was cool and open, and immediately I found a huge photo of my grandmother in a gaudy gold frame with her name on a plaque along with the years she had lived on it. I had seen the blown-up picture before. She'd gone to one of those Glamour Shots what had to have been twenty years ago at least, I guessed... She looked the way I remembered her the best: with her blonde-brown hair that I shared with her styled into short waves, her face full and highlighted by the brightest pink lipstick I'd ever seen. I had gotten my love of lipstick from her. She had never been afraid of some crazy fun color, and she never left home without it.

The thing that struck me the most though was that she wasn't smiling. She had never been one to smile, but her lips were pressed together into something resembling one. She looked proud and even a little snobby. It was weird to think that this successful hair salon owner, a single mom who had raised two children on her own, would also be related to two sons who would grow up to be mean, violent men. I had overheard her once say she was ashamed of them. I had been too.

How could I have gone the last six years without seeing her?

She had been the only one to show me kindness, even if it hadn't been warmth and comforting love, but it had been something.

If it hadn't been for her offering to take them when I'd finally gotten so desperate to leave, I might have ended up staying for longer in a place that was pretty close to Hell. And who knows what would have happened to my sisters if they had been stuck in that house for longer.

My grandmother had put the seed to leave in my head one day when we had gone over to her house to shower because our water had gotten turned off and told me *Go, Luna. I'll take care of the kids. But you need to go.*

I had gone when I couldn't stay longer... after doing the one and only thing that would ensure Lily and Thea and Kyra wouldn't be stuck in that house any longer.

I wasn't sure what would have happened if she wouldn't have called me when she found out my dad was getting out of jail so that I would go get my sisters.

I had sent her a birthday and Christmas card every year since, but she had never sent me anything back or called when I had left her my phone number in one of the cards. It didn't change anything though.

Grandma Gen, I'm sorry. I did love you, and I'm always going to be grateful for you helping me get out of here and taking care of the girls as long as you could.

Rip brushed against my arm as he stopped beside me. He was looking around the building, and if I wasn't imagining it, he was back to being tense again. I could see him lingering on the portrait of my grandmother.

EUGENIA MILLER
1945 – 2018

Seeing her last name was... weird. It hit me stronger than when I saw it on the end of my siblings' names. I hadn't seen it on my own since I had decided I didn't want a reminder of it.

A few people seemed to be hanging around a doorway

to the left of the portrait, and I watched them. They didn't look familiar though.

Now or never, right?

I could do this. I was going to. Then when this was done, I was going back to *my* house to see my sister, and then I'd have a job to go to the following day.

Breathing in through my nose, I told Rip, "We can go sit."

He glanced down at me, at six four compared to my five seven, and nodded. We walked forward, him beside me the entire time, as we headed toward the opened doorway. The man and the woman standing there both gave us a serious nod as we went by them. The room was filled with row after row of pews with a raised dais-like area at the front, where a casket lay. Opened. Like I had expected from the parking lot, only the first three rows of pews were filled, and I couldn't help but glance from the back of one head to another.

I stopped. With the back of my hand, I touched Ripley's loosely hanging fingers and whispered, "I want to go say bye. If you just want to wait back here, I won't be long."

His whispered response wasn't hesitant at all. "I'll go."

I raised my hand and rubbed at my brow bone with it, not because he wanted to go with me—that wasn't it at all—but just because... that casket and the backs of those heads made me feel hesitant and bad at the same time.

I still nodded at Rip, not able to even muster up any kind of facial expression that told him I was okay. Because I wasn't really feeling that okay. I wasn't bad, but I wasn't okay.

Ripley tipped his chin down at me, and it was that, that made me keep moving. We headed down the center aisle, where Rip walked to the side as I took a step up onto the raised area.

It was surreal, looking inside it, and it was more surreal —and honestly sad—to take it all in.

Thankfully, it was easy enough to ignore the gazes on the back of my head. Maybe I was imagining it, but I doubted it, and even then, I just couldn't find it in me to care as I looked at a face that looked familiar but didn't at the same time. It had been a long time.

A dozen thoughts went through my head, and I told my grandmother a few different things.

Thank you.

I hope you were okay.

Things worked out for me.

The girls are all doing great.

Lily is graduating at the top of her class.

They're all going to be in college.

Leaving was the best thing I could have done.

I'm sorry I didn't reach out to you more.

It was only the sound of the doors being closed behind me that made me realize how long I had stood there gazing down at the woman with her eyes closed. The familiar but not familiar face. The first person who had taught me that doing the right thing wasn't easy and would more than likely never be.

It was only then that I took a step back and gave my grandmother's face a bittersweet smile before I eventually turned around and immediately spotted Ripley maybe four feet away, standing with his back to the wall...

With his gaze on the pews.

I knew what I was doing as I glanced in the direction of what he was focused on. Some part of me knew that chances were I might not like what I saw. But I did it anyway.

It was my luck that the first face I landed on was the last face I would have ever wanted to see sitting there. Staring straight ahead. Face blank. Pretending like I wasn't even there.

My dad looked twenty years older than he had the last time I had seen him. Like my grandmother, he looked familiar but didn't. He looked like hell.

A lot could happen in a decade, I guessed.

The main one being that I didn't feel any kind of terror going through me as I took in his face. My knees didn't shake. Bile didn't rise up in my throat.

If anything, this coolness flooded over my skin and through my veins as I took him in.

When my eyes flicked to the woman sitting beside him, I wasn't sure what to think when I barely recognized her too. Her face was blank and dotted with sores. She was thinner than she had been before. A lot thinner. But if he looked twenty years older, she looked thirty years older. The years hadn't been kind to her. Not that they ever had.

On the other side of her was a man I had grown up with but barely knew.

My cousin.

Of course they were here. All of them—minus my older brother and my uncle, who was still in jail—but that wasn't shocking at all. These were the people who were at the top of my list for those human beings I didn't want to have anything to do with.

I didn't let myself think as I pivoted where I was standing and went to Rip just as a man in a suit walked down the center aisle. I was looking at Rip as his attention went from the people in the pews that I didn't want to look at for another second to me, then back to them. They finally went back to me just as I stopped a foot away, his jaw doing that tensing thing again.

Okay.

I nodded, and he blinked slowly enough to agree with me. We moved together down the aisle along the wall. My heart beat, beat, beat just faster than normal as we passed one aisle after another until I stopped at one only a couple of rows before the exit. Sliding all the way in, I took a seat as the man in the suit stopped behind a pulpit set up just to the right of my grandmother's casket. Ripley took a seat directly beside me, the material of the jacket he'd put on as we walked toward the building brushing against my bare elbow. I had rolled up the sleeves of the black button-down shirt I had tucked into my skirt.

The body contact did nothing for me.

I could see the backs of their heads in the second row, but I made myself focus on the man who started talking about my grandmother in vague, vague words that I wouldn't remember and that I had a feeling he had to have used generically for others all the time. My face went warm and stayed warm as I sat there, listening but only barely. This hum started buzzing around in my ears, but I did my best to ignore it and the way my heart seemed like it wanted to beat its way out of my chest.

Rip's arm moved, brushing against my elbow even more.

But I kept my gaze straight forward.

In less time than I ever would have expected, the man stopped talking and explained the instructions for the motorcade that would head to the cemetery where Grand-mother Genie would be buried.

And still, my ears buzzed.

I didn't mean to get up so fast, but I did, and luckily so

did Rip. We were the first people out and the first ones walking toward the lot. The tension in Rip's body was something I could have easily tasted. I felt it everywhere, even if I didn't understand it and wasn't in the mindset to as we walked out.

I knew something was wrong the second we got into his truck and he slammed the door shut, my name slithering out of his mouth, ending on a hard vowel. "Luna?"

I was looking out the window at the side mirror. My cousin was out of the door, his head swinging around the parking lot. Probably looking for me. "Yes?"

His breathing had gotten loud, but it was steady; I had no problem hearing it. "Is your last name really Allen?"

Shit.

This throbbing sensation instantly pierced right through my right eye sockct and had me rubbing my lips together. My fingertips even went numb before I winced—on the inside and the outside.

That was just about the last thing I would have ever, *ever*, expected him to ask.

Somehow, *somehow*, I managed to get the truth out, because there was no way I could lie. This wasn't the kind of thing I could try and hide when there were a handful of people who knew the truth. "Legally, yes." The pain from my head got stronger before I admitted slowly, "But it hasn't always been."

Had he recognized my grandmother's last name? The one I'd had for the first eighteen years of my life?

This was exactly why I had changed it. This was what I'd been trying to avoid. Only a handful of people— including Mr. Cooper—knew that I hadn't always been an Allen. No one else at the shop, not even the other guys who had worked there nearly as long as I had, knew about it.

They had no reason to know that my siblings had a different one. I was the only one so far who hated it enough to not want to keep it. Lily had mentioned before that she wanted to change it too, but she was still too young.

Rip had closed his eyes at some point. His forehead became lined as he frowned. I could see that great, big chest inhale and exhale, and his voice was incredibly calm as he breathed out. "Okay."

Okay?

Did he... know?

Had he read the paper and recognized the name and seen what my family looked like and pieced it all together?

It hadn't been a huge bust. Dad had only gone to jail for three years. His brother was a different story. But while I'd been growing up, everyone knew the Miller last name hadn't been the greatest. Maybe they hadn't known specifically about the meth, but they had known there was something, and no one ever did anything.

Until I did.

I couldn't even find it in me to be ashamed if Rip knew that part of the truth I had tried so hard to get away from.

"It used to be Miller." I tried to keep from making it seem like it was something I had tried to hide. Even though I had. "According to my birth certificate, my mom's last name had been Ramirez, but when I changed my name, I didn't want to choose anything that any of them might think of. You know Mr. Cooper's first name is Allen, and I thought Luna Allen sounded like a nice name."

The lines at his forehead and along his mouth got even deeper, and I couldn't miss the way he shook his head slowly, thinking who knows what. The skin at his cheeks changed color and got... pink? Why?

"I changed it eight years ago," I explained to him, glancing out the window to look through the side mirror again. More people exited the building, but none of them looked familiar.

I wondered if my dad had already gotten to whatever car he was now rolling around in, without me noticing.

"Mr. Cooper and Lydia drove me to the courthouse two days after my eighteenth birthday so I could start the process. They paid for the filing fees. The judge eventually granted my petition, and... I changed it," I explained, still looking through the side mirror, the pain behind my eyeball still sharp. "No one but my sisters, the Coopers, and now you, know I changed it."

The breath Rip let out was low and long, and the leather creaked as he shifted around.

I was a coward and didn't want to look at him. "Did you see it on the news?"

He didn't respond. The leather just creaked more, and the next sigh he let out was even louder than the last one. The deepest one I had probably ever heard from him.

Out of the side mirror, I watched a hearse pull around to the front of the building and a police officer appearing out of nowhere on a motorcycle.

It was time to go.

To go and see my dad, whose smallest offense had been selling drugs. The man who I would have forgiven for doing that, if he'd just been a decent person. If he'd just been... different.

"If you don't want to go to the burial, I understand," I found myself telling Rip as I fought the urge to scrub my face with the palm of my hand.

There was another sigh—not as deep but still off—and then he said, "We can go." The words had barely come out of his mouth when he started the truck and then put it into drive.

I could feel the wheels in his head turning. Could sense his tension. I didn't like it.

Did he think...

"I'm not... like them," I told him, just in case he was thinking that I was. I was reliable. I had never actually lied *to* him before. I hadn't stolen a single thing in years, and even then the stealing I had done was subjective. At least I thought so. "I've never done a single drug in my life. I rarely drink. I would never do anything to hurt anyone at the shop or anywhere else, even if they deserved it."

His scoff almost made me jump. His fingers flexed on the steering wheel for what might have been the hundredth time since he'd picked me up. "That's not what I'm thinking."

I held my breath and kept on looking at him and his facial features, but they didn't give a single thing away. "It's not?"

Rip scoffed again, shaking his head while his attention was on the other side of the windshield. "You're a good girl. Everybody knows that." He paused and a muscle in his cheek twitched.

"Nobody's fucking perfect, Luna, but I know a good girl —a good person—when I see one." His breath was more of a sigh. "And you are. I'm not about to start a fucking tally with you about the shit we've done in the past. I know you're not like... them in there."

My nose tingled, and I didn't... I didn't want to talk about those things I'd done. "I haven't seen them since I left when I was seventeen," I rushed out. "I told you, I'm not... it's complicated. We don't... like each other."

A line had somehow formed while we'd been talking,

following the hearse that had just driven off. Rip squeezed the truck in between a Chevy Impala and a small Toyota pickup. I looked behind me to make sure that it wasn't anyone I knew in the truck.

I wouldn't put it past the cowards I called my family members to do something stupid like accidentally run a light or look down. *That's* who and what I was related to.

Crap. What the hell had I been thinking? I had no business being here.

Yes, you do, Luna. You have every right. You think they were close to Grandma Genie? You think they'd be here if there wasn't some other motive? They never do anything unless they can get something out of it.

People don't change. Well. Most don't.

"I'm sorry I didn't tell you," I told him. "I guess I'd hoped that they wouldn't come."

He didn't say anything. He just drove, and as the silence stretched, all I could do was stay where I was and, after a moment, look out the window. The ache behind my eyeball got worse as we drove on.

We pulled into the cemetery and parked after a moment. I held my breath as we got out of the truck and walked in the direction of where two heart-shaped sprays of flowers were located. Rip walked beside me the whole time, the tension still just pouring directly off him. It said something about how much I distrusted the people I was related to that I kept glancing over my shoulder to make sure none of them were following us.

I was pretty sure if I looked up the Miller family history, the word "backstabbing" had to have been stemmed from an ancestor somewhere down the line.

Luckily, I didn't see any of them, at least not directly behind us. As we stopped at the gravesite, a hole that seemed too small for a casket, I kept my head aimed down, but I didn't close my eyes.

Rip's arm brushed my elbow as he settled in so close beside me I could feel the heat of his body. It wasn't unwelcome. The size of him, the knowledge that he more than likely wouldn't let anyone physically hurt me, even if he was unhappy about all of this—including finding out I was related to a felon—made me feel better. It was too warm for my long-sleeved shirt, and I could only imagine how hot he had to be in his jacket and dress shirt, but he didn't complain or act in any way like it bothered him.

I had a feeling it was him there that kept me from walking off as I watched the three people I hadn't seen in years approach slowly.

My sisters' mom didn't look at me.

But my cousin was staring. Beside him, the man who was half responsible for my existence acted like I was invisible.

I stood there and watched them both.

I wished that later on I could have looked back on that moment and been the bigger person. That I could and would have looked away from them while the chaplain or whatever he was said some more generic words about a woman he had more than likely never met. I wished I could have let myself focus on Grandma Genie and the few memories I had of her.

But I didn't do anything like that.

As the man went on, I stood there and took turns staring at my cousin and the man that my birth certificate said was my father.

My cousin basically snarled.

My dad looked right through me with those green eyes I saw every time I looked in the mirror.

Rip's arm brushed mine a few times, but I was too caught up in my own moment to worry about how bored he must be. Or how disappointed he might be in me for being related to these people. There were a million other things that he might have been thinking, and none of them were good.

It was only when the chaplain stopped speaking and the thirty other people around us approached the casket with mementos that I snapped out of it and took a step forward to drop the small picture of my sisters and me that I'd put in my purse the day before in the hole.

I was ready to leave, and it had nothing to do with the people on the other side of the casket.

I just wanted to go back home to the place that made me feel safe, to the people who made me feel loved, to the life that made me happy   that I swore from now on would only make me happier.

Turning to face Rip, who it seemed had his entire attention focused on me, I met his eyes and nodded.

He nodded back, his gaze flicking behind me for a beat, and we headed back toward his truck, avoiding old headstones and flowers.

Fortunately, I hadn't been able to relax or let my guard down, because I heard the hurried steps coming and was partially expecting the hand that wrapped around my wrist, the hold *tight and hurtful and mean*, a second before it yanked at me.

Or tried to.

Because I didn't let that happen. I'd spent years with Lenny at the gym so I'd know how to defend myself. That was how we'd met. She had taught a self-defense course I'd taken. Then kept on teaching me things after it ended. So I didn't hold back when I threw my elbow as hard as I could backward, and in a move that would have made her proud, I kicked my right leg out, feeling it connect with a left leg. The second the person behind me stumbled forward, I grabbed their right arm and extended it across my body into a straight armbar position—a submission move that hyperextended their elbow—his elbow, if you wanted to be specific, because I knew who it was.

It was the same move that Lenny and I had worked on time and time and time again, so many times, I had gotten sick and tired of doing it. She had done it to me *lightly* before and it had hurt for days. It had been totally worth it, I guessed, because instinct had just... kicked in, like she had said it would.

"What the fuck!" the voice I didn't recognize anymore hissed.

"Don't touch me," I snapped at my cousin as I took in his face, tightening my grip even harder, knowing I was hurting him and not giving a single crap.

I had seen Rip out of my peripheral vision jerk to a stop and turn around, but I had this.

I had always had this. Even when I was younger. Because maybe I was an Allen now, but I had been a Miller, and being a girl, being younger, didn't mean anything. I had gotten into fights with every single Miller kid around my age growing up, even some that weren't my age. They were all bullies and jerks. Every single one of them.

This one specifically had been the first one who had knocked me around. I still had a tiny scar on my forehead from one of those times. As I looked at his own cheek, I could see the one I had given him when I'd been fourteen and had punched him right in the cheekbone as hard as I possibly could.

"Put your hands on me again, and I will break your hand," I told him, dead serious.

His face, thin and oval, was pinched and in pain as he tried jerking his arm away, but there was no way he could. "Let me go, you fucking bitch."

I wasn't him, I reminded myself as I did finally let go, shoving him away at the same time so that the man who was only a few inches taller than me, stumbled back.

He looked terrible too. I could see the staining at his teeth, the gauntness at his cheeks, and the discoloration in his eyes.

This was what I'd avoided. This was what my sisters had missed.

Thank God. *Thank God*.

I took a step back and stopped only when I bumped into the hard mass of a body that belonged to Ripley. His hands didn't touch me. He didn't do anything but stand there.

Hopefully he was at least shooting my cousin that face that I knew damn well made the guys at the shop turn around and walk away.

"I only came here for Grandma Genie," I told my cousin as calmly as I could, even though I didn't feel all that calm. "Just leave me alone."

"Leave you alone?" my cousin snarled as he clutched his arm. "You came here. You knew what the fuck you were doing. We told you not to come back."

He was right.

It had been a mutual decision in a way.

But it didn't change the fact that he could have let me walk away.

"I came for the funeral. I don't want any trouble," I tried to tell him, but he was already shaking his head before I'd even finished the first sentence. "I'm never going to come back after this." I almost added "believe me" to the end, but I knew it would be pointless.

Honestly, I had an idea what he was going to say before he said it, and my cousin had never been the brightest or most creative crayon in the box. "You fucking bitch—"

My hand formed into a fist, ready.

But I felt it then. The hands on my shoulders.

I heard it then. The deep grumble from the man behind me.

Then I caught onto everything that came out of Rip's mouth, the rumbling rattle of each word etching themselves into me for the rest of my life.

"You can shut your fucking mouth."

Then I held my breath again as I took in the calm within Ripley's voice.

What I witnessed though was the way my cousin opened his mouth to say something, then he closed it. He made a face that said he didn't want to do that, but he had, and he took a step back. And another step back, the snarl on his face growing as he backed further and further away.

Keeping his mouth shut the whole time.

It wasn't until he was at least twenty feet away that the hands on my shoulders fell off them.

Only then did Rip take a step back.

By the time I turned around to look at the bodyguard I'd had to use my one and only favor on, his hands were at the scarf around his neck.

He was tightening it for some reason.

His cheeks were more flushed than any other time I had seen, and the tendons in his hands popped with restraint.

And his gaze... it had been on the ground, his lips thin.

I had made it. I was fine. I was loved. I had a home. I had everything I wanted and needed and more.

Yet knowing all that didn't stop my body from breaking into a shiver.

Maybe the adrenaline had disappeared and left me feeling shocked at the sight of what had happened to the people who I shared genes with me. Maybe it was at the reminder of what I had left. Of how desperate they had made me feel that I'd left their house at seventeen years old, not knowing what I was going to do, not knowing where I would live. Of how scared I had been *after*. Of how mad.

But mostly, maybe I just felt overwhelmed at how empty I had felt for so long. Of how much I had wanted things to be different. Of how much I had suffered from yearning for things that I had never been given.

It could have been any of those things and all of those things.

I'd felt lonely on and off for so long, the reminder that my little sister was finally leaving me soon hit me like a wrecking ball straight in the chest.

I wanted love, and even after all these years, I had found it, but I hadn't.

I was almost twenty-seven years old and I was still look-ing. I hadn't stopped wanting it after all this time. Here I was, not able to hug my sister because I was worried I wouldn't recover if she didn't let me. Because I had two other sisters who had pushed me away out of anger years ago, and I had never been able to get over it. This was who I'd become because of them.

I hated them.

I stood there, and all I could do was suck in a breath that sounded almost like a gasp.

I had never in my life done anything malicious just for the sake of being an asshole. I had sacrificed for my sisters. I had busted my ass for us, day after day. I had tried to be a good, decent person because that was who I wanted to be.

And here were these people who had treated me like total shit my entire childhood, trying to do the same thing after so long.

I hated them. I hated them so much I couldn't catch my damn breath. I couldn't catch my own freaking breath because of them.

If that wasn't bad enough, I hated myself too for letting my stupid cousin get to me now.

I didn't see Rip's eyes as they sliced over me, and I didn't watch as that hardened, rough expression turned into one that was still hard but surprised. I would never see the way his head reared back, his chin tipped down, and his nostrils flared.

"Luna..."

I grit my teeth as tears bubbled up into my eyes all of a sudden, but I made myself look up at him. I wasn't ashamed. I wasn't ashamed about any of this. All it did was piss me off.

I was choosing to be happy. I was choosing to be happy every day for the rest of my life, and nothing and nobody was going to take that away from me. No freaking way.

But why couldn't things have been different?

"You all right?" he asked, still taking his time with his words, his expression seeming like this mix of horrified and shocked as he watched me.

"Yes." I bit my cheek and then shook my head immediately afterward. "No."

Those eyes sliced to somewhere behind me for a split second before returning to my face. That foreign expression disappearing into that mean-muggin' Rip face that was my favorite. His chest expanded with a big breath, and he was totally serious as he asked, "Want me to go whoop his ass?"

"Yeah."

One of his big feet moved.

"But don't." I reached up to wipe at my eyes with the back of my hand, thankful I'd worn waterproof mascara and put a setting spray on my face that morning just in case. I knew better than to let this get to me. *I knew better.* I was better.

"Luna...."

I wiped under my eyes with my index finger and felt a shudder go right through me, violent and uncomfortable, starting at my shoulders and making its way down, and just... sucking. Just sucking, sucking, *sucking*. Had it really been that much to ask for, for things to be just a little bit different? To just come to a funeral and get through it without a reminder of what I had grown up around and tried my best to move on from?

I knew I had lost my damn mind when I asked him in a voice that wasn't totally steady, "Give me a minute would you?"

He didn't even think about it. "Sure."

I licked my lips.

When I had been a teenager, I had wondered what things would have been like if my mom hadn't died giving birth to me. If she would have been a better mother than the only one I had grown up knowing. I wondered if maybe our dad would have been different.

But as I got older, I realized that things might have been worse.

I had to accept I would never know how differently things might have been.

All I could do was stand there and slow my breathing, inhale and exhale.

"Just thirty more seconds," I told him, quietly, trying to ignore the ache in my chest.

But he didn't listen. He moved, and before I knew it, something warm and heavy fell over my shoulders and arms.

What had to be his hands draped themselves on my shoulders, over what had to be his jacket, and slid down over my arms, his hands molding themselves loosely over my muscles and bones. The skin on his palms and fingers eventually landed on my wrists. He was warm. Those palms kept moving downward until they were cupping my hands. His fingers lingered there. Holding them there.

Then they dropped away.

I always knew he was really a decent man.

That was when I forced myself to take a step back. To breathe. There at the cemetery, with Ripley's jacket on my shoulders, I sniffled and wiped under my eyes with my finger one more time, looking at everything and nothing at the same time.

It wasn't so hard to glance up at Rip as I wiped at my eyes again. His face was back to that cool, detached expression. Not mean. Not surprised. Just... cool.

"Thank you," I told him in a voice I was honestly proud of. "Can we go now?"

It was only his nostrils flaring that said something was going through that brain of his because his features didn't tell any other story.

The only words we shared over the next three hours were when he pulled up to a gas station and asked if I wanted to get something quick from the fast food inside, but that was it.

When he pulled up to my house after all that—my phone telling me I had an hour until Lily got home—I reached over and put my hand over his where it sat on the steering wheel. We hadn't done more than accidentally brush fingers in years, and here, twice in a day, we had done more than that. Weird how things like that worked.

"Thank you, Rip." I met those blue-green eyes and told him, "My sister is graduating on Saturday. If you'd like to come over after six, you're more than welcome to. We'll have food and drinks and stuff."

I gave it a squeeze, just one, and then pulled away.

I opened the door and slid out. Then I closed the door, took a step onto the curb and lifted my hand.

He didn't wave back.

But he waited until I'd opened my front door before he drove off.

I went to my room, changed out of my clothes and *then*, then, I cried.

For Grandma Genie.

For my sisters.

For the mom I had never met.

For the past, the present, and the future.

But mostly for myself.

CHAPTER NINE

While I didn't *love* Friday morning meetings, I didn't hate them on the same level that I did cooked carrots.

But that Friday might have been the exception.

The day before had just been... not the best day of my life, but not the worst either. Even after getting dropped off at home, it hadn't gotten much better. I'd cried for what I guessed was close to an hour before wiping my face off and reminding myself of how many wonderful things I had.

By the time Lily burst into the house screaming, "LUNA!" at the top of her lungs like she was expecting me not to have made it back home, my eyes had still been red and puffy.

She had run to my room and busted inside. My little sister had taken one look at me sitting on the edge of my bed and crawled onto it behind me, wrapping her arms around me.

"Did it go that bad?" she had asked.

"It was a C minus. It could have gone better, but it could have gone worse," I admitted to her, sneaking my hands up to rest over the forearms covering my neck.

Lily had just hugged me tighter. "You want to tell me what happened?"

"They were there," I told her vaguely. "Your mom is still on drugs. Dad looks like hell. Rudy grabbed my wrist, but I got him into an armbar, and Rip pretty much threatened to kick his ass, and then he left me alone."

My beloved little sister kissed my head at least five times before saying, "You should've broken his arm."

"I know."

"Kicked him in the nuts."

"Twice at least."

"Spit in his eyes."

"Vinegar would hurt more," I tried to make her laugh, and I did it. It wasn't a great, big laugh, but it was something.

"I'm glad Rip went with you," she kept going, her voice lighter than it had been a minute before.

"Me too," I told her forearm, resting my chin on it.

She hugged me even closer. "Tell me what your boss likes, and I'll make it for him. He deserves it for threatening stupid Rudy."

She didn't know what I had done and had no idea that we had basically performed a business exchange. I wasn't about to correct her. She had enough to worry about, so I had just nodded.

Her hand rubbed my back as she said, "Come on. Let's go to Red Lobster and take advantage of my employee discount before it runs out. My treat."

That was how we ended up going to Red Lobster for an early dinner and then going to the movies afterward. *To keep my mind off things*, Lily had claimed, and it had done the trick, at least until I tried going to sleep. Then it had all come back to me. The way my dad had ignored me, like I was dead to him. What my cousin had done. The hundred and one memories I didn't let myself think about from years ago.

Nothing helped me wind down, and nothing had kept me asleep when I had managed to doze off. I tossed and turned the entire night, thinking about all the things I should have done differently and all the things I wouldn't have done any differently.

I was healthy. I had somewhere to live. I had people who cared about me.

And I had found a brand-new lipstick in my underwear drawer that I'd forgotten all about.

Lily and I had had some good bonding time.

I managed to leave for work before my sister left her room. I had forgotten all about what day of the week it was and what it meant.

There were our weekly meetings, and then there were our *monthly* meetings. Our monthly meetings were that one time every four weeks where the *employees* got to vent, not just Mr. Cooper or Ripley. It was everyone else's turn.

I hated them.

Maybe it was mostly because of the day before, or maybe it was because I would have rather been in the booth working instead of sitting in a chair in the break room, listening to the guys complain about each other.

Because that's what the meetings were for: bitching. Lots and lots of bitching. I hated it.

The meetings were a necessary evil though. Over the years, I had seen things get so heated between the guys that fights would break out. I'd worked around this many men for so long that I got that they couldn't just get over things eventually. The problem was, if anyone got into an altercation, they would get fired.

It had happened before, and I was sure it was going to happen again, monthly meetings or not.

So, for an hour, maybe an hour and a half depending how stressed out and pissed off the guys were, I mainly just sat there and stared off into space so I wouldn't get called out for having my eyes closed. I'd spent most of my childhood zoning out people arguing; this was nothing.

Nothing but boring.

And annoying.

And honestly a little painful.

With the exception of Jason, I really liked everyone I worked with. I couldn't get why they didn't let the petty crap go.

"...and it's bullshit that I'm stuck doing all the sanding while everybody else pretends they're busy doin' somethin' so that they can jump in and do the filler. My fu—damn arm gets tired too," Jason muttered from his spot on the opposite side of the table, elbows on his knees, his face looking as irritated as his voice sounded.

Even I rolled my eyes.

It was Miguel who tossed his hands up in the air. "You're full—"

Mr. Cooper sighed and shifted in the seat beside me. I hadn't gotten around to telling him how the day before had gone, but he'd given me a hug when I sat down beside him, so I figured he had an idea from my body language that it hadn't been great.

There was a groan before Miguel continued talking. "You don't always do all the sanding. Quit exaggerating."

I kept from making a face and let my eyelids hang low.

"Seems like it. Everybody needs to pull their weight around and do equal work. I wanna do the body filler too. I do bodywork. I don't just *sand.*"

"And I don't just..." my coworker went on while I zoned him out to focus on the man who had held my hands and put his jacket around my shoulders not twenty-four hours before.

My eyes zeroed in on the sliver of tattoos along Rip's neck. I had brought him his coffee just like normal that morning, and he'd told me thank you just like normal too. There hadn't been anything that indicated things were different.

That had made me feel a lot better about the day before than I would have expected.

The guys babbled on for a while longer, but I took the time to go through my mental list of what I needed to pick up at the store today for Lily's graduation before I went home. She didn't want balloons because she didn't want us to waste helium on her. I had already called to make a reservation at a restaurant for a late lunch after the ceremony, but I knew that there would be at least a few people who went back to the house with us. So I needed to grab some snacks to feed them. Drinks. Ice. Chips—

"...spend this week in the booth."

The booth? The words snatched me right out of my head. I glanced over at Mr. Cooper, who had started talking at some point, and focused on my favorite older man.

"You good with that, Luna?" His eyes focused on me like he hadn't noticed that I wasn't paying attention.

Shit.

"What was that?"

His expression said he was fine with repeating himself. "Jason will be helping you out in the booth for the next few weeks, starting today."

Oh, no.

No, no, no, *no*.

"I'm not that far behind on things." I smiled, pressing my hand against my stomach subconsciously. "If I need help, I know I can ask." I made sure to keep my eyes on my boss and keep a smile on my face.

"We talked about Jason learning the booth, remember?"

Everyone in the room turned to look at Jason. Jason, the guy who purposely didn't finish projects so I would get stuck doing so. Jason, the one who got way too much enjoyment when I got in trouble. Jason, the jerk who had cheated on my little sister.

Jason, the guy who knew I knew he sucked and hadn't liked me since.

Great.

All I managed to get myself to do was nod and let my smile turn tight.

I didn't want to even look at him. I didn't like him, he definitely didn't like me, and the only way we worked together was by giving each other a ton of room and space.

Double great.

"I know you can catch up, but you don't need to stay late if you can get some help and knock things out faster," Mr. Cooper continued, giving me a warm smile like he genuinely thought he was doing me a favor.

I didn't need to glance at Jason to know why I would rather stay until midnight than have him help.

What was up with me and these jerks in my life? It was like God wanted me to meet the best and worst in extremes. There was no in-between with anyone I met.

"You good with that, Jason?" Mr. Cooper asked him.

From behind me, the guy I honestly couldn't stand said, "Yup."

Yup.

Of course this would happen.

I had survived my grandmother's funeral yesterday. My sister was graduating tomorrow. I guess I could make it through this too.

"Great," I found myself mumbling.

Today was going to be a good day. Somehow.

* * *

I COULD COUNT on one hand the number of people in my life that I genuinely hated.

Most of the people I could technically call my family.

Honestly, that was pretty much it.

Hating someone for me meant that if they needed a transplant and I was the only person in the world capable of giving them what they needed, I still wouldn't.

But I would more than likely give a complete stranger a kidney if they were nice and asked.

To me, there was a difference between disliking a person and hating them. There were plenty of people who I disliked for one reason or another—they were selfish, mean, rude, stuck-up, and any combination of all of those things. But if they absolutely needed something that I had, chances were, I would give it to them. Maybe I wouldn't smile as I did it, but I would do what needed to be done. If it was the right thing to do.

I'd met a lot of assholes in my life—I was related to most of them—but Jason... Jason was in a league of his own.

That was saying a lot.

I was pinching the tip of my nose so I wouldn't be tempted to pinch him instead that afternoon.

"Why did you do this?" I asked him slowly, trying my best to sound like Ripley, all nice and calm even though I didn't feel either emotion... On the inside, I'd kicked him in the balls at least four times in the last five minutes.

Maybe even twenty times.

The smirking-shrugging-useless papercut lifted his shoulders like he didn't know why he had clearly ignored the instructions I had left him to do while I'd been at lunch. They couldn't have been any more precise.

Two coats of primer. Two coats of primer. Two. Not one. Two.

And what had he done?

One coat.

And in the time it had taken me to go to the bathroom, talk to Mr. Cooper about what had happened at the funeral, and for him to tell me that he was pretty sure he'd found a replacement for the mechanic leaving, Jason had gone ahead and started adding color without giving the primer enough time to dry. I wasn't even sure where he had gotten the paint from.

It wasn't even a rookie mistake. It was an idiot mistake.

I had told him at least five times we had to let the primer dry for at least twenty-four hours after the final coat. Not ten minutes. Especially not when one coat hadn't been enough in the first place.

I could feel my left eyelid begin to twitch already. I took another deep breath through my nose and then let it out of my mouth. He'd done it on purpose. I knew he'd done it wrong on purpose. I'd bet my life on it.

"It looks all right," he tried to say, turning his back to me to do who the hell knows what.

My eyes took in the wheels and unease slithered right around the collar of my shirt. "Jason, it needed two."

"But it doesn't look bad."

I blew air into my cheeks and let them stay puffed out for

a second while I tried to think about what I could—and should—say. "That's not the point," I said as patiently as I could, before dropping to a crouch to look at the wheels sitting on top of a thick blanket. I didn't need a flashlight to see there was a line of uneven color all along the side of it. I could see hints of gray beneath the red, easily. I wanted to tell him he'd screwed that part up too, but... he had messed up enough by just missing the coat of primer in the first place. I had a feeling he hadn't even agitated the can of paint in the first place.

"I won't tell if you won't," my new—and hopefully very temporary—assistant tried to snicker.

I stood up and sighed. It was done. There was nothing I could do about it now. There was no point in being upset. I wasn't going to remember this ten years from now, but.... "Everything has to come off, and now we're going to have to do it all over again from the beginning," I told him, crushing his dreams.

I didn't need to look at him to know he had to be giving me a "are you fucking kidding me" face. But what did he expect?

I should have said something to Mr. Cooper the instant he mentioned this happening.

But I hadn't, and that was my fault.

"And it needs to dry properly," I explained, walking around the other side of the wheels and leaning back to take in another line of uneven color across the entire thing. He was rushing. That's why it was so bad. Why he'd decided to rush, why he'd decided to even do this in the first place, was beyond me.

We all had to start somewhere. We all screwed up. I could keep it together. I could give him another chance.

It was just going to be hard when every time I looked at

him, I thought about all the times in the past that I was pretty sure he'd tried screwing me over.

"Once it dries, I'll help you do some of the sanding if I have time, and you can try doing the primer again," I told him.

He gawked. "Help me do some of the sanding?"

"Yes." I glanced at him to find him making a face at me... and not doing anything with that face even afterward. "I'll help you. I can't fall behind now because of this. If I get a chance, I'll help you, and I probably can."

My coworker blinked, and the man who had to be twenty—too old to be such a crybaby—practically squawked. "But that'll take hours!"

Duh. I gave him the same shrug he'd given me. It was his fault he either hadn't read the instructions or had decided to ignore them. What was that saying? Measure twice, cut once?

"Mr. Cooper said I'm supposed to help you in the booth," Jason started, his voice already outraged and surprised.

Here we go.

I nodded. "This is part of it."

"But what about the body guys? Why can't they do it?" he tried to ask.

"Because they already have their own work to do." Which he *knew*. "They already worked on this. You can ask them if they'll help if they get a chance, but usually they're busier than I am, and I'm not going to ask for you. If I was the one who messed up, I wouldn't want anyone to know. I would do it all myself, but it's up to you what you want to do."

Maybe mentioning that I would be embarrassed if I

were him wasn't the nicest thing in the world to bring up, but...

This guy had gotten another girl pregnant while dating my eighteen-year-old sister. In the time he'd worked here, I had never heard anything about him having a son or daughter. But that was none of my business.

I couldn't find it in me to scrape up any sympathy for him. The other girl, sure. But Jason? Not even a little bit.

"But...," he started to choke.

I really wasn't anywhere near being in the mood to deal with him. "Look, Jason, go tell Mr. Cooper or Rip about it if you don't want to do it. I have too many things to do, to do it for you. I already screwed up this month and had to own up to it. I left instructions and they weren't followed. I'm not doing it for you. Period." Sorry not sorry, buddy.

Jason, who was about three inches taller than me at five ten and in decent shape, gulped. I saw the fury in his eyes, and I didn't like it. I never had. That was why I gave him about as much of a berth as possible.

But... Mr. Cooper, who never asked for anything, wanted me to work with him. I could do it for him. I would.

"I'm not trying to be a jerk. I can't be okay with you skipping two important steps. I would be furious if I paid thousands of dollars for a paint job that wasn't done correctly. Mr. Cooper wouldn't be okay with it either. We have a reputation, and I'm not going to let that come back on me. I'm sorry, but you have to do it again."

He was still giving me an angry expression and those beady, mean eyes.

Mr. Cooper, Mr. Cooper, Mr. Cooper. I could do this for Mr. Cooper.

"I've messed up before too. It happens," I added, trying to make him feel better. "It's fine. It can be fixed. It isn't a big deal." We didn't have to tell Rip, so he should be grateful for that.

He wasn't. "It's a lot of fuckin' work for a little bitty—"

All right, maybe Mr. C was going to end up owing me if I survived this.

"It isn't a little bitty mistake. It's a big one. I don't want to argue about it anymore," I told him, trying to keep my voice calm and my expression light and not like I'd just kicked him in the balls twenty-one times in my head. "Let's roll it out of here and into the room so you can get started on it, and I can keep going. I need to finish that hood sooner than later, and I still have to tape the lines."

He didn't move, and he didn't respond. All he did was keep giving me that ugly look I had seen too many times by people a lot better at doing it.

Oh freaking well. I pointed toward the wheels. "Let's do it now."

His jaw clenched, but he nodded after a moment, and it was only because of that, that I turned my back to head toward the big double doors that took up nearly an entire wall of the booth. They had to be big enough for entire cars to go inside easily.

And it was the second that I turned my back that I heard a mumbled, "Fuckin' bitch."

Maybe if he had been a teenager, I could have let it go.

If he wasn't always a douchebag to me, I could have let it go.

If I hadn't known he was a liar and a cheat, I could have let it go.

But that wasn't the case.

I turned around slowly, deciding whether or not I was going to tell Mr. Cooper afterward, when the door connecting my room to the rest of the facility opened.

Appearing there was the handsome face that had been pretty freaking nice to me less than twenty-four hours ago.

...and one more person who had a small idea of the mess I had come from. But he would never say anything to anyone. He wouldn't tell the rest of the guys at the shop who my dad was or that he'd been in jail.

But no one knew that had happened because of me.

Rip held the heavy door open with a shoulder, his coveralls buttoned all the way to the top. His face didn't reflect that he thought any differently of me. "Luna, you mind staying tonight and helping me with that GTO we found at the auction?" he asked in the same way he'd asked two hundred other times in the past.

I should have said no. After dealing with Jason, I just wanted to go home. I wanted to purge myself of how frustrated he'd already made me. Plus, I really did have things I needed to buy for tomorrow.

But... I still nodded.

That's what twenty-four-hour stores were for.

"I only need you for a couple hours. I wanna get it flipped as soon as possible," he went on, his gaze slid to Jason and rested there for a moment.

I wondered if he could sense the lazy-pain-in-the-butt vibe coming off him too, but Jason had worked on the floor long enough that I bet he did just enough for it to not be noticeable. Otherwise... well, otherwise, I figured Rip would have fired him.

"Sure," I replied.

"'Kay," he answered. His gaze stayed on the other man, but I could tell that notch between his eyebrows had formed. Maybe he really could sense it too. "Everything good?"

No, but I said, "Yeah."

Rip swung that gaze back to me.

I gave him a smile that, if he knew me even a little well, he would have seen right through.

"Let me know if anything's up," Rip said in a voice that was too calm.

Let him know if anything was up? Could he tell I was seconds away from putting this person on my permanent shit list? I had just literally been thinking about ratting Jason out to Mr. Cooper, but even for me, telling on him to Rip seemed a little harsh.

I wasn't in that bad of a mood.

I waited until Rip was out of the room before turning my attention back to the imbecile I was going to be stuck with for the near future.

I loved my job. I loved the people here. I was super lucky.

But I still couldn't stand this human hemorrhoid. "Well, let's get the wheels out there so you can get started."

* * *

"Rip?" I called out later that day as I looked at a small part of a panel of the GTO. There was lead on it, but I wasn't sure if he wanted me to burn it out—which I didn't want to do—or if he'd do it.

I got no response.

"Rip?"

Nothing.

Where was he?

I'd swear I had just seen him not even ten minutes ago; his cell phone had beeped, but I hadn't seen him walk off. I didn't need to look at the digital clock on the wall to know it was almost eight o'clock. I wanted to get home. Everything hurt today. I was *tired*. Exhausted, honestly.

But first, I really needed to ask Rip about the car, and the other builder, who had been here until an hour ago, had left. He wanted to eat dinner with his family, and I didn't blame him. I told him to go.

"Rip?" I called out again, this time even louder.

I listened, but there was nothing. Not a ting. Not a voice. Nothing.

Where the hell was he?

Standing up, with a hand going to the base of my spine because it ached from standing all day, I called out even louder and more annoying, "*Rippppp?*"

My voice echoed in the big, main room, making me smile.

"*Rip?*" I called out again, but still nothing.

It didn't take me more than a few minutes to climb up the stairs and check his office and the break room. Then it only took me a couple more minutes to go to my room, but he wasn't there either. Opening the door and calling out for him in the bathroom still didn't get me a response.

He wouldn't have left me here without saying a word.

At least he never had before. He didn't give me a hug and a kiss goodbye at the end of the day when we were working together, but he never left first. I doubted he'd start now.

Trying to guess where else he would be, I figured maybe he was outside. My lower back tightened up as I headed to the back door and slowly pushed it open, trying to listen for him. The fence and gate around the building kept out people who shouldn't be hanging around, but if someone really wanted to get over, they could jump the fence. The shop had automatic floodlights and security cameras all around the building that were triggered with any movement after six in the evening.

I'd barely opened the door a crack when I heard his low, low voice. "....that's not what I'm talking about."

I hesitated for a second, not sure if I should wait until he got off the phone, but... it was work.

Shutting the door behind me, more quietly than I needed to if I was going to be honest, I followed where his voice was coming from. The lot was mostly empty except for a handful of customers' cars waiting to be picked up, three clunkers that were on the list for restorations, my car, and his truck.

"Shorty said they brought you up. All I'm tellin' you is what he said to me, a'ight?" an unfamiliar voice spoke up, making me pause.

He wasn't alone.

Should I...?

"Why? I paid my way out. *I'm out*. I've been out. There isn't a reason for any of them to bring me up," Rip replied, confirming that I hadn't been imagining his voice to start off.

"Man, I don't fuckin' know. I don't want shit to do with it either. I got a life now. A real life. I got a kid on the way; I don't want a piece of it," the unfamiliar man spoke up. "I knew that shit was gonna blow up in their faces. They're getting desperate, I bet. It ain't like they got all that many allies."

"'Course we knew that was gonna happen. They would've too if they'd been paying attention. But it doesn't matter because there's no way for them to know where the hell I am. None of 'em knew my name. They know yours?"

"Nah. Why would they? S'not like we filled out IRS forms. Shorty's the only one who kinda knows I'm still around, and that's only 'cuz he's the only one who's got any business with me. I haven't seen him since we got out. Only reason he called today was to tell me what he heard. Warn us in case somebody tries to hit us up about coming back, I guess."

There was a tense silence that seemed to last longer than the two seconds it actually did. "I'm not going back."

"I'm not goin' back either. I'm done," the stranger spoke calmly.

Rip sighed loudly enough for me to hear. Then he said, "I'm too old for that shit. Liam's too old for that shit. I got a good thing going here I'm not about to fuck up, messing around with those fools again."

"Looks like it," the stranger answered with a quiet chuckle. "No wonder you were so fuckin' good at fixin' shit, man."

The "uh-huh" made me take a step back. "Fuck, man. I don't need any kind of shit coming back here."

"It shouldn't," the man tried to assure him. "I don't know why they mentioned you after this long, but Shorty'll let me know if anything else comes up."

"I fucking hope so. Say," Rip continued talking, "I was in San Antonio yesterday, but nobody saw me. Even if they did, it doesn't mean shit."

There was silence, then, "What the fuck were you doin' back there?"

Another pause. "Nothing. I was there for a couple hours. Don't worry about it."

"You're sure nobody saw you?"

"I'm sure."

But I could hear the hitch in Ripley's voice. It sounded different than usual, just a little, just enough for me to know that there was something big-time off about what he'd said.

Was he lying? Who could have seen him in San Antonio that he didn't want to see? Or be seen by?

I never wanted to see my family. I wasn't one to talk, but….

I took two steps back. Then I took a few more that got me to the door. I was quiet opening it, and I was even quieter closing it behind me once I was back inside the building.

Rip had paid himself out of *what?* What the hell was there to pay yourself out of? And why were they both worried about being found and getting pulled back into something? What was there to get pulled back into? And why didn't people know his real name? Who didn't have a real name in the first place? In what situation would it be possible to not have a real name? And he hadn't wanted himself to be seen in San Antonio?

What the hell had Rip been doing before he'd come here?

I couldn't even remember walking back to the main room of the building. I couldn't remember crouching down to sit beside the car we had been working on either. All I knew was that the next time I paid attention, I was there, trying to figure out what Rip was trying to keep from coming back to him.

Had he been in jail? Been running from the law? Had he done something… bad?

I had lied for him before, but my gut had said back then, like it did in that moment, that there was nothing for me to worry about. Nothing that could be bad.

Not that bad, at least.

He didn't have the most patient temper, but he'd never been remotely violent. His expectations were so high that I couldn't see him being a cheat. He was rough, but he was mostly fair.

"Luna?" the deep voice I could have recognized anywhere called out from close by.

"I'm here!" I yelled back, getting up to my feet just as I slapped what I hoped was a smile on my mouth.

He was already standing four feet away, a confused expression still on his features when I popped my head up. Then that expression went away and the closest to an easy-going expression I thought he was capable of took over that hard face. "Everything all right?" he asked, coming toward me.

I was still smiling at him as I said, "Yeah. I just got a back cramp."

He didn't look like he totally believed me.

Then I decided I needed to change the freaking subject. "There's some lead that needs to get taken care of, but I was hoping you might handle it? I can do it, but you'll probably do a better job at it." I forced a smile. "I'm not saying that to get out of doing it either or suck up, but... I would rather not do it if I don't have to."

For as much of a hard-ass as he was, he didn't look even a little put out by me pretty much trying to worm my way out of doing this. "Show me."

Luckily, I'd already been crouching right by where the spot was, otherwise... Well, I didn't know what I would have done, but I would have had to lie better about something. Crouching right next to me, I showed him what I was talking about.

"Yeah," he confirmed what I already knew. "I'll take care of it. Don't worry about it."

That's what I had figured. I gave him a little smile even as my heart raced over the words that my brain was still stuck on. *Paid his way out. Real name. Too old for some shit.*

What it all meant, I had no idea.

But my eyes strayed to the collar of his compression shirt and stayed there longer than they should have.

"You all right?" he asked randomly.

That time, my smile was genuine as I nodded.

"Sure?" Rip even went as far as to ask.

"Yeah," I told him. "I'm just tired is all. I slept like crap last night."

Those blue-green eyes watched me, and I figured he had a decent idea why that had been the case. Just as quickly, his eyes shifted to the giant clock on the wall. "Get home. I got this, and then I'll head out too. We got enough done."

I looked at him, pushing the words I'd heard out of his mouth minutes earlier out of my head. "Are you sure?"

It was his turn to nod.

"Okay. I was—" My phone rang from the back pocket of my pants, and I pulled it out and squinted at the screen. Then I stuck it back into my pocket.

His gaze had followed my hand, and his face was smooth when he tipped his chin up, his eyebrow going in the same direction. "You gonna get that?"

"No."

The corners of his mouth moved maybe a millimeter.

"My sisters have been calling me for the last two hours, even though they know I'm here," I explained. "They got to Houston earlier and—" I cut myself off, realizing what I was doing. This wasn't my other coworkers I rattled my business off to. I waved my hand in front of me and shook my head. "Anyway, I guess I'll get going then if you don't need me anymore."

Rip's little frown hadn't gone anywhere, but he nodded.

I took a step back, ready to turn away. "If you want to come by my house tomorrow after all, I won't let anybody bother you too much either," I offered him, knowing he wouldn't commit himself. "If not, I'll see you Monday. Have a good weekend."

At least I had invited him, like I always did.

"Luna," he called out before I got another step.

I stopped, half expecting him to tell me there was something else he needed. "Yeah?"

My boss stood there, hands on his hips, watching me with that gaze that I never completely understood.

I grinned at him. "You all right, boss?"

I watched his whole body exhale before his mouth twitched and he said in that low, grumbling voice, "Decide what you want as a favor."

"What's that?"

The next expression he gave me, I did understand. It was his *Luna's an idiot* face. Then he repeated himself.

And even after he repeated himself, I had no idea what the hell he was talking about. So I asked him once more. "I don't understand what favor you want me to decide on," I told him slowly, like it was him who wasn't understanding what he was saying.

Because that was the exact case.

I had used it up yesterday. He wasn't exactly a spring chicken anymore, but he wasn't *that* forgetful either.

Swiping at his eyes with the meaty part of his palm, he sighed my name. "Decide on a new favor."

"What new favor?"

Rip rubbed his face again, shaking his head as he did. "Your other one didn't count. Pick something new."

Eh... *what?*

He must have read the question on my face because Ripley muttered, "Luna, the other one doesn't count. Ask for something else."

A memory of Rip coming to stand behind me, of telling my cousin to shut up, filled my brain. The relief of it could still fill my mouth. But I could never take advantage of him. I would never want to in the first place. "Rip, I never wanted the favor. You don't owe me anything."

The handsome, stunning man let his hands drop.

"I don't need a new favor. You did more than I could have asked for. That was what I wanted."

He gave me that laser-like stare that I loved and hated at the same time. "I don't care," he tried to tell me in that *we're not talking about this anymore* voice.

"Rip—"

His shot me that *Luna is an idiot* look again. "It doesn't count."

"But I don't want anything else."

"And I don't wanna owe you shit, Luna," he insisted, watching me closely. "Something else, all right? You can come up with something."

I opened my mouth but felt my eyes narrow on their own. "Ripley, I don't want you to owe me anything. It was one thing I said for you. That's all."

That hand of his went up to tug at the collar of his compression shirt, showing me the skull there. His breath was deep. "I'm telling you how it's gonna be. Pick something else. Me going with you to that funeral isn't gonna be it." He pinned me with a look that almost might have taken my breath away. "That was nothing. Understand me?"

Of course he thought it was nothing. He was the one who didn't understand. "It wasn't nothing to me," I told him quietly.

My boss, this man standing in front of me, didn't say a word. He didn't move. He didn't twitch. He didn't flinch.

He didn't argue.

He just looked at me.

And all I could do was give him a flimsy smile back to show him that it had been more than enough. I didn't want him to feel like he owed me. He didn't.

"It doesn't count, Luna. Not today, not tomorrow. Pick something else or I will. You got me?" he asked me in that calm, cool, steady voice, piercing me with that unflinching gaze.

It was my turn to stare. My turn to watch him. Because I knew that tone and that voice and what it meant.

I might let people get away with a whole lot of things sometimes, but this wasn't someone with an attitude problem calling me a bitch.

This was my boss feeling indebted to me when he had no reason to. When I didn't want him to.

But all I could get out was his name before something moved across that hard face.

I definitely couldn't miss the way his chest expanded as he settled his irises on me mercilessly. "I pay back my debts, and what we did doesn't count." He tipped his chin up and started to turn away from me. Done. He was already done with me. "Go home."

I stood there for a moment and watched as he moved toward the chests, pulling a rag out of his pocket to wipe his hands as he did.

I sighed.

"Night, Luna," he called out over his shoulder, just a hint louder than a normal speaking voice.

"Night, Rip," I replied, shaking my own freaking head.

What was going *on* with him?

CHAPTER TEN

"Look at her. It feels like just yesterday we were talking about whether she should get started on pads or tampons," my best friend said with a sigh from her spot beside me.

I couldn't help *but* snort as I looked down the table in the same direction, eyeing Lily at the head of it, surrounded by a handful of her friends and our two sisters. Apparently, at twenty-six, I was too old to sit on that end at the restaurant I had reserved months ago. On my half, there was me, my friend Lenny, her grandfather, her grandfather's best friend, Mr. Cooper, and Lydia—the extended family we had made since I'd left San Antonio.

I'd been feeling pretty melancholic all day, and it had gotten worse when my sister had walked across the stage at the giant arena where her high school graduation was held. I loved all of my sisters, but Lily... Lily was the baby. She was the best of all of us.

I was happy for her, but it still made me sad that my little sister was growing up.

Fortunately, Lenny had snuck a blow horn into the

arena despite going through security somehow—I wasn't sure how, but I was going to ask later—and the minute that thing had gone *toot toot* and given everyone within a hundred feet an earache, I hadn't been able to help but feel joyful, just freaking happy and proud.

My little sister had graduated high school, and like our other sisters, in the top 10 percent of her class, with a three-fourths scholarship to a public university in Lubbock.

That thought especially made my chest fill with pride when I watched her lean back in her chair and laugh her butt off at something someone close to her had said.

"Don't remind me. I've managed not to cry, and I want to keep it that way," I said to my closest friend.

Elena DeMaio, or Len or Lenny as everyone called her, snickered and swung her gaze over to my direction. In a button-down cotton dress she had borrowed from me because she still couldn't lift one of her arms over her head after a surgery she'd had two months ago, she almost looked sweet with her sling on. Almost.

But we all knew she wasn't, and we loved her for it anyway.

She was one of my favorite people in the entire world, and I had no idea why this three-time Judo national champion and one-time world champion had picked me out of a self-defense class she'd been teaching and decided to make me her friend eight years ago. Lenny had literally walked over to me while I'd been toweling sweat off and asked, "You wanna get something to eat?" Maybe she had seen the loneliness in my eyes, because I'd been pretty freaking lonely back then, or maybe she had just been bored, but going with her had been one of the best decisions I had ever made.

Because of her, I'd added more people to my extended

family—her grandpa and his best friend. Getting to look at the hot guys at her gym was a nice bonus too.

"You never texted me back the other night," Lenny decided to change the subject instead of reminding me that I had a reason to be a little sad. "How did it go? Did you see you-know-who?"

I eyed my siblings down the table then made sure Mr. Cooper was in the middle of a conversation and not listening. He wasn't.

Plucking at a royal blue thread from my dress, I wrinkled my nose and whispered, "Yeah, I meant to call you, but I spent the rest of the day with Lily and worked all day yesterday."

She leaned forward. "And?"

I moved my gaze back to my siblings down the table. "Let's just say I went all Judo on my cousin and his elbow is going to be hurting for a while."

She punched me. She literally punched me right in the shoulder, and I didn't bother trying to pretend like it didn't hurt because it did. "You didn't!"

Rubbing at my upper arm, I nodded. "Yeah. Rip threatened to kick his ass, and that was the end of it." I winced. "Damn it, Lenny, you need to keep your Amazon strength to yourself. That hurts."

Lenny rolled her eyes and brushed my pain off. "Is that all that happened?"

I shrugged and glanced toward Mr. Cooper again. I had left that part of the story out when I'd told him. "Yeah, basically. My dad looks like shit, and the girls' mom looks even worse. Pretty sure she's on meth now. It's over with at least. I won't have to see them ever again." I smiled and tried to give her an enthusiastic "Yay."

She didn't "yay" me back or mutter a word, and that said everything.

Beside me, Mr. Cooper was in the middle of a conversation with Lenny's grandpa's best friend. On Lenny's other side, Lydia was talking to Grandpa Gus. We were all familiar with each other. Most of us had even had a few Thanksgiving dinners together when everyone was in town.

They were everything I had ever wanted.

Beside me, Lenny sighed, and I had to eye her.

"What's that sigh for?"

"No reason," she lied.

I made a face at her.

It was impossible to miss the way she shrugged her one good shoulder, the one that wasn't in a sling. "You got me thinking about how when I was little, I used to cry over how much I wished my mom would have stuck around, and how I probably got lucky that she didn't." She didn't need to say what her words really meant. I understood.

She could have had a family like mine. She could have ended up with my dad. Or with the person I had called Mom for too long. Or my brother, who hadn't necessarily been bad but had never been good either. Or any of the rest of the Millers.

She had heard enough bits and pieces to know I wouldn't have wished them on anyone.

As I looked down the table again at three sisters who I had busted my ass for everyday for years, this tiny part of me wept silently that I hadn't had the same opportunities as them. It was selfish and I knew it, but I knew more than anything that if I had to, I would never switch positions with any of them. Never.

I couldn't help the words that I whispered over to my best friend as I thought about how I never got to experience so many things other people took for granted. At least I had gotten a dinner the day my GED diploma came in. Mr. Cooper and Lydia and taken me to this very same restaurant to celebrate that day.

"I used to tell myself that I'd gotten switched at birth with someone else and my parents were off raising somebody else that looked just like me," I told Lenny quietly, keeping my gaze down the table on the two blondes and the one light brown head of hair. "I would think about how they took her to Disney and gave her ballet lessons and had dinner around a table every night... and how she was probably super happy.

"And at first, I'd want to cry, thinking about how she got lucky and how I'd ended up with *them,* and one day, after my dad had grabbed my arm so hard I thought he had broken it when he was drunk... I thought about how I was glad she had gotten the better parents because at least one of us could be happy. Maybe she—that girl—wouldn't have been able to deal with them. But I could, deal with them I mean, so it had worked out for the best."

I pressed my lips together as I tipped my head back and looked up at the ceiling. Not because I didn't want Lenny to see me cry—she had plenty of times in the past—but because I wouldn't even want to look at myself right then. I didn't want to remember that I was the same person who had dreamed those things. A part of me would probably always hate that I'd had to, and that was pointless and dumb because I *was* over it.

But still.

When you want to survive, your body and your brain will convince themselves of anything.

I wished I could have protected Little Luna from all of that. I could have stopped the *"Fucking Luna,"* and the

"Why are you always bothering me?" and *"Don't you have somewhere else to be?"* and *"You stupid little shit"* and *"Leave me alone"* when all I wanted was attention or affection from my dad or the only mom I had physically ever known. I could have stopped all the times my dad had called me useless and told me he regretted I was the one who had made it instead of my real mom. I could have deafened Little Luna's ears from hearing all the arguments and the fights that had nothing to do with her but ate her up all the same.

I mourned that.

I mourned for that girl like I couldn't put into words.

I sucked my bottom lip into my mouth and blinked.

I grabbed onto that knowledge deep in my heart that it was better late than never. I was loved, I had a home, I had money, and I had a job now. I was safe. I was happy. I had so much more than I might deserve—so much more than the people who should have loved me would have ever wished for me.

I packed up those thoughts, shaped them into the size of a basketball, and three-pointed that ball into an imaginary net far, far away from me.

I was here. I was fine. It was a beautiful day, and I was around people who gave me more love and happiness in a month than I'd had for seventeen years.

I would never have to see those jerks again.

And today was going to be a good day, damn it.

So I got it together and finally looked back down at my best friend to ask, "Did I tell you I stole a bottle of Visine once because I wanted to put a few drops into my dad's coffee, but I always chickened out?"

Lenny snickered. "No. Psycho. Did I tell you that one time I asked Santa to bring my mom back?"

I made a face. "That's sad, Lenny." I blinked. "I pretty much did the same thing."

"Uh-huh."

I raised my eyebrows at her. "Did I ever tell you that I wanted to have like ten kids when I was younger?"

The laugh that came out of her wasn't as strong as it usually was, but I was glad she let it out anyway. It sounded just like her, loud and direct and so full of happiness it was literally infectious. "Ten? Jesus, *why*?"

I wrinkled my nose at her. "It sounded like a good number."

The scoff that came out of her right then was a little louder. "You're fucking nuts, Luna. One, two, three, four, five, six, seven, eight, nine, ten-ten?"

"That's what ten means." I grinned at her. "I said that was back when I was younger, not any time recently. I can't afford ten kids."

"*Still*. How about... none?"

I glanced down the table again when I heard Thea's sharp laugh. "Okay, Only Child." I laughed. "I think four's a good number now."

My friend beside me groaned before reaching forward to grab a chip, dipping it into the tiny bowl of guacamole beside it. "Look, Grandpa Gus was basically my brother, my dad, my uncle, and my grandpa all rolled into one, and I had a bunch of kids to play with," she claimed. "Whatever makes you happy, but I think I'm fine with zero kids in my future."

I reached over and grabbed one of the pieces of fajita from her plate and plopped it into my mouth. "Watch, you'll end up with two," I told her, covering my mouth while I chewed the meat. "You've already got that 'mom' vibe going on better than anyone I know."

That had her rolling her eyes, but she didn't argue that she didn't, because we both knew it was true. She was a twenty-seven-year-old who dealt with full-grown man babies daily. She had it down. I was friends with my coworkers. Lenny was a babysitter for the ones she was surrounded with regularly.

"Like you're one to talk, bish," she threw out in a grumpy voice that said she knew she couldn't deny it.

She had a point there.

She picked up a piece of fajita and tossed it into her mouth before mumbling, "For the record, you should probably get started on lucky number four soon. You aren't getting any younger."

I rolled my eyes, still chewing. "Bish."

"Bish."

I smiled at her, and she smirked right back.

"Since we're on the topic of kids, and you can't have any on your own..."

The smile fell right off my face. This wasn't the first time we'd had a similar conversation. "I don't want to talk about it right now."

She ignored me. "Maybe it's time you started dating again."

I glanced down the table. Thankfully, no one had decided to start paying attention. "I don't want to talk about it," I insisted.

Still, Lenny ignored me. "How long has it been since you dated that silver fox?"

"Do you have to talk so loud?" I glanced around again before whispering, "And three years, you know that."

"So it's been how long since that one guy who wanted you to call him Daddy?"

And she'd gone there.

I burst out laughing, which I knew was the last thing I needed to do when every person at dinner was nosey. "*Shut up, Len!*" I tried to whisper, but it really came out as more of a laugh, damn her.

I had almost forgotten about the one and only "rebound" in my life. The thirty-six-year-old to my back-then twenty-three.

Of course, she still ignored me as she thought about the dates before answering her own question. "Three years too, right?"

"Can we talk about this later?" I basically begged her, even though I was still cracking up over the memory of that short and weird relationship that I'd gone into with almost no expectations.

Lenny's snort told me we weren't going to talk about this later. We were going to talk about it now. Because when Lenny DeMaio wanted something, she got it.

It all went to hell the moment Mr. Cooper turned and smiled over at us. "What are you two cracking up about?"

Oh hell. I started to shake my head. "She's being—"

It was too late.

"I'm trying to tell Luna that she needs to start dating again if she wants to have four kids someday, and we're going down the list of her exes."

"There's only been one and a half, and that half was debatable," I said, but I knew it was pointless.

Still, she ignored me. "And I reminded her about the first one."

Mr. Cooper's face instantly fell. "I didn't like him."

At least she hadn't brought up—

"Was that the one who wanted you to call him Daddy?" Grandpa Gus, who had been in the middle of a conversation when I had looked at him two minutes ago, asked out of nowhere.

It was my turn to punch Lenny in the shoulder, and I never did that.

Unfortunately, she didn't flinch or even act like she'd felt anything as she nodded in agreement to her grandpa's question.

I didn't even know why it surprised me she had told him about him.

Out of the corner of my eye, I watched Mr. Cooper flinch. The man was for all intents and purposes, my adoptive dad. There had been a reason why I had told him that we had broken up after a month because *things weren't working out*. Not because me and the man I had briefly dated had wanted me to call him freaking *Daddy*.

"I didn't like him either," the man, who was right around Mr. Cooper's age, if not a year or two older, agreed. "Now the silver-haired one I did like, Luna."

I had too.

"He was all right," Lenny sort-of agreed but then shook her head. "But it's been more than three years, and I think it's time we found 'someone' a new boyfriend." As if the *someone* wasn't obvious enough, she had the nerve to point at me.

I just shook my head, my gut telling me this was spiraling out of control too fast. "I'm fine," I tried to insist, even though... well, even though I did want someone in my life.

Joining in on the conversation now, Lydia leaned forward from her spot two seats down and reached across to pat my hand. "Lenny's got a point, Luna. You would be happy by yourself, but life is always better with other people to share it with, don't you think?"

I blinked.

"I know a few nice men I could set you up with," the woman kept going, her face thoughtful. "Let me make sure they aren't in relationships, and I'll get back to you."

I was going to kill Lenny.

"That's all right, you don't have to—"

"ARE YOU TRYING TO START DATING AGAIN, LUNA?" Lily basically shouted across the table.

Scratch that. I was going to drag out her torture. For years.

I shook my head at my sister then

forced myself to smile. "Lily, why don't you show everyone pictures of the house you're going to be living in while you're at school? It's pretty nice—"

My traitor-butt little sister pretended like she didn't hear me as she kept going. "MY P.E. TEACHER THOUGHT YOU WERE REALLY CUTE, AND HE JUST BROKE UP WITH HIS GIRLFRIEND."

Did she have to shout that? But how she knew he thought I was cute, much less why she knew he'd broken up with his girlfriend, was beyond me.

"Nope, that's all right—" I started to say before Lenny's bish self cut me off.

"There's a guy or two at Maio House who aren't total pieces of shit I could introduce you to." She was referring to the mixed martial arts gym where we had met. The same gym that her grandfather owned and that she worked part-time at. Someday, when Grandpa Gus finally decided to retire, she would end up taking over running it.

I could already imagine how her fixing me up with someone from there would go. That idea probably caused me more panic than Mr. Cooper knowing some guy—the second man I had ever slept with—had wanted me to call him Daddy while he'd been... doing it. God. He was probably scarred for life now. I really was going to kill Lenny. I really was. I would miss her for the rest of my life, but it had to be done. It really did.

"Or you could not. Just throwing that out there," I told her, focusing on that for the time being instead of Mr. Cooper's future nightmares.

She gave me a face I knew too well. "I know other people not from there I could set you up with. My people know people. It'd be easy. Right, Grandpa?"

My people know people.

These were my loved ones.

This entire conversation was my fault. I should have never brought up wanting to have kids someday. If I would have just kept my mouth closed....

"I've got a couple men in mind...." Grandpa Gus trailed off, getting a distant and way too thoughtful look on his face.

All right. This had gone on long enough. "Thank you, everyone, even you yelling over there for the entire restaurant to hear that you can fix me up, but I can find my own dates."

I didn't even believe that myself, and by the silence that responded to me, neither did they.

I was going to take it as a compliment that none of them laughed.

"I know people too," I told them then stopped. "Stop looking at me like that. I do know people, and I get hit on sometimes. Thank you for your optimism."

Still, none of them said a word, and that felt nice.

Not.

"I'm not that ugly. I can find someone to date me if I want," I told them, dryly.

It was Lily who chose to ignore I'd said anything. She

slapped the flat of her hand against the table before yelling, "SO HOW ARE WE GOING TO DO THIS? I CAN SEND EVERYONE A LINK TO A GOOGLE FORM WHERE WE CAN SIGN UP LUNA FOR DATES ON CERTAIN DAYS OR WE CAN DO A GROUP MESSAGE."

Oh hell.

Lydia reached over and set her hand on top of mine, giving me a big smile. "Let us do this for you, Luna, honey. Maybe it'll be fun. You can trust us. What do you say?"

What did I say?

What did I say?

I held my breath and took a look at the way too eager faces around the table. All of them. Faces of people I loved. Faces of people who loved me—with the exception of Lily's friends, of course.

But the rest of them....

Lenny punched me in the arm again, just as hard as she had a moment before. "Do it, Luna," said the woman who had never dated anyone in all the time we had been friends. Not once.

But that was another story.

They wanted me to trust them?

I glanced at the faces again, and I said two words I was worried I might end up regretting big-time. "I guess?"

CHAPTER ELEVEN

———————————————

THE REST OF THE WEEKEND WENT BY IN A BLUR.

After staying at the restaurant so long that the waiters gave us some serious side-eye, everyone made their way over to my house like I had expected. Our group of fifteen turned into thirty at some point in the evening, and we'd ended up ordering everything off the nearest pizza place's menu. The Coopers spent a small fortune buying bags of chips and drinks from the gas station, I saw, after they had snuck off for a moment and come back loaded with bags.

I had been in such a good mood that it had only hurt me a little when my sister Lily had come up to me at some point, thrown an arm over my shoulder, and said, "Sugar tits, my friend's aunt needs help at her restaurant in Galveston this summer, and she said she would hire us. Her parents have a beach house, and she said I could stay with them. She said the tips during the summer are *really* good, like more than I make now. A lot more."

She hadn't been asking me for permission, but she hadn't been *telling* me she was going to do it either.

I knew what it meant. Galveston was a beach town a little over an hour away from where we lived. She would be going to stay there. Making money. And while she listened to me, I wasn't her mom. I was lucky to even be her guardian. Our relationship had always been this weird dance between me being the closest thing to a mom figure she had, and me not wanting to cross the line, balancing being a sister and... her caretaker.

I had never seen myself as being in any position to tell any of my sisters what they should do or how they should live their lives. I had made a thousand mistakes on my own. I was nobody to try and give them advice, much less be any of their role models. Unless something was absolutely a crap idea, I usually kept my mouth shut over what they wanted to do.

I didn't *want* her to leave for what I would figure was the rest of the summer.

But...

I had hidden my sadness and smiled at her. "That's great, Lil. When do you start? Are you going to put in your two-week notice at the restaurant or just call and tell them you aren't going back?" I asked her, referring to the waitressing job she'd had for the last almost two years.

She had said she was going to put in her two-week notice but claimed her boss would end up firing her when she did. It was what that boss always did, apparently. As long as that happened, then she would be leaving on Friday, she had told me, giving me a kiss on my cheek as she went on about how tan she was going to be and how I could come visit on the weekends and we could hang out on the beach.

Lily hadn't been wrong. I had been sitting at home the day after her graduation, when she left for work and was still sitting at home when she had come back four hours later, telling me her boss had told her she didn't need to bother finishing out her two weeks. So, she was leaving.

After spending the rest of Sunday at the house with just Lily, since Thea and Kyra had left early in the morning—one to Austin and the other back to Dallas—the next few days went by fast. I helped her pack a couple of boxes of clothes and went with her to buy a new bathing suit. We went out to dinner with Lenny and Grandpa Gus on Wednesday. And that very morning, on Friday, I had gone to wake her up before I'd left for work and given her about four kisses on her cheeks before we'd said goodbye, with her being half-asleep.

She promised to drive up every couple of weeks, and I had promised to go visit too, but I knew how that went. My other two sisters had promised the same thing, and now I barely saw them but three or four times a year. When I offered to go visit, they didn't have time for that either.

So my seventeen about-to-be eighteen-year-old sister at a beach house in a party town coming back on a weekend when she probably made the most amount of tips?

I wasn't going to hold my breath.

Lily would still text me every day. And she was only a phone call away.

So that Friday, a day where I had requested to leave early months ago for a gynecologist appointment, I was trying my best to cling onto every little bit of happiness I could find, which probably explained why I was trying to be extra enthusiastic about decorating for my coworker's going-away party that day. I had just finished taping up the last chunk of black streamer when a big figure stopped at the door to the break room.

With my arms stretched as high as they could go over my head, and with pieces of tape stuck to my fingers, I turned my head to shoot Ripley a closed-mouth smile. I hadn't even been remotely surprised he hadn't stopped by on Saturday. It wasn't the first time I had invited him to something and he hadn't shown up. It was no big deal.

"Hey, boss."

The big man stood there as he looked around the room. "What's all this?"

"Today is Rogelio's last day," I said, pointing at the cardboard letters that spelled out BYE BISH going across the bottom of the break room's cabinets.

He scratched at his temple.

"I'm on my lunch break," I threw in before he tried to say something about me not getting paid to decorate for someone's going-away party. It had been a gray shirt kind of week so far, and I didn't want to jinx it.

His eyes drifted to the sign and then the two black balloons directly beside them, and all he said was "All right" in that low voice.

Turning back to the streamer, I pressed my finger against the tape one last time to make sure it had stuck and then hopped off the top of the two-step ladder I'd had to drag from my room up here.

"Where'd all this come from?" he asked, surprising me.

I folded the ladder in on itself and propped it up against the counter. "I brought it from home. I used it for my sister's going-away party two years ago." I glanced back at him and gave him a smile.

"I have some blue streamer at home if you want me to use it for your next birthday," I tried to joke around.

His snicker as he stood there made me smile even wider.

"There's cake. If you want a piece, Rogelio said he'd come up here in—" I glanced at my watch. "—ten minutes."

My boss didn't move, but he wasn't done asking questions. "What kind?"

"Angel food."

One of those hands went up as he scratched at his throat, exposing maybe a millimeter more of it than usual. "You make it?" he asked in that calm voice that was probably my favorite of all.

"Nope." With Lily leaving, I hadn't wanted to waste thirty minutes I could have with her on something else. "I got it from the grocery store. I'll save you a piece and put it in the veggie drawer if you aren't around," I offered before tearing my eyes away so I could finish picking up my mess. Everything had been so hectic, I'd barely gotten a chance to think about the last long-ish conversation we'd had—the one that included Rip telling me he still owed me.

I decided right then still wasn't the right time to think about it. Maybe tonight when I got home. Maybe later in my room when I tried to zone Jason out.

In the meantime, I stashed all the bags I'd brought from home and took the cake out of the fridge to set it on the counter. I'd barely stacked up the paper plates—because I sure wasn't going to wash them and none of the guys would either if they were real plates—when Miguel came into the room and claimed, "You didn't decorate for my birthday."

I slid him a look. "It's Rogelio's *going-away* party. You know I don't put up decorations unless the birthday ends in a zero. And you've got what? Five more years until your fiftieth?"

The older man slid *me* a look. "Don't remind me."

I laughed.

He finally laughed too as he made his way inside. "What kind of cake did you get?"

"Angel food, but hold your horses. Ro gets the first slice."

"He's leaving, and you know he's going to want half of it, Luna. You know how he is," Miguel tried to reason, even as he opened the fridge and started poking around inside.

Rip, who had warmed up his food while I'd been cleaning and talking to Miguel, pulled a chair out from the table and dropped into it, setting a container in front of him.

Done, I picked up the last lunch I might ever get from my little sister and took a seat down the table from him. I'd been eating it in bits and pieces as I decorated. Salisbury steak, mashed potatoes, and steamed spinach. Man, I was going to miss her.

Miguel took the seat beside mine, opening up his lunch bag and pulling out a sandwich and a bag of chips.

I nudged him. "Isn't it your wife's birthday today?"

He froze, and then he looked up so slowly, straight at the wall ahead, that I knew the answer. "Today is the sixth?" he whispered.

I glanced at Rip, and even he was looking at Miguel curiously. "Yes."

Miguel cursed long and low in Spanish before glancing at me with a horrified and panicked expression.

"I wondered why she was giving me a dirty look this morning." He muttered almost thoughtfully, his eyes wide. "She's gonna kill me. I thought her birthday was tomorrow."

"She's not going to kill you," I tried to assure him, not fully believing the words myself. I'd met her. We were friends. She really would kill him.

The face he made said he didn't either.

"Okay, maybe, but I know what you can do. Did you buy her present already?"

He hadn't. He didn't need to say it, I could tell. "I was going to take the kids with me tomorrow to get it."

"Okay, good." I forked some more food into my mouth. "I know this florist that can deliver flowers by three if you order them soon."

That had added some coloring to his face. "The same ones you ordered for Owen last month?"

I nodded and got a nod in return. This wasn't the first time the same thing had happened with one of the guys at the shop. I had half the guys' credit card information saved on my phone. I usually helped them buy Christmas presents for their wives and girlfriends too since they were such slackers.

"What are her favorites?" I asked him.

Silence.

"Miguelito, what flowers does she like?"

He was back to staring blankly.

We both laughed.

"What do you like?" he asked me like that was help.

It wasn't. "Oh, I don't care. Don't ask me."

Miguel blinked. "Luna, what have your boyfriends sent you?"

Boyfriends. Like that was *really* plural. I gave him a funny face before pulling my phone out of my pocket and looking through the contacts for the florist that some of the other guys had used before. "They didn't. Thanks for reminding me," I said, trying to say it lightly and playfully, like it wasn't a big deal.

Because it wasn't.

If I wanted flowers, I could buy them myself.

"None of them?" my coworker asked, not letting it go.

I found the contact and set my phone on the table between us. "Nope."

"Not even the old one?"

I snickered and shook my head. "Stop." I pointed at the phone. "Call and order the flowers."

He grinned and brought out his phone too, dialing the number quickly and then, putting his phone over the receiver, asking, "What about your sisters?"

I wasn't exactly sure why I shot a look at Rip, but I did, and luckily his attention was down on his food. So I shook my head.

"Your high school graduation?" he threw out next.

"Ah, I got my GED. I didn't... finish high school the... normal way."

Miguel blinked, and fortunately the florist answered, because he started rattling off a request and then an address.

I managed to eat the rest of my steak by the time Mr. Cooper made his way into the break room, one hand rubbing his stomach like he was starving, his eyes sweeping across the room. He shot me a big smile. "Looks nice."

I smiled back at him just as Miguel hung up the phone and let out a big sigh.

"He said he can drop them off at her job by three."

"See? She'll only kill you a little now."

Miguel slapped me on the back twice. "Thank you, Lunita. You're a lifesaver."

"You would have figured it out yourself."

But freaking Miguel wasn't done. "Luna?"

I tipped my chin up at him as I ate some more mashed potatoes.

He took a bite out of his own sandwich. "I think we need to find you a boyfriend."

I stopped chewing at the same time that Mr. Cooper

started laughing and set what looked like a chicken salad sandwich in the spot in front of where I was sitting.

I shook my head. "Ignore Mr. C, Miguel."

Unfortunately, this conversation interested the man who had known me for five years. "What? Why you laughing, Mr. C? You think she needs to find a boyfriend too?"

I jumped in before Mr. Cooper could. "We had this conversation on the weekend. All I agreed to was maybe going on a few dates. Maybe. That's it."

Miguel nodded thoughtfully, popping a chip into his mouth. "I know five—no, three—"

"Oh, no. I've been to your family reunions."

The other man started laughing.

I was going to use that moment to change the subject. "*Anyway,* what ended up happening with the guy you interviewed that you liked? Are you hiring him?"

I regretted the question the second it was out of my mouth.

Especially when Mr. Cooper's eyes slid to Ripley's direction. The much older man smiled anyway, his nostrils flaring just enough to tell me it wasn't totally genuine. "He came in today. I think it went well, but we're going to talk about it."

"Is he nice?"

Mr. Cooper's smile turned into a genuine one. "You think I'd hire somebody who wasn't?"

I grinned at him, but all I could think about was that the only reason I was having a decent day was because Jason had a sore throat and wasn't talking as much as usual.

But I kept my mouth shut on that topic.

* * *

I HAD JUST FINISHED GIVING Jason instructions for the rest of afternoon, my purse and keys in hand so I could leave for my gynecologist appointment, when I heard the yelling coming from upstairs.

Crap.

Really?

Everyone should have gotten a slice or two of cake. It should have been a pretty decent day. None of the guys in the shop had even come to my room to complain about anything either.

And Jason had barely annoyed me. Considering I was dreading going to an empty house, it had still been an okay day. We had made it through lunch without an issue. The rest of the day should have been free of issues too.

I made my way down the hall toward the main part of the building and found all of my coworkers there, busy, but two of them had stopped and were looking up, like they could see through the ceiling and into the office over our heads.

I stopped there with my bag over my shoulder and looked in the same direction.

"You gonna go do something about it?" Miguel, one of the ones looking up, asked.

I glanced at him. "Why me?"

He scoffed. "I'm not their favorite."

I blinked again, ignoring the way Owen, the other guy who had been looking up, snickered.

"I don't have your magic touch," Miguel added.

"I don't have a magic touch."

He looked at Owen, and they both nodded and agreed at the same time, "Yeah, you do."

"I need to go. I have a doctor's appointment in—" I glanced at my watch. "—thirty minutes."

The yelling got louder for a brief moment, making us all focus up at the open staircase and the landing that fed off from it.

"Do something, Luna," Owen said. "It's Rogelio's last day. I don't want today to be my last day. Miguel doesn't want it to be his last day. Nobody else but Rogelio wants it to be their last day, either. You know how they get."

I wanted to argue, I really did, but I knew when to pick my fights, and in this case, this wasn't one I had any chance of winning. I already knew none of them were going to go upstairs and say anything.

"Chicken shits," I groaned and couldn't help but smile when they laughed.

I shouldered off my bag and dropped it on the floor by my feet. "You guys owe me," I mumbled under my breath as I ignored my coworkers and headed up the stairs, shaking my head.

"I'll buy you a Sprite tonight!" Owen shouted up.

"What's going on tonight?" I stopped and called down to him.

"We're getting together at Mickey's. I told Jason to tell you hours ago," my coworker claimed.

That freaking fart face. Man, he sucked.

Shoving that aside, it kind of answered my predicament for being home tonight, so I gave him a thumbs-up. "I'll see you there then," I told him before continuing up the stair-case, listening.

The voices stopped for a second, yet still managing to be a loud, muffled buzz of anger, but right as I got to the top of the stairs, it started up again, less of an unidentified mumble and more individual words laced together.

"*—so goddamn disrespectful!*"

"I'm fucking disrespectful? Are you fucking with me?"

"No, I'm not fucking with you, Ripley! You hurt Lydia's feelings! We went because she told me I should go."

Ooh. I winced at that. I thought it had been long enough that they wouldn't bring up Rip walking out on them during his birthday celebration. I was wrong. I took one step forward and then another. Still listening.

"I don't give a fuck why you went or why you took her with you!"

"Because she's my wife, and she has been for almost twenty-three years!" my favorite boss shouted back.

I took another three steps, passing the break room and approaching the office door when the words got real.

"Yeah, the wife you married a year after your last one died. You want to talk about fucking disrespectful."

Mr. Cooper had been married before?

I blinked at the door, feeling... I don't know. Shocked? Taken aback?

I had worked for Mr. Cooper for nearly ten years and had never heard anything about another wife.

There were plenty of reasons why people wouldn't share information like that, I told myself as I raised my hand. If his wife had died and he didn't want to talk about it... it wasn't my business to get why, much less to judge.

There were more than enough things in my life I would rather not talk about with anyone.

But the knowledge that he'd had another wife before the one I knew.... That we had known each other for so long and I had told him things I didn't tell most others, when he hadn't ever said anything to me about this....

This isn't about you, I reminded myself. It wasn't. Not even close.

Then I knocked.

The voices went quiet.

The "Luna?" from Mr. Cooper was low and beyond strained.

Of course he knew it was me. No one else was dumb enough to come bother them while they were yelling. Or I could think of it like I was the only one brave enough to.

Those scaredy cats were downstairs hoping for a miracle.

What they were getting was me.

"I'm leaving for the day. I have my doctor's appointment, and I left Jason in my room. Do either one of you need anything before I go?" I called out, rolling my eyes at my own words. I wasn't even trying to be subtle about breaking their argument up. Did they need anything? When had I ever asked them that when I was about to walk out? Never, that was when.

There was a pause that I was pretty sure consisted of them either sitting or standing on opposite sides of Mr. Cooper's desk, glaring at the door or at each other.

Then Mr. Cooper called out, "No, I'm fine. Thank you for asking."

I made a face at the door, because we both knew that was BS.

Then there was a rumble of a "Go to the doctor, Luna" that I barely understood.

"Okay," I called out again, wincing at just how fake happy I sounded. "Have a good night!"

I took three steps away and stopped. Then I listened and waited.

But there wasn't a single sound from inside the office.

Until the doorknob turned suddenly and the next thing I knew the door itself was being opened.

Crap.

There wasn't a point in hiding or running. It was just going to make it that much more obvious and worse. So, I walked like normal toward the stairs to go down, only glancing over my shoulder when I actually made it to the landing. That was when I saw that it was Rip who had followed me out.

His expression was that usual one that seemed like bottled-up thunder under skin and bone.

Screw it. I waved at him.

"See you tomorrow, boss," I called out to him, knowing I wouldn't get a response. He was a grumpy little goose.

My phone vibrated from my pocket, and when I picked it up, my sister's name flashed across the screen.

It was a picture message of what she'd told me earlier was Jamaica Beach in Galveston.

Then another message came through.

Lily: WISH YOU WERE HERE

My poor little heart honestly ached, but I still texted her back.

Me: Me too. Love you and be safe.

I typed another message and then let my fingers linger over the screen, deciding whether to send it or not.

I sent it.

Me: Don't forget about me.

Her reply was instant.

Lily: I could never forget about my FAVORITE SISTER.

Her favorite sister.

Well. Okay. She had never called me that before, but I liked it. I liked it a lot.

Just as quickly as I decided that, the idea of going home

to an empty house seemed like hell. With my phone still out, I shot out a quick text to Lenny.

Me: I've got a gyno appointment in thirty. You free later? My coworkers are getting together after work, and the girl is gone, and I don't want to go home too early.

CHAPTER TWELVE

"Look, *look!*"

I was already looking at Lenny, who was behind the wheel of her car, gesturing to me with one hand as we left the Greek place we had gone to have dinner at. "No," I cut her off. "I did look, and he's out of my league."

She groaned.

I looked down at the picture of a half-naked man on my phone and shook my head. "He is, Len. I can *see* it. He probably has girls hitting on him all the time. Just look at him."

She didn't bother arguing that the man she had apparently set me up on a date with—a retired MMA fighter—had plenty of girls hitting on him. She'd be a freaking liar if she did, and Lenny was a whole lot of things, but not a liar. That was me. The route she did decide to go down was, "Give me a break. *You're* out of *his* league."

I would have laughed, but she kept going like she knew exactly what I was going to say and wasn't about to let me.

"You're the fucking best, Luna."

I smiled at her and lifted a shoulder. "I've got my moments," I tried to joke.

"What have you got to lose? He's hot, but you've got that Cinderella thing going," she tried to say.

I rolled my eyes because I hated when she used the Cinderella example on me. I was usually dirty, cleaning up after others, working too much, and taking someone's shit. The Life of Luna.

"If he gets hit on during our date and leaves me there for another girl, I'm blaming you," I told her.

She snickered. "If he sucks, blame Grandpa Gus. He's the one who picked him out."

Oh, Grandpa Gus.

"He's really proud of himself, by the way. I swear he had a list and was checking names off of it over the last few days. I saw he had a comment next to one guy's name that said 'too hairy.'"

It was my turn to snicker. "I love that man,"

Lenny shook her head. "Me too, but I swear the only person who loves him more than I do is himself."

She so had a point. While Mr. Cooper was calm, easy-going, and had every personal trait that was fatherly and comforting, Lenny's Grandpa Gus was... something else.

"Hey, we're going to Mickey's, right?" she asked, refer-ring to where I had told her my coworkers were getting together after hours to celebrate Rogelio abandoning us.

"Yup."

After my gynecologist appointment ended, I had headed over to her gym. Grandpa Gus had waved us off, telling me to take her away. We had left and gone shopping at the nearest strip mall, and then gone to eat afterward. Now, I was dragging her along with me to Mickey's. Except we'd ditched my car at my house because she was the worst back seat driver, and I didn't feel like getting griped at for driving too slow. Should she be driving with one arm in a sling? Probably not, but I wasn't going to be the one to tell her that.

"Is Rip going to be there?" she asked.

"Doubt it."

Her muttered "shit" made me laugh. She'd been trying for the last three years to make seeing him in person finally happen. I couldn't exactly get her to come over while I was working.

"I just want to see him. Just once," she said.

"I've shown you pictures." Pictures I had maneuvered to get him into the background.

It was her turn to make a noise. "It's not the same."

"It's the same," I tried to argue.

"Maybe it'll be my lucky day and he shows up."

"Don't hold your breath or you'll end up passing out."

We both cracked up just as her phone started ringing from where she had set it in the cupholder between our seats. Connected to her car's Bluetooth, GRANDPA GUS came up on the screen of her dashboard. She didn't hesitate to hit answer.

"Grandpa."

"Can you head back to Maio House?"

Concern flashed across my friend's face. "What happened?"

There was some rustling, then just barely the sound of Grandpa Gus whispering, something like *I will pop you if you ever use that tone of voice on me again* filled the car, but he wasn't talking to us.

I had to press my lips together to keep from laughing, and it was obvious that Lenny was too because she shot me a funny face.

"There was an accident," he came back on the line after a moment, his tone mysterious.

"What kind of an accident?"

There was a sigh and another whisper that sounded like *I don't want to hear it* before he came back on the line to respond with, "S*omeone* needs a couple stitches and doesn't want to go to the hospital, and Peter says he's not doing it."

That must have been enough of an explanation for Lenny because she groaned, obviously knowing who *someone* was and why her grandpa's best friend didn't want to give *someone* stitches. I'd heard enough from her over the years to know he set noses regularly, glued things back together, and could fix just about every kind of dislocation without a visit to a hospital.

"All right. I'll be there in twenty," she agreed with a grimace.

"Okay." He didn't even say "bye" before he hung up.

Lenny sighed, but I beat her to it.

"You know I'd go anywhere with you, but you know I'll faint if I see blood." That was a true story. I was really squeamish. "Can you drop me off at Mickey's since we're closer? If you get a chance to come back, then come. If not, I'll catch a ride home with someone." Or take an Uber. I wasn't planning on drinking.

Her fingers were already up at her nose, pinching the tip of it. For one brief moment, I wondered who that *someone* was. "You're sure?"

"Of course I'm sure, bish. Keep my stuff, and I'll get it from you this weekend."

She was still pinching her face. "I have to work at the gym tomorrow but text me after your date. We can do something Sunday," she said, just as she got us a block away from Mickey's.

I sighed at the reminder I had a date the next day. I already didn't want to go. That wasn't a good sign.

Lenny pulled her car up to the curb right outside the bar and gave me an almost half-ass wink that told me how aggravated she was that she was going to give someone stitches... or take them to the hospital. I didn't really want to ask. "Let me know when you get home, okay?" she asked. "I can come get you if you're still here when I'm done."

I smiled and nodded at her. "Drive safe."

Lenny blew me a kiss. "If Rip shows up, call me."

I shook my head as I got out of her car and slammed the door shut behind me, clutching my purse to my chest.

She honked the horn the second I was on the curb, and we waved at each other before she busted an illegal U-turn that made me shake my head as she sped away.

It only took me a second to find my license and flash it at the bouncer who didn't even look at it. He'd seen me enough times to know I was over the age. It was already eight o'clock by the time I walked in and found six people I knew: three coworkers and three wives and girlfriends.

I waved at them before making my way over and giving them all hugs, and it was just as I was turning around to see who else was there that I spotted the small table directly beside the one where I was standing at.

Sitting there, all alone, was Rip.

He'd come?

The surprise must have been evident on my face because Owen shrugged at me and said a little too loudly, "I didn't think he liked Ro that much."

Honestly, neither had I.

But he *was* there.

It made me sad that he was sitting by himself, when it only took me a moment longer to spot four more people I recognized. The thing was, none of the chairs at the table he was at were pulled out. He really was sitting alone.

He'd come and no one wanted to sit with him.

I was sure the argument he'd had with Mr. Cooper earlier hadn't helped but....

I knew what I was going to do before my feet moved. I shrugged back at Owen and tipped my head to the side to tell him where I would be. He gave me the same look I gave Lily when she ate steamed carrots in front of me. Like *really?*

And, yeah, really.

I was going to need to text Lenny and let her know she'd jinxed herself.

Trying not to come off too aggressive, I headed toward the bar first to get a Sprite. Then I turned around and headed back the way I had come. Rip hadn't moved. He was still sitting there, not on his phone, not doing anything else, but *sitting there*. Present. I thought it was a lot sweeter than I had any right to think.

"Fancy seeing you here," I told Rip as I crossed around the front of his table and stopped there.

My boss, who I wasn't positive had seen me up until that point, blinked at me. "Luna."

So much enthusiasm.

Just as I was about to ask if I could sit with him, I decided not to even bother. I pulled out the chair and took the seat anyway. "I didn't know you were coming."

That stubble-covered cheek kind of twitched. "Didn't know you were either."

I lifted a shoulder as I took a sip out of my Sprite. "My sister left, and I don't want to be home alone."

He lifted his own glass up to his mouth, some amber-looking liquid, and took a sip. I didn't expect him to say, "Thought college didn't start till August."

I didn't mean to give him a sad smile, but it happened, and I tried to cover it up by keeping my voice light. "It doesn't. The plan had been that we were going to move her to Lubbock at the beginning of August so she could get settled in and find a job before everyone goes back to school, but... her friend's family has a restaurant in Galveston and they invited her to work there for the summer."

"Galveston?" he asked in that amazing voice, still surprising me by keeping our conversation going.

"Yeah. Staying at a beach house and everything. Totally slumming it and having a miserable time, you know?" I gave him a real smile that time.

Rip just raised his brows.

"I promised her I would go visit, and she promised she would come up too... What's that face for?" I surprised myself by laughing. "I don't believe it either. I'll get lucky if she comes once. I'm not that delusional."

I didn't imagine the way his cheek twitched again, just a little, just enough to keep the smile on my face.

"I'm stuck making my own lunches from now on. I have nobody to watch scary movies with who's more dramatic than I am screaming at the scary parts. And my house is empty," I told him, going on a roll.

"Your lunches?" was what he picked up on.

I wasn't sure how much he'd had to drink that he was asking me so many questions, but I wasn't going to complain. "I can't cook to save my life, boss. I thought everyone knew. Baking is the only thing I can handle."

"You serious?" he asked in a surprised tone.

I nodded.

"For real?"

"Yeah," I confirmed. "I can't even make rice in an Instant Pot. It's either way too dry or it's mush." Oh. "An Instant Pot is—"

"I know what it is," he cut me off.

It was my turn to make a face, but mine was an impressed one. He knew what an Instant Pot was but not a rom-com. Okay. "Sorry."

He didn't react to me trying to tease him, instead he asked, "You can't even make rice in that?"

"Nope."

"You know there's instructions online."

Was he messing with me now? I couldn't help but watch him a little. How much had he drunk already? "Yeah, I know."

"And you still screw it up?"

I blinked, soaking up Chatty Cathy over here like a plant that hadn't seen the sun in too long. "I wouldn't say I *screw it up*. It's more like... you either need to chew a little more or a little less."

It was his turn to blink.

"It's a surprise. I like to keep people on their toes."

If I hadn't been guessing that he'd had a couple drinks before, what he did next would have confirmed it.

His left cheek twitched. Then his right one did too, and in the single blink of an eye, Lucas Ripley was smiling at me.

Straight white teeth. That not-thin but not-full mouth dark pink and pulled up at the edges. He even had a dimple.

Rip had a freaking *dimple*.

And I wanted to touch it to make sure it was real.

I couldn't help but think it was just about the cutest thing I had ever seen, even though I had zero business thinking anything along those lines. But I was smart enough to know that I couldn't say a single word to mention it; otherwise, it might never come out again.

What I did trust myself to do was gulp down half of my Sprite before saying, "You can make rice, I'm guessing?" If he wanted to talk, we could talk. I was good at talking.

"Uh-huh," he replied, sounding almost cocky about it.

All I could get myself to do in response was grin at him, and for another five seconds, his dimple—and his smile—responded to me.

"Big plans for the rest of the weekend?"

He gave me that smug face. "No" was his short answer, which could have meant a thousand different things. "You think of a new favor yet?"

We were back to this.

Well, if he wanted to play this game, we could play it. "I don't know what you're talking about."

The smug face turned into my favorite smart-ass one. "Luna."

I smiled. "Ripley."

"You think of one or not?" he grumbled but not in a mean way.

I scrunched up my nose at him and leaned forward a little as I lowered my voice and said, "For the thousandth time, boss, you really don't owe me anything."

"I really do," he quipped back immediately, lowering his voice too.

"No, you don't. We're even."

That dimple popped up and disappeared again so fast I thought it might have just been wishful thinking that I'd seen it again. "We're not even until I do another favor for you," he tried to claim.

"That's what I'm trying to tell you. You don't have to do another favor for me. You didn't have to in the first place."

He blinked. "Think of a favor, Luna."

I blinked back. "You think of a favor."

He stared, and I definitely wasn't imagining that his voice dropped into this thing that was too low to be called a whisper. "You want me to think of one?"

I ignored the way *that* went straight to my chest and lifted a shoulder, keeping it calm, keeping it cool. "Sure. Why not?"

That got me no response. Just like I thought. *It's not that easy, is it, Rip?* I thought to myself before giving him a break.

"Do you know how to do tile work?"

"Tile work?" he asked slowly.

I nodded. "Yeah. How about you help me tile my bathroom?"

"Tile your bathroom?" he echoed, fueling up my inner pest.

"I'm just throwing out ideas since you're being all desperate and needy about wanting to get this favor over with."

If Rip could have sputtered, I was pretty sure he would have right then, because his expression.... "You say I'm being desperate and needy?"

Okay, so maybe I just wanted to screw with him a little. So I kept my mouth shut and took a small sip of my Sprite before adding, "It's okay if you don't know how to do tile. Not many people can tear a car apart and build it back together like you can."

The silence yawned between us for a moment and then three before... "How much have you had to drink?"

I burst out laughing. "It's Sprite, boss. I don't drink that much, and especially not in front of most people."

Those eyebrows went up. "You don't?"

He was still asking me questions. Okay. "Drink?"

Rip dipped his chin.

"One or two is okay, but even that's rare. But get *drunk*? No. I've done it… twice, and it was for special occasions," I informed him.

His finger drew a circle around the rim of his glass as he asked, "What were they?"

Was Rip trying to get to know me? I wanted to be excited about it, but… well… I wasn't sure why he was doing it. But it was fine, I wouldn't overthink it. "My twenty-first birthday and my best friend's grandpa's seventieth birthday."

Rip looked at me. "Huh."

Plastering a smile on my face, I went with changing the subject again. "But seriously, Rip, everything else aside, I want you to know I'm being serious about this favor thing. You don't owe me anything. You don't have to do anything. Going with me to the funeral was more than enough."

"I don't care what you think. I still owe you."

I crossed my eyes and didn't bother holding back a sigh. I didn't even know why I was bothering insisting. Like he was going to change his mind. I could only wish.

And really, why was he being so freaking talkative? I liked it. I liked it a lot, but it didn't make any sense.

Just as I was opening my mouth to tell him *fine*, someone called out "Luna!" right behind me.

I barely managed to glance over my shoulder when a male body stopped directly beside me. Tipping my head back, I found a familiar face grinning down at me.

"How's it going?" the late twenty-something-year-old asked.

"Hey, I'm good. How are you?" I asked the guy back.

"Good, good. Owen invited us to come by."

I smiled at him.

"I wanted to tell you. I did that rice thing you said to do with my phone last time I saw you, and it worked like a charm. Let me know if you want a drink. I got you," he offered, sliding Rip a quick glance before dropping his hand off me. "Least I can do."

"I'll let you know, but I'm glad it worked."

"See ya," he said with a grin before turning around and heading back toward the bar, disappearing into a small group of people.

Turning back to Rip, I raised my eyebrows. "He works at one of the parts stores we order a lot of things from," I explained when I noticed his gaze was in the direction the guy had gone.

That had my boss glancing back at me with that remote face.

"He's nice," I added for some reason I wasn't totally certain of.

His fingers brushed over the stubble covering his chin, eyes zeroed in on me almost thoughtfully.

"What?"

"Nothing."

"What?" I insisted.

"Nothing, Luna."

Okay then. If he didn't want to tell me, I was fine with that.

"Luna!" another familiar voice shouted in the bar.

Glancing over my shoulder, the group of coworkers I had greeted when I'd first walked in—who were behind me

—waved me toward them. "You can have my seat!" one of them offered.

"I'm okay!" I yelled back. "I'm all right over here."

"You sure?"

I gave them a thumbs-up.

When I glanced forward again, Rip was taking another drink, and he was watching me.

"What?" I asked.

"Do you know everybody here?"

I rolled my eyes, hoping he'd know I was just playing with him. "Not everyone. Just like half of them," I joked.

Honestly, it looked like he believed me, but what I didn't like was the way his jaw kind of ticked to the side and how his voice went from tight to honestly a little sharp as he said, clearly, "I don't need a babysitter."

I couldn't help it. I frowned.

"I'm not being a babysitter."

"You don't have to sit with me," he said coolly out of nowhere.

What the hell had crawled up his butt? "I know that. I came over here and sat with you. If I had wanted to sit somewhere else, I would have," I told him, trying to process his words and tone. "But if you don't want me to sit here, I can get up and go. It won't hurt my feelings if you don't want me around. I don't want to wear out my welcome."

Damn it, why hadn't I just said that he wouldn't hurt my feelings if he wanted to sit by himself instead? I didn't mean to make it... about me. But regardless, I didn't shove my stool back and get up. I wasn't going to show him his words and his tone bothered me.

Because they didn't.

Much.

Before I got a chance to say anything else, my phone

started to ring from inside my purse. Rip didn't say a word to confirm or deny that he wanted or didn't want me to sit with him. He didn't tell me to leave either, but that didn't make me feel much better. Phone out, I saw THEA flashing across the screen, and I answered it, cupping my hand around my mouth so she could hear me.

"Hello?" I pretty much yelled anyway.

"Luna," her watery voice came over the line. "I got broken into."

I froze. "What?"

"My place. It got broken into," she explained with a sniffle that was so loud I managed to hear it despite the loud background. "What do I do?"

Shit. "Call the cops but not the emergency line," I rattled off, trying to think. "You're sure no one's still in the apartment?"

"Positive," she confirmed, her voice wobbly and honestly sounding pretty freaking panicked, not that I blamed her. "Can you... can you come?"

"Yeah," I agreed, quickly. "I'm not home, but I'll leave in a little bit. Call the police and start making a list of what they took. But whatever it is, don't get upset, okay? It's just stuff. What matters is that you're fine."

"Okay, I'll call now, but hurry, please."

My stomach turned as I took in the fear in her voice. "I will. Maybe don't touch anything. I don't know. Ask the dispatcher who answers, okay? I'll be there as soon as I can." I swallowed. "I'm glad you're okay though. But don't stress. Everything can be replaced. Text me your address, Thea, okay? It'll save me time from looking for it."

Giving me a broken goodbye, my sister hung up, and I shoved my stool back and got to my feet.

Poor Thea. I couldn't imagine how she felt, much less

that she called me first before calling the freaking cops. I was honestly surprised she wanted me to come, but I would never tell her no if she needed me. Not to any of my sisters. Or anyone I cared about. But that didn't change the fact that my relationship with the oldest of my three younger sisters had been strained since before she had moved out. Since the night I had tried to give her a hug and she'd pushed me away, telling me to leave her alone. I hated that string of words more than any others. I really did.

Why was I thinking about that? I had promised myself I wouldn't again.

Taking in a calming breath, I unlocked my screen and quickly started going through the apps on it.

"Everything good?" Rip asked, honestly reminding me he was there. I wasn't sure how I'd forgotten, but I had.

Opening the app I needed, I glanced up at him and rushed out, "My sister's apartment got broken into."

The little notch between his eyebrows popped up. "She all right?"

"She doesn't sound like it," I told him, glancing down at my phone as I put in the address I was going to need to get a ride to. "She asked me to go see her, so I need to get back home, and drive up there."

"Drive where?"

I didn't glance over to him as I hit the search icon to find a ride on the app. "Dallas. She lives in Dallas." I grabbed my purse and watched the screen blink as it searched.

"What are you doing?" Rip asked instantly.

"Trying to get a car to take me back home," I told him, still looking at my screen. "My friend dropped me off."

I heard him shove the stool back instead of seeing it. "I'll take you."

That had me glancing up at him. "You don't have to."

"I'll take you, and don't say anything about the favor either." He was already up and making his way around the table. "Let's go."

I blinked, but... I hit the icon to exit the app.

Maybe I should have argued with him a little more, but... maybe he'd count this as the favor once he really had a chance to think about it. Not that I held much hope since driving me to San Antonio hadn't counted, so I doubted driving me a few minutes away would, but...

His choice.

I nodded and took off toward the door, waving absent-mindedly at the coworkers who watched me leave, giving curious glances, probably because Rip was right at my heels behind me. It took seconds to get out of the bar. Rip pointed down the street, and half a block down I spotted his yellow truck. In no time at all, we were at it and he'd unlocked the passenger door to let me in. The second my seat belt was on, he pulled onto the street.

"You good?"

I took a breath, not realizing that I was staring out the windshield. "Yeah, I'm fine. Just a little worried about my sister," I explained, thinking he didn't know her name. "I'm just surprised she called me, I guess. Not that surprised her place got broken into. Her apartment isn't in the greatest neighborhood I've ever been in."

"She lives by herself?"

"No, she's got a roommate." I took another breath in and out of my nose. "I'm sorry, Rip, do you need me to give you directions?"

"I know how to get there."

Another breath in, another release of it. "Thank you so much for driving me," I told him.

"Uh-huh."

I eyed the clock and swallowed back a yawn. It was going to be after midnight by the time I made it to her house. I'd gotten up at 5:45 that morning. I could make some coffee, and I'd make it just fine. Well, as close to fine as possible. Worst case, I'd roll down the windows and let the air wake me up.

I must have been in my thoughts longer than I imagined because the next thing I knew, Rip was pulling his truck into a driveway.

My driveway.

I needed to get it together. Calm down. Focus and get going as quickly as possible.

"Thank you so much for the ride," I managed to tell him.

Rip's gaze was pretty intent on me as he put the car into park and leaned back in the seat, and I watched as his eyes flicked to my house over my shoulder before returning to me. He licked his lips before he said in that boss-man voice that told me not to argue, "Get your things. I'll wait out here."

Uh. Maybe he had had a little more to drink than usual. "You don't have to wait. My neighborhood is pretty safe."

I doubted anyone would ever give me a slower blink than the one he shared with me in that moment.

I watched as he paused and looked at the bracelet I'd put on that morning. My fun thing of the day was an old bracelet Lily had made me years ago that said LOVEYOU in white beads with black lettering. He sighed and flicked his eyes back toward my face. "Luna, I'm taking you to Dallas. Get your shit."

CHAPTER THIRTEEN

"You really don't have to do this."

Rip didn't even huff or roll his eyes as I said the same words I'd already told him five different times since he'd pulled up to my house and dropped the bomb on me.

Luna, I'm taking you to Dallas. Get your shit.

Of course I'd reacted the way any sane person would. I had sat there and stared blankly for about a minute until he'd raised his eyebrows at me and said, *Night's not getting any younger, baby girl. Let's go.*

And that, *that* had snapped me out of it.

Which then started us into a five-minute back and forth discussion about why he didn't have to take me and why he was going to. I mean he could barely get through a conversation with me without huffing and shaking his head. I hadn't even known he'd had a dimple until tonight. Yet he wanted to drive me to Dallas?

I wasn't the kind of person to tell someone not to help me, but it just didn't make sense.

And yet, I still found myself in his truck twenty minutes

later with a bag filled with a change of clothes, my tooth-brush, contact case, and solution.

I sighed and leaned my shoulder against the window. "Rip...."

"Luna."

I pressed my lips together, watching his profile in the dark cab. "Turn around and take me back. I shouldn't have even gotten into the car in the first place. You don't need to do this. I'm sure you have better things to do."

"I don't."

I blew out a breath that had him swinging his eyes to me.

"I don't," he repeated himself, those long fingers flexing on the steering wheel.

I sighed again. "It was just one little lie, Ripley."

"You lied to the fucking cops for me, Luna. That's a felony if you didn't know. There's nothing little about that."

I guess there was no arguing *that*. I put my hand over my face and took a breath, sliding my gaze over to him, trying to be sneaky about it so he couldn't see me doing it. Who *was* this man? Not that I was complaining that he was actually talking to me and asking me things and trying to be nice, but....

"Why are you being such a pain in the ass about me going with you?" he asked all of a sudden, forcing my thoughts back.

I stopped trying to be sneaky with my glances and just stared. "I'm not being a pain in the ass. You are." I flexed my fingers, remembering *this was my boss*. "I say that with all the respect of you being an owner of Cooper's and me being your employee, by the way. Please don't fire me."

He shook his head, and I wasn't sure if it was because he wasn't going to fire me or if I was just getting on his nerves.

Knowing Rip, it could be either.

"Look, I do appreciate you coming with me. I really do, Rip. I like your company. You know that." I didn't miss the way he turned to glance at me, just for a second, just for one single split second, but I didn't miss it. The thing was I didn't know what to think about the wary expression on his features when he did it. "But I told you, you don't owe me. Honestly, I would have probably called my best friend to go with me if you hadn't... volunteered." I wasn't sure I would call him telling me to get my shit as him volunteering, but close enough. "I really do appreciate you coming with me, but I don't want to be an inconvenience."

Those long fingers flexed again, but his attention stayed forward then. "You're not."

"You're screwing up at least some part of your weekend off driving me to Dallas."

"I'm not screwing up shit, Luna." He flicked his gaze toward me and shook his head again. "Who told you that you're an inconvenience?"

I didn't mean for my body to get tight, but it did. "No one," I tried to tell him as brightly as possible.

The look he gave me said he thought I was full of it.

He would have been right, because I was, and as much as I didn't want to admit it, I didn't like that he got that idea, especially so quickly.

"I don't like to bother people, that's all. I don't like asking anyone for a favor, and if I can...."

Dear God.

I realized what the hell I had just said.

I didn't like asking anyone for a favor. It was the truth. I would rather go without than ask anyone for anything.

And for three years, I'd been holding this favor that Rip felt he owed me, over his head.

No wonder he wanted to get it over with. It made total sense.

Hell.

"I'm sorry you feel like you owe me, and I get why you want to get this favor over with," I muttered, feeling my face heat up as I accepted what I had done and why it was stupid of me to keep arguing with him over a favor that he was never, ever going to forget about. No matter how much I might try and talk him out of it, he'd gotten it into his thick head and nothing was changing.

"You're not asking. I offered," he suggested like I would really look at it like that.

I shifted my gaze out the window and nodded. "You're right."

There was a sigh, then, "You're not gonna give me a hard time anymore?"

"Nope."

His "huh" had me side-eyeing him.

"I appreciate your commitment and how... patient you've been with me over this," I told him, a little more grudgingly than I needed to.

Rip hummed.

"I'm not sure how long this is going to take. If you want to drop me off and then—"

"What is with you always trying to get me to drop you off?" he snapped all of a sudden.

I made my eyes go wide at his freaking *attitude*. "Because, I told you, I don't want to bother you. I don't like to bother anyone. Don't take it personal, okay?"

I wasn't 100 percent sure, but I was pretty freaking positive he frowned at me.

Rubbing my hands against my pants, I decided to mess with him some more by muttering, "At the rate you've been going lately, I'm going to start to think that I don't get on your nerves as much as you make me think I do, boss."

The laugh that burst out of him literally had me clutching the door I was leaning against. It was so sharp, so out of the blue, like a freaking firework going off right inside the cab.

I jumped. Then I grinned.

And I kept it going, because why not? I'd made him laugh. Rip. *Laugh.* "Next thing I know, we're going to be friends," I kept muttering, barely able to keep from laughing.

His reply was a shake of that handsome head and a chuckle that continued on.

"But really, thank you for coming with me. And taking me home. And for having enough pride and honor to keep your word when you insist on doing me a favor that I really don't think you owe me," I told him, smiling even though he couldn't see it.

The deep inhale of breath he took was loud and clear. That time for sure, I knew without a doubt he did look at me. "I don't have that much honor, Luna. Don't give me that much credit."

I watched him, seeing he meant it. "Well, I think you do. Most people would have just given up and pretended like they forgot if someone told them a thousand times that they didn't need anything."

His "hmm" didn't sound that convinced, but I knew I was right. There was no point in me forcing it down though.

Bringing out my phone, I pulled up my messages with Lenny and sent her one.

Me: Hey, going to Dallas. Thea's place got broken into. Can you ask Out of My League if

we can reschedule? Not sure if I'll make it back in time tomorrow.

I couldn't even say I was really that heartbroken about missing my first date in... six months? Maybe even a little longer? I doubted I'd be that disappointed if he couldn't change the date either.

Lenny texted me back not two minutes later as Rip fiddled with the radio.

Lenny: She okay? I'll send him a message. Sunday work for you?

I knew there was no way I would stay until Sunday with her. I was definitely going home at some point tomorrow. Unless she insisted, but I wasn't going to hold my breath. She was busy. At least that's what she always said. It would take all of my fingers and Ripley's to count the number of times I had asked her over the years if she wanted me to visit with the answer always being the same: it wasn't a good time for her.

Lenny: Don't answer that. Sunday is good. Let me see what I can do.

Dang it. That's what happened when someone knew you too well.

Me: She's fine. And yeah, sure, Sunday is good. The earlier the better.

Lenny: :]

At least that was done with.

Music played softly in the background the entire drive to my sister's, now that Rip and I were done arguing at least. I dozed off a couple of times, but he didn't complain or give me a hard time. I'd left my phone between us with the navigation going. When I checked the arrival time and saw that we were only five minutes away, I sat up straight and started paying attention.

I hadn't realized that my sister had moved.

When I had first trailed her up to Dallas three years ago, I had just followed her.

The place I had been to was a decent apartment complex that hadn't looked *too* sketchy. It hadn't been anything fancy by any means, but it had been all right. It had basically been the same kind of place that we had lived in after moving out of Mr. Cooper's.

But *this* place, this place was *nice*.

Too nice.

Way too nice if the Mercedes and Audis and BMWs that were on the other side of the gate meant anything.

I gave Rip the code for the gate—Thea had texted it to me along with her address— and I couldn't help but feel really weird about everything that I saw. Every single car was a late model luxury car, with a handful of Hondas and Kias thrown in. Now that I thought about it, Thea hadn't driven herself to Houston in forever. She usually met up with Kyra in Austin and rode with her.

Why wouldn't she have told me that she moved?

"I thought you said your sister was in college," Rip said as he slowly drove past one building and toward the other, following the complex's signs.

I spotted a Range Rover just as I told him, my own voice sounding off and weird, "She is."

"This is the nicest complex I've ever been in."

"Me too," I muttered, feeling really uneasy and maybe even a little hurt that she wouldn't have told me. Did she think I'd be jealous or something?

But really, how the hell did she afford something like

this? She had a job at the university. She took summer classes. She had an internship and loans.

I paid for her meal plan at school.

There had to be a reason she hadn't told me she was living somewhere else.

Maybe she had gotten a new roommate who was rolling in it?

That would make sense. I was still living in my house that I was fixing up, and she didn't want me to know that she probably had a walk-in shower and granite countertops while I was still saving for mine. Thea had never been the kind of person to be *that* humble but....

"What number is it again?"

I told him the apartment number she'd given me.

Right by it, Rip turned the truck into one of the spots that said they were reserved for guests. Based on the apartment number, the place was on the third floor. We got out, and he let me lead the way as I looked for the stairs or an elevator. I found the stairway first and headed up, with him following behind. On the third floor, it didn't take long to find the number I was looking for.

I rang the doorbell and took a step back, bumping into Rip's side. Peering up, I found him looking down at me, and I smiled at him. "Thank you again for coming with me."

He watched me with those blue-green eyes. His voice was low, "Sure."

"Let me see what she wants to do, and I'll see if I can get a hotel room or something for you to stay at." My eyes slid toward the door that still hadn't opened and something that was pretty close to unease slid over me. "I had planned on just staying here, but I don't know if that's going to happen."

Why hadn't she told me?

I punched my finger to ring the doorbell again, then

knocked on it too. It wasn't even one in the morning yet. I knew she wouldn't be asleep.

The door still didn't open.

"Call her," Rip said.

I pressed the buzzer again.

Still nothing.

Pulling out my phone, I dialed her number from memory and *heard* it ring inside. Abruptly, the chiming stopped like she had hit ignore or silenced it.

Was this really happening?

I glanced up at Rip and found him still looking down at me, this strange expression on his face.

Frustration and hurt built up in my chest *instantly,* and the next thing I knew, I raised my fist and banged the outer part of it against her door as hard as I could. Then I did it again, yelling "Thea!" into the door.

That did the trick.

Two seconds later, what sounded like a deadbolt turned and the next thing I knew, the door was swinging open to show my sister standing there. In a robe, with her blonde hair down and her eyes big and puffy and rimmed in red, she looked like a mess. Not that I was one to talk, but she genuinely looked like a mess, and she never did.

"Luna," she muttered, genuinely sounding surprised.

"Hi," I told her, trying not to sound awkward.

My twenty-one-year-old sister wiped at her face with the back of her hands, and I watched as she glanced at Rip behind me and let her eyes linger for a moment, this weird, *weird* expression coming over her before she took me in again. "I wasn't sure you were coming," she tried to claim in her equally weird voice.

I blinked. "You asked me to. I texted you twice while we were on the way." I tried to give her another smile, but I wasn't sure I succeeded. *Had she really been about to ignore my call?*

"Yeah, I know, I just—" She shook her head and took a step back, sniffling as she did. "Come in."

I took a few steps inside, Rip directly behind me. She barely closed the door when I looked over at her and gestured at Rip. "Thea, this is Ripley. Rip, this is my sister Thea."

It was my sister who put her hand out first, Rip shaking it firmly but quickly before stepping back beside me. Her eyes slid to mine, and I didn't like the sigh she let out. "The cops came and left about an hour ago."

I nodded. "What'd they say?"

"Come on, come into the living room," she said, her gaze sliding back to Rip for a second before leading us down a short hallway that opened into an airy living room and kitchen. Three pieces of velvet navy blue couches decorated the room with a nice glass table in the middle. There were lamps and pretty knickknacks decorating side tables, a huge TV mounted to the wall with floating shelves holding what looked like a DVD player and some kind of sound system.

It was nice, really nice.

And nothing looked... out of place. Or missing. It was all immaculately clean, like I knew Thea liked her things.

"Want something to drink?" she asked, clasping her hands in front of herself. Almost wringing them.

My throat suddenly felt dry. "I'd like some water."

"I'm good," Rip replied, his voice not like him, but I didn't overthink it.

Thea nodded and headed into the kitchen, pulling out a bottle of water from the fridge. I noticed it wasn't a no-name brand either. When I had left Thea in Dallas three years ago, everything in her pantry had been generic brand. Hell, most things in my pantry were the generic brand unless Lily insisted. Even when I bought organic stuff, if there was the generic label, that's what I would get.

My sister handed me the bottle of water and just stood there.

I took it from her, unscrewing the lid and sucking down half before putting it back on. Glancing at the man to my side, I held the bottle out to him, just in case he really was thirsty. He was. He took it from me without hesitation and chugged the rest.

In any other circumstance, I would tell him that friends shared bottles of water, but... well, that wasn't the time, and I wasn't in the mood when my sister was being so strange.

"The cops came by and asked what was taken, made a list, and then they left," Thea said, biting her lip every few words. "They didn't take fingerprints or anything. They said they would talk to the property manager to look at the cameras, but I don't know if they did."

Exhaustion hit me right in the shoulders as I stood there, and I couldn't help but glance around the rest of the apartment. There was a doorway right across that seemed to lead into some sort of hallway, and closer to where we were standing, there was a cracked door that showed like it had a half-bath, and another few doors that might have led to a pantry, maybe another bedroom, and I wasn't sure what else.

But nothing seemed out of place.

The place was *clean*.

Too clean?

"What did they take?" I found myself asking my little sister.

Her hand went up to her face to wipe at her eyes again. "My laptop. Some clothes. Some jewelry."

What jewelry did my sister have that was worth stealing?

"They went through my room and all my drawers and opened up everything in the kitchen, but I already set everything back where it was supposed to be," she explained, shakily.

Oh. "Thea, I'm so sorry." If she had been Lily, I would have hugged her, but it was my heart that wouldn't let me raise my arms, and my brain that wouldn't let me embarrass myself if she didn't accept my comfort. Again. "What do you need help with?"

My little sister bit her lip again, shaking out her hands, and swallowing so hard I was sure her throat had to hurt. "I'm sorry, Luna. I don't really need anything. I don't even… I shouldn't have even called you." She swallowed again, and I couldn't help feeling my eyes narrow. "I shouldn't have asked you to come. I was just freaked out, and you were the first person I thought of to call. I'm fine."

"You don't have to apologize for asking me to come," I told my sister. "I'd come if you just asked me to for the hell of it, Thea. You know that." But….

Her hands flexed at her sides and she nodded, giving me a watery look. "I know, Luna, but I shouldn't have asked you to. I just freaked out."

None of this felt right. None of it. "It's fine. You're all right though, yeah?"

My younger sister nodded.

"Do you have rental insurance?"

She lifted a shoulder.

I pressed my lips together and ignored the growing ache in my chest. "What about your roommate? Did they take anything from her?"

Her "no" was the sharpest one she'd ever given me.

I held my breath. "Where is she?"

She did it. She scratched at her cheek. If I hadn't known her as well as I had once upon a time, I wouldn't have known that was her tell when she was full of BS. But she sounded pretty freaking convincing as she said, "She's out. She'll be back in a little while. She had to work tonight."

Work? At midnight? With a place like this, she wasn't exactly a waitress.

Thea lifted her hands and scrubbed at her eyes, putting me more on edge. "I'm sorry for making you drive all the way over here for nothing."

It wasn't that easy not to flinch.

"I'm fine. I know... I know it's just stuff they took. I'll find out if we have insurance that'll cover it. The only thing I'm worried about is my laptop."

Her laptop. For school. I tried to push down my disappointment in her lying—because I'd seen that scratch—and her regretting making me drive so far to come over... and told myself that I loved this person. I wanted the best for her even though she was making my chest hurt and it wasn't the first time she had done so.

"How much is a laptop?" I managed to ask, clinging onto that thread of love like it was going to save me from falling off a cliff.

"You don't have to do that, Luna. It's fine. I can figure it out," she said.

"But you need it for school. I can send you some money over—"

Thea shook her head sharply. "No, it's fine, Luna. I've got it."

She had it? *How?*

"I promise," she insisted, just making me even warier. And hurt.

Okay. I forced my hands loose, forced myself to stay calm. To stay focused on that love inside of me. "What can I do then? What do you need?"

"I don't need anything," she said, but it felt more like a slice to my Achilles.

Beside me, Rip shifted and his voice was low as something touched my lower back briefly, so lightly I almost didn't feel it. "I'll wait in the car."

I ignored the sandpaper-quality filling my throat, focusing on the woman in front of me. Because she was a woman. And for some reason I didn't, and more than likely wouldn't, understand, I told him, "You don't have to. You can stay if you want."

"Luna." Thea's voice went a little too soft. "I promise I'm fine. I'm sorry for wasting your time."

She might be a liar, she might be hiding things from me for some reason, but I loved her. *I did.* "I'd do anything for you. You know that."

"I know, but I really am sorry." Her eyes slid to the side, the way they had plenty of times while she'd been younger. "My roommate will be here in a little bit, and I need to talk to her." She rubbed at her eyes again, still averting them. "I have to be at work at eight tomorrow, and I'll be there all day."

"Okay." I knew what she was trying to say. *I knew it.*

"We agreed not to let people stay over...," she kept going.

There it was.

"I'm so glad you came. Only you would. You're the best half-sister I could ever ask for."

It was the half-sister that finally, *finally* made me flinch.

She had only called me that every once in a while, and only over the last five years. Before I had always been *her sister.* Her *big sister.* And now, now I was her half-sister.

"I wish I didn't have to work tomorrow, but I need the money."

She needed the money.

"I don't know when I can come down again, but I'll try to real soon." My sister gave me a smile that fell flat, that sliced me again, this time straight across my stomach. "I miss you. I wanted to stay longer this last time, but I just couldn't."

All I could do was stand there.

With my heart feeling awfully close to breaking.

With a knot in my throat that seemed to be growing by the second.

I loved my sister. I genuinely loved Thea with everything in my heart. She had been the first person to be put into my life that had loved me back.

And she was, in few words, asking me to leave after I'd traveled almost four hours to come and see her.

My mouth watered and not for a good reason.

But I wouldn't pitch a fit. I touched the LOVEYOU bracelet on my left wrist. I wouldn't beg.

I just... nodded and gave her a smile that didn't feel all that understanding, but I hoped it didn't make her feel guilty either. She had just hurt me, but that didn't mean I had to hurt her right back. What I couldn't let go of right then was that freaking ache in me. I wasn't going to give her a hard time for kicking me out.

But...

But I couldn't just walk out of here, letting her think that she'd pulled a fast one on me. As much as I might want to believe she wouldn't do that... she had. Or at least, she was trying to, and I couldn't let that small thing go away. Not this time.

"Why didn't you tell me you moved?" I asked her, ignoring how numb my voice sounded.

She paused, and the face I knew so well grimaced just a little but just enough. "I just..." Was she trying to think of a lie? "I... I didn't want to bother you."

She didn't want to bother me.

Maybe I had literally hours ago said those exact words to Rip, but that had been because I didn't want to ask him for help.

My sister moving out of her apartment wasn't *bothering*. Why would that be bothering? How would that be bothering?

Thea must have realized how weak that excuse was because she gave me a smile that time that was just as fake as her last one had been. "My roommate invited me to come live here with her, but she doesn't like people coming over, so I didn't see a point in telling you and then...."

Having to tell me I wasn't allowed to spend the night? After I had paid for our apartment all on my own while she had lived with me for three years? I would have understood.

She knew that.

I wasn't unreasonable. I could have stayed at a hotel.

But she had always shut down every time Lily and I brought up coming to visit. Every single time. Instantly. Over and over and over again over the years.

Hadn't Kyra come and stayed with her a few months ago? I wondered for a moment before deciding I didn't want to know. In case she was lying to me.

I scraped my tongue against the roof of my mouth as I stood there and nodded like I understood. But I really didn't. Not even a little.

Thea watched me carefully, back to wringing her hands.

I bit my bottom lip.

I was loved. I was happy. I had my own place. I was a decent person.

And Rip had driven me all the way to Dallas to come see my sister because she had asked.

I wasn't going to feel ashamed or bad. I wasn't going to let this get to me. Even if she was one of the last people in this world who I would have ever expected to hurt me the way she just had.

I was going to choose to be happy after this.

"Okay, Thea," I told her carefully, not able to muster up more than just a smile that consisted of a twisted cheek. "Let me know if you need anything, all right?" I still found myself offering.

She... she just nodded.

I took a step back and thought about that hug I wished I could or would have given her, but she didn't step forward or make a move to make it seem like she wanted one either.

So I let my hands drop to my sides.

"Take care," I told her, hearing how wooden it came out.

She didn't even flinch. "Drive safe," she told me like she had a hundred other times when things between us were fine and normal. The scratch she made to her cheek was the only thing that told me that she might feel a little bad. And just a little. I didn't expect much more than that.

I thought I was a strong person. I was forgiving. More patient than most people I knew. I wasn't really *that* petty. I didn't expect a lot from anyone, ever.

But as I walked around my sister with my eyes glued in front of me, I felt shittier than I could ever remember in the last ten years.

It honestly, genuinely, felt like my heart was breaking. Or maybe the fracture had always been there and it was getting wider and deeper, cutting into me even more than before. I hadn't thought it was possible.

I went down the hallway and opened her door, fisting my hands at my sides and breathing in through my nose and out of my mouth.

She didn't call out after me.

She didn't change her mind about me leaving.

I felt Rip's presence, heard the door slam shut behind us. I bit the inside of my cheek and jogged down the stairs, not running but not walking. And when I hit the first floor, with Rip's steps close by, I stopped there, giving him just enough room to go around me.

I wasn't going to feel bad. I was going to be happy. I was fine.

My hands went to my hips, and I took a deep breath in through my nose, feeling myself shaking my head more than actually being aware of the decision that I did it.

There was no way for me to ignore the subtle but sharp pain going on right in my solar plexus as I stopped there.

"I just need a minute," I told Rip quietly, still in front of him so that he couldn't see my face.

His "all right" was just as low and soft as my request had been, but I was in no condition to analyze it in any way.

I nodded, hoping he'd seen it, and I started walking again.

I was choosing to be happy. I was choosing to be happy. I was—

Not.

I wasn't happy. I couldn't even wrangle a little bit of it. Not a speck of it.

My feet took me into the parking lot, past Rip's truck.

They took me down the middle of the lot in the muggy Dallas air. I walked to the end of the building and back, breathing in through my nose and out of my mouth, shaking my head every once in a while. The entire time, not letting myself think about how sad and hurt I felt. Not letting myself think of how not happy I was in that moment.

I tried with everything in me to force my mind blank as I turned around and walked back in the direction I had come.

I wasn't going to cry. I wasn't going to get upset.

This was not the worst thing that had ever happened to me. My sister telling me I couldn't stay with her. My sister referring to me as her *half-sister*. My own fucking sister not wanting me around for whatever reason.

I had driven out here because she had asked. Not because I expected anything.

But I had expected more than to get sent home after ten minutes of being inside her place after she'd called me upset.

I specifically didn't let myself think of how she had disregarded me.

Pushed me aside.

I bit the inside of my cheek again and cracked the knuckles of my hands as I kept walking.

Rip didn't care. He would never shame me for what happened or make fun of me, I knew that in the center of my bones.

Nope, this burn had nothing to do with him.

Nothing.

One single tear slid out of my eye and right along my nose, brushing the side of my mouth as it kept slipping down and over my chin.

I blinked.

She hadn't even tried to hug me.

After everything—

She didn't even bother wanting to take a second and talk to me. Just in and out. Out you go. Bye.

I squeezed my hands harder into fists as I approached Rip's truck and found him leaning against it, arms crossed over his chest, him watching me. His face was blank, for all intents and purposes. He even had one foot crossed over the other.

I tipped my head back to look at the sky, covered in charcoal gray clouds and lit up by city lights.

And I took a deep breath.

Then I took another.

But those breaths didn't do a single thing.

Not one single thing as another tear escaped my eye and followed the track the first one had left for it.

This croak built up in my throat, and my instincts tried their hardest to keep from letting it out. I even had my mouth closed, but this tiny sound escaped, sounding like a whine. Sounding pathetic and sad and like a note something made when it broke.

And another tear came out.

Then another.

And another closed-mouth noise escaped.

"One more minute," I slipped out, sucking in a shuddering breath that probably mutilated the words and had them sounding like something totally different.

I heard his "all right" just as I sucked in another breath, just as another tear slid out of my eye.

I had no reason to cry.

My sister loved me, I knew it. She was just... I didn't know what she was doing or why she was being that way.

Sometimes you outgrew people.

Maybe that's what she had done. Moved on from her high-school dropout sister who painted cars for a living. Her half-sister since that's how she thought of me now.

And it was that *half* that was the prick I needed for more tears to roll out of my eyes. One after another, after another, until I had the meaty parts of my palms tucked into my eye sockets, diverting the flow of one traitorous tear after another.

"Luna," came the deep, deep grumble of a voice.

"Fifteen seconds," I tried to tell him as I told myself to *stop*. Stop.

Stop, Luna.

You're fine.

Quit being dramatic.

You're taking this too personal.

Stop it.

I'd swear I heard a muttered "Fuck" from somewhere too close, but I could never be sure.

What I could be sure of was the body that stepped right up to mine. The body that didn't give me a chance to stop crying or even drop my hands because that body wrapped itself around my own. An arm curled over my shoulder, another right below it, draping itself across my shoulder blades.

The body was warm and hard and molded to mine, crushing my arms between us like they weren't even there in the first place.

Legs and thighs pressed against me, and something warm grazed my cheek as gentle, almost delicate words filled my ears. "It's all right, baby girl," they started.

"You're a good girl."

"A nice girl."

"The nicest."

"Sweetest."

And more tears just came right out of my eyes with each thing said into my ear, spilling over my fingers and wrists, down my arms as I stood there, letting my boss, a man who barely talked to me on a good day, hug me and tell me I wasn't a sad, pathetic person who deserved to feel so small.

You're such a dumbass, Luna, my dad had told me so many times, it sounded like he spoke the words into a tap that sent him directly into my brain.

"You got your 'love you' bracelet on. You're all right." The arm closest to the top, directly over my shoulders, tightened, and warmer, soothing words tried to drown the old ones away. "I've got you. I'm here," the man holding me said.

He had me.

Maybe just for a minute. Maybe for ten. And even though I knew it was dumb and that I had no right to and I needed to get it together, I leaned into him. I went a little limp against his body, even tilting my head forward until it rested right between his neck and collarbone.

For one moment in time, I let Lucas Ripley hold me up while tears just dropped out of my eyes, making the ones I'd shed in my bedroom after my grandmother's funeral seem like nothing.

All I had ever wanted was to be loved.

And one of the only people I had expected to give me that unconditionally for the rest of my life had let me walk right out of her place, without as much as just... talking to me about how school was going. Or work. Or anything.

We had driven all the way over here and....

One of the arms around me moved, and what had to be his hand landed on the back of my head, fingers dipping into my hair, running through the ends before coming back up to do it all over again.

"Ten more seconds," I mumbled into my hands, into his shirt, into him.

"Ten more seconds," he agreed into my cheek, his hand cupping the back of my head again.

I sucked in a breath through my nose and pressed my face even closer into the high point of his chest, feeling bones and hard muscles beneath it—a reminder that this man was immovable. Tough. Hard. Even leaning into him with more of my weight than I had ever let someone support, he held it without an issue.

His fingers worked their way through my hair to touch my nape.

Those rough, calloused fingers worked their way to straddle the back of my neck, to hold my head in place, right where it was.

Thea loved me. I knew it. But it didn't feel like it. *It didn't feel like it.*

"I just... I just...." I tried to say but couldn't find the words.

"I know." Those fingers kneaded my muscles lightly, the band around my shoulders tightening. "I know. You're good. You're fine."

I *was* good. I *was* fine.

I sucked in a breath through my nose and nodded against him.

I *was*.

I had food. I was fine. I had everything I wanted and needed.

I wasn't going to be upset over Thea.

I wasn't.

I wasn't.

I was good. I was fine. I was loved.

I was—

"Five more seconds," I told him, knowing somewhere in the back of my head that it was more like five minutes after my initial request.

Those fingers went through the ends of my hair some more. "Five more," that gentle voice agreed.

I sniffed, fighting the urge when more tears popped up in my eyes again. *I was fine, I was fine, I was fine.* But I still didn't move. When his fingers went through my hair once more, I whispered, "That's really nice, Rip," hearing it sound all broken and chopped.

I was fine.

I would be fine.

"It always made me feel better when my mom would do it for me," he told me, doing it all over again, so soft, so naturally. "Didn't matter if I was scared or sad or mad; everything always felt better after she did it."

It was hard to picture Rip as a little kid having his mom soothe him.

But it was even harder to picture that it was him soothing me right then the only way he knew how. Maybe. Possibly. I didn't know. I was starting to think I didn't know anything.

"She'd put me to sleep doing it too," he kept going in that gravelly voice that felt like a secret itself. "Two more seconds?"

It wouldn't be until later, much, much later, that I'd realize he had been teasing me.

But I still said, "Yes, please" as my sniffles stayed sniffles, but the tears slowed down.

I was fine. I was all right. I didn't need to cry. This

wasn't going to kill me today, tomorrow, a week from now, or ever again.

So what?

So what if my sister had changed her mind after I'd driven all the way here?

So what if she had lied to me? I had lied a hundred times in my life.

I was fine.

But I still said, "One more."

And Rip still replied, "All right."

Sorrow so deep I didn't think I was capable of, covered everything around me. The tips of my fingers, the tops of my hands, right between my shoulder blades, right at the center of me.

But I wrapped it up, the memory of my sister pretty much telling me to leave, and I threw it into the trash so it wouldn't hurt me anymore.

I had no idea what was going on with her, but there was something. I could only hope it had nothing to do with me.

I was choosing to be happy. I wasn't going to let this bother me anymore. I wasn't.

"Thank you, Rip," I whispered, still catching those notes in my voice that reminded me I *had* been hurting, and if I lingered on it any longer, I would again.

When the arms around me loosened a little, I dropped my arms from where they were between us. I was going to pretend like my hands didn't shake—just a little—before I set them on his hips. Swallowing hard, I reminded myself I was fine. I was.

"Thank you," I repeated, forcing myself to tip my head back so I could look him in the eye.

That brutally handsome face was focused down on me. Those blue-green eyes moved, looking from one of my eyes to the other and back again. The arms he had around me slowly dropped back to his sides, sandwiching mine where they were on his hips.

"You're good," he told me.

"I'm good," I confirmed.

Those teal eyes still bounced back and forth as he said in that perfect, boss-like voice, "I know."

Lifting my hands off his waist and trying not to make it seem like it was a big deal they'd been there in the first place, I used the backs of them to wipe at my face as I asked, pretty timidly, "What else did your mom do when you were upset?"

There was a pause and then, "She'd give me ice cream."

I couldn't help but smile a little at that as I dropped my hands and sucked in a breath through my nose.

I was fine. I was fine, I was fine, I was fine.

"That was probably the best ice cream ever, huh?" I asked him with a swallow. "But I'm starving, and if you don't mind driving us, I'll treat you to food and a hotel room for the night. I'm sure it's way past your bedtime. I know it's past mine."

Hard eyes and a hard mouth watched me closely for a moment before nodding gravely. "I'll drive."

It was my turn to nod, and I pressed my lips together before telling him carefully, "I'm sorry you brought me all the way over here for no reason." I tried to give him a smile, but I wasn't sure I managed it. "At least we're even now, huh?"

CHAPTER FOURTEEN

I KNEW SOMETHING WAS REALLY WRONG ON MONDAY when I showed up to work and found the lights in my room were already on.

There had only been one car in the parking lot when I'd showed up, and it had been one I knew well. The owner of it had never, in the years we had worked together, gone into my room that early in the morning for no reason. If I really thought about it, he had probably never gone into my room when I wasn't in it, period. There was no reason he would start now.

Even after everything we had done together this past weekend after leaving Thea's.

"Everything" being us going to the closest twenty-four-hour diner and eating burgers, fries, and a sundae each; then staying in a hotel close by. In different rooms. The ride back to Houston the next day hadn't been awkward... but instead a nice, easygoing quiet with both of us humming along to the radio. It had been okay—more than okay, considering Friday had sliced me deeper than anything else had in a long time.

I hadn't cried over Thea since then. Even if she hadn't called me or bothered texting me to make sure I made it back to Houston safely. Even if I did ache a little still from it, kind of like a papercut that you knew wasn't going to kill you, but it still stung like hell.

But I wasn't going to linger over any of that longer than I needed to. I had better ways to spend my energy, and in that moment right then, it was trying to guess why the lights in my room were on.

Approaching the door, with the lights on through the square-shaped window at the top of the door, I balanced my tote bag, holding a container full of funky-looking stir-fry I had made to last the entire week. I couldn't help but wonder why Rip would be in there. To help me? No way. He had enough things to do. Check something? Maybe.

I had left Jason with only a small project before I'd left on Friday for my gynecologist appointment, but he should have gotten it finished before he'd bounced. Chances were, Rip was double-checking his work. He had done that to mine from time to time when he'd first come to CCC, doubting I could do what I had assured him I could.

So even though my gut knew something was off, the rest of me tried to push that nagging feeling aside as I turned the knob and pushed the door open. There was no way I could be surprised when I found Rip inside, standing just outside the booth's opened doors, looking in. I didn't worry when I found him with his hands on his hips, doing that.

But when I said, "Good morning" as I came inside, my purse over one shoulder, tote in my hands, and he didn't look at me... that's when something in me confirmed that there was something wrong.

He didn't look at me.

He didn't say anything.

Okay.

Not like I had cried into his body after my sister had shot a freaking arrow into my heart and made me feel about three inches tall.

I hadn't *let* myself think of how nice it had been to lean up against him and have him hold me.

I wasn't about to start now. I knew he was my boss, and I knew he owed me a favor and that's why he'd gone with me in the first place. Maybe comforting me hadn't been part of it, but I knew he didn't hate me. Maybe somewhere inside of him, he was a little fond of me.

But that was all there was.

He was a good enough person to be there for me when he didn't need to.

But none of that reflected on the face that was aimed at me. Any bonding, any connection we might have made with each other, wasn't reflected there. At all.

I watched him as I set my things down on top of the desk and didn't bother putting my purse into the compartment where I usually left it. He still hadn't moved. He was too busy looking at whatever was inside the booth.

The only thing in there should have been the parts Jason had finished days ago.

Oh, God. He'd messed something up, hadn't he?

But how? What? I really hadn't left much for him to screw up.

"Rip?" I called out again, taking my time to approach him.

From where I was, he took a deep breath, and I saw the muscles on his forearms get tight. His attention did waver though as he said, "What the fuck is this?"

Fucking Jason. Fucking, *fucking Jason*. I knew it. I should have known it.

Hadn't I learned to trust my gut? And hadn't my freaking gut told me that Jason would find some way to screw things up?

Hell.

Freaking *hell*.

I walked faster toward my boss, cutting the short distance between us until I stood a couple feet to the side of him. I held my breath as I took in the sight before me.

Before I'd left, I had finished up the last coat of primer on two quarter panels. Jason had promised to get them out of the booth so he could finish the four sets of wheels for another project. I'd had to get to my appointment, and I'd been trying to give that pain in the butt an olive branch; I'd given him something he could do to earn a tiny bit of loyalty. To show me that maybe I could trust him.

But as I looked into the booth, the panels were definitely still in there.

Panels to what I knew were a 2010 Ford Mustang. The same make and model of the car I had left on Friday. Only, it wasn't the solid gray I had left it. And it wasn't the so-dark-green-it-looked-black color that I had locked away to use this morning.

It *was* green. A spotty green that had been applied so badly, I could tell from the distance I was at. It was terrible.

Just... freaking... terrible.

"Crap," I whispered to myself, stunned. *Stunned.*

"You do this?" he asked slowly like he couldn't even believe he was asking me that question.

I reared back to look at him. "No!" I had screwed up recently, sure, but nothing like this. Not actually skill-wise.

He was still focused on the car inside when he let out a deep breath that made me think of the hug he'd given me outside of my sister's apartment. "Then who did?" he asked, not sounding at all like we had overcome some barrier between us less than two days ago.

In fact, it sounded like before. Like worse than before. And I didn't like the way it made my chest feel funny.

"I don't know for sure," I started to say, "but it had to have been Jason. I finished the primer before I left on Friday, and he was supposed to stay and do the rims, not work on this." After our Friday morning meeting, Mr. Cooper had told me to leave whenever it was time and let Jason finish whatever was needed.

"Where's the order at?"

The work order?

I looked around the room and tried to find the folder with all the order information for it. I didn't see it on my desk. I'd left it there for sure that Friday, so Jason could have access to it if he needed. "Let me find it. I know I left it on my desk before I left, but he was only supposed to do the rims. I told him three times."

I couldn't stop looking at the freaking car I had spent hours on. I'd seen people's DIY paint jobs look a hundred times better than this. Taking off the color was going to be a major pain, especially after I'd had to do the same thing so recently.

"You left him here alone?"

I kept going through my desk, knowing I was a little bit of a coward for not looking him in the eyes as I answered. "Yes." Mr. Cooper had known. He'd been the one to tell me to go before he and Rip had gotten into that crappy argument.

Rip let out another deep breath that unsettled me.

And still, I couldn't manage to look at him. "I didn't do it, Rip," I said, giving myself away. "I've started triple-checking orders to make sure I'm doing the right color after that other time a few weeks ago. And I've definitely never done *that* to any car, even when I was learning."

He let out another breath, and I'd swear I heard his jaw crack.

Jesus Christ. This was... what? Three screwups in his eyes? In just a matter of weeks? Three times now that something had gone wrong?

And hadn't he put down those times on my record or whatever it was called?

Fuck.

Calm down, Luna. Calm down and think.

Did I want to get Jason fired? No. But did I want to get fired when he'd specifically done something like this even after I had told him not to?

No.

I stopped looking through the desk and closed my eyes before rubbing at my forehead with the meaty part of my palm. "Jason's been acting like a real prick lately," I started to tell him, not letting myself feel bad for throwing him under the bus. "But I didn't think he'd do something like this. I told him all he had to do was work on the rims, not anything else."

Rip's hand went up to go over his forehead.

Oh, no.

"I think he's trying to get me fired. You can look at the cameras and see he stayed after I'd left. I didn't come back into the building. I left for my appointment, and you know where I was the rest of the evening."

He closed those blue-green eyes, and I could see the tension all over his upper body. Oh, man. I barely noticed right then it was a white compression shirt day.

"Rip, I didn't do it. I swear," I told him, opening my eyes and hoping I didn't sound as desperate as I felt but getting nervous that it might be a good idea that I did. I didn't want anyone's pity, especially not Rip's. Especially not after everything.

But if I did the math correctly in my head, this might be three strikes for me.

"I swear on my life I didn't do it," I rushed out, dropping my hand as more nerves shot straight through my chest.

"Stop talking, Luna," he said in the quietest voice he had ever used on me before. "Just stop fucking talking."

I did what he said, feeling nauseous the entire time.

He couldn't blame me for it... could he?

I shouldn't have left Jason alone, okay. But I had. The same way the man who had the head paint position before me had left me alone countless times when he wanted to take off from work four hours early. There was no "I" in team. I'd had to go to my appointment....

I was just making excuses.

So, I didn't want to get blamed, but I didn't want to get fired more than that. I knew that for sure, accepted it for sure. Was a little bit of pride worth losing my job? A job I really did love?

No, it wasn't.

"Rip," I started up again before I could stop myself. "I'm so sorry. I can fix it."

He stood there, still like a statue. Breathing in, breathing out. Still. Utterly, completely unmoving. Until, "What did I just say, Luna? I don't want to fucking hear it right now," he replied calmly, which just made it worse. He was furious. He didn't need to yell at me for me to know that.

And the dread in my stomach just got worse.

"We can fix it. It'll just take—"

He finally turned that massive body toward me to explode.

"I don't give a shit if you can fix it or if we can fix it! I just want you to stop fucking talking for a second!" he hissed, just about the closest thing to yelling as he was capable of, I'd bet.

It was the loudest I had ever heard him talk before.

That had to be why I sucked in a breath; a breath that I didn't let go. I felt the urge to make some sad sound form in my throat. Then in my heart. After a moment, I was blinking quickly without even meaning to.

Maybe it was my fault that I had left Jason alone, but it wasn't my fault he had done this. It wasn't my fault that Rip was in a bad mood and was now being mean.

What was my fault was how betrayed I felt right then. I hadn't had enough time to build up any expectations between us, but *this?* This hurt. Just a little, but still.

"Please don't fire me." My voice cracked despite the fact I was basically whispering. "I'll fix whatever needs to be fixed. It's my fault. You don't have to pay me, but please don't fire me. I love working here," I told my boss—the man who had hugged me and called me baby girl forty-eight hours ago—my voice shaky, keeping my eyes trained on the button of his coveralls that was directly in front of my face, somewhere in between his pectorals.

I was loved. I was fine. I wanted this job, and I didn't want to lose it.

"Please, Rip," I added, hearing the hoarseness in my voice and not letting it shame me.

The silence after those words were out of my mouth could have burned the skin and muscles off my bones it was so oppressing.

I wasn't going to cry, but if it happened, I wasn't going to be ashamed of it. I'd dealt with enough of that in the past, with my parents telling me to quit being a baby when they'd say something that upset me and then didn't want to deal with the consequences.

A person gets to pick what constitutes their pride.

I had used to think that my parents stomping my ego to pieces as a kid had been a disgrace, but now... now I thought it had been a gift. I knew what I could take without breaking. Bending hurt. It was uncomfortable. It was terrible. But I knew that bending didn't kill.

If the fact that it was Rip treating me like this was the reason why I was struggling with keeping it together...

I wasn't going to think about it.

He was my boss, and I had forgotten that again. That was on me. No one else.

No. I wasn't going to think about Rip being the cause, because I wasn't going to feel this way longer than... five minutes. I'd do this for five minutes, and that was it.

That was it.

This ache in my throat... five minutes.

This BS sense of betrayal... five freaking minutes and that was it.

I'd been yelled at enough in my life. Rip was going to get to be just another person who succeeded in making me feel this way.

I didn't want to start over. I had screwed up. Fine. But I hadn't screwed up *that* badly.

"Please don't fire me," I repeated myself, hating myself for even being in this position in the first place.

A minute dragged by. Maybe even two minutes. Just as I started to accept that he wasn't saying anything for a reason, I took a step backward, feeling... nearly as bad as I had Friday night. Then, finally, Rip spoke up. "I'm not firing you," he claimed in a voice that was pretty damn close to a growl.

It didn't seem like he wasn't firing me.

"I'm not," he repeated himself.

The saliva in my mouth started to taste sweet as I stayed right where I was in every way. "Are you sure?" I forced myself to ask.

Rip's voice was low as he murmured, "Yes."

Okay then.

He wasn't firing me for someone else's mistake.

Feeling the frustration—and the hurt—in the backs of my eyes, I sucked in a breath and nodded. I could feel my nostrils flaring as I took another step back. Then another.

I'd gotten what I wanted. I had no reason to be upset. Not because this was unfair. Not because he had just hurt my feelings by reminding me that he was my boss and that was all there was between us.

Not because he had held me while I cried over my sister shooing me out of her life.

"Luna," came my name in that murmured, rough voice that I usually enjoyed, except in that moment.

I ignored it.

"Will you help me carry it out of here?" I asked him instead, my own voice low.

There was a beat of silence, and I had no idea if he was looking at me, doing the sign of the cross, or rolling his eyes. I wasn't fired, and that was all that was going to matter then.

Lenny had rescheduled my date for that night, and even though I wasn't super excited over it, it was something to look forward to. That could be the best part of my day, even if nothing came of it. Because at least I was trying to make my life better. Every day, I tried to make my life better, and that had to mean something. It would.

"Luna?"

My heart started beating faster, but I ignored that too and managed to ask, "Can we please do it so I can start?"

There was a pause and then a soft, "Sure."

I swallowed and kept my gaze on that little button. "Okay. Let's do it."

There was a deeper sigh. A longer one. Another "Luna..." that reminded me of a shooting star with a long tail behind it. A dying meteor. That's what it was in a way. I would forgive him. I would move on, but that *Luna* wouldn't change what it really was.

A reminder that he was my boss first and foremost.

A dying little dream that was burning itself out.

"It's fine," I told him, noticing how flat my tone sounded and getting frustrated over it. "If you wouldn't mind helping me move it, please."

Silence.

There was another sigh.

His gradual "All right" wasn't what I expected. It was soft. So soft it slid right off me and onto the floor, lost forever.

And then we moved the panels.

CHAPTER FIFTEEN

"How was it?"

I set my food on the table beside Mr. Cooper and gave his shoulder a pat. "How was what, Mr. C?" I asked, pretty certain he wasn't asking about the reaming I'd given Jason *again* that morning just in case the first one, the day before, hadn't been enough.

I was still mad about it. Bitching him out the morning before, then refusing to speak to him the rest of the day hadn't been enough to get the anger out of my system. I had gotten to work that morning, still unable to forgive him, and when he'd decided to go out on a limb and ask me a question about an hour ago, I hadn't been particularly nice in my response to him.

I only felt like a tiny bit bad about biting his head off.

Then again, I had gotten my head bitten off because of him, so I knew I shouldn't.

Mr. Cooper smiled at me, not giving me a single clue what he was referring to, as I pulled out the chair next to him. "How was it?" he asked again.

I plopped into it and gave him a smile right back. "Mr. C, I don't know what you're asking."

I hadn't complained about what had happened the day before. As far as I knew, only Rip, Jason, and I knew about his screwup, and I highly freaking doubted he had found out about Rip going with me to Dallas over the weekend. The only people who knew about that were Thea, Rip, and me. As much as I was willing to share with Mr. Cooper, my sister's crap was one of those rare things I would rather keep to myself. On top of that, I hadn't overheard a single argument between him or Rip either so....

He tipped his head to the side. "How did your date go, little moon? I thought you told me you were going on one on Saturday."

Oh. *Oh*. That.

I had told him about it. "Oh. It didn't happen on Saturday, but I did meet up with him yesterday."

"Did it go well?"

I lifted a shoulder as I pulled the top off my container of food. The noodles were from the batch I had made on Sunday. They were overcooked, the vegetables were soggy, the meat didn't have enough seasoning, but... I had made it. And it hadn't given me the runs yesterday, so I could only hope they wouldn't today either.

"He was... decent," I admitted.

Mr. Cooper snickered. "It didn't go that well then?"

I set the lid of my food between us with a sigh. "I went in with zero expectations, Mr. C, and I'm glad I did."

That was the truth. I hadn't gone to the bar expecting to meet the love of my life, but I had gone with my hopes up that my day couldn't get any crappier after what had happened with Rip.

It hadn't. But it hadn't made it any better either.

The Out of my League man had been in his forties and very good-looking, just like Lenny had shown me. He had been outgoing and talkative.

I didn't mean to laugh as I thought about how the night before had gone, but it happened.

I lifted a shoulder as I shot Mr. Cooper a look and snorted then shook my head. "It wasn't total crap. Maybe 50 percent."

The expression on his face was so overprotective it warmed my heart about a hundred degrees. "That bad?"

Well...

I didn't want to bother with all the details. I had called Lenny on my way to work that morning to let her know that the man Grandpa Gus had set me up with had spent the entire time telling me all about how he had just gotten divorced and how he was so excited to *move on with his life* and *do all the things he hadn't been able to do for all those years*.

I took it as: I'm single and not looking forward to reliving marriage any time in the next decade.

I had only been in one actual relationship in my life. I had dated one other man for a little while but didn't count that. Since then, I had gone on another handful of one-off dates. I had even tried the online dating app that was more of a hookup site, and that was where I had met the Daddy guy. So, I thought I was pretty good at recognizing the look in a man's eyes when he wasn't ready for commitment.

At least not commitment with me.

The man who had sat across from me hadn't been looking forward to settling down in any way in the near future. Not even close. None of his words had given me the impression he felt otherwise either. He'd said all the right words and told me just how "cute" he thought I was, but that had been it.

"Nothing bad happened?" he asked carefully. A little too carefully, really.

Honestly, I loved it. It was a nice reminder after yesterday.

I shook my head, my ears picking up on the sound of two familiar, heavy footsteps coming from down the hall. Nothing had happened except for the fact he kept trying to get me to agree that I was basically looking for a booty call, but I wasn't about to tell Mr. Cooper that, at least in those words. I lowered my voice just a fraction. "No, he just wasn't looking for something serious, and I could tell. And I'm not... trying on clothes that I don't want to buy, you know?"

Mr. Cooper's smile was gentle as he nodded. "I don't envy you this adventure, little moon."

"I wish I didn't have to do this, Mr. C, trust me, but hey, maybe the next guy will sweep me off my feet and treat me the way you treat Lydia." I took a bite of my food and ignored all the things that were wrong with the taste of it. "Maybe my luck will finally take a turn for the better," I covered my mouth and told him.

Bad dates happened. I'd heard about them enough from the guys at the shop. I'd heard it enough from my sisters. I wasn't going to give up after the first one.

I was just not going to trust Grandpa Gus again to fix me up any time soon.

I'd only gotten one more bite in when a voice I was too familiar with spoke up. "Luna, you got time to go with me to the store and pick out some paint?"

Go to the store and pick up some paint with Rip? For

the first time ever? After the partial weekend we had spent together?

After he had given me so much crap yesterday?

I chewed the rest of the lo mein I had in my mouth and turned my attention to my other boss, finding him standing there with his hands on his hips over his coveralls, his undershirt a navy color today. Heading into the kitchen, he moved that big body behind the chair I was in to grab something from the fridge, before he kept talking. "I wanna pick out some paint for the GTO and the SS you found, but I don't like anything in the catalogue or the samples you got."

To give him credit, he hadn't been even a little weird with me that morning. I had brought him his coffee, muttered a "Hi, Rip" that was more out of good manners than anything. He had been working and had called out behind me, "Luna." Like nothing had happened. Then I had said, still grumbling, "Leaving your coffee on the bench." And he had replied, "Thanks."

And that had been that. Normal. Fine... as if yesterday hadn't happened.

So it was with that, that I told him, sounding pretty freaking nonchalant, "I can get you the address to my favorite shop."

Out of the corner of my eye, I saw Mr. Cooper glance between the two of us—probably surprised I didn't immediately say yes—but I pretended like I didn't see his movement.

What neither one of us could ignore was Rip saying, "I want you to go with me."

He wanted me to go with him.

Mr. Cooper eyed both of us again, and I wasn't sure who was more surprised by Rip's words. Me or him. He was always such a stickler for *people getting paid to actually work*. Two people going for paint? That was unheard of. Him inviting me twice to go somewhere with him in less than a month? It was practically a miracle.

My gut said he was doing it because he felt bad.

"You want me to go with you?" I echoed, still trying to process his invitation and why he'd even extended it.

His "Yeah" came out more like "duh."

I picked up some more noodles with my fork and shoved them into my mouth. Because I was hungry, not because I was at a loss for words.

Definitely not because a part of me wanted to be petty and tell him that *no*, I didn't want to go anywhere with him because he'd been so mean the day before.

Not me. I was better than that. Yup.

He was still hanging out by the fridge when he kept going. "You got time, don't you?"

If I said I was just busy enough, it would sound like I didn't have enough to do. If I said I had time, it would sound like I didn't have enough to do. And if I told him I was barely catching up after the crap with the Mustang, then I would sound like I was harboring some resentment toward him.

So...

How was I supposed to answer him?

Did I *want* to go?

I didn't have to think about it too long. The answer was: not so much. Normally, I wouldn't mind going. I really wasn't very busy, and I didn't want to be around Jason more than I needed to since we were on thinner ice than usual. On top of that, I didn't want to talk to Mr. Cooper about the day before and cause another argument between him and Rip, because that's what would happen. I had already planned on going to bother the guys on the floor to see what I could help them with.

But if I insisted I didn't want to go, he would know I was butt-hurt, and I was almost never butt-hurt. If he thought that, he would know he had gotten under my skin.

Rip had just been my boss. He did to me what he would have done to any of the guys. I had no logical reason to take it personally.

But it was really hard to know that *and* accept it.

It was hard to tell your heart what your brain was smart enough to understand.

"Nothing's pending?" he asked when I still hadn't replied.

There was always something pending, technically.

He didn't wait for me to answer. He didn't give me a chance to give him an answer. "Finish your lunch, and then we'll head out."

I didn't need to go with him. I actually wasn't even sure why he wanted me to. He might listen to me sometimes, but not that much.

But...

I was better than this. I wasn't going to let him get to me. I wasn't going to let him *know* that he had.

"Okay," I finally got out, shrugging. I had made myself let Jason do what was on the schedule for the day since it had only been small projects, and I'd watched to make sure he did it right. I hadn't wanted to, but that's why Mr. Cooper had stuck him with me. To learn. Me leaving would be good, for both of our sakes. There were only a couple things left the rest of the day that needed to be done.

I could be a mature, reasonable person and put the day behind me.

I was loved. I had a good job. I had everything I needed.

I'd had a decent date the night before, but I had another one coming up.

Every day was a new day that gave you the opportunity to have your entire life ahead of you.

And that was what I was going to keep telling myself.

* * *

"What do you mean you're leaving?"

I tried to control my temper—a temper that I didn't normally have unless it was provoked, a temper that this guy seemed to stoke like a snake charmer, like it was his superpower, while my superpower was that I was easygoing and didn't get mad that often.

But I guess even Superman had his kryptonite.

Mine was a coworker with an attitude problem who had cheated on my sister. An attitude problem that I had unfortunately noticed mostly only flared up in my company.

That seemed to be a running theme throughout my life for some reason that I wasn't about to focus on.

"I'm going with Rip to pick out paint," I said again as I unlocked the cabinet in the desk that held my purse. I'd only started doing that since Jason and I had gotten stuck with each other. I didn't trust him to not eat the snacks I kept in there or rub my toothbrush along a toilet rim if he had the chance. The booth was mine. I wasn't sure what I would end up doing if they tried to put him with me permanently, like I had been Mack's assistant for years, but I'd make sure it didn't happen.

Somehow.

"Why?" he had the nerve to ask, like the last time we'd exchanged words, I hadn't wanted to strangle him.

Did I need to give him an answer? No, but I did

anyway. "Because he asked me to," I responded as I locked the cabinet back up. He didn't need to know that I had tried to get out of it.

"But now I'm stuck here doing your work," Jason complained, like he wasn't paid to do just that. He'd been acting like an abused puppy since yesterday. All meek and whiney, but not in a cute or likable way.

I made sure my back was to him as I made a face that couldn't hide how much he was getting on my nerves. "Going with him is part of my job. You also get paid hourly, so you'd either be in the booth or out there helping out the other guys. If you would rather go back out there, go tell Mr. Cooper. He won't force you to do something you don't want to do," I told him, not able to totally hide my irritation.

But man, I hoped, *I hoped, I hoped, I hoped* he would go tell Mr. Cooper he wanted out.

If he wasn't out of here by the time my birthday came around, I knew exactly what I was going to ask for.

There was a moment of silence and then, "I can go with him."

Oh, boy.

I was choosing happiness and patience.

I was choosing happiness and patience.

I was choosing happiness and patience.

So I bit my cheek. "Ask Rip. I'll stay if he's fine with you going." I mean, I was going to get paid anyway. I didn't care if I'd end up staying instead of him.

Then again, I was also 99 percent sure Rip wouldn't say yes even if Jason had the balls to invite himself. I had seen the way he took him in, and I'd bet he'd heard him complain enough on the floor to know what he was like. After yesterday, he had firsthand experience of the mess that was this turd.

I hoped that, if he hadn't already, he would eventually chew him out. Or even fire him. I had been more than a little disappointed he hadn't yesterday.

The lack of response he gave settled that he either saw the point I wasn't making or understood that maybe he shouldn't try and change the boss's mind.

"Can't you ask for me?"

"No, she can't, and you're not coming," came a voice we both recognized.

A voice that startled both of us, because somehow we'd both missed the door opening. Missed getting eavesdropped on. But only one of us was embarrassed by it, and that person wasn't me.

"Luna's going with me," Rip confirmed, sounding bored.

Fortunately, unlike with his conversations with me, Jason managed to actually shut his mouth and not argue or beg or be a passive-aggressive jerk. His head had snapped over to Rip's direction the second we'd heard him speak up, but at our boss's decision, he dropped it.

Sucker.

But had Rip given him a hard time yesterday after giving me one? I wondered.

"You ready?" that deep voice asked.

I nodded, gripping the strap of my purse tight.

He stood there, holding the door open.

I didn't say anything to Jason as I walked by him, but I did smirk.

Like usual, neither one of us said a word on the way out of CCC. Rip didn't ask if my sister had called to check in with me—she hadn't—and he didn't comment about anything else this past weekend, which all worked for me. The only words out of my mouth on the way over were the instructions on how to get to the business, which wasn't far, but it was still a nice twenty-minute ride away in Houston traffic. It wasn't until we were only a couple minutes away that I asked Rip what he had in mind.

Because I wasn't going to give him the idea that he'd hurt my feelings. Staying quiet would do just that. Fortunately, it worked.

The problem was, he didn't have anything in mind. He wanted to look and see what could be mixed for him in person. Fine by me. We had never gone to the store together, but there was a first time for everything, from the looks of it. I enjoyed going to pick up paint. It was one thing I didn't mind leaving the booth for, even though most of the time it got dropped off in our weekly deliveries.

Rip parked his truck in the nearly empty lot and we both got out. I was busy thinking about what colors he might be interested in—trying not to think about the day before too, if I was going to be honest—that I just barely managed to tell him "thank you" when he held the door open for me.

Once we were both inside, I finally asked, "Are you feeling a light or a dark color?"

His eyes seemed to scan the shop, and I had to ask myself if he'd ever actually been here, period. I didn't think so. He usually just chose colors from samples. It was Mr. Cooper who had come with me in the past if he wanted something custom, but even then, that was rare. Custom paints were a lot more expensive than the thousands of options you could choose directly from a catalogue, but sometimes with certain types of cars they bought, it was worth doing something really custom. The two cars he had bought at the auction were totally worth it, so I didn't blame him for wanting to do something original.

"I'll know when I see it," he answered as he turned down an aisle that held brushes.

I almost crossed my eyes. Then I asked myself why he was in the brush section to begin with. Then I reminded myself that I didn't need to wonder over it.

"Sup, Luna?" a voice called out from behind the counter at the back of the store.

I couldn't help but immediately smile as I craned my neck toward the counter along the far back wall of the paint store. "Hi, Hector."

"I had a feeling today was gonna be my lucky day," the really good-looking man, who had worked at the shop for as long as I could remember, replied from where he stood. He was already smiling that giant, white smile that had to be one of the nicest I'd ever seen.

I snorted. "You say that to everybody."

"Only you." He grinned. "Whatcha need?"

I stopped right in front of the counter and took a peek over my shoulder as I said, "My boss wants to do something custom for two cars he's going to start working on, so I had to bring him to the best." Standing on the tips of my toes, I called out, "Rip?"

What might have been a grunt answered me from the direction of where I had last seen him. The storefront was pretty small. I wasn't positive what he was looking at, or why I couldn't see him, but all right.

I turned back to my friend and rocked onto my heels. "He'll be here in a sec."

Hector leaned forward, planting his elbows on the counter between us, and asked the same question he always did when I came to see him. "What are you doing for lunch?"

Then I told him the same thing I always did. "I already had lunch. What are you doing for lunch?"

He laughed, like this was new, and it was just as nice as his smile. Just as nice as everything about him. "Nothin' now that you aren't coming with me."

"You're so full of it." I snorted again and glanced over my shoulder once more. Rip still hadn't come. I turned back to the other man before asking, with my eyebrows raised, "You got one?"

He raised his eyebrows right back. "I always got one for you," he said, making it sound way flirtier than it was.

He always had them, period, but this was our game.

I dug through my purse for a dollar, then thought twice about it and grabbed another one before holding both between us. "Can I have two, please?"

"Two?" he asked as he took the bill, then opened a drawer on the other side of the counter and pulled what I wanted out as he traded it for the money. "She's saving for a bike now."

"A bike? What happened to the cell phone she wanted?"

Hector snickered as he closed the drawer. "That's how long it's been since you dropped by. She already sold enough of those things to buy her cell."

"No way!"

"You probably paid for a quarter of it," he said.

The sound of a throat clearing behind me told me Rip had appeared, and when I turned, I was more than a little surprised to find him looking past me. He was staring.

At Hector.

And because I knew his features well enough, I knew that face that might look carefully blank to everyone else was a lie.

He was irritated.

But by what, I had no clue.

And it wasn't any of my business.

"How's it goin'?" Hector asked, being as friendly as usual. "What can I help you with?"

When a moment passed and my boss didn't say anything, I glanced at the other man and said, "Hector, this is my boss." Like that would explain everything. "Rip, this is Hector."

Rip though, didn't respond, and his eyes still didn't stray from the dead-eyed stare he was shooting the man on the other side of the counter.

Okay.

I needed to get this in gear.

I gestured toward my boss. "Ah, Rip? You want to come over here so you can narrow down some ideas?"

He didn't move, and he didn't look away from the other man. *All right.*

"Here you go, Luna," Hector said from the other side of the counter, tapping what I knew were mango-flavored chili-covered lollipops against my forearm.

I bought one from him—from his *niece* to be exact—every time I came in.

Taking them, I smiled and said, "Thank you," before pulling the plastic off the top off one and shoving the whole thing into my mouth before holding the other one out toward Rip.

His body still hadn't moved, but those blue-green eyes had. To the lollipop. Then back over to Hector.

"I got it for you," I told him around the pop as I balled up the wrapper with my other hand and handed it to the one man in the room who had never hurt my feelings.

"Luna said you were wanting a custom color for a couple of cars," Hector piped up as he threw the trash away.

Rip took the lollipop from me and shoved it into his free pocket.

His eyes slid to me, and somehow I managed to raise my eyebrows at him because I didn't get what had irritated him. "You okay?"

He tipped his chin, and I noticed the way he let out a deep breath. Noticed the way his shoulders were shoved back as he came toward the counter. Then I definitely couldn't miss the way he stood next to me, his upper arm touching my shoulder. His boot against the side of my boot.

Maybe he did feel bad about yesterday.

It wasn't like he ever jerked away from me before, but he'd never come up to standing right beside me either unless there was a reason. That reason being me being upset if the last two times counted. That was something to think about.

"Any ideas what you're lookin' for?" Hector asked, his eyes bouncing back and forth between Rip and me in a way I wasn't sure how to take.

Just as I opened my mouth, Rip beat me to it. "Red. Blood red."

I'm sure I looked up at him with my mouth open in surprise. Where the hell had that come from? I had literally asked him in the car if he had any ideas.

"Almost black, but not," Rip kept going.

Hector seemed to think about it for a second before he nodded. "I can work with that. What about the other one?"

That handsome face tipped down to look at me, those intense eyes lingering on my hair for a moment before they finished the trek down to mine, and he asked, "What's your favorite color?"

My favorite color?

Hector answered for me. "It's white, isn't it?"

I nodded, but I was going to blame the lollipop in my mouth for why I did. We'd had plenty of conversations about colors over the years. Of course he knew.

Rip's gaze swung back around to me, his forehead furrowed. "White?"

I nodded again.

"Why?" he asked like even he couldn't believe it.

I shrugged and took the lollipop out of my mouth long enough to say, "It's classy. Everything looks good in white."

He blinked.

"If you mix the three primaries together, you get white. I think it's cool." I smiled at him, for real that time. "And I've only painted one white car in years. I'm not sick of it yet."

"What kind of white can you do then?" my boss asked the other man, but his gaze remained on me.

"Don't do it because of me. You can do any color you want," I threw in, not liking the pressure of him putting my favorite color on a car he was going to be selling.

His face was super serious. "I know."

Okay then.

"Show me a pure, bright white with a blue undertone then," Rip told the other man after finally turning to face him again.

Hector bobbed his head before pecking at the computer keyboard.

Well.

He really must feel bad.

Good.

* * *

It took about ten different tries to get the shade of red Rip had envisioned in his head, which took hours because mixing colors was literally a science that Hector had a doctorate in, and it took half as long to get the shade of white that he liked.

When Rip said I could spray a fine layer of metal flakes onto the car that was going to be the shade of white he'd chosen—white with some hints of light blue—I had "oohed" and "ahhed" because I *loved* doing metal flakes and didn't get to do them all that often; cleaning up the booth and the gun afterward was time consuming and a giant pain in the butt but totally worth it.

I had barely closed the truck door as Rip loaded the paint into the back of the truck—he'd given me a look that said I was nuts when I'd gone to pick up the first container— so I'd backed off, put my hands up, and let him do it. It wasn't like I hadn't carried my own paint to the back of the CCC truck a thousand other times, even though Hector always offered, but if Rip wanted to do it now, so be it.

The door had barely been shut when my phone started ringing from inside my purse. I pulled it out and frowned at the screen. It was the shop's number. "Hello?" I answered.

Instead of Mr. Cooper's voice, or even Miguel or anyone else's, the one I dreaded said, "When are you getting back?"

I tipped my face toward the window to my right and bit the inside of my cheek. "Soon. Why?"

"Something doesn't look right."

I thought about the work I'd left him with and didn't understand how it was possible for him to screw up any part of it. He should have been done by then. He should have been helping out on the floor. "How?" I heard the edge in my own voice. I really was fed up with him. I was so fed up,

I was almost to the point of being past caring about whether or not he got fired for messing up so often.

"Look... you need to get back so you can fix it," the man-child claimed.

Just the words I wanted to hear.

I kept making a face. "Tell me what you think you did wrong, and I'll tell you how to fix it before I get there."

The driver door opened, and I didn't miss the teal-colored eyes that swung toward me as Rip got in.

"It's easier to show you. How much longer are you going to be?" he repeated.

"I don't know. Probably not that long, but I need you to tell me what happened because a lot of things you think might be messed up, can be fixed," I said, trying to sound calm, but just thinking about how much him screwing up might eat up my time when I got back left a tight feeling in my gut. It was already almost five, and I wasn't too crazy about staying late. Not today at least. I was supposed to go to the gym with Lenny.

Jason decided to pretend he hadn't heard me. "How long? Twenty minutes?"

Kill him with kindness, kill him with kindness, kill him with kindness. The words alone felt like a boulder right in the center of my entire freaking existence. I'd been having to tell myself those exact same words way too often lately, and they weren't being as effective as usual. "Jason, tell me what you did."

He ignored me like he always did. "It doesn't matter. You're going to have to fix it."

The truck starting up broke through my thoughts, but I kept my gaze forward on the building we were parked in front of. "I'm not going to fix anything. You need to learn how to fix it. So even if I get there, you're still going to have to do it, okay?"

There was silence on the other end and then, "This isn't my job."

Oh, *no*.

A big hand landed in front of me, palm up, and I glanced over to see that obviously it was Rip's.

He opened and closed those long, forever-stained fingers despite the bulk-sized Orange hand cleaner in every bathroom.

Did he...?

Screw it. Fine. I had already come in between these two, I wasn't about to volunteer to do it again.

I dropped the phone into his hand, and he didn't waste a second bringing it up to his ear and grumbling, "What did you do?"

I wasn't sure if I'd answer that question if I were Jason. Honestly, I'd probably hang up.

"You're calling Luna when you know she's busy, with me, so I wanna know what you did that's making you call.... You didn't do anything? Then why are you calling?.... So you did fuck up?.... That's what I thought.... Again? What did I tell you yesterday?.... Go upstairs, tell Cooper what you did.... Yes, Mr. Cooper. Yup, the one who hired you. That one. Go tell him right now. Don't wait until she gets there. She's not doing shit." There was a pause and then, "The fuck did you just say?" Rip snapped, and I had to press my lips together, if only to keep my mouth from opening... in almost glee.

He blinked.

I blinked.

Then he pulled the phone away from his face and stared down at the screen.

"Did he hang up on you?"

He was still staring down at the phone when he muttered, sounding *pissed*, "This motherfucker...."

He'd hung up on him.

And... it made me laugh.

Maybe it was Rip's facial expression, maybe it was the idea that he was genuinely outraged, but I laughed, and I didn't stop laughing. The frustration I'd felt toward that *motherfucker*, in Rip's words, instantly disappearing. Maybe because it was nice to see that I wasn't the only one who got treated like crap. I seriously couldn't believe he'd hung up on him. It made me cackle and forget I was supposed to be professional and stuff. "Watch, he's going to pretend the phone dropped the call, but he's on the landline," I warned him.

Rip kept his gaze down on the black screen before thrusting the cell back in my direction. His tone was freaking grumpy as he asked, "He always this much of a piece of shit? He already knows he's got one strike against him after yesterday. Now he's gonna have two after this bullshit. He can't play the dumb card too much longer."

So he had gotten in trouble then. That made me feel just a little better about yesterday. But I would have liked it more if he'd gotten the ax. I mean, Rip had gotten rid of people for less, but that was none of my business.

Fortunately, he didn't wait for my answer, probably knowing that was a *yes*. "He always act like that with you?"

I closed my eye, still looking forward. "What do you mean exactly?"

I was pretty sure Rip clucked his tongue. He rephrased it, bless his heart. "He always act like a prick like that?"

"Well..." I trailed off, but inside, I thought *yep,* which

was why he had reamed me the day before—because Jason was a prick.

There was a rough, "Hmm." Ripley's cheek did that twitch thing, and I almost laughed again at the reminder of how mad he'd just been. "He gives you shit like that again, you tell me. Got it?"

I made a face to myself, telling myself to let the day before go—and only partially succeeding—but still managed to say, "Sure." If it came out sarcastic, that hadn't totally been my intention.

Those blue-green eyes swung to my direction, exposing something in them I couldn't pinpoint. "Luna, just fucking tell me, all right?"

Like I wanted to deal with Jason's attitude more than I already did. Rip could have him if he wanted him. I felt a little like I was cheating on Mr. Cooper by going through Rip to get rid of him, but I had told Mr. C about how he acted around me, and he'd still thrown him my way. "Sure," I agreed again, knowing I didn't sound convincing.

I was choosing happiness. I was going to move on and forgive Rip for the day before. He would have done it to anyone.

I shouldn't take it personally.

I could see his hands flex on the steering wheel, but it took a minute for the next round of words to come out of his mouth. "Say, think of something else you want."

My body froze, instantly choosing that quat to focus on instead of... before. Because, we were back to this? *Again?* "Rip," I almost groaned. "No, we're done. We're even. We're fine, whatever you want to call it." I almost started to say we were good, but that felt like a little bit of an exaggeration. In a few days, we'd be good. Right now, we were just fine.

He didn't look at me though. "We're not."

"But we are."

"Nah, Luna, we're not. Choose something else," he insisted, still focused ahead.

Was he being serious? He'd spent fifteen hours in my company, including the time he slept in a room down the hall from mine. If that didn't count as a massive favor, a favor that should make us totally even for all intents and purposes, I wasn't sure what else would.

Unless....

Did he really feel *that* bad about getting mad at me?

"Rip, it counted. Just because—" *My sister kicked me out*, I thought but didn't say. "—we didn't end up having to stay or do anything, doesn't mean it doesn't count. You went with me. That's more than enough." I just wanted to... move on.

He had other ideas though.

"Too fucking bad." Those blue-green eyes slid back to me for a split second, and I could see the tightness at his jaw. "Figure it out and let me know what you want."

"Nothing. I promise. There's not a single other thing you need to do." Because there wasn't. There really wasn't.

Those long fingers tapped along the steering wheel, and his jaw did that tightening thing again. "Yeah, there is. The other one doesn't count. All we did was take a fucking ride and eat a late dinner. Figure it out, Luna. I don't wanna be sixty when you decide."

I pressed my lips together.

Don't do it, Luna. Everything is not fine and dandy. Don't do it. Don't—

Let it go. Let it—

I didn't.

"So I have... two years... before then?" I whispered,

grimacing at the joke that I shouldn't have made so that we could focus on the serious topic of our conversation. So I could hold on to the distance I was supposed to put between us because he was my boss.

What I got was silence.

Freaking silence.

The sigh that came out of him reminded me of what I figured a hot air balloon would sound like if it deflated. "I should've fired you the other day."

I sucked in a breath, and my entire upper body turned to him.

He was smirking.

He thought he was being funny.

He was... joking.

These mocking, laughing eyes I had never seen before slid over to me, and the second they spotted my expression, they changed. My name came out a grumble. "I was playing."

Sure, he'd been.

His mouth went so tight, it was edged in white. "I was messing with you," he insisted, seriously.

He was messing with me.

Those long fingers flexed again. "You that mad at me?" he asked.

"I'm not mad at you."

"Upset with me?"

I didn't look at him as I said, "No." I wasn't. *I wasn't.* "I just..." What could I say? "You don't ever joke around with me. I'm just surprised." I started to crack my knuckles but stopped. "Okay, maybe I am a little upset with you, but I'm almost over it."

Out of the corner of my eye, I watched him glance at me

again, and I could barely hear his voice when he spoke again. "I joke around outside of work," he said softly.

I wasn't going to overthink it.

Did that come out defensively, or was it my imagination? "That's good." I was such a sucker. I really was. He was trying, and I didn't have it in me to brush him off. "You can joke around with me whenever you want," I replied just as softly as he had. "I wouldn't tell anybody. I know it doesn't mean anything, and I'm really good at keeping secrets. It can be another one of ours."

I doubted I would ever forget the way he turned his head to look at me, slowly, so slowly, those eyes like hot freaking coals, raking me over. Seeing me. His eyebrows were knit, like he was deep in thought, and he just—

"RIP!" I shouted the second I spotted the car pulling out in front of us all of a sudden.

The brakes he slammed were *instant*. So instant, so unexpected, so forceful, I barely had time to suck in a breath and throw my arms up over my face. I closed my eyes just as the seat belt jerked across my chest, and I felt something slap me right between my breasts as someone's brakes *screamed* in the background. But I knew I hadn't made a peep.

I couldn't have.

My entire brain just... shut down.

My upper body went forward...

And the truck made contact.

I wouldn't be able to describe the sound of metal meeting metal. Of the truck careening into the car that had pulled out of what I would figure out later was a gas station. Even if someone had played me samples of crashes, I wouldn't have been able to pick out what I had heard. It had just been noise.

But I felt my body jerk. Felt the seat belt dig into my shoulder. Felt what I didn't know until seconds later was a big palm right in the middle of my collarbones.

Later, I would feel the painful fucking ache across my neck and shoulders.

And just like *that*, it was over.

The truck had stopped moving, the brakes had stopped squealing, and nothing but panting filled my ears.

My panting.

It was mine.

"Rip?" I sucked in a breath as I opened my eyes and found a totally intact windshield in front of me.

The weight across my collarbones moved, making me look down to see it had been a hand—his hand—there. Holding me back. There. Just there.

Dragging my eyes up his wrist, to his elbow, to his shoulder and then his face, I noticed his cheeks were flushed. That not-thin but not-full mouth was parted. But it was the thin red slice across his upper eyebrow that held my gaze.

"Are you okay?" I panted, not sure if I'd even be able to hear him above the roaring of blood and adrenaline and who the hell knew what flooding my ear canals as my brain registered that the danger was over and I was pretty sure we were okay.

Rip blinked. Those curly black eyelashes just dropped, once and then twice to cover his eyes briefly. His nostrils flared.

"You okay?" I asked again, the hand closest to him—which I'd tucked into my body by reflex—reached out. I set my palms and fingers on his forearm, only briefly feeling the goose bumps under them. "You all right?"

He let out a sharp exhale and then nodded.

I squeezed his arm again, just barely noticing that it was shaking. "They just pulled out of nowhere." I sucked in a breath, trying to slow down my heartbeat. "I didn't see them until it was almost too late," I admitted, hearing that shaking in my voice as my brain refused to slow down and instead said *you were in a car wreck in case you didn't know*.

We had been in a car wreck.

Shit.

I sucked in a breath through my mouth and let my head fall back against the headrest, moving my eyes forward again to see that the truck's front end was smashed up against the driver and rear side doors of a late model BMW. I'd detailed them enough over the years to recognize the body frame.

"Holy shit," I hissed, everything about me starting to tremble. We had been in a freaking car wreck. My heart was going to beat right out of my damn chest, it felt like. "Holy fuck."

I swallowed. Tried to take a deep breath. Then I swallowed again.

I was fine.

Rip was fine.

That was all that mattered.

Glancing down at the seat belt across my chest and waist... it hadn't clicked until right then that Rip had done some restomodding, which meant he'd modified his truck. Which meant he'd added safer seat belts since his truck had been made before the age of airbags. And based on the screeching, he'd updated the brake system too. If he hadn't....

That wasn't a nice thing to think about.

Movement inside the sedan told me that the driver of the other car was fine too. The door seemed to be jammed from the way the person inside was moving, but by the time I managed to think clearly enough to decide to get out of the car, that driver had managed to get the door opened and thrown a leg out.

The sound of a seat belt clicking had me glancing to my side to see Rip's hand lingering over that part at my hip. He looked a little pale, and his hand wasn't what I would call steady as it hovered there. I wasn't sure what the hell I was thinking as I slid mine over and set it on top of his, everything going up to my elbow not much less shaky than his.

He was watching me, and all I could muster up was a smile that was probably just as wonky and off as the rest of me was.

"Son of a bitch!" a voice outside the truck yelled, and I didn't need to look out to know that it had to be the driver of the BMW, who I had seen out of my peripheral vision circling his car.

My heart hammered away inside of me. I was shaking a little. My shoulder was starting to ache, but I was okay, and so was the man next to me. That was all that mattered.

"Motherfucker!" the driver outside yelled. I didn't notice that Rip hadn't answered me.

But somehow, I managed to focus enough to say, "I'll— I'll call the cops, but let's get out of the truck first."

Still, he said nothing.

Pulling the seat belt off from around me and letting it fall to the side between the seat and the door, I tried my best to get my arms under control enough so that they would stop trembling. I had goose bumps everywhere too, but I ignored those as well.

That had been close. Too freaking close.

"Luna, get out of the truck," Rip finally managed to say, his voice soft and... off.

I nodded.

I was fine. My adrenaline was just crashing. I was pumped up, and now I was falling. We were safe. Everything was okay.

Not looking over at the man to my left, I got myself together enough to push open the door to the truck and climb out, only barely managing to remember my purse from where I'd left it right next to my feet. Luckily, I had zipped it, so nothing had fallen out and gotten strewn all over the floor. It only took a moment to fish my phone out and hit 911.

It took all of me to pay attention and answer the dispatcher's questions, watching as Rip stood at the front of his mangled truck, talking quietly to the owner of the BMW, a man in a heather gray suit who looked around the same age as Rip. The guy in the suit looked *pissed*, and Rip, he just stood there, a couple inches taller and a lot broader, with his arms crossed over his head, palms cupping the back of his skull. A few cars had pulled over, the drivers getting out to make sure everyone was fine, but a couple lingered, those people saying something back to the man in the suit.

In the background, I could hear the wail of a police siren, but I kept talking to the dispatcher who wanted me to wait until the police got there to hang up. My shoulder didn't ache worse than it had a few minutes before, but it felt stiff.

Deep breaths. Calm down. Everything was okay.

The driver of the BMW started talking louder, and I heard him say something like "stupid-ass!"

Rip didn't even bother replying. He took a step to the side and walked away. Even with the sun blasting all over the road, I could see his eyes moving around the wreck, not lingering, but continuing to slide from one direction to the other until he spotted me off to the side, one hand holding the phone to my face but both my arms tucked in close to my sides and chest.

Those long legs ate up the concrete as he headed in my direction, as the other driver kept raising his voice to argue with the three other people who had more than likely seen what happened and were telling him that he was in the wrong.

Because he had been.

I didn't feel like putting in my own two cents and telling him that I'd seen the entire thing happen and that he was the one who was at fault.

All I could do was stand there, watching as my boss stalked toward me with flashing blue and red and white lights somewhere in the distance, beyond the busy street we were on. When he was maybe ten feet away, I finally gave him a weak smile as I held the phone to my face. When he was five feet away, I noticed the frown that had taken over his features.

It was right then that I noticed the muscles in his arms jumping, the twitching at his wrists, the veins popping at his temple and throat.

Rip was shaking.

Not kind of trembling like I was—and had been—but full on shaking. He was pale. Even his lips had lost their color.

I said something to the person over the phone that I hoped at least included a "thank you," but I would never know for sure, because the next thing I was aware of was ending the call and shoving my phone into my purse, which was sitting against my hip.

That entire six-foot-four, two-hundred and something pound body was literally shaking.

He looked like he hadn't just seen a ghost, but a hundred of them.

I didn't intentionally set out to grab his hand or pull him toward me, but I did. Once, I had shaken the same way he was doing right then, and all I had wanted afterward was someone to hold me.

And for me, there had been no one to do that.

But I could be that person for someone else now.

I led him to the curb I was standing on and watched as he sank onto it, those long legs bent at the knee, his hands loose at his sides, his nostrils flaring with deep, deep breaths that could have passed for pants on anyone else. He scared me. Right then, watching his normally tan face go so freaking white, watching the biggest and most no-nonsense man I had ever known shake, scared the hell out of me.

"You're okay," I told him, ignoring everything else around us.

His eyes were straight forward, on me but not on me, and I just barely noticed it.

I squeezed his hand and got nothing but another bone-rattling shake.

"Rip, you're okay. That guy's an idiot," I said softly.

He still just stared straight ahead, right at the top hem of my leggings since it was what was directly in front of him.

Dropping into a crouch, my worry kicked up threefold, and I took his other hand, giving both of the much bigger palms and fingers a squeeze. He still didn't react.

I let go of one of his hands and raised mine to his face, only letting my fingertips graze his stubbly chin. "Hey, you're good. Nothing happened."

Nothing.

Even knowing I had no right and no business to touch

him, and that he probably wouldn't like it, I palmed his cheek, tiny whiskers grazing my skin. He was clammy and too cool. "Rip?"

Nothing.

I let go of his other hand and cupped his face between both of mine, trying to catch his eyes, but they were still straight ahead, unfocused and zoned out.

What was I supposed to do?

I could still hear the sirens coming from a distance, but I knew that other than the cut on his face, he was probably physically fine. The worst he'd have were some bruises and possibly his shoulder hurting just like mine was.

I tried again. "Rip?"

Nothing.

"Hey, you're okay," I told him, still holding his cheeks. "I'm okay. Take a deep breath."

He didn't. He didn't do anything.

I tried to think about what I would want if I was in his shoes, and I hesitated. But it only took one glance at his zoned-out face to know I was going to do it even if he pushed me off and cussed me out later.

At least I'd be ready for it.

So before I could talk myself out of it, I swept my hands from his cheeks toward the back of his head, then moving one hand to do the same gesture over the top of it too. When he didn't flinch, I dropped to my knees, ignoring the shooting pain that the concrete sent through them, and I wrapped my arms around his neck, and I hugged him.

I pressed the side of my cheek against his, and I hugged him even tighter, not letting go.

But it still wasn't enough. He still shook, these shivers that flowed from the center of his body down toward his fingertips.

"You're okay. Everything is fine," I repeated, still hugging him. I swept my hands from the nape of his neck, across his trapezius muscles, over his shoulders and down his arms, applying light pressure. Then I did it again and again, before moving them right above his chest, starting there before going up to continue the route up to the base of his neck, across and down his arms.

The shaking only got a little better.

Screw it.

My knees creaked as I got back up to my feet and then did something I had never done before. Nothing I had ever even dreamed of doing with Rip, ever. But desperate times called for desperate measures.

I took a step closer to him and settled myself, my butt, my entire body, high up onto his right thigh, pulling his opposite leg in so that I forcefully made him sandwich me in between him, and I wrapped my arms and hands and as much of my body around him as I could. My palm went straight to the top of his neck and dragged my hand down his spine, making circles at the base while my other one held the back of his head.

"Rip," I whispered right beside his ear since I had set my cheek a millimeter away from his. "Everything is fine."

My hand circled his back again, and I hugged him tighter to me, his own shakes moving me too.

"It's me, Luna," I told him. "You're okay. Everything is okay."

I grazed my fingertips through the short, soft hair at the back of his head like he'd done for me outside of my sister's apartment.

"Talk to me, Rip," I asked him. "You're safe. You're okay. Nothing happened. I need you to take a deep breath."

Nothing. He still gave me nothing.

I ran my fingers through his hair again, hearing the near-desperation in my voice. "You're scaring me. Talk to me, please. I don't like you shaking like this."

I rubbed his back. I promised him he was fine. I told him I'd take care of him.

Over and over again until the big man in my arms settled... a little more, but it was more than nothing. At least we were getting somewhere.

"We can go get ice cream after this if you want." I kept talking to him, not sure if that's what was helping. "That sundae this weekend was pretty good, but I know this really good place close to the shop with the best ice cream. They make it in small batches every day. If we can't go today, I'll bring you some on my lunch break soon."

I slid my hand back up to rub the back of his cool but damp neck. The thigh under me flexed and tensed, and I put a little more force into rubbing the hard muscles on his nape. "You know, I always imagined that if my mom had been around, she would have hugged me and rubbed my back when I needed her. I tried looking up information on her a few times, my mom, I mean, but there are so many people with the name Teresa Ramirez, it was like searching for a needle in a haystack. That's why I'm on top of you right now in case you're wondering. I bet she would have made me flan too.

"One time, I bought those little packages of flan when I lived with my dad, and he found them and lost it. I figured my mom probably liked it and it set him off, but I don't know. Everything used to make him mad. Maybe he just hated flan, but I think it was more than that. I don't know," I kept rambling, not even sure what the hell I was saying in the first place, but sensing it was doing something.

"If you haven't had flan before, I'll bring you some from

this bakery I go to sometimes. I'd say I would make it for you, but you really don't want me to even bother trying. It would probably end up burning the pot and my entire kitchen down." I dragged my hand up his spine and rubbed his neck, alternately. "Oh! Wait a sec."

I dug inside my T-shirt and undid the clasp of the necklace I had on. I'd seen it that morning and had a feeling about it. How about that? Even with my fingers still a little shaky, it only took a second to slip the chain around Rip's neck and redo the clasp to keep it on him. I pulled back just enough to see the ice cream charm on it fall right on top of the notch of his throat. It looked ridiculous there, but I patted it down in place anyway. "Look. See? It has a little ice cream cone on it. To make you feel better."

His whole body tightened for a moment before a loud burst of a noise exploded from his chest. And in the time it took me to process the sound, it was gone, and his muscles had relaxed even more. I'd swear his breathing slowed too.

"There we go," I told him, putting pressure on his back and neck again. "You're good. You're all right."

For some reason, that only made me want to hug him tighter. He was so big, it was hard to try and wrap him up; my arms could barely reach. I palmed the back of his head and lightly scratched at his scalp the way Lily used to like when she was little. She had done it to me too every once in a while when she'd been falling asleep, and I had loved it too.

From the way his body loosened, muscle by muscle, I figured he did too.

So I kept scratching.

Slowly but surely, that big body relaxed against mine, not totally, but it was something.

"You okay?" I asked when the only movement I felt come out of him were deep, deep breaths.

Part of me expected him to snap at me, to shove me off his lap, to tell me to fuck off.

But none of that happened.

One of the arms he'd had at his sides came up and his hand settled at my hip, giving it a light squeeze. His forehead dropped to that spot where my shoulder met my neck, and I could feel his soft puffs of breathing on my collarbones and chest. His hand squeezed my hip again. And my heart... it didn't know what to do.

"Tell me what you need," I asked him.

He shook his head against me.

It was the sound of footsteps coming that had me glancing over my shoulder to see a police officer walking around the cars, heading straight for us.

Rip must have too because he tensed. Everywhere. From the thigh under me to the bulk up against my chest, Rip became granite. I took a sniff that told me he smelled lightly of a clean-scented soap and the crispness of a sporty deodorant.

"Nothing hurts?" I whispered the question.

Rip shook his head again.

"I'm sorry about your truck."

"It's just a truck," he replied quietly, surprising me. The weight at my hip moved up until his fingers spanned around my lower ribcage, his fingers molding themselves around my bones.

"The cop is coming," I warned him, letting my hand drag down his spine once more. I gave him one last hug before loosening my hold, beating him to it. I pulled back, his hand still on my ribs, and met his now bright blue-green eyes. I smiled at him, this knot in my chest forming when I thought about how pale he'd been. "You saved our freaking faces installing those seat belts, boss."

The body under mine grew hard, but not in the same way it had a moment before. The hand on my rib didn't move, and the arm connected to it didn't loosen up either. Rip sat there, letting me stay on his thigh like we had done this a hundred times in the past—me sitting on his lap.

"I'm glad you're okay and you're not mad about your truck. I'll help you fix it if we can."

The hand on my ribs decided to give me my own squeeze.

He got the next words out of his mouth before the cop interrupted, quietly, gently, and more earnestly than I ever would have imagined. "I'm glad you're good too, baby girl."

CHAPTER SIXTEEN

LILY HAD WARNED ME I WAS GOING TO BE HURTING. She had been in a car wreck two years ago. Her friend, the driver, had blown right through a stop sign and gotten T-boned. My little sister had gotten a face full of airbag, two black eyes and a swollen nose, but in all the ways that it mattered, she had been fine.

So when I had texted her the day before to tell her that I'd been in a wreck—because she would have found out somehow and I would have rather been the one to tell her than some other way—she had warned me. Before that, she had chewed me out for *texting* her something so serious. *What happened?* She had basically shrieked at me.

To give them credit, Kyra had texted me immediately afterward too, and Thea had sent me a message just an hour later. She didn't bring up anything about the weekend, and I hadn't had the heart to bring it up either.

But going back to Lily, she had said, *It's gonna hurt, sugar tits.*

Yet I was still surprised when I woke up that morning and felt like what I'd imagined a person who had gotten run over would feel like. My neck hurt so bad I couldn't turn my head in either direction. My shoulders ached. Honestly, everything hurt, even the spot right in the center of my chest where Rip's hand had been.

It took me twice as long to shower and get dressed, twice as long to even go down the stairs, because I swore even my knees had taken a hit. I felt like a robot as I made my breakfast and thanked everything in the world that I'd made enough lunch to last for a few days, even if it wasn't the tastiest thing I'd ever eaten.

Two painkillers later, I headed toward the door, grabbing the rest of my things and keys.

For one second, I thought about calling out of work. Mr. Cooper knew we had been in an accident. I had called him while the cop had talked to Rip to get his statement. He'd been the one to drive to where we were and pick us up. He had given me the biggest hug ever, giving me the opportunity to feel a faint tremor that shot through his body.

I had seen the long, long look he had cast Rip's way, as the man made it a point not to look at Mr. Cooper once while I had been around. His eyes had been trained on the tow truck that would be taking his pickup to the shop.

Afterward, the older man had dropped me off at my house and sworn to have someone drop off my car later, giving me another hug and telling me he was glad I was fine after walking me to the door.

But as soon as I thought about calling out, I told myself *no*.

I wasn't dying. There was nothing I could do at home to make it worth staying. If I had to go slower, no one would complain.

Except Jason, but I wasn't going to waste my time or patience on him. Today was not the day for him to give me a hard time. Not with his two strikes. I opened my front door and took a step out, only to stop dead in my freaking tracks. Because parked in my driveway, behind my car, was a brand-new black double-cab pickup truck.

Sitting clearly in the driver's seat was Rip.

I blinked. Then I blinked some more, making sure my eyes weren't playing tricks on me.

I mean, I knew I wasn't imagining things. This wasn't some déjà vu, I'm-in-an-oasis-seeing-a-mirage moment. This was real.

Rip was in my driveway.

Fortunately, I managed to keep it together enough to lock my front door and make my way down the steps, eyeing my car sitting there after one of my coworkers had dropped it off about an hour after Mr. Cooper had walked me to my front door. Rip was already watching me as I headed toward him, and I couldn't help but feel even more surprised when the doors were unlocked, and instead of the window being rolled down, he leaned across the seats and shoved the door open.

I wasn't sure why I smiled exactly, but I did and I said, "Morning." Only barely not asking *what are you doing here?*

Rip, who had sleek black sunglasses on, tipped his head to the side away from me. "Get in, Luna."

Get in. Not *good morning*. Not *I'm here to pick you up* or anything like that.

Just... get in.

I managed to stare at him for a second before snapping out of it and taking in the height of the pickup. It had a lift kit on it for sure. Tucked into the sides were retractable running boards to give passengers a boost. Black leather covered the passenger seat.

It was literally brand new.

And I just stood there.

Because Rip was in my driveway.

Again.

Because he wanted to make sure I got to work.

"Not that I'm not happy to see you, but whatcha doing here?" I threw the question out before I could stop myself, sure I was giving him a loopy smile.

"Here to get you," he replied like it was obvious.

I didn't need to point out that my car was right in front of the truck, but I still slid my eyes to the side anyway. Because *yep*, my car was definitely there. It hadn't adapted camouflage technology randomly overnight.

Behind his glasses, my boss's eyebrows rose slowly, and his question came out at the same speed, marked with a little more sarcasm than I knew what to do with. "Need a boost or not?"

He was my boss, and under no circumstance was I about to throw myself into his car like I was desperate.

"I can drive myself."

Those thick, dark eyebrows stayed up, and that was *definitely* sarcasm in his tone. "Bet you can't look over your shoulder," he tried to dare me, surprising me even more.

Like the sucker I was, I latched onto his unexpected playfulness anyway as I asked back, "But you can?"

"Uh-huh. I didn't have time to tense up." His eyebrows dropped, and he gestured me into the truck. "Get in, I'm giving you a ride to work, and we're already running late."

I guess I hadn't thought about it in that light, but he did have a point. I couldn't turn my head, not well enough to be a safe driver at least. And was I *really* going to be stubborn over not wanting a ride to work from the man who might have been a jerk to me two days ago but who I knew in my heart would have behaved the same way with any of the rest of my coworkers? The same man who had let me hug him and comfort him after he'd had some strange breakdown after the accident? A breakdown that I didn't understand, but one I had thought about last night while I lay in bed and had only managed to come to one conclusion.

That wasn't the first accident Ripley had been in.

I wasn't going to ask what the first had been. I wanted to know, but I also knew that someone didn't react the way he had for no reason.

I sighed but couldn't hold back the smile on my face as I told him the truth. "I can't raise my arm up over my head, boss. I can't get in." I started to raise my arm up so I could show him, only getting a few inches in before I had to stop with a groan. "Yeah, that's not happening." How I was supposed to work, I had no clue, but I'd figure it out.

The expression he gave me, a slight frown and a tiny head shake, said, "that's what I thought." But fortunately he didn't rub it in my face as he touched a button somewhere by the steering wheel that had the running boards dropping into place. Then his door opened and he got out, circling around the front of the truck before I had a chance to realize what exactly was happening.

The next thing I knew, Rip was behind me and those big hands were high up on my thighs, just below my butt, and he was lifting me *up*. Not straining. Not grunting, nothing. Just a lift up until my feet were over the running board, and then, and only then, did he let me go.

I didn't need help ducking into his car, barely suppressing a moan at the movement that shot pain around my neck. If Rip noticed, he didn't make a comment as he let go and took a step back, slamming the door closed. In the time it took him to get back into the truck, I had run through all the reasons why this was happening.

Then I accepted there was only one reason that should matter, and we needed to get it sorted out as soon as possible.

I waited until he'd reversed out of my driveway and started heading toward the shop before I shifted my body into the corner of the seat to get a view at him that didn't require me to turn my neck. He looked fine to me. And it was a navy shirt day.

"How bad's your neck?"

Luckily, he wasn't watching my face twist up into a grimace every time he drove over even a tiny pothole, because he would have known I was full of it. "Bad enough," I told him, fighting the urge to reach up and try and massage my neck.

His nod was a slow tilt forward of his head.

That was when I knew I needed to strike. "Say, Rip?"

"What?"

What. I wasn't sure why that amused me so much. "I'm all right, okay? My neck hurts and so does my shoulder, but it'll go away. You don't have to come get me from home because you feel guilty."

He cut me off. "I don't feel guilty."

"Oh," was the super smart thing out of me. Well. Okay. "All right then."

Then I thought to myself *liar*, because why the hell else would he show up here to get me? Because he wanted to? Because we were friends and he cared about me? Nah. I flip-flopped almost daily on the signs he gave me that he might be a little fond of me. Then he would do something like what had happened on Monday and make me rethink it all.

"It was the other asshole's fault," Rip stated after a second. "I know you're gonna be fine, just like I knew you'd come to work today even though you've gotta be in pain and probably won't be able to work long before it gets too bad."

I made a face to myself. "I can work the whole day." I had worked with the flu before. I could survive a day with a little strain.

A little strain that had me hiding a groan when he went over a speed bump a little too fast.

One glance at his face had me wondering if he'd done it on purpose to prove a point.

Those teal-colored eyes slid toward me, and I'd swear one corner of his mouth went up a fraction of a millimeter. "I know."

He *had* done it on purpose. I wasn't sure how I knew, but I did. Fine. He didn't want me to suck it up? I wouldn't. What I would do was continue being a decent person. "I'm glad then that you don't feel guilty, because there's no reason for you to be. But I promise you didn't need to come get me. I can drive myself."

Rip waited so long to say "Luna?" that I half expected him to change the subject.

That didn't happen.

"Yeah?"

"If I want to come get you, I'm gonna come get you. Deal with it," he stated, or more like *told* me. "You wanna stop at that donut place you like or what?"

I jerked a little in place, telling myself to not take his first comment too seriously. "We can go to the donut place if you want."

"All right."

I faced forward again. "Okay."

"Sure you're not mad anymore?"

"I'm sure."

He glanced at me. "Do you even know how to sulk?"

I gave him a little smile. "No, not really."

I heard Rip take a breath before his voice filled the cab. "Luna?"

"Hmm?"

"My mom died in a car accident when I was eighteen. I was with her when it happened," Rip said, making me freeze in place as his words settled in. "That's why I... that's what happened yesterday. Just wanted to say thanks for what you did."

His mom had died in a car wreck? The mom who scratched his head and bought him ice cream to make him feel better?

Then he kept talking, and I didn't know what to say. "Add that to our secrets, all right? Just thought you deserved to know."

* * *

As MUCH AS I tried telling myself that I had made the right choice coming in to work, the truth was, it turned out to be a terrible decision.

I was in pain. Physical pain, if you wanted to be specific, that had nothing to do with the ache that Rip's confession earlier had given me. The confession that I purposely wasn't going to think about until I got home and could ponder it in private. I wasn't sure I could handle thinking about Rip basically losing it after the accident because of a traumatic experience in his life.

So, later. Later I would think about it. For now, I was going to focus on how bad I physically hurt.

I had learned real quick that there was no such thing as looking over my shoulder or looking down. I had to turn my entire body one way or the other to do any of those things, and even then, I still hurt. I had murmured "fuck you" to myself when I'd bent over to tie my boots earlier. The pain must have been so apparent on my face that not even Jason gave me the slightest bit of a hard time. Either that or he knew I still wanted to kick his butt after my Monday incident with Rip.

The over-the-counter painkillers I'd taken hadn't done a single freaking thing. By the time lunch came around, I had resigned myself to the idea of visiting the doctor to make sure I wasn't ignoring a bigger issue.

I left Jason in the room as I headed down the hall with the intention of going up the stairs to eat my overcooked, total crap lo mein.

I almost ran into Miguel by the bathrooms when he burst out of the men's room.

"You're a damn ninja, Lu—" he started to say before cutting himself off with a blink and followed that up with a wince. "You look like hell."

Well. "Thanks, Miguelito."

He didn't even crack a smile at my response. Instead, he looked me over in a way that someone would a turned-over trashcan. "You okay? Mr. Coop said you were okay yesterday, but you look like you're ready to die."

Oh, Miguel. "Everything hurts," I told him. "It's making me a little nauseous."

The wince turned into a grimace as he wrapped up his inspection by wrinkling his nose. "Looks like it."

I couldn't help but laugh, even as it sent sharp pain shooting up my neck and had me cutting myself off with a groan. "Oh, my God, don't make me laugh."

His disgust at my nausea instantly turned into concern. "Take something. For real. You look like shit." He went thoughtful for a second before dropping his voice. "I know where there's some vodka if you want to take the edge off."

I only barely managed not to laugh but gave him a smile instead. "That's okay. I might see if they'll let me leave early and go to one of those urgent care places."

My coworker patted my shoulder. "You know they will. But you know I know where the vodka is. You need a ride, tell me," he offered. "I didn't see your car in the lot. Mr. Coop will let me take you."

I kept my face neutral. "Rip picked me up."

"He doesn't look like anything happened to him," Miguel confirmed, back to watching me too carefully like he was expecting me to projectile vomit all over him suddenly. "The devil's not taking him back."

I shook my head. "Don't be mean. But I'll let you know about a ride to the doctor if I go."

He gave me one last pat. "You feel like you're gonna vomit, aim at Jason."

I snickered as I ducked into the bathroom and quickly did my business, ignoring the ache that shot through my quads as I squatted to pee. Finishing up, I kept walking down the hallway.

"Luna!" Mr. Cooper's familiar voice boomed from just up ahead, where he was standing just on the other side in the main room. There was a man I didn't recognize beside him in jeans and a T-shirt.

I lifted my hand only about waist level and waved as I approached them. "Hi, Mr. C. Hello, other person."

The other man's instant grin matched Mr. Cooper's. "We were just about to come visit," my longtime boss told me.

We were about five feet away from each other when I finally managed to get a good look at the other guy. Not much taller than me, with dark blond hair, in shape and with a face that was so boy-next-door good-looking, it kind of surprised me. I had to glance back at Mr. Cooper to see if he was going to give me a sign who this was. He didn't do it fast enough though. "I'm taking my lunch break now, but Jason is in the booth if you want to drop by," I explained, stopping a few feet away from them.

"I was going to take Ashton by to show him around the shop, but really, I was going to see if you wanted to go to lunch with us afterward," Mr. Cooper explained. "Luna, this is Ashton, our new Rogelio. Ashton, this is Luna, our head painter who does a little of everything around here."

I held my hand out first toward him, smiling at him and Mr. Cooper as he took mine and gave it a firm shake, his own mouth pulled up into a lopsided grin that was pretty cute.

"Nice to meet you," the new man claimed just as he let go.

"Nice to meet you too," I told him before trying to point over my shoulder and failing miserably when that hurt too. I groaned and didn't do that good of a job hiding it. "I work back there if you need anything."

"Hurting that bad?" Mr. Cooper asked, concern lacing his face and words.

I gave him a grimace-like smile. "Little bit," I lied. "I was going to eat something, take a couple more painkillers, and see if it helps any." I almost brought up asking if I could leave early, but I didn't want to set a bad example in front of the new guy, making him think he could just ask to leave early over a little boo-boo. I'd just do it in secret later.

"Come have lunch with us," my boss suggested, still frowning at me, his eyes looking me over just like Miguel's had done. "Let's see how you feel after. What do you say?"

Did I *want* to eat my food? Not really. Would I? Of course I would. But I was still going to take up Mr. C on his offer. I would never say no to spending more time with him.

If the new employee was going to be there too, well, I wasn't going to complain. I liked getting along with everyone I worked with—Jason being the exception.

"Sure," I agreed, letting myself glance at the guy named Ashton for a split second again. "Give me a second to grab my purse."

"You don't need that thing," my boss claimed.

Under normal circumstances, I would have grabbed it anyway, but I really didn't feel like walking all the way down the hall to get it from my desk. And I felt zero guilt for letting Mr. Cooper pay for my food.

"In that case, I'm ready."

Mr. Cooper put a hand on my shoulder and gestured in the direction of the exit for the shop. I led the way, smile-grimacing at the coworkers we passed by. We were halfway across the floor when I sensed Mr. Cooper stop, and definitely heard him say, "We're going to lunch with Ashton. Would you like to come with us?"

I knew he was talking to Rip, the man who had bought me not just a twist donut that morning but a kolache too. I hadn't even been hungry, but I'd eaten both things on the ride to work since he had driven with one hand, holding his own kolache in the other.

The same man who had helped me carry my things inside the shop and then turned around and walked right back out of my room, only throwing out over his shoulder, "Take it easy today." If I had been harboring any more resentment toward him from two days before, those feelings would have disappeared after all that.

But at Mr. Cooper's question, I braced for Rip to give

him a rough response. At least yesterday, they hadn't said a single word to each other. The tension in Mr. Cooper's car after he'd picked us up had been uncomfortable, and that was saying something considering the arguments between them that I had broken up.

Instead, what Rip gave him was a "Let me wash up first."

He was coming? With us? If I could have moved my neck, I would have, just to see if hell had frozen over.

Did he know Mr. Cooper was actually going or...?

The way Mr. Cooper said "Okay" meant I wasn't the only one shocked he'd agreed. I mean, as far as I could remember, the older man took all of his new employees out to eat when he hired them. In my case, he'd done that and saved me from living in a crappy motel room, and then gotten stuck with me for years living under his roof.

I remembered when he hired Jason, I didn't go—because I had been too busy—and neither had Rip, for whatever reason he could have had.

So....

Mr. Cooper's muttered "huh" made me smile. "Let's wait for Ripley then," he stated, sounding different but not in a bad way. More... totally surprised. In a good way.

Not bothering to turn in a circle to face them, I just stood there until the Ashton guy spoke up and asked, "How long have you worked here, Luna?"

Then I did have to turn all the way around to face my boss and newest coworker. "Nine years." Did I sound proud of myself or what?

"Luna here has been with us the longest now, isn't that right?" Mr. Cooper asked.

I remembered not to move my head and said, "Yep" instead.

"If you need anything, this here's your girl. She knows everything, and if she doesn't, she figures it out," the older man kept going, sounding like a proud dad. Man, I loved him.

"Ready to go?" came Rip's deep voice from behind the other two men.

Mr. Cooper startled but nodded. "I was planning on driving, but if you want to..."

I could see Rip's face as he replied, "You can drive."

What was going on with him being so agreeable and nice? I took in how calm Rip's face was but made sure not to let mine reflect the surprise there. I would have figured they would have argued even over that, but...

They didn't even argue over going to eat burgers.

I led the way toward the exit and only held the door open long enough for Rip to reach out and take the weight from me.

"Are you okay?" came the question from behind me, specifically from Ashton's mouth.

I didn't bother turning around to say, "I just strained my neck."

"We were in an accident yesterday," Rip explained in that low, low voice of his.

"They're both fine," Mr. Cooper told the new guy just as I stopped right in front of his car. "Other than Luna's poor neck."

Poor everything, but I didn't need to be specific.

He unlocked the door and moved the seat forward, so I climbed in and sat behind the passenger seat. What I wasn't expecting was that, instead of the new guy climbing into the back, it was Rip who managed to wedge himself in beside me. In the process, he pretty much took up three-fourths of the seat, forcing me to squish into the corner as the entire left side of my body ended up pressed against his.

Even the tip of his elbow rested high up on my thigh.

Those blue-green eyes met mine as Mr. Cooper and the other guy got in too. Rip eyed me. "You good?"

Hadn't I asked him those same words at least three times the day before while he'd been having his moment after the wreck?

"I'm okay," I assured him. "You?"

He threw up a look like "no shit."

I glanced at the cut above his eyebrow.

I couldn't stop myself. I poked at a spot just above it, ignoring the flash of pain at my shoulder. The cut was already totally scabbed over.

"I'm really glad that's all that happened," I whispered as I dropped my hand with a barely contained groan. "Did you call your insurance?"

His eyes moved over my face for a moment. "They gotta come take a look at the truck, but it's totaled. Not sure I'm willing to fix it."

That made me sad, his truck was beautiful. Had been beautiful. "For sure?"

His cheek did the twitch thing. "For sure."

I scrunched up my nose. "I'm sorry."

His nostrils flared. "Just a truck. No big deal."

It was only the car doors slamming closed that told me we were heading out.

The head in the driver's seat turned to look around the seat, and Mr. Cooper asked, "You going to the doctor?"

"I don't know," I answered, glancing down at the length of thigh lined up with mine. It was easy to remember just how hard and muscular it had been under me. *And* I needed to forget that had happened. Just like I needed to shove aside what Rip had told me about his mom. "I might end up going, but nothing's really messed up. I'm pretty sure it's just whiplash."

It wasn't at all my imagination that Rip leaned into me or that his fingers grazed the top of my hand as he asked, "You want to go to the doctor?"

There was something about his voice that had me wanting to close an eye. "I'm thinking about it. I'm sure that jerk's insurance will reimburse me for it."

"It will," Mr. Cooper claimed from his seat up front.

The fingertips went back to the top of my hand. He didn't even try to lower his voice. "I'll take you when we get back."

I didn't tense up my forearm as his fingers lingered over my knuckles, and unlike him, I did tell him quietly, "I'm okay." Especially with him touching my hand.

He wasn't quiet back. "I'll take you when we get back."

I blinked and tried again, quietly, "You don't have to take me."

It was his turn to blink. "Luna."

I blinked right back. "Ripley."

"I'm taking you to the doctor," he told me just as loudly as he had said every other word before.

He really must feel terrible.

I had no business being so touched by his concern. He was my boss. If I wasn't well, I could potentially do my job horribly.

"You're being very sweet," I managed to say without cracking a smile, just to be a pain. "But—"

He didn't let me finish my statement, and I'd swear he leaned into me even more. "I'm not being sweet."

His mom had died in a car wreck, I thought, before pushing that aside again for later like I had promised myself.

I could act normal. So, I closed an eye and brought my index finger and thumb pretty close together. "Little bit."

His jaw did that twitch thing again. "I'm not, but you're going to the doctor, and I'm driving you there," he tried to claim. Tried to tell me.

But I just stared back at him. "You don't have to."

His elbow landed on the top of my thigh, and I wasn't sure if he was doing it to intimidate me—which I doubted— or if he was finally feeling how tight the space was. "I'm taking you to the goddamn doctor."

I opened my mouth to keep arguing with him, but that was when my phone rang. Pulling it out of my pocket, I looked at the screen and couldn't help but frown when Thea's name popped up. I happened to look up at the rearview mirror and found Mr. Cooper's blue eyes on mine through the reflection. He had a funny look on his face. I smiled at him before poking at the screen.

"Hello?" I answered, trying to whisper since Rip had already put enough of my business out there in front of someone I had barely met and another man who might not understand why or how Rip and I were talking to each other so... almost friendly.

"Luna," my sister said my name all funny.

"Hi, Thee." I bit the inside of my cheek when she didn't immediately say anything else. "You okay?"

"I'm fine," she rushed out. "Are you?"

"Yeah. I told you in my message, remember? I'm okay," I promised, not liking the way she sounded. I could appreciate her being worried about me but....

She kicked you out of her apartment.

So there was that.

"Yeah? Nothing else happened?" she asked, sounding too... different.

I took in the back of the seat in front of me, trying to ignore the unease her tone made me feel. "No, it was only the accident. Just a little whiplash," I promised her, telling myself not to think this over too much. "Are you all right?"

"Yeah, Luna. Yeah," my sister replied a little too quickly.

She didn't sound like it. I lowered my head. "Did you get your rental insurance sorted?" I made myself ask.

Thea made a weird noise I hadn't heard before, which put me even more on edge. "Um, yes. They're covering my things."

"Good."

"I'm glad you're fine," she muttered, sounding distracted then. "Well, that's all I was calling for. I just... wanted to make sure you were okay."

In the three years since she had moved out on her own, she had never, not once called to *make sure I was okay*. I wasn't much better at calling, but I did text her at least once a week.

"I'm okay." I lifted my head and stared at the back of the seat, something about this feeling wrong and weird. "Thee, is everything all right with you?"

"I'm fine, don't worry about me. But I gotta go. I'll talk to you later," she answered quickly.

"Okay." I paused. Then added, surprising myself, "Love you, Thea."

"Yeah, me too."

Then she hung up and left me holding the phone against my face, frowning over our conversation.

What the hell had that been about? Thea and I had always had the rockiest relationship. We had never been as close as Lily and me, or in her case, as close as she was to

Kyra. But... I still loved her. I always would, regardless of the things she had said or done.

The car hit a speed bump right then that sent Rip's elbow straight into my thigh.

"Your sister?" he asked quietly, forcing me to swing my eyes to him.

"Yeah," I told him, leaving out the part where I thought something was off because... well, why wouldn't I? I didn't need to ask his opinion to know that he probably didn't have good thoughts about her in the first place. Honestly, if our roles had been reversed, I wouldn't have thought well of his family member if they had done to him what she had done to me.

But I wasn't going to worry about that.

Instead, I looked over and slanted him a look. "And back to our conversation, I'm not letting you take me to the doctor, boss, but thank you again for offering."

CHAPTER SEVENTEEN

ALL MY HOPES AND DREAMS FAILED ME THE NEXT morning.

I had told myself I was going to be better. *Way* better by the time I woke up the following day. Maybe I would have still been in a little bit of pain, but nothing I couldn't have handled.

At least that's what I had genuinely believed.

In reality, everything hurt even more. All it took was about five seconds after my alarm went off to realize just how much more. "Shit," I muttered to myself as I laid there, wanting to reach up to massage myself and then stopping because lifting my arm would more than likely only make me choke up.

And I didn't really feel like finding out for sure.

I was never going to tell anybody how loud I moaned as I rolled onto my side and then forced myself to sit up. Then I peeked out the window to make sure there wasn't a black truck parked in my driveway. There wasn't.

After he'd dropped me off at home yesterday evening, I had told Rip that he really didn't need to pick me up. He had settled for giving me a look, then lifted a shoulder and said, "'Kay." I still didn't totally believe him that he wouldn't come by, but at least his truck wasn't there.

It took a long time for me to shower and stiffly pull on clothes; there was still no truck when I peeked out, and then it took even longer for me to make breakfast and fill a Rubbermaid with another serving of lo mein that somehow managed to look even mushier. I hadn't thought that was possible.

It was thirty minutes later than I usually left when I opened my front door, juggling my things, and found a black Ford F-250 there.

Sure enough, through the windshield, I spotted a familiar dark brown head of hair attached to a massive body behind the driver seat.

In the minute it took me to lock my door and head down the steps, my boss was out of the truck and already holding the passenger side door open, all the while giving me a look that said "shut up, Luna."

"Morning, boss man," I called out as I walked in his direction, feeling pretty resigned.

He had his sunglasses on again, and his voice was just as low and hoarse as always. "Morning, Luna."

I stopped right in front of him, noticing that he didn't have on a compression shirt. Instead, in the middle of June, he had on a thin long-sleeved white T-shirt that ended right at the notch of his throat, showing off a whole lot of thick neck.

I met his gaze and raised my eyebrows. "Whatcha doing here?"

"Picking you up," he answered, even as his hand took the bag from me.

Could I have held on to it? Sure. But I wasn't going to.

But still…

"You don't need any of this though," Rip told me.

Now that had me hesitating and narrowing my eyes. "Why?"

He gestured me to get into the truck. "You're not going to work. We're going to the doctor."

I stared at that handsome face, taking in the fact that he wasn't trying to avert his eyes or be sneaky or anything like that. He was being serious. "But I don't need to go to the doctor," I told him carefully.

"You're not going to work. Worthless can handle whatever needs to be done." He motioned inside the truck again. "Let's go."

Worthless? Is that what he was referring to Jason as? Because if it was, I could be all about that. Instead of picking at his nickname though, I didn't move, and he noticed.

And when he noticed, he frowned. "Why you being stubborn? You're hurting. You were in a wreck—"

"So were you."

That frown didn't go anywhere. "I'm not in pain," he claimed before gesturing toward the inside of the truck once more. "Go to the damn doctor and have them check you out. You could have some other issue later on, and the car insurance won't cover it if you don't have a record that you weren't feeling good from the start," he explained.

He had a point.

But I knew there was nothing actually wrong with me.

One of those hands went up to his head and he smoothed it over the curve of his skull before letting out a deep breath and saying, calmly, "Get in. Cooper made an appointment for you yesterday for eight in the morning today."

Mr. Cooper had done that?

I didn't even need to think about it then. If Mr. Cooper wanted me to go, then... that made this whole thing different. He was only trying to get me to go because he cared about me.

I would have traded anything to have a father who cared about me when I'd been younger. I'd take it now.

"Fine," I agreed, trying not to sound all put out about it, because I wasn't, especially now that I knew the entire story. Plus, the only reason I hadn't gone yesterday was because Jason had almost screwed up, and I didn't trust leaving him alone. He really was like a little kid I constantly had to babysit, except he wasn't cute, curious or had the excuse of being a kid.

If he was feeling smug about it, Rip didn't say anything. What he did do was point at the inside of the truck.

I pointed too, just to give him a hard time. "Give me a boost?"

I didn't miss his cheek twitching. I also didn't miss his response, because there wasn't one. All he did was lower my bag to the ground, come right up behind me, and just straight-up lift me like he had the day before until I could reach the running boards. I got in and watched him put my things on the floor by my feet before going around to the other side and getting in too.

We had barely gotten out of the driveway when Rip asked, "You're not pissed?"

I glanced at him, taking in the thick ink I could see along the side of his neck that almost looked like... flames? Huh. "What would I be pissed over?"

"The appointment."

I was pretty sure those were definitely a skull and flames. Kind of artsy looking flames but flames. "No. I would never get mad over someone worrying about me." The words were barely out of my mouth when I realized how pathetic they sounded.

Oh well.

"You're sure you don't need to get checked out just to be on the safe side?" I asked him, just to mess with him.

His snicker wasn't a surprise at all. "No."

"You're sure?"

"I'm sure," he insisted, the tiniest trace of amusement in his tone.

I smiled only because I knew he wouldn't see it. "I can call and make an appointment for you if you want," I kept going.

"Anybody ever told you that you're a pain in the ass?" he asked, as he kept his attention forward on the drive.

I smirked just as my phone vibrated from my lap. There was a message from my little sister Lily.

Lily: Morning. Got a breakfast shift today. Miss you so much.

I loved that girl.

Me: Miss you so much too, sugar lumps. Have a great day at work. Make some tip money.

I hesitated then typed up another message before I could talk myself out of it.

Me: I love you

Thirty seconds might have passed before I got a response.

Lily: I LOVE YOU SO MUCH <3 <3 <3 <3 <3 <3

"Good news?"

I moved my eyes toward him.

"You got a big smile on your face," he said as an explanation.

Oh. "Just a good morning message from my little sister." I thought about it, then thought about his comment about his mom yesterday. Then, before I could think twice about what I was about to ask, I went for it. "Do you have any brothers or sisters?"

His "no" was immediate. Then he tipped his head to the side and kept talking. "My mom wanted to have more, but it never happened. Don't know why, but it's only me."

Only him. I wasn't sure why that made me sad, but it did. His mom was gone. He didn't have any siblings, and I had no clue what was going on with his dad.

If he'd even known him.

It wasn't like I had known my mom. Or wanted to know my dad after a certain point.

But I wasn't going to bring up that subject. Nope. So I stuck to a safe one. "Did you want any?"

He thought about it for a moment before shaking his head. "No." Before I could get another question out, he beat me to it. "You talk to your sister again?"

"Which one?" I asked, even though I had an idea who he was referring to.

"The one in Dallas."

I'd been right. "Just yesterday." I bit my cheek and didn't understand why I kept talking. "But that's been the first time since we went... to see her. It's not unlike her though. She never calls me—" *unless she needs something,* but instead, I told him, "—during the workday unless it's an emergency."

His "hmm" sounded loaded enough to grab my attention.

"What?" I couldn't help but ask.

Rip didn't drag it out. "You get a good vibe from her?"

That had me instantly getting defensive. "What do you mean?"

He must have sensed something because he slid me a look. "I'm not talking shit about your sister, Luna," he stated calmly. "All I'm saying is that there's some fishy shit going on with her, and you know there is."

So I hadn't been the only one imagining it. "What do you mean by fishy?"

He made a face. "You're not gonna get all pissed off, are you?"

"No," I answered, sounding like I was lying, but I wasn't. Because I wasn't going to get mad. There was nothing *to* get mad about. He said he wasn't talking shit about my sister. So...

"Look, I didn't wanna say anything, but some shit with her just doesn't add up." He shot me a look that was like a dare for me to contradict him.

I wouldn't, because his comment had something inside of me perking up. "What doesn't?"

He blew out a breath that should have been a warning I might not like what he was going to say next. But in true Rip fashion, he didn't hold back. "You didn't notice when we went to her apartment that there was nothing wrong with her front door?"

What?

"Her front door," he repeated, like I'd literally asked the question out loud. "She said her place got broken into, but there was nothing wrong with it. I've seen places that got broken into, Luna; it didn't look like anybody had fucked with her shit. The doorframe was intact. She had an alarm system, for fucking sake."

It took me a second to process his words. To *think*.

But when it came down to it... he was right.

There hadn't been anything wrong with the front door. I had rung the doorbell. I had knocked on it. Banged on it. And she lived on the third floor. How would they have gotten in unless they went all Spiderman and climbed up the balconies, but for what though? To get in through the sliding door? All that effort to steal a thousand-dollar laptop, which I didn't even think was that expensive in the first place? Wouldn't they have broken into more apartments to make it worth it?

Rip grumbled out as I sat there. "Just saying. It doesn't add up."

Huh.

Huh.

He had a point.

And that point made my ears buzz. Because something hadn't felt right about the entire thing, but I hadn't been able to pinpoint what or why. I had just thought it was Thea acting weird, but it wasn't.

Or maybe I just wanted to assume that was it.

I didn't expect her to be my best friend, but I hadn't taken her to lie to me either, not after everything we had been through together. But she had. For whatever reason, she had started lying to me from the moment she had moved out of her place and not told me.

...maybe even before.

That betrayal felt worse than anything else. Why would she make something like that up? Had someone broken into her place after all?

I wondered if Kyra knew something was weird with Thea. I doubted Lily did.

For once, I didn't know what to say. All I could do was... think about it.

And feel disappointment.

It was that disappointment that robbed the words from my throat for a long time after that.

* * *

"Thanks," I mumbled to the receptionist after settling my bill for the doctor's visit, an hour and a half later.

The woman reminded me again, "The pharmacy will have your prescription ready in about thirty minutes."

I repeated my "thank you" before escaping through the door that led into the waiting room, where I found Rip. He was sitting sprawled out in one of the chairs, arms crossed over his chest, basically bursting out of the poor seat. For a second, I wondered what his couches at home looked like; then I told myself to stop. He climbed to his big feet and looked me over, like I'd have a sign on that gave my diagnosis. "Ready?"

"Yeah," I told him, giving him a smile that was only partially forced. I wasn't mad at him for bringing up Thea's... thing, but it weighed heavily on me. So heavy I really didn't know what to say to him. What to think, more than anything.

I rarely let people hurt me, but Thea not being honest with me... it hurt more than it should. I mean, hadn't I lied to enough people over my life to be an enormous hypocrite over someone doing the same thing to me? I knew the answer to that. My lies weren't always white.

I needed to snap out of it though.

So I balled it up and set it aside. For now.

I was fine. I was loved. I had everything.

Just not my sister's honesty. And possibly her loyalty.

And there I went again.

LUNA AND THE LIE   333

"I'm okay," I made myself tell Rip as we walked out of the office and down the hall toward where he'd parked his truck earlier. "They did an X-ray. The doctor says everything is fine, but I'm just a little banged up." I kept the *like I told you* to myself. "He called in a prescription for me that'll be ready in half an hour, but I don't see a point in getting it. I won't take it."

"Why?"

What more pride did I have? He already knew enough of the bad bits and pieces of me. What was one more, really? "I don't trust myself around anything that could be addictive. I don't want to risk it, and the pills are an opiate. I looked them up while I was waiting."

I didn't need to look at him to know he'd sobered. I could feel it. Could sense him shoot me a glance.

I shrugged so he'd know it wasn't a big deal. "Anyway, if you want to—"

"You're not going back to work," he shot back before I could even finish.

It was hard not to smile. "I know. Mr. Cooper sent me a message while I was waiting for an X-ray and told me not to bother coming in the rest of the week. I was going to see if you could give me a ride home, boss."

His grunt made me smile again. "I'll take you. I didn't wait around for no reason."

I rolled my eyes.

Then I wondered what I was going to do now. I had never taken a day off just for the hell of it. It had always been for something with one of my sisters or on the rare occasion I was sick.

But now? The first and only thing I thought of was Lily. Lily and only Lily.

And Rip, doing that thing where I swore he could read my mind, asked, "You gonna take it easy?"

"*Yes*. I was just thinking maybe I could go see my little sister in Galveston."

"Galveston?"

"Yeah." And before he could say anything, I threw out, "If I go, I'll take an Uber or something. I'm not going to risk my life or anyone else's trying to drive, okay?"

He held the door open for me that led outside, and I brushed by him, feeling the hard muscles across his chest and abs graze my arm. Sheesh, the man was buff. Tight. Hard.

And *my boss*.

My boss who I needed to keep messing with so he wouldn't think I was thinking about his body.

"Unless you want to come?" I threw out for the hell of it as I went down the steps that led into the building.

He didn't respond as we headed to his truck, and I didn't take it personally. It wasn't like he ever took me up on any of my invitations, and I'd asked, what? A hundred times over the last few years?

Pulling my phone out of my pocket while I walked, I found Lily's name under my messages and smiled at the last one she had sent me.

I sent her a new one.

Me: Taking today and tomorrow off, and I was thinking about coming to visit if you've got some time. Let me know. No pressure.

If she was busy, I'd understand. No big deal.

"You gonna spend the night or go for the day?" Rip asked as he unlocked his truck.

Oh. "I'm waiting to hear back from Lily, but if I go... I

guess I could spend the night. I don't think I've ever spent the night in Galveston before, now that I think about it."

He opened the passenger door before going to stand directly behind me, hands going to that familiar place really low on my hips again. "Haven't been to Galveston in twenty years. Feet up."

"You don't like the beach?"

"I like the beach. I don't like sand up my ass."

Don't do it. Don't do it. Don't—

I couldn't help myself. "Is there something you, uh, do like up there?" I asked.

Rip choked.

I laughed as I tucked my legs up right as he lifted and put them down when it felt about right. He slammed the door closed as soon as I was in the seat, and I couldn't help but smile at how unnecessarily nice he was being. The second he was behind the wheel, I told him, "Rip, you know you don't have to be nice to me because of the accident. It wasn't your fault."

He didn't even bother sliding me an annoyed look. "We already talked this shit over."

This shit.

And he didn't blame himself.

Yeah, sure.

"Good, I'm glad you don't blame yourself, but seriously, you don't have to drive me around. I'm not Miss Daisy. We're even. We're good. I would still go to work if you and Mr. C let me, if that's what you're worried about."

What did he pick up on? "We're still not even," he had the nerve to try and claim, using that dry tone with me.

I didn't want or mean to glare at him, but... what the hell? "Why?"

He shrugged. "'Cause we're not."

Right then, my phone vibrated, and I glanced down to find a new message from my sister. Then another one came in.

Lily: I have to work until 5 but COME SEE ME. I MISS YOU SO MUCH.

Lily: You can hang out at the restaurant with me.

Another one came in before I finished reading the first two.

Lily: My room is really small but SLEEP-OVER. We can share a bed like old times.

And then another one came in, and I couldn't help but smile at her messages.

Lily: Are you already on your way?

I loved her. I loved her so much.

Me: Not yet but I will.

"What's that smile for?" asked the man beside me.

Slipping my phone back into my purse, I still couldn't wipe the smile off my face. "My little sister has to work, but she told me to come see her, so I guess I am going to get a car to take me." Just thinking about her made me feel better. "I miss her so much," I told him with a sigh. "And even though I'm really sorry about your truck, and I feel bad I have to take time off, I'm excited I get to go see her. I could use a few dozen of her hugs."

He "hmmed" me.

Making a list in my head of what I should pack, I was genuinely surprised when my phone started vibrating, but not in the way it did with a message. It was a call. Half expecting it to be Lily, I paused when I had it in my hand and saw the San Antonio area code on the screen. Was it the lawyer guy again?

I only hesitated for a second before answering. "Hello?"

There was a loud noise in the background before a man's voice came over the line. "This Luna?"

Okay. That didn't sound at all like the man I had spoken to weeks ago over Grandma Genie. "Yes?" I replied, knowing I sounded uncertain but not really caring.

"Fucking finally," the man on the line muttered, and I had to pull the phone away from my face to look at it, because who the hell was this?

"Excuse me?" I asked when I brought it back to my face.

He didn't make me wait. "We need to talk," the man went on, shooting the words out quickly. "Sooner the better."

Wait. *Wait.*

I was fine. I was loved. I had everything I needed.

Except for this conversation with a man who I suddenly knew, some way, somehow, was my father.

How the hell had he gotten my number?

My father was calling me. After nine years. After telling me he was going to kill me. After holding a—

Calm down, Luna.

I was calm. I was calm. I was fine. I could think.

"Don't ever call me again," I said into the receiver slowly, cutting off the man on the other end.

What did he do? He cursed. He cussed like he had every time I had ever asked him for anything growing up. Like I was an inconvenience, and his next words confirmed that nothing had changed. "I'm only fucking calling you because of your sister, don't think it's because of anything else."

Because of my sister? Which one?

"Tell her she needs to quit that fucking job she's at. She's not taking my calls anymore."

Taking his calls anymore? She was taking them in the first place? Since when? Why?

Why would she do something like that?

I wouldn't hold it past him to lie, but... why? Why would he do that?

"Just talk to her. She doesn't have any business doing that shit," he went on, rambling, talking too fast.

Shredding me a little word by word. Or maybe it was my sister who was doing it with every word that came out of *his* mouth.

My hands started to shake. *Mine*. And just as I was about to shove the empty one under my thighs, I stopped. Then I made a decision.

"I don't know what you're talking about," I told him honestly, because I didn't, and I wasn't going to hide it. "But I don't ever want to hear your voice again. Don't call Lily or Kyra either. If you do, I'll call your parole officer. Don't think I won't."

And I hung up.

Then and only then, did I shove my freaking shaking hands under my thighs as I let out a deep breath.

What in God's name was Thea into? What the hell was she doing? Why the hell was she talking to him of all freaking people?

Just when I thought things couldn't get worse...

I found *this* out? *This?*

"You all right?" Rip didn't wait to ask.

I wanted to say I was fine. I really did. But that wasn't what I responded with. "Yes. No. I think... I think you're right about my sister doing something fishy. That was my dad who just called."

My dad. What a joke.

"I haven't talked to him in years, and he just said..."

Why the hell was I telling Rip all this?

Slipping one of my hands out from under my thigh, I lifted it up to my head and rubbed the palm of it across my forehead pretty freaking roughly, like that would erase the conversation that had just happened.

Rip's voice was low and gravelly, and so, so serious as he asked, "What he say?"

Keeping my gaze forward, I could barely tell him. "He said my sister doesn't have any business doing something, but he didn't say what, and..." Bitterness, honest to God bitterness, swelled up in my throat for the first time I could remember. I wasn't bitter. *I wasn't*. But I felt it then. Understood it then. I got why people could hold on to resentment for the rest of their lives. "He said she's been ignoring his calls, like that was new."

How could she? After everything he had said and done to me? She'd been the oldest. The one who witnessed more than the rest of my sisters just how our relationship had been.

And she was talking to him?

"I'm sorry." I picked my phone back up and instantly hit the speed dial number I needed, my heart in my freaking throat. "I need to call her."

He didn't reply as I hit the icon to start the call. But I sat there, listening to it ring, then ring some more, then ring a little more. Until her voice mail picked up.

Then I called her again, and again she didn't answer. Screw it. I'd leave a message.

"Thea, it's Luna. I just got a call from... back home. Are you okay?" She had been talking to our dad behind my back. God, I was *pissed*. But more... more than anything... it felt like a stab. It hurt me so much I could barely talk and barely keep it together. I could barely *think*. "Look, I don't know what's going on, but I'll help you any way I can. Just talk to me, all right? Call me back please. I'm not going in to work today. Call me any time." I breathed in through my nose and back out of it. "Be safe, okay?"

Only then did I hang up, feeling weirdly... numb.

What was she doing?

Pulling my hand out from under my thigh, I fisted both of them on my lap and stared down at them, trying to put my thoughts back in order. She wasn't dying. Nothing terrible had actually happened to her. There was no reason for me to freak the hell out and go back up to Dallas to see her—not that she'd even open the door to her apartment for me.

I took another deep breath that honestly sounded like a backed-up muffler on the way out.

Calm down. I needed to calm down.

It was only the rocking of the truck that had me noticing we had stopped. Right in front of my house.

"Luna," Rip drew out my name slowly and carefully. "You good?"

I bit my bottom lip and heard the lie that wanted to come out of my throat. I replaced it with the truth. "I will be."

Familiar, long, and tattooed fingers crept over the top of my hand and stayed there, brushing the LOVEYOU bracelet I'd put on that morning. Lucas Ripley's voice swept over me as he said, "I don't know what's going on with your sister, but you tell me if there's something I can do. You're not alone, you hear me?"

I pressed my lips together and nodded.

But he wasn't done. "You're not, Luna, and I gotta tell you, you don't need to be letting anybody run all over you or try to get away with shit—"

"I don't do that," I cut in.

It was only because of the soft face he gave me, all those normally harsh features without tension for once, that I didn't let his words, or what he was implying bother me. "All I'm saying is, you don't have to take shit, and you need to quit believing you do. Think about that, all right? Have fun with your sister but think about what I said."

CHAPTER EIGHTEEN

"Happy to see you back, little moon," Mr. Cooper said as he headed into the break room with his cup of coffee in hand.

I leaned back in my chair and grinned. "Me too, Mr. C. It feels like I've been gone a week." But it was really only two full days. I could have stayed home an extra day and no one would have said anything, but I wasn't about to milk anyone's kindness.

That and I had only been home alone last night for a few hours and hadn't known what to do with myself. I had learned real quick while I had gone to visit Lily that if I had five spare seconds, I would end up thinking about Thea and my dad. And if I wasn't thinking about them, I thought about Rip and his secret friends and his mom. Once and only once did I let myself think about the last words he'd said to me before he had dropped me off at home, about not taking people's crap.

I didn't want to think about either of them, especially not since my own sister couldn't find it in her to call me back but had zero issue texting Lily. It was only because she was texting her back, and because I had called Kyra to see if she'd heard from her, that I knew she was at least alive and decent. If things were bad, she wouldn't be working and going to school, according to what Kyra had told me. I'd had to lie and tell her we had gotten into an argument and she was mad at me.

It had happened before.

The older man set his hand on top of my head as he walked behind me, pulling me back into safe, nice thoughts that weren't centered around my sister emotionally betraying me or my dad being a prick. "You back to normal?"

"Mostly," I answered, finally able to turn my neck—at least more than before. The massage I'd had done on Wednesday while I waited for Lily to get out of work had helped. "How are you doing? How's your lady?"

He set a sandwich beside me. "Everything is good. She's great. She misses you and told me to have you call her. Other than that, no complaints from me."

"Your blood pressure?"

That had him sliding me a look.

I grinned and whispered, "The new guy?"

"Good," he confirmed. "He works hard, very respectful and professional. I'm happy."

"Good."

"What'd you do on your days off?"

I had decided I wasn't going to tell anyone about the Thea thing, including Mr. Cooper. "I went to see Lily and stayed with her for the night. I spent last night watching TV and doing laundry."

"Gone on any more of these dates?"

Hell. If it hadn't been for my little sister sending me a message that morning, I would have forgotten all about it, even after she had brought it up a dozen times while we had been together. "Tonight actually. I'm going out with Lily's old teacher."

"A teacher?"

Did he sound skeptical or was I imagining it?

I nodded anyway.

"I could see you with a teacher," he said, thoughtfully. So he wasn't skeptical about it. All right.

"I can't. She said he's nice. We're meeting at Mickey's, so hopefully it goes well," I replied, glancing to the side to see Rip halfway into the break room. I hadn't even heard him come in, he was so sneaky.

He shot me a stone-faced look I wasn't sure what to think of.

When I had walked in that morning, he'd already been working. And when I brought him down his coffee not too long afterward, we'd had the same exchange we always did, except he'd asked if I felt any better. I had told him, yes, and that had been the end of that.

He hadn't asked about my sister after offering to help me out with her situation if I needed.

Not that I would.

Well, unless it was absolutely necessary.

"Feeling better, Luna?" another voice asked, drawing my gaze back toward the door as Rip walked right behind me.

It was the new guy, Ashton, at the door, holding what looked like a bag from the burger truck that was a block away from the shop.

"Yeah," I said, shooting him a smile. "I can finally turn my head a little. See?"

The blond man smiled as he dropped his bag into the seat in front of mine. "Nice."

"Thanks," I told him.

Out of my line of vision, Rip stuck something into the microwave.

"Everyone was complaining about you not being here," Ashton kept going as he pulled his seat out.

"Aww, they don't have anyone else to pick on is all," I joked.

Two bites of food later, the scrape of the chair on my other side being pulled out had me preparing for Rip to drop into it, and he did. He had a reusable glass container with what looked like... chicken, brown rice, and veggies. Then I looked down at mine and found the same sticky, tan noodles, and wilted brown vegetables that still didn't taste any better than they had the first day.

He must have peeked at my food too because our eyes met, and I had to shoot him a grin.

The cheek closest to me went up—it was the one with the dimple too—and I couldn't help but feel a little triumph at our inner joke.

I nudged my container an inch closer to him and asked, totally serious, "You want some, boss?"

That cheek went up a little higher as he replied very clearly, using all the depth of that deep voice, "I'm good."

"You're sure?"

His eyes swung back to my food, and he seemed to think about it for a moment before he took the fork in my hand, dug it into the container, and like he'd done it a dozen times before, scooped the food it into his mouth in the time it took me to process what he'd done. His jaw worked... Those teal eyes went wide...

And he gagged.

Ripley freaking *gagged* before his throat bobbed forcefully and he swallowed it.

I opened my mouth wide as I watched him shake his head afterward like he was trying to erase the memory from his brain.

"Rip," I managed to get out while still having my mouth open.

"What the *fuck* was that?" he asked, reaching for his bottle of water and gulping down half of it before shooting me what I was pretty sure he meant to be a horrified expression but was just adorable instead.

"Lo mein," I told him, starting to laugh.

He looked at me. Then he grabbed my Rubbermaid, shoved his chair back and dumped everything in it into the trash.

"Rip!" I hissed, laughing. "What are you doing? That's perfectly good food!"

Already pushing his chair back in closer to the table, he shot me a look as he set the now empty container down and picked up his own. "There's nothing perfectly good about any of that, Luna," he grumbled, shaking his head as he scraped half of his meal into my bowl. He scooted it back toward me with a lift of his chin. "Eat that."

I blinked, ignoring the prickly feeling that popped up on my arms as I took in what he'd done. "I don't want to eat your food."

"Luna."

"What if you get hungry later because you only ate half?"

That handsome face changed, just a little, but then he rolled his eyes and said in that bossy voice, "Eat it."

It hadn't hit me until right then that neither Mr. C nor Ashton were saying a word or had been since Rip sat down next to me and we had started talking. I wondered what Mr. Cooper would think.

But Rip talking again made me focus on him. "You're really going to argue with me over eating?" he had the nerve to ask.

I pressed my lips together and muttered, "No." Then I stopped doing that, curled my finger over the top of the bowl, and dragged it over. "Thank you for sharing. You didn't have to."

His warm reply was a grunt.

If it hadn't been for my phone beeping from its spot on my table, I would have kept going, but I glanced down to see I'd gotten a message from Lily.

After the call from my dad, anytime the phone went off, it made me paranoid.

I unlocked the screen and tapped her message open.

Lily: Are you ready for tonight?

Okay, at least it wasn't anything else. Just that date. Tonight.

Did my neck start hurting again all of a sudden or was I imagining it?

I texted her back.

Me: Yes...

Me: My neck hurts though.

That was more of an exaggeration than it needed to be, but....

Lily: Don't turn your head then, silly.

Peeking at Rip, I could see he'd pulled a magazine out of somewhere—his pocket?—and unrolled it beside him. But it looked like he was dragging his tongue over his teeth, making a face as he did it. My food had that effect on people.

I thought about what to write her back, before finally glancing down at the new food in my container. It was exactly like what I had thought: stir-fried rice with veggies and a chicken thigh. I scooped up some rice with my fork and shoved it into my mouth, blinking as I chewed and swallowed.

I slid my gaze over to Rip and took another bite.

It was freaking *delicious.* I wondered if he'd made it or— or what? Unless he had a cook who went over to his place— or a woman who made his food—he'd made it.

Maybe it was a woman who made it for him. I had no idea if he had a girlfriend. Or maybe not even a girlfriend but just a... friend. Maybe with benefits. No one had ever mentioned him having a woman in his life, and it wasn't like he brought anyone over to the shop other than the guy he'd met in the lot.

"Did you make this?" I asked him.

He didn't even glance at me. "Uh-huh."

Okay then. I texted Lily a response while I scooped more food into my mouth.

Me: I really don't want to go, Lily.

Lily: Come on. Do it. Who knows, maybe you'll hit it off. I promise he's really cute.

I knew he was cute. She had shown me a picture of him at least three times. That wasn't the point though.

Lily: But I'll see if he can go another day if you want.

I didn't feel like going in the first place, but... I was supposed to be trying. So...

I glanced at Rip again, watching as he flipped through the magazine while digging his fork into his food without looking at it. He'd shared his food with me. Food he'd made.

The heart wants what it wants, but the brain knows what it can get.

And it was with that thought that I wrote her back.

Me: Yeah, if you can.

Lily: Okay, I will.

I only slightly felt like a jerk after that, but at least I wasn't outright cancelling. I was still trying. Just... not today.

For some reason, I glanced to my other side to see what Mr. Cooper was doing since he'd been so quiet, and I had to pause, looking at him when I saw the smile he had on his face while he ate his sandwich.

"Is it that good?" I couldn't help but ask him.

His blue eyes came to me, that smile still on his face, and Mr. Cooper chuckled lightly. "Yeah, it's that good, Luna." His smile grew even wider right before he moved a hand to pat the top of my head. "Best sandwich I've ever had."

* * *

Hours later, when it was five o'clock and I was pretty much done with my work for the day, which consisted of me barely talking to Jason, who had been eerily decent, I checked my phone again and found more messages from Lily spread out over the afternoon.

Lily: I emailed him but haven't heard back.

Lily: Still nothing

Lily: No response, mama Luna. I gotta get to work, but I'll see if he writes me back. Sorry. <3

He hadn't responded?

What if he'd gone to the bar we had agreed to meet at and was going to wait?

I sent my sister a text and told her it was fine then grabbed my things to head out. Rip was busy talking to a couple of the shop guys, so I couldn't even wave goodbye to him. I did call out bye to Miguel, who was still watching me like I was going to hurl vomit at him from across the room.

By the time I got home and Lily still hadn't messaged me to confirm that my date was off, I felt bad. I really didn't want to go, but I wasn't about to leave him hanging either. I forced myself to get dressed and head to the bar.

Worst-case scenario, I'd text Lenny and tell her to call me in an hour if things went bad.

Best-case scenario, he'd stand me up.

* * *

I'D BEEN at the bar for only a few minutes when I accepted the fact that the teacher had either gotten my sister's message and been too much of a butthole to write her back or he had died. It had to be one or the other. At least that's what I was going to tell myself.

But on the very small chance that he hadn't gotten her email and was only running late…

I was waiting. It was the nice thing to do.

About five minutes into sitting there, checking my phone about every minute to see if Lily had messaged me, I was kicking myself in the ass for not just staying home in the first place and running the risk that the teacher would be the one sitting around instead. But I had ordered a glass of Sprite and took in each person who walked into the bar, hoping one of them looked like the picture my sister had shown me of the guy.

After fifteen minutes, I would have taken anyone attempting to look around, so at least there had been some hope that someone was looking for me. But the only looking-around going on was people coming in groups looking for a table. I had taken up a two-seater in the middle of the room.

There wasn't anyone though. Just me, sitting alone, watching other people. The story of my life.

I checked my phone one more time and didn't even bother sighing when nothing had changed on the screen. One of the waitresses walked by me with a tray of potato wedges covered in melted cheese and what I was pretty sure was broken up bits of bacon. My stomach grumbled. I should have gotten at least a snack before I'd come.

Ten more minutes. Ten more minutes and I'd leave and not feel guilty because I had come. That was it. I wasn't going to stay a minute longer; I was starving. If I wanted potato wedges, I could settle for a stop at the Jack in the Box on the way home.

Across from me were a group of men standing right by a dart board, already halfway trashed if how bad their aim was meant anything. One of them threw a dart that hit about three feet to the right, bouncing off the sheetrock covered wall that already had a bunch of holes on it from other drunk guys in the past trying to play the same game. The men in the crowd started laughing, but the same man went again and did just as bad.

I glanced at my phone.

Three minutes down, seven to go.

"All alone?"

I must have been that distracted that it took me a second to process who was standing there in front of me, holding something dark and amber in a glass. It was the big hand with fingers covered in tattoos that I caught onto first. Then it was the long sleeve ending right at the man's wrist that I took in next.

There was only one person I knew who would wear a long-sleeved shirt in the summer. And when that wrist connected to a big, muscular arm, and then a wide chest, a thick neck, and finally a face I had seen countless times...

I'm sure my eyes were bugging out of my skull.

"Rip?" I might have gasped like I didn't know his name.

Those teal-colored eyes didn't shine, and his mouth didn't form the shape of a smile. He went right on looking at me as he stood there, tall as ever, broad as ever, and just too handsome as I sat there, getting stood up. "You here alone?" my boss asked.

Was... was I here alone?

I had lost my mind. Crap. I must have been that surprised I couldn't think straight. "Hi. Yeah." I smiled, confused as to why he was here. "I was supposed to have a date, but I don't think he's showing up," I babbled

He scratched at the side of his nose with the thumb of his free hand. Then he pulled the only other chair at the table out and wedged that huge body into it. His forearms went to the top, and those eyes came back to me.

Did he have a funny look on his face or was I imagining it?

"What are you doing here?" I asked, looking around—I wasn't sure for what, a beautiful woman with giant knockers coming toward us or something.

But no one was even paying the smallest bit of attention toward our table.

Rip had his focus on the group of men throwing darts as he replied, casually, "Getting a drink before I head home."

Well, that made sense.

Grabbing the tip of the straw in my drink, I fidgeted

with it as I kept an eye on the man on the other side of the table. "Do you live close to here?"

He was still looking at the group of men. "No."

So.... "Are you here by yourself?"

"Yeah."

Rip turned that perfectly profiled face over to me as he took a sip of his drink. Lazily, those dark eyebrows went up a little. "This is a shitty place to meet a stranger, baby girl."

See? There was that tiny bit of fondness again. "It's public."

"It's dark," he countered.

I blinked. "There's a lot of people here."

"A lot of people drunk or about to be."

"The bouncer is almost as big as you are," I told him.

That other eyebrow went up and he said slowly, "The parking lot is fucking dark."

I'd swear on my life that he smirked, and I ignored the little pleasure I felt at it. At being the one he would do something like that with. *But it didn't mean anything.* I couldn't forget that. He was my boss, and... he *was* fond of me. He was. I knew it. He'd shared his lunch with me. If that wasn't fondness, I didn't know what was. I knew how to share, and everyone knew that. But Rip? Rip had hidden his birthday cake so no one else could have any.

"Why'd you choose this joint to meet up at?"

It finally hit me right then that he was here watching me wait around for my date. Watching me get stood up. Fantastic.

Absolutely fantastic.

Why was he always around when my Luna Luck kicked in at its worst? Literally, my cousin trying to hurt me? He was there. My sister kicking me out of her apartment after a four-hour drive? He was there. Me screwing up at work? He was there. Me getting lied to by the same sister? He was there.

I wasn't sure I believed in signs, but if I did, those would have been major ones. At least that's what I'd figure.

I sighed, shoved those worries aside, and sipped out of my straw just to kill time before I told him the truth. "Because it isn't that far or that close to my house."

I didn't imagine that his look was pretty freaking close to him being amused. "Pretty smart."

I tapped my temple.

Wanting to change the subject, and taking advantage that *he'd* come over to sit with me, I leaned forward and put my chin on top of my opened palm. "Will you tell me where you live or is that too personal? I can put it in our box of secrets, if you want."

He moved his head from side to side before replying with two major streets I recognized being further up north.

"House, duplex, apartment, or complex?"

"Shithole."

I shouldn't have laughed... but I did, and when I caught him smirk-smiling, I knew he had said that on purpose. He was playing again. Why now? After all these years? I wondered, but did I care that much? No.

"It's shit. Just somewhere to sleep and eat," he explained, smoothly.

I took a quick sip of my Sprite. "How long is your lease?"

"I don't have one."

He lived in a shithole, but it wasn't a rental. I didn't want to say that didn't make sense, but... it didn't.

"It's not that kinda place." His mouth twitched, and he said out of the blue, "I got a mobile home on a lot."

"It's yours?"

Rip nodded.

"That's not a shithole then."

"Whatever you say," he said, keeping an eye on me. "It's shit, believe me, but it's a place to sleep, shower, and make food."

"That's all mine has too," I told him. "My place isn't amazing or anything, but it's mine, so I think it's pretty awesome."

The little smile that he gave me at my words egged me on to keep talking.

"You should have seen my house when I first bought it. It looked like it could have been the setting for a movie about a family who moved in and the children get possessed by poltergeists that had been in the house for the last two hundred years. My little sister, Lily, used to shove a chair under her closet door because it freaked her out. I slept with a lamp on for like the first year, but don't tell anyone I told you that. I always told them all they were overreacting, but it really was creepy in there. Half the time I expected something to grab my foot off the edge of the bed and pull me under."

Ripley's eyes lit up and my chest filled with pleasure. "That bad?"

He had no idea, and it made me laugh. "Yeah. I couldn't shower in peace without opening up an eye every two seconds just to make sure nothing was lurking in the bathroom with me."

Rip made this hoarse noise that *almost* sounded like a chuckle, and I wasn't about to let myself react. Nope.

"You can come over one day if you feel like maybe getting possessed or want to get an idea even though a lot of it looks pretty different now. There's still a lot I want to do to it though." Was he smiling? "But it's mine, and as long as

I pay the mortgage and the property taxes, no one can take it away but the ghosts and the little kids who live in the walls."

He chuckled at me. For real. And that dimple was kinda-sorta in full view when he asked, "How long you had it?"

"A year and a half. How long have you had your place?"

"Three years," he replied without thinking twice.

Since he'd come to Cooper's.

Then he decided to switch the conversation on me. "You were pretty young, getting your own place."

I took a sip of my Sprite. "I didn't want to live in an apartment longer than I needed to. We moved around a lot when I was a kid, and I hated it. So when I got a job, I set aside as much money as I could, even if it was only twenty bucks a week. My goal had been to buy something when I was twenty-two, but after my sisters came to live with me, there was always something else to spend money on. Mr. Cooper offered to cosign for me if I needed it, but I got the house for such a good price and had built up my credit over the years, so I didn't have to. They'd already done enough, cosigning my car loan for me when I was eighteen." I smiled at him and hesitated with what I wanted to say next. But screw it. "I know you two aren't exactly best friends, but Mr. C is the most generous man I've ever met. He's been better to me than my own dad, but I'm sure you've put that together by now."

Strangers had been better to me than my own dad, but nobody needed to bring that up.

Luckily, Rip didn't get all hot and bothered by my comment. He just looked thoughtful for a second before he seemed to shrug it off and aim that intense gaze on me again. Even his body seemed to lean forward as he asked, "Why you here, Luna?"

"Because my sister has bad radar for men and she set me up with someone who couldn't even find it in his heart to reschedule our date or at least tell her he wasn't interested anymore?"

His gaze didn't move away from me. Nothing about him did, and it made me wonder if that wasn't exactly the question he'd asked.

"Or are you asking why I'm trying to go on a date period?"

The look he gave me confirmed that had been his original question.

Well. "Because" was my brilliant freaking answer.

That got me an eyebrow raise. "Because?"

Why did I feel so uncomfortable all of a sudden? I lifted a shoulder. "Because. Why do you date?"

He blinked. "I don't."

It was my turn to blink. "What do you mean you don't date?"

"I don't date," he confirmed.

I stared. "Why?"

Those teal eyes were totally centered on me. "Because I don't know. Never wanted to. Didn't want to be tied down. Didn't like anybody enough, you choose," he replied easily, like it was a fact. And maybe it was for him.

I couldn't help myself, especially not when he was being so open. I figured he'd turn this around on me sooner or later, I knew how persistent he could be, but I was going to milk this as long as he was willing. "You've never had a girlfriend?"

That got me a nostril flaring. "No."

"*Never?*"

He gave me one of his "duh" looks. "No."

I made a face that had him doing that low barely a chuckle thing.

"Have I seen the same woman a few times? Yeah…"

That wasn't jealousy or anything that made my stomach tense.

"But a fucking old lady? A girlfriend? Like we're friends and talk about shit and go over to spend time with each other? Nah." He shook his head. "Nah."

Sex. He was trying to tell me the only interest in women he had was only if it was sex-related. I couldn't say that it didn't leave a weird feeling in my gut, but… it explained some things. I wasn't going to worry about that bitter thing in my stomach at the idea of him having sex with people.

It wasn't like I was a virgin.

But his comment and his look helped me understand why I needed to settle my expectations for what they were.

He was here, talking to me, and he could be kind and nice and caring when he wanted to be, but that was it. It wasn't like that should be a surprise or anything. If I looked at it a certain way, maybe it would actually make me feel nice that he saw me in a different light… in a way.

I guessed.

"Why you here, Luna?" he asked again, going back to the topic of me a lot sooner than I had hoped.

I shoved his previous words aside and focused. "Because I'd like to meet somebody to be my friend and spend time with me." I turned his words around on him.

He rubbed his fingers against his glass. "Why don't you already have somebody?"

Why?

"Thought you were dating somebody when we first met," he kept going.

Oh… "We had already broken up by then, but… you

know, things just ended. He wanted something that I didn't, and we broke up," I told him, knowing it was coming off as mysterious, but hoping he wouldn't hook onto the bait.

He was nosey enough that he did, and I couldn't help but feel his surprise. "What he want?"

I had walked right into that, hadn't I? I fidgeted with my straw again. "Between us?"

He nodded.

"A threesome."

Nothing on his features registered surprise.

"With his ex-wife," I finished, giving him a smile and kind of raising a shoulder. I was over it. Now it just made me laugh.

Rip blinked, took a drink, and then took his time with his next question, making an almost stunned face. "Say that again."

I finally did laugh. "He wanted us to have a threesome with his ex-wife. Apparently that's something he did sometimes with other people, even after they divorced, but I had no idea until he asked."

That big body leaned back in his chair, but that funny face didn't go anywhere. "He broke up with you over it?"

I fiddled with the straw again, looking down into the Sprite before raising my gaze back to him. "I broke up with him over it. He said he was sorry and that he shouldn't have asked, but it was too late. It hurt my feelings, and I couldn't get over it. I mean, I don't think I was being overly dramatic, but it's a little weird that a man still has sex with his ex-wife. They had two daughters together. You know?

"He swore it wasn't a big deal if we didn't, that they were over for a reason and that it didn't mean anything, it was just sex, he'd said. But back then, he'd been the only one I'd ever..." Crap. He didn't need to know where the rest of that had been going. Did he? Nope. "He was really nice, and he treated me really well, and I know he cared about me, but in that question... he broke my trust, and I knew I would never be able to get over it. What, he'd bring up having a threesome with her again later on? Or get bored with me and then find someone else to suggest? I don't think so. So I broke up with him, and that was that."

That story stung a lot less this time than it had every other time in the past I had retold it.

He hadn't broken my heart, but he had my trust.

I had been sad for about two days, and then I got over it. I didn't let people take too much of my time away, and that's what mourning and whimpering were. Time and energy wasted.

Maybe some people would be able to have a threesome... maybe I could have if we hadn't been in a relationship and he hadn't been the same man I had lost my virginity to... but I was pretty sure that there was something in me that wouldn't let me ever be in that kind of relationship.

I'd had to share so much in my life. I thought that if I wanted to be selfish every once in a while, there was nothing wrong with that.

I shrugged again. "And right after him, I saw this one guy for a few weeks... kind of like a rebound, I guess... and that's been it, except for a couple of dates here and there every few months, but none of them ever worked out." I plastered a smile on. "But now that Lily is gone, everyone talked me into giving it another try. So I'm here, getting stood up. Yay."

Rip's nostrils flared again, and one of those thick fingers went to the rim of his glass, circling it while his eyes strayed to mine. "But why are you here, baby girl?"

Why was I here?

That wasn't a loaded question.

I glanced at the group of men still trying to play darts. "I'm happy, but I know people who are even happier because of the people in their lives, you know? I've always liked seeing elderly couples walking around, holding hands and stuff; I want the same thing, or at least I want to try for it. I want a partner. I want someone I can rely on. Someone to snuggle with would be nice. I like snuggling.

"And if I have to meet a bunch of guys and sit at a bar getting stood up a few times until I find one who makes me feel... happier than I am by myself, then it'll be worth it someday." I smiled at him to make the conversation not seem as heavy as it felt for me.

But it was all the truth. I just... wanted somebody. Not just anyone, but someone special. A best friend and a lover. A partner. A *life* partner. I was fine being alone, but I didn't want to be lonely, and there was a clear difference.

Rip watched me, and I mean, he really watched me right then. Whether he was trying to figure out if I'd lost my mind or if I was something to be pitied, I had no idea.

Maybe I should have kept my mouth shut. "Anyway, I should probably get going."

That big, beautiful man leaned forward in his chair, his eyes sweeping over my face and the hair that had gotten pretty wavy because of the humidity. I had almost forgotten I'd put a silver glitter clip into it that morning to keep it out of my face. "You're gonna leave me here alone?"

"You really want me to keep you company?"

His response was a long, long look.

For some reason, it made me feel oddly vulnerable. He thought I was pathetic. I knew it. But pathetic or not, well, he was kind of hinting he wanted me to keep him company. "I can stay if you want."

He didn't say he wanted me to, but... he just kept right on looking at me.

So I took it as a yes. "Okay, I'll stay."

It was the right answer.

He took a sip of his drink. "Good."

Well, it looked like I was staying a little longer now. With our conversation still nipping at the back of my head, I asked him again, "So, you've really *never* had a girlfriend? Not in forty-one years?"

"Nope."

"Not even in high school?"

He shook his head.

"Not *once?*"

"Nope." He gave me this face that almost seemed like a challenge. Like a dare. "I've got two numbers on my phone that don't belong to somebody who's got a dick. One's the lady that cleans my place once a week..."

"Who's the other?" I asked, trying to ignore the edge of jealousy waiting around the corner of his answer.

That got me another snicker. "You, who the hell else?"

"Me?" I leaned forward then. "Since when? You've never called my cell."

"Since always. Just 'cause I don't call you doesn't mean I don't have it."

I couldn't help raising my hands up to my heart and settling them there, this huge smile coming over my face. "Does this mean... Boss, are we friends? Outside of work, of course."

His face went totally serious for a moment before he tossed his head back and *laughed*. "Get the fuck outta here, Luna. Christ."

We were. We were so totally friends. He was my boss too, but that didn't mean we couldn't be friends when we weren't at the shop. Or during lunch. Or when my life tried to fall apart on me a little.

Me and Rip.

Friends.

I'd take it. I'd take it every day of the year, forever.

CHAPTER NINETEEN

"You're dead," I laughed at Miguel as we walked toward the booth.

"Why do you think I brought the car with me?" he asked.

"She's going to kill you either way. I'm still surprised she didn't do it on her birthday," I confirmed, referring to his wife's car at first. We had just spent the last ten minutes looking it over and setting up a plan for fixing it. Apparently, he'd backed his car into hers that morning, and he hadn't had the guts to tell her, so he made up a lie and drove hers to work today so that we could repair it without her finding out.

The thing was, we both knew she was going to find out anyway. Now or later.

"I know, but if I buy her some flowers and some *conchas* from the bakery by our house, I think I can get her to take it easy on me," he stated with a laugh.

I shook my head just as we stopped in front of the door to the booth, and he reached forward to open it for me. "I'll call my guy right now since I have the code for the color, and he should have it. It's a standard stock color. I might be able to go pick it up for you on my lunch break."

I had been expecting to see Jason in the room when I walked in, but I wasn't expecting to see the new guy too. Between the two of them, they were carrying a panel into the booth. Jason, to no surprise, pretended like he didn't see us walk in.

Little jerk.

He'd been surprisingly tame lately—at least with his words, eye rolls, and griping—but he couldn't hide the fact that I could sense he still wanted to do those things. I knew I had Rip to thank for that.

"You're an angel, Luna," Miguel said, giving my head a pat, since that was the way all the guys showed me affection. Like I was a puppy. A very loved puppy. I'd take it.

I smiled at him. "I know."

"Tell me if you can get the paint pen. I was going to skip my lunch and buff out the scratches." The older man did something that made me feel like he was fluttering his eyelashes. "Can you do the paint?"

I grinned at him. "You know I will."

He patted my head again. "An angel."

"I'm just your friend, and I don't want you to die."

Miguel laughed. "Thanks, Luna. I owe you one."

I shrugged him off. "You're welcome. Let me call and find the pen first, and I'll come bother you when I get an answer. If he doesn't have it, the dealership should. I'll find it somewhere."

Miguel started to back out of the room with a grin on his face, like he thought he was getting away with his accident. "I love you more than my own sister," he called out.

I laughed. "I'm gonna tell her you said that next time I see her."

"I'll tell her you're drunk," he called back before opening the door and sliding back out of my room.

I snorted as I turned around and headed toward the booth to see what exactly was happening. Inside, Jason and Ashton were setting the panel they had been moving onto some old tubs we used to prop things up. "Need help?" I asked.

The new guy grinned up at me. "No."

While the other pain in the ass muttered, "Not anymore."

And that's what I got for jumping the gun and thinking he'd been behaving better.

I just ignored him.

"How's your day going?" Ashton asked right as they set the panel down.

It was only nine in the morning, but I thought it was nice of him to ask. "It's great so far. How's yours?"

"Good," he replied, brushing his hands on his pants.

"My day is going great too," Jason mumbled.

I didn't even bother giving him a glance. "You liking the shop so far?"

"Yeah," he agreed, in the middle of shooting the human wart a confused look for his little comments. "It's great."

I smiled. "Thank you for helping Jason," I said like he was my child who needed assistance.

Which I guess in a way he kind of was. He was my little shit, spoiled kid that I was still trying to mold into a decent person.

You know, without talking to him more than I needed to.

And he was twenty years old instead of an impressionable three.

"Sure," the new guy said.

I'd swear on my life that Jason snickered as he turned around and left the booth. I really just wanted to smack him sometimes.

"Do you know any good places to eat around here?"

"Yeah. There's a food truck about a block down with really good burgers, but I thought I saw you with a bag from there already. There's also a Mexican place about four blocks down that a lot of us really like; it's a little hole in the wall place, but it's great. If you go between eleven and one, there are lunch specials. And two blocks away, there's a barbecue place that's pretty good."

He shifted on his feet. "The Mexican place is your favorite?"

"Yeah. I don't go there that often, but it's the best around here."

"You doing anything for lunch?"

"She's gonna be busy," a deep male voice answered from somewhere behind me.

A deep male voice that could have belonged to only one person.

As I looked over my shoulder, sure enough, Rip was there, standing at the entrance into the booth with those giant biceps crossed over his chest and a bland, bland look on his face.

I was going to be busy? Since when? I had just talked to him that morning when I brought down his coffee, and we hadn't talked about any kind of projects he needed me for.

But he had given me that smirk I liked and asked, "Did you fuck up your lunch?"

And I had smirked back at him, remembering the two hours we had spent at the bar on Friday and mocked him with, "It's only a little burned, thank you."

He had let that smirk stay on his face as he shook his head and went back to work.

And that had been that.

More than anything before. And maybe I didn't understand why he was being, at times, so much friendlier, but I wasn't going to complain.

So, when Rip said I was going to be busy, all I could do was stand there and wonder what I was going to be busy doing.

Ashton was a good sport because he smiled at me and said, "That's all right. Maybe tomorrow."

Over my shoulder, Rip spoke up again. "Luna's gonna be busy tomorrow too."

Uh.

I saw Ashton make a funny face before he shrugged, easily, and said, "All right. I should get back to work, but I'll come back later and see if you need more help."

I didn't have the heart to tell him that if I did need help, he would be the last person I would ask. I would always bother the guys who had been here longer first. But it was nice of him to offer.

And nice to invite me to eat, if that's what he'd been about to do.

Even if I had a feeling that maybe it wasn't as friendly as I thought it would be. Especially not because of that blush.

I thought he was cute, but that was the beginning and the end of that. Hector at the paint store was one of the hottest guys I had ever seen in my life, and that didn't mean I wanted to date him. My eyes liked him. My brain liked him. But my heart wasn't in it in that way.

"See ya, Luna," Ashton said. Walking right by our boss, he dipped his chin toward him. "Rip."

I blinked and followed Ashton on the way out. The second I couldn't see him any longer, I looked back at Rip, who had moved his gaze back toward me by then. "What am I busy doing at lunch?" I asked. "Did you want to go pick out some more paint? Because I thought you were still working on the GTO and the SS."

"No," he answered, not moving an inch, but instead, just watching me. "I brought you fucking lunch."

He brought me—*did he just say lunch?*

"There's a thing in the fridge with your name on it," Rip kept going, watching me steadily. "I could use your help later if you've got time."

All I heard was something about him needing my help if I had time, but what I really focused on was the container in the fridge with my name on it.

"Come get me if you do," he said, taking a step back like he hadn't just surprised the crap out of me.

But I could still get a few thoughts together, at least enough to call out, "What am I going to be doing tomorrow?"

He was still walking backward as he told me, "I'm bringing you lunch tomorrow too."

What was happening?

What was happening?

"You don't have to bribe me to be your friend! I've been waiting for this for years, Rip," I hollered after him, ignoring the way my stomach had just felt like we'd started a descent from a steep roller-coaster ride.

I'd swear I heard a chuckle as he answered, "Get to fucking work and come get me if you've got time to help me out."

We were friends.

We *were*.

Favor or not, you didn't bring someone food who you weren't fond of.

I really didn't want to smile, but I couldn't freaking help it as he walked back out of the room. I was still smiling as Jason went to stand exactly where Rip had just been and asked, "If you're done flirting, can I get started on those panels?"

That wiped the expression right off my face. "Say something like that to me one more time, Jason, and I will go rat on you, all right?"

The younger guy sneered, apparently back to freaking normal. "What I do with my fucking life is none of your business."

So that's where we were going today. "What are you talking about? I'm not bringing up what you do with your life, Jason. You said something rude, that's what I'm talking about."

"I'm talking about you not liking me and now *he* doesn't like me either," he tried to argue.

It was my turn to sneer at him. "If he doesn't like you, it's not because of anything I've said to him. Maybe it's because you hung up on him that one time you called me, buddy, or you doing things you had no business doing. Have you thought about that?"

His mouth pinched, and he rushed out, "I didn't hang up on him."

I freaking knew he was going to lie about that. I hated to call people dumb, but he really was dumb. I didn't feel like arguing with him over it. What I did instead was shrug at him. "I know you know why I don't like you—and I'm sorry for saying that because I've never said that to anyone before, but you have never been nice to me. But I've never gone out of my way to be mean to you because of it. I don't have to like you to work with you, but I wouldn't whisper about things you did two years ago to make Rip not like you."

"Look, you don't even know what was happening between me and Kyra."

I raised up both my hands between us and said, "I don't care. You don't have to explain anything to me." Even if it made perfect sense, I still wouldn't like him. "I wouldn't like anyone who made my little sister cry, for whatever reason."

"I'm not an asshole," he tried to claim.

I stayed quiet.

"*I'm not—*"

My phone ringing from my desk had me shaking my head as I walked way around him and out onto the floor. "Start on the panel, Jason."

He cursed, not loudly enough for me to hear clearly, but I ignored him and pulled my keys out to unlock my desk and pull out my still ringing phone, hitting the Answer button.

That was where I screwed up.

I was so riled up by Jason that I didn't look at the screen first before I hit answer.

"Hello?"

I heard the "Don't hang up" just as I was turning back around to make sure Jason's annoying butt wasn't flipping me off behind my back. "Luna, don't you fucking hang up," a semi-familiar male voice spat on the other end.

And maybe my brain didn't automatically recognize it, but my instincts did.

It was my dad.

"I already told you not to call me," I whispered into the receiver as I made sure Jason wasn't close by.

"You heard from Thea?"

Had I heard from Thea?

I pulled the phone away from my face and ended the call.

Fisting my free hand, I didn't hesitate dialing my sister's number and trying to call her. Again. Like I hadn't already called her every single day since the first time this man had contacted me.

I shouldn't have been surprised when she didn't answer, but I was.

Screw it.

I dialed Kyra's number and fortunately at least she did.

"Luna-face, what's up?" my middle sister answered.

"Your sister's what's up. Have you talked to Thea?" I asked her straight out, hearing the tremble in my voice. Because, *this again? Dad calling again?* I didn't need this. I didn't want it.

"Yesterday actually," she replied a little uneasily. Maybe she heard the shakiness in my tone. "Why?"

Did I want to tell her about our dad? Hell. I had no choice, did I? "Dad just called me."

There was a pause and then, "Why?"

"He was asking about Thea, Kyra. He told me to tell her to quit her job."

There was another pause. "Ah..."

Something hard hit me in the chest.

"I know that she had talked to him..."

I held my breath.

"Luna?" she said a little too sweetly, her voice a little too high.

"Yeah?" I muttered, trying to tell myself to calm down. To not get riled up. To not get mad.

I was going to be patient. I was going to be calm. What-ever it was wouldn't be the end of life.

"Don't get mad," was what she decided to start with,

and of course my body decided to react the exact opposite way of what she was asking. My blood pressure was already starting to climb. "We both thought it was a bad idea if we told you about the calls."

They had both been keeping it from me.

Both of them.

That's what she was trying to hint.

Two of my sisters had been hiding this from me.

I must have sucked in a breath or *something* because Kyra made a sound that sounded strangely like a gulp. "Oh, Luna. I promised her I wouldn't say anything about her job. But about Dad... Don't be mad. It's no big deal. He calls her sometimes and they talk. I've talked to him a couple of times—"

What?

And I stopped listening. I stopped listening because my ears were buzzing, and genuine freaking fury and hurt like I didn't think I was capable of feeling filled my chest.

Kyra said something about how it had been going on for *only a year or two.*

She said something else about how they both loved me and how it had nothing to do with me.

Told me not to worry about whatever it was that Thea was doing for work that even our dad disapproved of.

It had nothing to do with me.

I wouldn't say it was fury that stole the words from my soul. Wouldn't say it was anger that made my heart break even further. But I lost something then. Something I wasn't sure I could or would ever be able to put into words.

Somehow though, I managed to ask the one other question that had been eating away at me lately. "Kyra, what else is she hiding from me?"

The silence was a better response than any of the words she might have used could or would ever be.

Even though a part of me didn't want to ask and was honestly scared to pry... I couldn't help myself. I was tired of the secrets. Tired of so much stuff I wasn't ready to think about everything. "Did she tell you her place got broken into? Because I didn't even know she moved, and if she needs help, you all should know I will always help you. I just want to know what's going on, okay?"

What I got was another dose of a pause.

Another response that said that the trust I thought was between us was just in my imagination, and her next words changed everything between us for the rest of our lives.

"I'll tell her you called and that she needs to call you back," Kyra went on, ignoring my question, but the only thing I was aware of was hanging up eventually. Of standing there, numb and pretty much shattered by the knowledge they had gone behind my back to talk to someone who had treated me worse than trash. Someone who would have let them starve if it hadn't been for me. Someone who had never washed a single load of their clothes ever in their lives. Someone who had never, ever bought them a single birthday present or Christmas present. Who had never supported them in school or much less encouraged them to go to college.

And if I would have been the kind of person who smashed their phone, I would have done it.

What I did instead was take a deep breath that included that part of me that I had lost, then turn around and kick an empty five-gallon bucket across the room.

I made a decision right then, as I pulled at the bracelet of unicorns at my wrist. I wasn't going to let my dad ruin this day for me. Not when he had already ruined my relationship with my sisters in the two shortest phone calls of my life.

* * *

I TOLD myself that I wasn't in a bad mood even as I slammed the door closed to my car.

I wasn't mad.

I wasn't.

Not even a little.

Nope, not me.

But I must have been the only person to believe that because even Hector asked me what was wrong.

Nothing was wrong, I had told him.

It was just that two of my sisters were talking to the one man in this world who I hated. That the two girls I helped as much as I could with their college expenses had gone behind my back to do something that they knew would wound me. That they had kept it to themselves *so that I wouldn't get mad.*

No. I wasn't mad over that at all. Not even Hector's niece's lollipop took the edge off my anger.

So it was because of that, that I wasn't paying even a little bit of attention as I walked toward the building, holding the paint pen for Miguel's wife's car in one hand and clutching my purse in the other.

And it was because I wasn't paying attention that when someone hollered, "Hey!" I froze.

Turning in the direction of where the voice was coming from, I spotted a man standing just on the other side of the fence, right by a lowered red pickup truck. Forty-ish with a handful of tattoos spotted across one arm, I blinked and said, "Hey."

The man grinned. "Can you do me a solid?"

I took a step forward. I had no reason to be mad at him or take it out on him. "Depends on what it is."

His grin spread wider. "Can you get, ah, Ripley out here?"

I dropped my pleasant expression. "Who?"

"Ripley," the man repeated, that grin going nowhere.

Never, not once, had Rip ever had anyone come over. Well, except for that one guy who I had caught him talking to, but... I hadn't gotten a good look at the man. Was this one standing in front of me the same one as before?

I didn't know, but if it wasn't...

"I don't know a Ripley," I told him quickly.

His grin was this gap-toothed thing that magically got even bigger. "All right. Well, my name's Gio, and I'll be sitting out here for another—" He glanced at his watch. "—twenty minutes." He winked.

I raised both my eyebrows. "Nice to meet you, Gio."

He smiled and said, "Nice to meet you too, Luna."

I was pulling open the door of the shop when I realized what exactly he'd said.

He'd called me by my name. I didn't wear coveralls with my name on them, and even if I did, I wouldn't have left the shop with them on. I was too paranoid for that.

How did he know my name?

Inside, I looked around the main floor for the biggest man at the shop but didn't see anyone with the height or the right hair color. I didn't need to look at my watch to know that I had twenty minutes to eat—eat whatever Rip had brought me—before I needed to get back to work. Or at least, should get back to work. I worked so much overtime it didn't matter if I took another fifteen minutes, but as lonely and quiet as my home was, now that was where I would rather be.

Up the stairs, I heard two voices coming from the break room. Sure enough, Ashton was in there talking to one of the other guys, and right at the end of the table, sitting there quietly by himself, looking through a magazine, was Rip.

I smiled at the other two guys and watched as Rip lifted his head, watching me in return.

I kept the smile on my face as I opened the refrigerator and immediately found a glass container sitting on the top shelf with my name scrawled on a Post-it. Through the side, I could see what looked like noodles, beef, and vegetables— exactly what my lo mein should have looked like when I had made it.

Grabbing one of the plastic forks from a drawer, I pulled out the seat right beside Rip and took it. Popping the top off the container, I lowered my voice as quietly as I could, knocked my knee to the side until it hit Rip's, and whispered, "There's someone named Gio outside asking for you. I told him you didn't work here, but he said he was going to wait out there for another twenty minutes five minutes ago."

I could feel Rip freeze.

Then I saw him out of my peripheral vision lift his head and give me a funny expression that had his cheek going up that millimeter. "You told him I don't work here?"

I picked up my fork and speared a piece of beef with it before whispering, "Yup."

You couldn't trust anybody these days, hello. Not even your own—*Stop.*

Rip shook his head before he shoved his chair back and got to his feet. I flashed him a closed-mouth smile that I was pretty sure he recognized as not being totally authentic.

But he lifted his hand up, and before I could even blink, his fingers pinched a loose strand of hair off my cheek and tucked it behind my ear, the pad rubbing against the sensitive skin right behind it.

And just that quickly, his hand dropped. "Watch my food for me, yeah?" he asked.

Had he just tucked my hair behind my ear or was my anger making me delusional?

I managed to get out a nod before he disappeared through the door. I only sat there for maybe five seconds staring after him before I turned my attention back down to my food and stuck a piece of beef in my mouth.

It was just as delicious as the chicken last week had been.

CHAPTER TWENTY

I KNEW I'D MADE A MISTAKE WHEN THE GUY CALLED ME "sweetie" twice in a row.

Because I was pretty sure the man I was on a date with couldn't remember my name.

If I was going to be honest with myself, the pool of pity and hurt and anger that I had been swimming in for the last few days didn't help anything either. As much as I told myself to suck it up and handle what I had learned about my sisters—as much as I told myself to forgive them—I hadn't. Not yet. I hadn't even been able to tell Lenny about any of it, much less Lily. I was so... just... on edge. I hadn't said a word to anyone over it.

So that entire situation didn't help anything at all.

It didn't change a single thing either, which was why I hadn't cancelled the date I had been set up on.

Like a whole lot of things in my life, it was turning out to be a giant mistake. A giant freaking mistake.

That knowledge only settled even more in my head when my date kept glancing around the round table we were sitting at, and asked, "You sure you're not married?"

I only barely held back a frown. "Yes." I paused. "Why?"

He was taller than me, with dark black hair and a smirk I had thought was okay when I saw it on my phone—Lydia had sent me a sneaky picture of him. Apparently, he was a physical therapist at the same clinic that she worked at. You would have figured that by making his living dealing with people, he would have been warm, but he was just kind of... aggressive and not charming at all.

He'd tried to kiss my cheek the instant he'd come over, and I wasn't about that life. I liked making people feel comfortable and welcomed, but I didn't want some stranger putting his saliva on me. If we had been friends, that would have been a different story.

But this guy and I were not.

"Some guy has been staring over here like he wants to kill somebody for the last thirty minutes," my date answered, still flicking his gaze around Mickey's.

"I'm not married," I confirmed, not bothering to tell him that I hadn't had a boyfriend in years either, so the chances of me having a jealous ex stalking me were slim to none.

The man's eyes locked on something over my shoulder. "You sure?" he asked for confirmation again, shifting around in his seat. Squirming, he was squirming.

"Yeah." I almost turned completely around to see who he was talking about but decided not to.

We were only thirty minutes into this date, and I was about ready to get home.

If I was going to be honest with myself, I'd been ready to get home before I'd even left it.

"Huh," the guy hummed before tearing his gaze back to my direction. "What were we talking about before?"

That confirmed it. He had no clue what my name

was. That was for sure. "You were telling me about your job," I responded, hearing the enthusiasm in my voice. Not.

He shrugged. "Oh. Nothin' much to tell. That was it. Lydia said you... paint?"

"Yeah."

"Like art?"

I knew for a fact I had told him specifically what kind of painting I did fifteen minutes ago when he'd first asked me this exact same question. I decided to spell it out for him. "No. Cars. Trucks. Automobiles."

He blinked. "No shit?"

"Yeah," I confirmed, watching his face as he got really thoughtful. He was attractive, but there was something about him that was just....

"Like you paint cars a different color?" he asked.

There was more to it than that but... "Yeah."

He was still squirming. "Isn't that—"

I knew exactly where this crap was going.

"—you know, more of a man's job?"

"No," I told him patiently. "I do it too, and I'm not a man."

I should have stayed home. Being alone was better than being here with a man who didn't know what my name was.

"Why?" he asked all of a sudden.

I finally couldn't suppress my frown. "Why what?"

"Isn't there something else you can do?"

I narrowed my eyes. "I like it. I'm good at it. Why would I do something else?"

This jerk had the nerve to *laugh*.

I bit the inside of my cheek and grabbed the Sprite between us, taking a long sip and wondering how the hell I had gotten myself into this position. Why? Why were my dates just such major fails? Was everything in my life destined to—

Stop.

I was fine. I was loved. I had a good job. I had everything and more. Patience. Patience. I was going to choose patience.

"You the only girl where you work?" he asked, back to looking around, and I guess not letting this topic go.

I raised my eyebrow at him as I said, "Uh-huh."

The face he made was like *see?* Like he thought he was making a point.

But he didn't know the only point he was making was that he was a big douchebag who might be a bit sexist.

"I don't think I could let my girl work with a bunch of horny guys," he said, still giving me that patronizing expression.

I snickered. "Why would they be horny?"

"Because."

What an imbecile. "Yeah, I don't work with any guys that have constant boners. I don't know what kind of guys you work with, but mine... never. And if they do, they don't go around whipping them out for me to look at."

The dead-eyed glare he gave me had me expecting the worst, and his next comment didn't surprise me. "Lydia said you were really nice... something wrong with you?"

I shook my head and couldn't help but raise my hands up to my face and laugh. "Yeah, I think maybe this is over. Can we agree on that?"

I should have been thankful he responded with "I think you're right" almost immediately.

But instead, I was relieved and still numb.

I hadn't exactly been looking forward to tonight, but I had expected... something better than this. I would have rather gotten stood up than this. I needed to just get home, call Lily, and let her cheer me up.

Neither one of us said much as I hailed the waitress and she brought us our check, splitting it Dutch when he didn't offer to pay for my one and only drink, because that's what kind of date it had been.

The topping on the sundae was the man getting up and leaving with a "Yeah, see ya."

And by the time I stood up and turned around, I forgot to look around at whoever he'd been talking about that was staring over.

I didn't care.

There was never a big guy or a small guy or any kind of guy there for me either, and it made my heart hurt just a little. I was just feeling pretty darn sorry for myself, and that didn't help anything.

I wasn't about to give up on dating even though this wasn't exactly going so well, but what did I expect? To find a soul mate in two dates? In weeks? Months?

Lily liked to watch this show on TV about people who were set up in arranged marriages, and I had never really thought it was that weird, contrary to her beliefs that she could never marry a total stranger. But now... I could definitely see the appeal in it. What was wrong with someone who wanted to be in a relationship? Someone who cared about you and wanted the best for you, wanted to have a family with you. What was a relationship if there wasn't respect in it?

I wanted someone who wanted to be with me, and not just as a booty call.

In the meantime, I had a nice comfy bed at home I could go to bed early in.

* * *

My spidey senses went off the second I parked my car in my driveway.

For one, I knew I'd left the porch lights on. I was paranoid about someone hiding in the dark and attacking me from the bushes. I wouldn't play around with my safety.

Two, my front door being wide open, like a gaping maw in the dark, would confirm that something wasn't normal. Under no circumstance would I have left the door open. I was known for getting back out of my car and checking the front door if I couldn't clearly remember tugging on the handle after locking it.

And third... if the lights I knew hadn't been left off and the door being wide open hadn't been enough, bits and pieces of broken wooden frame being all over the porch would have confirmed that someone had broken into my place. Through the front door.

Someone had broken into my place.

Someone had broken into my place.

Shit.

SHIT.

Pressing my fingertips over my brow bone, something ugly and warm and... just horrible... instantly filled my chest. And my throat. And my mouth. And the urge to throw up blew up in my throat and—

Think, Luna.

Trying to calm that beast in my body, I pulled my phone out of my purse, searched for the number to the police department, and hit the call icon.

Then I ignored how bad my hand was shaking and how bad I wanted to throw up and how worried I was at the fact that someone had broken into my house. It wasn't a bad neighborhood. It was quiet. If the house had been fully remodeled when I'd moved in, it would have easily been four times the price I had gotten it. Even the realtor had told me I had scored it as a foreclosure.

It had been old, but steady.

While I would have been perfectly happy with any style of house, the instant Lenny had driven me by the dilapidated bungalow in desperate need of a paint job and a remodel to bring it up to this century, I had fallen in love.

And now, someone had gone into the one and only place that had only ever been mine. They might have stolen things I'd worked my ass off for. They might have gone through my drawers and personal things.

Don't cry. Your insurance should cover everything. It was just stuff.

You're happy. Healthy. You're safe. You're alive. You still have a job.

It's just stuff. It's just stuff. *It doesn't matter.*

But one glance at the kicked-in door made all the hairs on my back stand up.

A door can be fixed. An alarm can be set. A deadbolt put on.

"Thank you for calling the Houston—"

It took about twenty minutes to talk to the police department and let them know what had happened.

Stay there, they had said.

But all I had to do was look up at that door....

I shivered. Then I shivered some more as I stood there, staring into the darkened house....

Another wracking shiver down my spine had me reaching for my phone. Had me dialing the number in my phone. There was one ring before the voice mail picked up. *"This is Allen Cooper of Cooper's—"*

I had forgotten he turned off his phone while he slept.

Okay. All right.

Focus, Luna.

I took a breath and dialed another number. It rang. It kept ringing and ringing and ringing, until, *"The voice mail box you have reached is full—"*

Lenny was asleep too. Okay. That was fine. I could do this. I could—

Someone had broken into my house. Someone might have taken my things. Gone through my laundry. Been in the room I slept in. Someone had kicked in my door. Someone could do it again... this mean, evil voice in my head whispered, making me swallow as I stared at the front door.

I'd locked it without a shadow of a doubt. The same lock I had always put on every night. The lock that was supposed to keep people out, supposed to keep me safe.

Tears swelled up in my eyes all of a sudden, stinging, uncomfortable, shitty tears that made me glad I was all alone. I was a sucker. I was a sucker with terrible luck. I should have been used to it. You'd figure I would be.

But I'd be fine. I would. I'd be all right. Things could be worse.

Taking a breath through my nose, I glanced back toward the wide-open door leading into the place I had felt so safe at for so long. I didn't let myself cry.

But if a couple of tears slipped out of my eyes, I sucked in a breath and pretended they hadn't.

I stood there and just stared at the door, telling myself to go in. What were the chances there was someone inside?

Someone inside. How could there have been someone in my house? What if I'd been in there too?

Crouching down, I just stayed there, staring at the dark

hole. The police would get here when they got here. I wasn't going to go inside. Not alone.

My hands went up to my cheeks without thinking, wiping at my face slowly. I set my hand on my chest and for some reason thought about the necklace I had put on Rip. He still hadn't given it back. Just as quickly as that thought came into my head, it slipped right back out as I focused on the front of my house again.

Everything would be fine.

It would.

CHAPTER TWENTY-ONE

I WASN'T AT ALL SURPRISED WHEN I GOT ZERO SLEEP
that night.

I figured it wasn't unheard of when the only thing
keeping your front door closed was a console table you had
dragged over. If I'd had anything heavier that I could have
pushed on my own, I would have. But there was only so
much I could do alone, and I didn't have that much
furniture.

So, I hadn't slept. I'd been too paranoid, lying in bed
and listening to make sure no one pushed the door open.
When I wasn't worried about that, I laid there thinking
about my sisters talking to my dad.

It hadn't exactly been the greatest night of my life.

So when the alarm clock went off, just as I had barely
started to sort of doze off, I had *almost* cried. *Almost.*

*Why did things like this always have to happen to me?
Why? Why couldn't I catch a break every once in a while?*

I knew I was being dramatic. I knew there were worse
things in the world than having your home broken into and
your things stolen and broken. At least I had a place to call

home. At least I had insurance. But... it all still felt like a donkey kick to my freaking soul.

You get one step ahead and then have to take five back. That was life sometimes, wasn't it? For everyone, not just me.

I was just sulking, and I didn't know what to do with myself or how to wear it right.

I didn't cry as I dragged myself off my damaged mattress —because they had even messed with that. I hadn't even had the heart to fix the fitted sheet so it would serve as a barrier between me and the bed that had been the first bed I had ever bought, so I'd been all about splurging a little. And now, it was seriously injured. Someone had taken a knife to it, dragging that blade from one end to the other.

Because some asshole had broken into my house and torn it up for no reason.

Did I look like I was rich? Or some spy with secrets I had stitched into the mattress? It just seemed so... senseless. Even the cops had agreed. They had gone as far as to ask if there was anyone who could be upset with me.

I told them, no, but I knew there were. Just not anyone I figured would be upset enough to do something like this. Trip me? Slash a tire? Kick me while I was down? Yeah.

But break into my house? I wasn't that bad of a person— at least I didn't think so.

Getting dressed and ready for the day took longer than it should have, and when I went to check the door and couldn't because it had been kicked in, I'd almost cried again. I did what I could to secure it from the inside, and then snuck around to the back door and went out the through the yard. I headed to work, trying so hard to focus on driving and not what was waiting for me back home and... failing.

My heart, and every part of my body, felt heavy as I walked into CCC. I put my things in the desk, then headed up the stairs to make the coffee I didn't really feel like drinking. If I was going to be honest, I didn't really feel like doing anything. Sure as hell not working. But I knew I was going to need money and the only way to get it was by going to work. Even if only for a few hours. A small paycheck was better than no paycheck.

I made coffee and was relieved there wasn't any arguing in the room next door. When I heard noises coming from downstairs, I sighed and prepared the other mug of coffee, because no matter how crappy I felt, not making Rip his would be like... not putting on deodorant—even if I was pretty sure I might have forgotten to put on deodorant that morning once I thought about it.

I wasn't going to cry.

Losing my things wasn't a big deal because at least I was okay.

I went down the stairs, making faces so I wouldn't lose it. I could make it through the day. I would. During my lunch break, I could call around to some handymen and see if any of them could go by the house once I got off work and fix the door for me. I was pretty sure there were a decent number of projects on the schedule, but Mr. Cooper would let me leave once I told him. I knew he would.

I swallowed and would have pinched the tip of my nose if I'd had a free hand.

Down on the main floor, I looked around and found Rip standing by one of the tool chests, opening and closing drawers as he looked for something. Thankfully. Maybe I could get away with making it back to my room without him glancing at me. That happened often enough, didn't it?

I needed to quit. What had I told myself about things

out of my control? There was no reason to get hung up on them.

But my luck decided to remind me it was never that great.

Because I had barely set the mug down when Rip muttered, "Thanks, Luna," then he happened to flick his gaze in my direction.

I could tell it had meant to be fast. Just a glance. But no sooner had his eyes gone back to what he'd been looking at, that they returned to me. Rip straightened as a frown took over his mouth and his eyebrows drew together.

"What's wrong?" he demanded, those incredible eyes moving over my face quickly.

I tried to give him a smile but only got about half of it on my face before I gave up. "Nothing."

His eyes stopped moving, and I'd swear his voice got deeper as he asked again, "What's wrong, Luna?"

My mouth strained in its weak position as I repeated myself. "Nothing."

He shut the drawer he had opened without looking down and turned that huge body toward me. "Tell me what's wrong."

"Nothing is wrong."

"I can see it on your face," he claimed in that rough voice, taking a step forward.

I pressed my lips together and let myself blink twice, quickly. When my voice came out like an almost whisper and it was huskier than normal, I tried not to let the frustration show on my face. "It's nothing you need to worry about," I tried to tell him.

And just like *that*, his face clouded over and he took another step toward me. "I wanna worry about it. Tell me what's wrong."

He—

I felt my nostrils flare. Felt myself press my lips tighter together, and I blinked even more. Keep it together. *Keep it together.* "Rip, it has nothing to do with work. I didn't mess up."

His eyes moved over my face even more, and he took yet another step closer, that frown not going *anywhere*. "What happened?"

With my free hand, I reached up and did pinch my nose that time, letting myself close both my eyes briefly before they decided to betray me like everything and everyone else in my life, apparently.

Stop.

I was fine. None of this was worth crying over. I was okay.

"I didn't get any sleep is all," was all I could get out, and even to me, it sounded like I was full of it.

Rip breathed, and I didn't need to look to know he was even closer to me than he had been a moment before. "Why?"

He wasn't going to drop this. Okay. All right.

I wasn't going to cry. I could just tell him. Quick like a Band-Aid. Rip it off. "My house—"

And, I was going to cry. Yep. There was no denying it.

"What happened to your house?" he asked slowly.

My voice wavered like a flag on a windy day. "It got broken into." There. I said it. I had survived it. "They stole some things, tore up other things..." I had to stop again after that. My nostrils flared, and I pinched my nose again, opening my eyes. "I'm a little upset about it."

I tried to smile, but it immediately toppled over.

One of Rip's hands went to scratch at his forearm through the material of the coveralls he had on, but his eyes stayed on me. His Adam's apple bobbed, and even his voice was off as he asked, "They fucked up your things?"

I nodded, keeping my lips together.

A nerve in his cheek started to tick. "Bad?"

All I could do was shrug and hold my breath.

"How bad?"

I bit the inside of my cheek and didn't bother curbing my croak of, "Bad."

His Adam's apple bobbed again, and his head ticked to the side. His hand came up and he scrubbed his cheek with the back of his hand. Rip's voice was tight. "How'd they get in?"

Tension filled my entire soul as I thought about all the things those jerks had taken from me, not physically but... "They kicked in the door."

"You call the cops?"

I nodded.

One teal eye narrowed, and I couldn't miss the low anger in his voice as he asked, "Who went into the house for you?"

"The cops." The more I talked about it, the worse it got. How had I thought I would get through the day?

Maybe I should ask him to give me the day off. Or at least the morning. Or the rest of the week.

"You clean up already?"

A frog seemed to take up residence in my throat because what came out of my voice next was for sure a croak. *Don't you, cry, Luna. Don't you do it.* "I didn't. I got home late and the cops took so long to come..." I was going to cry. I was going to cry and there was no stopping it. I just needed to hold it in a little longer. Just a little longer until I was home alone, or at least in my room by myself. *I was fine, I was fine, I was fine.* "I should have tried cleaning since I couldn't fall asleep in the first place, but I'm going to get started on it tonight. I was going to call some handymen about coming to fix the door—"

I saw his face cloud over before I heard the change in his voice. *"You slept there?"*

"It was late," I kept on croaking. "I tried calling my best friend and Mr. C, but neither one of them answered."

And, oh, my God, wasn't that another reminder that I was alone. I could have tried Lydia's cell or Mr. Cooper's home, or Grandpa Gus's number. Hell, I could have even called Miguel. But I hadn't wanted to bother anyone. It was my house. My things.

Rip pierced me with that intense gaze, giving me no preparation for his next question. "Why didn't you call me?"

Call... him?

That time I was able to shape my mouth into a smile but only because it wasn't a happy one. "I wasn't going to call you because my place got broken into. It has nothing to do with the business—"

"*Luna,*" he growled through his teeth, taking another step forward. That big body seeming to expand before my eyes. "It's my business. You are my business."

What?

"You slept in that goddamn place with your door not properly locked?" he asked, but didn't wait for my response. "Christ, what were you thinking?"

What had I been thinking? "I didn't want to bother anyone," I managed to get out, shrugging just one shoulder at him, feeling embarrassed, but mostly... over-whelmed. "I was upset, Rip. All of my stuff—" My voice got higher and higher until I forced myself to stop because...

It had been all of my stuff. Mine. For the first time ever, everything had been mine. And someone had—

I didn't realize I'd made this squeaky noise, and I definitely didn't realize that at the tail end of it the tears were just going to burst out of my eyes.

It wasn't just stuff. They had been my things. *Mine*.

Right there. Standing right there, with a cup of coffee in one thermos, with Rip in front of me looking like thunder, I started bawling. *Bawling*. My shoulders hunched in and I started shaking. My hands went up to my face, and even though I told myself to *stop*, told myself that it wasn't the end of the world, reminded myself that a billion other people in the world had problems that made mine seem absolutely insignificant... I still cried. Tears dripped over my fingers and down the palms of my hands.

And I cried.

Because I had worked so hard for what I had only for someone to come in and screw everything up.

Because I was tired. Tired of getting shit on time after time.

I had my place where I had felt happy and proud and safe, and someone I didn't know had decided to take that away from me.

Take, take, take. That's what people did to me. Because I let them. Because they were greedy.

And it was so fucking unfair.

It was *bullshit*.

"Ah, fuck," I heard muttered as I stood there, feeling so sorry for myself, so hurt, so frustrated....

What had to be two hands covered my own for a moment before moving to cup my ears, framing my face. I didn't need to look up to know it was Rip. Who else would it be? But I kept on crying, because not even having Rip right there, being nice to me, was enough to ease how crummy I felt.

Why?

"Why would someone do that to me?" I asked him, sure my tears were probably going down his wrists as he held my face, his thumbs going over the little bones on the backs of my hands. "I don't have anything worth stealing. I haven't done anything to anybody lately. I don't know why this would happen." My voice broke. Broke, broke, broke.

Why did anyone do this kind of crap?

"It's just stuff, but it's my stuff, and somebody just broke in like it's nothing. And it just feels like... some people have bad days, but it's like I'm having twenty-six years of bad days, and I hate feeling helpless, and I'm sorry I'm taking it out on you. And crap, I hate crying. I'm sorry."

Shaking, I curled in on myself even more, trying to retreat. Trying to protect that part of me that didn't feel like it had gotten beat with a bat because it was all I had left that held hope. Foolish. I was so damn foolish.

Two big arms wrapped around me, cutting my thoughts off. The next thing I knew, my face was at a very warm neck and my chest was against a broader one... and I did the only thing I knew how. My hands went to hips that weren't my own and my fingers curled into the coveralls he had on.

And I kept on crying.

Whether it was because of my things, or the idea of someone coming inside my place, or I didn't freaking know. I had no clue. Maybe I felt like life was unfair and this was BS, but I wasn't positive.

All I knew was that I felt like crap and I was tired of things not working out, and I was even more tired of people taking their mess out on me. Life was unfair, and it was total BS sometimes, and even though I had known that fact for a long, long time, it didn't make it any easier. If anything, it felt even harder.

"I don't know what I did in another life to deserve this," I coughed and choked into his chest, pressing my nose as close as possible to that warm, familiar-smelling column of a throat.

Heat touched the top of my head lightly, and what I knew had to be a palm spread across the space between my shoulder blades, pulling me in even closer to that coverall-covered body. Rip's voice was low, as he said, "S'all right, Luna. Don't cry."

The hand on my spine moved up and down, up and down.

"I'm sorry."

"You got nothing to be sorry about," he said into my hair, his arms strong. "Not a single fucking thing."

I didn't say anything. I just stayed there, inhaling and exhaling him... mostly on accident, but on purpose too. Like medicine but for all the other little hurts. The big hurts too. And the medium-sized ones...

Days from then, maybe I'd remember how his skin smelled like Irish Spring. How he smelled like the shop somehow too but better. I'd remember how he smelled so good in this way that had nothing to do with cologne or aftershave.

But for then, for that moment, I'd take him in for what it was. Just a man I trusted, who cared about me at least a little bit and made me feel better. At least, he made me feel less alone.

"Wanna take the day off and deal with it?" he asked my hair.

I shook my head and barely got out, "Not right now." Thinking about everything I'd need to do... "I can wrap some things up this morning and maybe this afternoon..."

Everything was ruined. I needed to call my insurance. Needed to call a handyman. Buy trash bags...

Don't cry.

Too late, wasn't it?

I felt myself put my face back into Rip's neck and heard myself make a desperate noise into his skin.

Damn it. *Damn it.*

"Go when you wanna go, Luna," he whispered, his hand stroking up my spine and staying between my shoulder blades even as I let out a shuddered breath. "Everything's all right, baby girl."

I nodded.

"You're gonna be good."

I was going to be good. He was right. So I nodded again.

His hand slid higher up to palm my neck, and his voice was soft as he said, "You should've called me."

No, there was no reason to. He knew that, he was just being nice. Just like he was being right then, by holding me.

But I was going to take it because who knew when the next time I would get held again would be.

Unfortunately, I knew it wouldn't be Rip doing it.

I HAD BEEN STANDING outside in my yard, staring at the front door for the last ten minutes, trying to talk myself into going back in.

I'd been freaked out enough last night but had managed it, mostly because there hadn't been any other option and the cops had been with me. But now there wasn't anybody to do it with me.

You can do it, Luna. You can do anything.

And I could. I just didn't want to.

The thing was, I didn't want to call Lenny or Grandpa Gus or Mr. Cooper, or anyone else to go in. I wasn't their responsibility. I could do this. I could.

I was in the middle of pumping myself up to climb the stairs onto the porch when I spotted the black Ford pickup pulling into my driveway and parking behind my car. I didn't need to look through the windshield to see who was behind the wheel. I knew it like I knew my own freaking name.

It was Rip.

Who must have left work five minutes after me.

I knew that massive body. I knew the man slamming the door closed to the truck before stomping around, his gaze sweeping across the front of the house. Back and forth, behind him and in front of him. Looking.

His gaze landed on me just standing there, holding my hands to my chest. I could see his eyes narrow. See the great big breath he puffed out of his mouth. I could tell his shoulders dropped, his hands going loose at the same time.

"You didn't tell me you were leaving."

Something inside of my freaking soul stuttered. My throat seemed to choke on every letter in the alphabet, and all I could do was press my lips together and, after a second —after that thing inside of me stuttered then stuttered some more—I nodded.

But I managed to get the words out. "I didn't want to bother you."

And Rip... Rip blinked. His nostrils flared. His chest went in and out, and he said with all the calmness I had never witnessed out of him before, "How many times I gotta tell you that you're not a bother?"

I held my breath.

He made sure to look me right in the eye. "You need me, you call me. Any time. Any day. It's that easy."

Why did that make me uncomfortable?

"You don't gotta do everything alone."

"I've never wanted to, Rip."

And something on that striking, handsome face seemed to splinter. Ripley's chin dipped down once, and then one of those long, massive thighs went forward. One size twelve or thirteen foot set down on my grass, and then Rip was stalking toward me. His hands at his sides, his nostrils wide, and that gaze locked on me.

And before I knew it, before I could process where he was going, he was there.

Standing directly in front of me, so tall I had to tip my head back to look up at that face that was easily eight inches taller than me.

I didn't realize I was tearing up until I felt the tears pooling in the corner of my right eye and then felt something brush them off just as quickly.

It wasn't my hand that did it though. It wasn't my fingers that swept beneath that eye and then swept beneath the other eye.

It was Ripley's fingers that did so.

Before I could get another word out, and before I could blink at that, that huge hand slipped into mine like it was nothing and he tugged me toward the side of the house.

I opened my mouth to tell him I appreciated him coming out here, but that he didn't have to stay. But even though I opened my mouth, nothing came out of it. I wasn't dumb or stubborn enough to tell him to let go of my hand. I needed it. I wanted it. So even if it was for these crappy circumstances, I'd take what I could get.

I could more than likely remember everything that happened afterward if I bothered trying hard enough to. But when something feels more like a terrible dream than reality, most of the time, some things go into your memories forever and other things, you just decide to live through.

Sometimes you have enough shitty things in your life you're forced to remember without adding more. I was picking and choosing at this point. It was all I could do.

Going through my house, room by room, with trash bags was one of the single most painful things I had ever done before. Worse than packing up my things when I was seventeen, shoving what I could into a duffel bag and two plastic grocery bags, and leaving my parents' house without a single clue what I would do or where I would go.

But what I could and would remember was how Rip stood with me, his hand holding mine the entire time we threw things away.

It was all some weird memory I wasn't going to pick up and go through any time soon, or ever if I didn't have to.

My whole body tightened as I took in the television I had saved three months to buy that now had a massive crack through the center of it. That was only the beginning. Broken dishes, four flipped dining room chairs, my mattress, and drawers that had been ripped out and gone through.

I didn't let myself cry as I realized hardly anything had been stolen with the exception of about one hundred dollars in cash I'd hidden in my drawer and two hundred under the bathroom sink. My laptop was missing and so was my tablet. There was just so much... destruction. *What was the point?*

My chest ached, and it felt like I couldn't breathe for a long time.

It was enough to remember the night before when I'd

kicked my clothes aside on the floor, trying my best not to imagine some stranger going through them, putting their hands all over things I had bought with a whole lot of love.

And so much of it had been destroyed.

My safe place had been ruined, and I didn't know what to do.

* * *

HOURS AND HOURS LATER, after filling up ten contractor-sized bags, after cleaning the hell out of everything while Rip went to the home improvement store to buy the things he needed to fix my door, after ordering Vietnamese food while he fixed the door because I had to feed him for doing all these things for me... when I was exhausted and wanted to go to bed, a hand went for my wrist and Rip gripped it.

"Come on," he said in that voice that wanted to lull me to sleep.

"If you're still hungry, I can order some pizza."

"I'm not hungry." He tugged again. "You can't stay here tonight."

I didn't want to stay there tonight. Or the next night. But I didn't want to leave it either.

"You're coming with me."

I was?

I was what?

"Come on. I'm not in my twenties anymore. I'm usually in bed by now."

What? I glanced at my watch and saw the time. It was almost midnight. Holy crap. How had this taken so long?

How was *I* even awake?

Rip tugged at my wrist again. "You're not staying here. Don't give me that face."

Me making a face? Was he serious?

I didn't want to stay, but I didn't want to leave either. He'd already done enough. He had already done so much more than a boss should do for his employee, which only reminded me that I hadn't told anyone what happened yet. Not even Mr. C. And man, that made me feel guilty. What had Rip told him as the reason why I left?

His thumb swept over the back of my hand, and his voice was genuinely really tired. "Come on. I'll get you a hotel room if you don't wanna stay with me."

All I could do was stand there and blink.

He blinked back. "Now, Luna. I'm too tired to give you shit."

I wanted to tell him that I was fine. That I didn't need to go home with him or stay at a hotel, but my mouth didn't move.

God, I was such a wuss. It was pathetic. I could sleep here. There was a lock on the door again.

It would be fine.

I would make sure it was fine.

I wasn't—

"Luna. I'm tired, baby." Rip sighed, giving me a gentle squeeze.

I looked up at him, exhaustion weighing down my eyelids. I watched as his hand came toward my face and his finger slipped across the bottom of my eye. There weren't tears there. There couldn't be. I had already done enough crying for the next decade. But his finger didn't go anywhere else; it stayed there, under my eye.

"Let's go." He was still speaking softly, his face genuinely exhausted. "You're not staying here. You're going to be fine. You don't want to stay at a hotel? Stay at my place. You don't want to stay at my place? We'll get you a room."

I stared.

"It's nothing nice, but I got a bed you can take, and a lock on my door, and some food in my fridge."

I didn't say anything.

The hand around my wrist loosened and he slipped his fingers through mine once more. "Let's go," he tried insisting again.

But I didn't "go." I just stood there, trying to imagine what his place looked like, what his bed looked like... and I still didn't go anywhere. I didn't want to stay at a hotel, and for some reason I didn't understand, I didn't want to stay at his place either. He was my boss first and foremost. *My boss.*

But Rip was even more tired than I was or wanted to go to bed earlier because he sighed, "All right, baby girl. We'll stay here."

* * *

LOOKING AROUND MY BEDROOM, I blew out a breath that felt like it would have weighed a ton if it had any mass to it, and I wrapped my arms around all the blankets I'd managed to collect from around the house. Lord, I could finally feel every hour I'd been awake in every inch of my bones.

Making my way to the living room, I held everything as tight as possible. The blankets, two pillows... I was going to sleep on the floor, I'd decided. Luckily, the couch was a pull-out sofa, and the assholes who had broken into my house hadn't bothered doing more than stabbing at a few cushions.

But the same question I'd been wondering over since

last night remained. Who the hell would do this to me? Why would they?

The idea of it made me want to throw up. It was so *mean*...

It's just stuff.

It was just stuff.

And I had insurance. That was something. I had called them while Rip had gone to the store, and it had taken almost an hour to get everything sorted and in motion.

Something was better than nothing.

I found Rip sitting on my couch with his arms crossed over his chest, staring at the television sitting on the small entertainment center across from it.

If he looked exhausted, I didn't want to know what I looked like.

"I'm sorry, Rip," I said, really feeling like a thoughtless ass right about then. How many times had he brought up how tired he was?

"If you want to go home..." *I'll survive alone.*

He simply shook his head, and I'd swear on my life his eyes drooped for a moment. "I'm staying here," he repeated for what had to be at least the fifth time since he'd brought up that option.

"Yeah but..." I made myself say it. "You can go if you'd rather go home."

"I'm staying."

Did I really want to beg him? Not really.

"Okay." I swallowed. "Thank you then." Focus. "Let me help you make up the sofa bed then—"

"No sofa bed. I can sleep on the couch."

I eyed the ruined cushions and the length and then weighed the chances of him actually getting any sleep on it.

"Eh, Rip, you're size ginormous and my couch is size normal."

He slid me a look that under any other circumstances might have made me laugh. Without another word, that long body unfolded itself from the furniture, getting up to feet that I knew were long, and he turned to me, that handsome face aimed right at me. "Couch is fine, Luna. I've got it."

He had it.

With a nod that I wasn't completely feeling, I walked up to the couch, beside him, and dropped the mound of sheets and blankets, and extra pillow on the end. I watched as Rip got to his feet as I shook out the sheet and then tucked it into the cushions.

But he didn't say a word as he watched what I did for long moments before finally asking, "You wanna sleep here too?"

Did he...?

Numbly, at least that's how I felt, I thought about his question for all of fifteen seconds—if that—and said "Okay" before I could stop myself.

Okay. To sleeping on the couch too.

Who does that?

Me. That's who. Someone was going to feel really dumb and needy later.

But I'd worry about that afterward. Way afterward. My pride wasn't so big that I'd try to be tougher than I really was.

Because the truth was: I didn't want to be alone.

And I was a dummy for thinking that.

But oh well.

"All right," Ripley said softly... so softly, I couldn't help but glance at him, wondering where all this tenderness was coming from.

He just feels bad, my brain whispered.

"Come on," Rip kept speaking, and I looked up to see him dropping onto the couch and leaning back with a big sigh. His arm was up on the back of the seat as he let out a deep, exhausted sigh. "Stretch out here, I can sleep in this corner."

I blinked, the exhaustion hitting me hard. He wanted me to lie down while he slept sitting up?

"I can sleep anywhere. Come lay down. I need to get some rest."

I didn't say anything.

"Everything will be fine," he said.

Pressing my lips together, I nodded. He was here. I was going to lay down beside him. Okay.

God, how I wished that was true.

It wasn't, but for tonight, I would take it.

Rip patted the spot beside him. "Come on."

I did.

I took two steps and plopped down on the couch, one cushion down away from him.

He yawned, watching me the whole time. "You all right?"

"Yeah," I told him pretty half-heartedly, toeing off my boots. I had forgotten I'd put on Pac-Man socks that morning. It was the most fun I'd wanted to go. That, and all my jewelry had been strewn all over the place.

Before I could realize what he was doing, he reached across the couch and grabbed my hand, pulling it—and me —toward him. I stopped what I was doing and blinked at the sight of his big hand, those long fingers, perfectly short nails, engulfing mine. Then he pulled again, making me stretch out on the couch.

Rip got to his feet, grabbing the pillow and blankets from the armchair. He shook out the blanket right before throwing it on top of me. I just watched him as he stood over the couch, kicking off his shoes, his hands going to the top button of his jeans and undoing it. It was my turn to yawn as he walked to the end of the couch, directly beside where I was laying and plopped down. I could feel the heat of his thigh and the weight of him make my couch sink.

What I wasn't ready for was the hand that snuck beneath my head and lifted it—Rip lifting my freaking head —, before effortlessly sliding the pillow under my head before his fingertips touched my forehead. "Go to sleep. I'm here," he said to me.

I looked up, or tried to look behind me, and I saw him stretch out from upside down.

Rip was too busy yawning to notice I couldn't take my eyes off him. "Sleep, Luna. I'm not going anywhere."

I didn't say a word. I didn't know what to say. Mostly though, I felt exhausted.

Stretching out on the couch, I thought about telling Rip that he should lie down and that I should be the one to sleep upright. I could have slept on the floor.

I rolled over to my side, tucking my hands beneath the pillow under my head. I didn't think of anything. I just... lay there, listening to Rip's deep breaths. But I still couldn't wind down.

When the clock had changed to tell me that ten minutes had passed, a low groan came from the man beside me, and a moment later, fingers settled right in front of my face, palm up. "Nothing's gonna get you," he rumbled quietly, his voice rough and mellow.

I stared at those big fingers, taking in the calluses all over them and the palms. They were strong hands. Solid hands. And they made my own itch.

"You think I'd let that happen?"

I rolled onto my stomach and propped my hands under my chin, so I could look up at him. I mean, if he wasn't falling asleep yet either... "No."

His head was back against the couch, his eyes heavy and low. "Good, 'cause I wouldn't." Those impressive fingers squeezed mine. "You talked to your sister?"

I knew exactly which one he was asking about and couldn't play stupid. "No. She's still ignoring my calls."

"Anybody else heard from her?"

Lord, he was digging that dagger deep when I felt like I'd already gotten the crap kicked out of me. "Yeah, it's just me she's ignoring." I took a deep breath through my nose and slid that dagger in deeper myself.

He made a grumbling noise. "I thought you all left that house because your dad was a piece of shit."

That made it worse. "We did, but my dad was at his worst with me. He just didn't give a crap about my sisters. That was the difference."

This pause hung in the air in between us. Then, "What's that mean?"

"I told you things are complicated. My dad used to tell me that he should've pulled out. Him and his wife... even though now that I think about it, I'm not even sure they were legally married... they were the worst people I've ever met in my life. They were mean and unhappy and selfish. I don't... I don't know why they were together in the first place. Misery invites misery or whatever that saying is." I took a breath, thinking about them. "And my brother never did anything. He was never really around in the first place.

He never defended any of us. I know he hated them as much as I did; he left the second he graduated high school and never looked back."

I didn't tell him the rest. About all the times my dad told me I was stupid and worthless. About that woman saying those same, exact things. About all the rest of the things I didn't want to remember. Not ever.

Those eyes locked on mine and his grip tightened. "I thought you only had sisters."

"No, I have an older brother too, same mom and dad. I just never talk about him. I haven't seen him in eleven or twelve years now. I couldn't even make it until I turned eighteen, you know. I left a couple months into my senior year of high school." But I didn't leave my sisters. That part I didn't tell him.

"They kicked you out?" he asked in that quiet voice.

I sighed. "Not exactly."

"What's that mean?"

I scrunched up my toes beneath the blanket. "I mean, they had been counting down the days until I turned eighteen since I was like three. And one day they gave me no other reason but to go. So I left."

"What happened?"

I squeezed Ripley's hand and thought about that time in my life. "I did something," I told him in a very small voice.

There was a pause. "What'd you do?"

I scrunched them again. "I don't know if I want you to know."

"Why?" he asked relentlessly, lowly.

"Because I don't feel bad about it. I don't even feel a little bad about it," I admitted.

His breath was soft as he said, "I've done some bad shit

too, Luna. I'd be the last person to judge you for anything you did."

I held my breath.

Then he added, "Tell me another time, whenever the hell you want, yeah? Put it in our... what do you call it? Box of secrets?"

I didn't think twice about it, or the fact he was acknowledging our box of secrets. I just agreed. "Yeah, okay."

"Where'd you go after?"

I almost sighed in relief. I could tell Rip this at least. "I had made a plan with my grandmother that she would take my sisters since we both knew their mom couldn't and wouldn't want or be able to take care of them." *Oh, Grandma Genie.* "She gave me some money, and I had some too, and I took the bus to Houston right after I left that house. I think I told you that. I stayed in just about the shittiest hotel in Houston. It was the dirtiest, crappiest place in Houston probably, but they didn't ask for ID or a credit card or anything. I was so scared that I had to shove the dresser in front of the door the entire time I stayed there."

I swore my heart started beating just a little faster thinking about those days when I worried so much about getting caught and sent back to San Antonio. Of not knowing how long I could really stretch the money my grandmother had left me. "I applied at just about every job opening I could find on Craigslist. About two weeks after I got to Houston, I applied here for a job as a receptionist, actually. Mr. Cooper had decided to take the listing down the day I showed up, but he didn't tell me until I got there."

"He told me he changed his mind about needing a receptionist and would be better off hiring another mechanic instead. I started crying in his office, you know. He asked me if there was something he could do, and I told him I really needed to find a job and asked if he knew anyone hiring. I didn't tell him that no one would hire me for a full-time job because I wasn't eighteen. I hadn't even told him I was seventeen, but I've always looked pretty young so...."

There was a pause and then, "He found you a job?"

Thinking back on him taking on some random person to do a job that didn't really need doing, was a risky business decision. Mr. Cooper hadn't needed me, but he had taken me anyway. So I nodded at my newest boss. "He warned me that I might not like a lot of the things I'd have to do around the shop, and he said he wasn't going to treat me any differently because I was a girl, but if I was fine with that, that he'd take me on as kind of a community assistant instead of hiring a mechanic after all. But I told him that I learned fast and that I'd do just about anything he or anyone else asked, and that he wouldn't regret it.

"I literally would have scooped up crap with my hands at that point. I didn't care what he asked me to do as long as it didn't involve something weird. He asked when I wanted to start, and I told him I could start right then. He found me the smallest coveralls he could find, and I started cleaning up the shop." I scratched my upper lip remembering that day, taking in the confused looks from my new coworkers who wondered what I was doing.

"That day, at six, when everyone was going home, Mr. C told me it was a tradition for new employees to go eat at his house... He promised me he was married and that it really was for dinner and that his wife would be at the house. I'd been eating off the dollar menu and those noodles in a cup every day at that point. So I went, and Lydia fed me. They said they would give me a ride back to my hotel, and even though I told them they didn't have to, they did anyway. They took one look at that motel and both of them went into the room with me, got my things, and told me I was going to be staying with them until I decided to move out."

I swallowed thinking about how they had lied about the tradition for new employees to come over and eat. He had to have known I needed a meal. He had to have known something was wrong. And Mr. Cooper had stepped up to the plate. "I stayed with them for four years. I could have stayed longer, they told me, but my sisters had already been living with them for a while too by that point, and I didn't want to take advantage... and I moved out afterward. Mr. Cooper begged me not to, but I did. We lived in a two-bedroom apartment for the next few years, and then I bought my house. And now I'm here."

Rip's big chest went in and out as I spoke, and stayed sucked in while he said, "I can't see you ever taking advantage of anyone."

I smiled at him. "That's nice but I wouldn't. I've had too many people try and take advantage of me to do that to someone else."

Rip let out a breath so deep and slow, his chest reminded me of a balloon that had been pierced with a needle, slowly losing all of its air.

I didn't expect the next question out of his mouth. "Why do you still work at Cooper's? And don't give me some bullshit answer about owing Cooper or liking your coworkers either."

It only took me a second to think of the truth. "I like fixing things and making them look nice again." I bit the inside of my cheek, not sure how that sounded, but at this point, I was beyond worrying what impression Rip had of me and the things that came out of my mouth. He should have been used to it by now. "Like... it's no big deal they aren't perfect anymore—you know, if they were in an accident—because they're still going to run. The cars I mean. They're going to look and run better than before and still have a long, perfectly good life ahead of them. It's like we're giving them a second chance." Well, hell. "I can relate to it a lot, I guess."

He watched me for a long, long moment.

So it surprised me when he asked slowly, "What's up with you and wearing your fun shit everyday?"

Oh. "I read a book a long time ago about being happy." I didn't care how that sounded or came across. "One whole chapter was dedicated to self-care," I explained with a little smile. "Wearing something I think is fun everyday reminds me that things are all right. That I deserve to be happy. That I get to choose how I handle things. It made sense to me. I'll take what I can get. I'm not going to die sad and miserable if I can help it."

Rip didn't say a word, but he watched me so closely then I didn't know what to say.

And in the time it took him to form his mouth into a shape that words could come out of, I had sat up. His arm burned against mine. I didn't know if he minded me sitting beside him, practically plastered to him, but he didn't tell me to move away either.

"I know that face. Don't feel bad for me," I told him, carefully.

He was looking me right in the eye as he said, "I don't. Not even a little, baby girl."

Well. I smiled. "Okay then. Thanks for helping me today." Then I went for it because why not? "You know, I think you're pretty freaking wonderful when you aren't mad at me."

He didn't smile back. His voice was warm as he said, heavily, "You're welcome. Go to sleep, Luna."

I looked at him for a second, as he looked right back at me with that face and voice I had no clue what to do with, and I said, "Go to sleep, Ripley."

CHAPTER TWENTY-TWO

I woke up mostly because my phone's alarm clock was wailing right by my ear, but the crick in my neck that shot through my shoulders and spine helped too.

"Oww." Groaning as I tried to fish my hand around for my cell, I forced myself to open an eye when I didn't immediately find it.

And it was all of a second after I'd opened an eye that I realized where I was.

On the couch. Where I'd fallen asleep the night before. Or, really, more like four hours ago.

My hand found my phone tucked under my chest, and I dragged it out, tapping my finger across the screen from muscle memory to get it to shut up, just as something moved out of my peripheral vision. Something...

They were fingers. Long, thick fingers. And there was only one person I knew who had what looked like an M and C on his ring finger and pinky finger.

Those fingers were Ripley's.

And Rip's fingers moved right by my face as I lay there, on the couch, on my side.

He'd spent the night with me. Slept on the couch directly beside me. I'd barely had that thought when the pillow under my head moved.

The pillow under my head moved?

"Fuckin' tired," Rip's voice—this even deeper, huskier sound than usual—said from close by as the "pillow" under me moved some more, almost like it was... stretching?

I had my head on his thigh, didn't I?

"You all right?" that incredible voice grumbled.

I nodded, still trying to put my thoughts together. How he was there. How I had my head on his lap. Mostly *how he was there.*

He made this husky sound that could have been illegal. "Time is it?"

I peeked at my phone with my one open eye that was more than likely bulging now at my realization. "Six."

The man I was using as a pillow grunted.

I moved my head to press my ear flat against the leg beneath me. I needed to get up. I needed to tell him thank you for everything he had done. And I needed to get up just because.

But I didn't do any of those things.

What I did do was slide the tips of the fingers of my left hand under his thigh, like I was settling in to go back to sleep. Like he really was my pillow. Or like I had the right to touch him.

"I don't wanna get up either," Rip yawned, the fingers by my face lifting up... and landing on my shoulder, cupping it.

He didn't say anything and neither did I. I couldn't even hear him breathing. But I lay there, just for a minute, and thought about all the things I needed to do, starting with *getting up and off him*. But instead of all that, my mind said *later*.

The hand on my shoulder gave it a light squeeze that had my eyes going just that much wider. "Take the day off, baby girl. I gotta go into the shop for a few hours, but I'll come back and help you after that."

That had me opening both my eyes and staring straight at my cracked television. My beautiful, beautiful television. Okay, it was time to focus on what I needed to do. But I still didn't immediately move. "I should get to work too. I can't really afford right now to take a whole day off, but thank you."

He yawned once more. "I thought you said you had homeowners' insurance."

"I do, but I've got a feeling they aren't going to cover everything, and I don't know how long it'll take for them to cut me a check," I explained. "I don't want to end up being in debt for the next ten years buying everything on credit..." And there went the money I'd been saving for my granite countertops, I realized. Oh well, I guess. They weren't going anywhere, and mine still did their job and would continue to.

Rip let out another yawn.

"Plus, I'm behind on what I didn't do yesterday, and Jason never called me, so I have no idea what he did or didn't do. I can deal with the rest of this stuff—" Never "—after work and during the weekend. I'll make it work."

There was silence, and the muscle under me hardened. The hand on my shoulder gave it another squeeze, just as gentle as the one before it. And Lucas Ripley moved his hand from above my arm to graze my cheek... and I held my breath as those rough fingers stayed there. "All right then, let's go to work."

Somehow, I managed to stir up a tired smile against his thigh—it was lovely to meet it, and unfortunately we would never meet again unless something like this happened in the future, but I hoped that wasn't the case—and then I pushed against the cushion under me and sat up. Rip was sprawled as much as possible in a relaxed seated position on my couch, pretty much as melted into it as possible. I had gotten it because it was comfortable, not to be pretty, and with him on there... it was the best-looking couch I'd ever seen, if I said so myself.

With one arm sprawled on the armrest, his shirt was plastered completely to his entire upper body, wrinkled and rippled along his wide ribs, with stuffing from the ruined couch stuck to different places along his sides. His jeans were tight on his thighs... and opened in a V at the crotch, showing just a tiny triangle of black material underneath. That rough, handsome face had "sleepy" written all over it.

I don't think he'd ever looked better. This sense of longing just...

Sheesh. How was he so freaking good looking all the time? I didn't need a mirror to know I looked like hell. I'd been looking at myself in the mirror for the last twenty-six years. I knew my eyes were puffy, my face swollen, my mouth swollen. I hadn't tucked my hair under my head before I'd fallen asleep, so it all had to be sticking out in random directions.

Oh well.

I smiled at him before slapping my hand over my mouth to yawn. "I don't have anything your size to wear," I told him as brightly as possible when I was done.

His blink was even lazier than before. "I got a shirt in my truck. S'all I need."

I lifted my hands over my head to stretch and yawned

out, "My shampoo isn't too fruity, and neither is the soap, if you want to shower."

Those teal eyes strayed down for a moment before coming back to my face, reminding me I'd slept in my clothes and hadn't even bothered putting on pajamas.

"The bathroom is down the hall and to the right, in my room, in case you forgot. There are towels in the little closet in there," I told him as I dropped my arms with another yawn. "I can get the shirt out of your truck if you want."

Today was going to be rough. I needed ten more hours of sleep, easy. Maybe I could nap during my lunch break.

Rip watched me carefully for a minute before getting up to his black sock-covered feet with a nod.

"Holler if you need anything," I said to him, still smiling, because why not? Maybe a lot of things sucked, but he was here, doing what he didn't have to.

He hadn't brought up the favor in a while, but I wasn't holding my breath that he'd forgotten how he felt about it. Maybe he still thought he owed me something, but I hoped he knew he didn't. For once, I didn't want to remind him.

He shot me a long look, even flicking his gaze down to my socks before turning and heading in the direction of my room. Sitting there, I took a deep breath, smacked my cheeks a little with my fingers, and got up. It didn't take long to find his keys and then do the same to the T-shirt in his backseat. Then, I followed in the same direction Rip had gone, heading toward my bedroom to pick out some clothes from the pile I'd set on the bed yesterday. We had thrown away so much stuff the night before, I honestly wasn't sure what I had left. I hadn't wanted to look too closely or think about it too much.

But things could always be worse.

I looked at the door connecting to my bathroom and

imagined, for just one little second, the naked man on the other side. Then I sighed.

ON MY LUNCH break hours later, I headed up the stairs to the second floor of CCC to find two of the guys exiting the break room with funny expressions on their faces.

"Awkward," the taller one of the two muttered.

"I wouldn't go in there," the shorter one said in a whisper.

I frowned.

"They're fighting," the taller one explained, still whispering.

Well, it had only been a matter of time.

The other one raised his eyebrows as they passed by me, disappearing down the stairs, as I kept going forward. I had planned on grabbing one of the frozen meals I bought and left in the freezer for emergencies since I still hadn't gotten around to making my own lunch, and Rip hadn't gone home, so I couldn't expect something to magically appear.

I didn't even need to take a step inside the break room before I heard the arguing.

"That's fucking bullshit."

"It really isn't."

"No, it really is. You had no right to make that decision without me."

"I had every right to make that decision without you. You didn't need to jump the gun—"

"They needed an answer and I gave them one. I tried calling you over and over again, but you didn't answer."

"I was busy."

There was a pause. "So I saw from you taking the day off without saying anything."

Oh no. It was my fault?

"I get here before everyone else and stay here later than everyone else. If I need to take the day off, it shouldn't be an issue." There was a pause and then, *"I'm not a kid and you're not my fucking boss. You don't get to tell me when I can take time off and when I can't."*

Mr. Cooper didn't reply immediately, and I stood there, right outside the break room door, listening and wondering if I should interrupt them or not. Them arguing drove me crazy. It really did.

"I'm not trying—"

"Yeah, you fucking were."

"Cut me some slack. We're in this together. I don't want you getting into trouble."

"You think I'm doing something to get into trouble?"

"I don't know, Ripley. I don't know! You don't tell me anything!"

"I need to?"

"Why are you trying to—"

Okay. All right. With a sigh, I kept walking, but instead of ducking into the break room, I made it to the office door and knocked before I could stop myself. I didn't know what the hell I was going to do exactly, but I knew I wanted them to stop and it was up to me since the rest of these chickens never did.

Sure enough, a millisecond after knocking, the voices cut out altogether.

"Mr. Cooper, it's Luna. Have you seen Rip?" I called out, rolling my eyes at myself for being such a bad liar.

"Sure, Luna, come in," Mr. Cooper called out after a second.

I wondered what faces they were making at each other. Or at me for being an inconvenience. But I was doing them both a favor. They just didn't know it.

I didn't wait for them to change their mind, I turned the knob and peeked my head inside, making sure to put a surprised expression on my face when I spotted Rip immediately. He was standing right by the door, those massive arms crossed over his chest. I gave him a smile that wasn't totally bright—I was too tired for that—but it was good enough to pass.

I still hadn't told anyone at work what had happened, and if Mr. Cooper thought it was strange that I hadn't come into work yesterday, he hadn't bothered calling to check. I figured right then, that Rip had told him something about me separately, but hadn't said where he would be for some reason. I was going to tell him obviously, but the day was going rough enough. I didn't want to cry about it again so soon.

"I was looking for you to see if you wanted to go to lunch," I said quickly, aiming my gaze right at Rip. "I owe you for yesterday."

I didn't miss the confused look that Mr. Cooper sent Ripley, then me.

I also didn't miss the way Rip's body tightened at my question.

He was going to say no, I knew it, and I was going to be fine with it. The only reason why I'd even said anything was to break this up.

"So?" I asked, giving him another smile that was as big as he was going to get, trying to tell him with my eyes that it was fine for him to say no.

But he didn't do that.

"All right." He uncrossed his arms and let them drop to his sides. "But you're not paying."

I pressed my lips together and blinked. Okay, then. All right. "Then I wouldn't be paying you back for helping me, would I, boss?" I asked him sweetly.

Mr. Cooper's head swung from me to Rip and back again, and I felt bad for leaving him in the dark.

I'd tell him as soon as I had a chance.

"You don't need to pay me back for shit." He took a step forward. "I've got it. Let's go."

I kept that annoying sweet smile on my face, watching him get closer to me. "But really, you should let me pay."

"Really, I shouldn't," he replied sarcastically, brushing his shoulder against mine as he passed by me.

Now he was joking? Okay. All right.

Breathing in through my nose, I swung my gaze over to Mr. Cooper, not sure if I was going to do the right thing or... not. But I knew that if anyone deserved my loyalty, it was Mr. Cooper. It was bad enough I hadn't told him the other things.

"Would you like to go eat with us?" I asked him, purposely turning my back to his business partner so I wouldn't see his face if he was making one.

But of course he was.

The question must have surprised Mr. Cooper because he stood there for a moment. I didn't miss the way he slid his gaze to Rip for maybe a second before going back to me. He plastered on a smile that wasn't totally fake as he said, "Thank you, Luna, but I already had lunch."

Had he wanted to go though?

When we had gone to eat on Ashton's first day, the two of them had gotten along all right. Part of me thought they had been on their best behaviors in front of the new guy.

They hadn't talked directly to each other once, or even made eye contact, but it had gone okay. I'd watched them like a hawk the whole time, expecting something to happen, but nothing had.

Nothing had in a while.

"Next time then?" I asked, giving him a smile that felt more honest than the rest of them before. I really needed to tell him the truth.

Mr. Cooper nodded, his expression pretty freaking curious but... okay. Bright, but okay.

I glanced back at Rip finally, keeping that expression on my face so that hopefully he wouldn't think I was trying to pull a fast one on him even though I had been. "Ready?"

His eyes bounced on mine, something in them that I wasn't familiar with, but he nodded eventually.

With a wave to Mr. Cooper, I headed out the door and down the stairs, Rip following behind me. We made it to the bottom before I realized I wasn't ready to go, and I glanced over my shoulder to find him literally a foot away. "Give me one second to grab my purse, okay?"

Those blue-green eyes slid toward me. "You don't need money."

I opened my mouth, but he cut me off.

"You don't need money. Let's go," he insisted.

I opened my mouth again, but he did the same thing, giving me that exasperated expression.

"You can pay me back some other way, all right?"

"I didn't invite you so you could end up paying for someone else's food."

He stared at me.

"You've done enough. I don't want to take advantage of you," I told him for what felt like the hundredth time lately, knowing he would understand that.

Those eyes focused in on me, and I watched them go to my ears. I'd put on the first set I'd found in the ruin of my bedroom: fake gold teddy bears. "I'll tell you if I feel like you're taking advantage of me. But let's go, I'm hungry. Those kolaches this morning went right through me."

Oh, man. He wasn't going to let this go. "Fine. But I'll pay you back for my food at least." I squinted an eye. "Somehow."

He didn't agree, but he did give me another side look before he shook his head. "Come on."

I was going to lunch with Ripley.

I was going to tell myself that wasn't excitement or crazy high anticipation going through me. Just two coworkers going out to eat in public. No big deal. It wasn't even the first time we did it.

I led the way out the doors, noticing that no one even looked at Rip and me as we headed out. We had barely gone out the door when those long legs caught him up to me and we walked side by side toward his truck. He'd insisted on driving us to work that morning, even shoving my keys into his pocket so I wouldn't get any ideas. I swear I didn't know who this man was anymore. Neither one of us said anything as he beeped the locks and opened the passenger side door, and then went around to do the same on the driver side. He slid in while I buckled up. In no time, we were on the road.

To go out to eat together.

"What do you want to eat, boss?"

"Don't call me that when we aren't at work," he said, his voice easy, not mean or anything like that. Just... him telling me not to call me that.

For some reason.

I made a face. "Okay... what can I call you then when we aren't at work?"

His grunt was his reply to that, but he didn't look at me as he asked, "What do you think about barbecue?"

"I think I can eat a half pound of brisket," I told him as I genuinely thought about what else I could call him instead that would be pesky but not too pesky.

His cheek twitched, and I'd take it as a smile. "You hear anything from your insurance?"

Ah. "Yeah, I talked to them earlier. They're sending out an adjuster, and I have to send some paperwork to them, so I'm betting I'll be fifty by the time I get a check."

His fingers stretched out again on the steering wheel and his head ticked to the side.

"It's fine. I'll make it work. You fixed my door enough for me to be okay, and it isn't like the people who came in are going to come back. They already took all the good stuff," I tried to joke, but really, it sounded like anything but one.

Everything was fine. Things were just... stuff. They weren't everything. I could live without them. I had survived with less before. But...

"Luna..."

"I'm okay. I know it's stupid to be worried they'll come back or the same thing will happen."

"It ain't stupid."

It was and we both knew it.

"You don't feel safe. Nothing stupid about that," Rip tried to tell me in that voice I had no defense against. "Thought about getting an alarm?"

"I've *thought* about it," I told him. "But the company that came by my house once was more than I could afford. They were asking for three hundred dollars down for the equipment. That's the cost of the fancy tile I want for my kitchen backsplash."

His fingers flexed on the steering wheel and he tapped them. "I know someone. Let me give him a call and see what he says."

I couldn't help but eye him. "You don't have to do that, Rip." Because he didn't.

"I'll get back to you after I talk to him."

Of course he was going to ignore me.

Well, I couldn't do anything about it if he was going to insist. He'd have to understand if I couldn't afford it. The cops had said there had been a couple of break-ins around the area.

So, it was supposed to be... normal. Getting your house broken into wasn't unheard of. Even if I hadn't heard a single thing from any of my neighbors over them hearing about break-ins.

"Thanks for offering," I told him. "You—"

That handsome face turned toward me, and he rolled his eyes, shaking his head. "Quit thanking me for everything."

I made sure he watched me roll my eyes right back at him. "Okay, but thank you anyway."

He shook his head again, turning back to face outside the windshield. "You don't need to thank me."

"You don't need to do all the things you've done for me either but—"

"Stop," he grunted.

I would have crossed my eyes if he'd been looking at me. "I appreciate it, okay? You're being really nice, and you don't have to. I just want you to know I'm grateful, so suck it up."

We happened to come up to a stop sign when he glanced at me with those blue-green eyes and said, not softly but not roughly either, just... different, "I want to, all right?"

As quickly as I opened my mouth, I closed it.

He wanted to?

Lucas Ripley wanted to be nice to me?

My first thought was: why?

My second one was: who was I to tell him no? *No, sir, please be a jerk and don't care about me.* I wasn't that dumb.

I HAD JUST FINISHED FOLDING the clothes I pulled out of the dryer, when there was a knock at my front door.

I glanced at my phone and took in that I hadn't missed any calls or texts. No one I knew was coming over; otherwise they would have messaged. I grabbed my biggest kitchen knife, because luckily those had survived the jerks, and headed toward the front door.

But when I got to the peephole, I took a step back afterward.

Then I took another step forward to look into it again. The person was still the same one, and the face on the other side hadn't magically morphed either.

I couldn't even think as I flipped the lock and pulled the door open, finding a duffel bag sitting on my porch and a tall man with wide shoulders and a wide chest standing there.

He didn't even give me a chance to say a word. "You gonna let me in?"

Well. "No," I told him with a grin even as I moved to the side to let him inside.

He didn't even try to sneak by either; his entire side brushed my front as he did.

"You eat dinner already?" he asked as I was closing and locking the door.

"Yeah, did you?"

I mean, he'd dropped me off two hours ago. We had both worked late, and he'd offered to take me home whenever I was ready. He was the one who had come by my room right before seven asking if I was done for the day, and I had been. Or at least I'd been pretty close to it.

"Nah," the man replied, dropping the duffel at the bottom of the stairs.

My eyes focused in on the bag, putting together what he was doing at my house at nine o'clock at night with *that*.

He was going to spend the night.

"Want me to order you something? I ordered pho, but I ate it all, I'm sorry," I apologized, still looking at that navy blue bag that had some miles on it.

"No," he replied, bending over to unzip it and pull out the same kind of container he'd brought me lunch in. But then he pulled out three more just like it too, stacking them up carefully in his hand as he straightened. "I brought food. I'll put the rest in your fridge, all right?"

"Okay," I basically croaked.

Those eyes caught mine for a second before he disappeared down the hall that led into the kitchen.

Just like Lenny did when she came over. Or when Mr. Cooper or Lydia came over. Or when my sisters were here.

Like it was normal.

And he'd brought me food. Again.

Man, I could fall in love with this man if I let myself. I really, really could. But only dummies fell in love with their bosses—bosses who didn't do *girlfriends* or *relationships*.

There was no use dreaming about things I couldn't have. There was no use thinking I could fall in love with him even though some tiny part of me quietly whispered that I already was. That was for sure. It was with that thought that I yelled down the hall, "Rip! I'm going to shower but make yourself at home!"

"'Kay," he called out just as loudly, doing whatever it was he was doing in the kitchen. Eating?

I stopped where I was. "Want some company while you eat?" I yelled.

"I'm good," he replied.

Okay.

I headed into my bedroom, grabbing the clothes I had organized while I waited for my dinner, and pulled out a navy short and tank top pajama set with pink hearts that Lily had bought me.

It didn't take me long to shower and get dressed as I did my best to ignore how tired I was. I'd gone on maybe five hours of sleep over the last three days, and I was feeling it. Honestly, all I wanted to do was fall face-first onto my bed. I was too sleepy to even care about the tiny possibility someone might decide to come back.

And... Rip was here.

I even brushed my teeth then moisturized my face, giving the circles under my eyes a sigh. I really needed to get some sleep. And using one of those gel eye masks wouldn't hurt either. At least the stress hadn't made me start breaking out.

Sighing again, I opened the bathroom door and stopped.

I stopped right there in place and took in the man sitting on the edge of my bed.

The man sitting on my bed, pulling off his socks, giving me a nice view of pink soles.

The man who looked up the second I opened the door and flashed me a smile that was almost as tired as mine was.

"If you get hungry in the middle of the night, I left food in your fridge," he told me quietly, folding his socks and dropping them on top of his work boots. "You need to hit the store though. There's nothing in there."

"I know, but thank you," I told him, standing there. "I'll make time to go this weekend." I paused. "Did you cook everything yourself?"

His eyes never left mine as he answered, "Yeah."

I wondered if his mom had taught him how or if he'd had to learn after she was gone.

"Did you want to shower?" I asked, choosing that to focus on.

He shook his head. "I did before I came over."

Well.

"I can't make it through another night on your couch again," he let me know, still speaking in that calm, quiet voice that I didn't know what to do with.

Oh.

I thought about that. "Lily's bed is too small, it's just a daybed, and my other sisters took theirs."

Oh.

Oh.

I didn't need to look at my bed to know that while it wasn't a king-sized mattress, it was a queen. And the biggest in the house.

"You can sleep on my bed. There are some tears in the mattress, but I covered them with the sheets. It'll still be better than last night," I offered, giving him a smile. "I'll sleep on the couch."

...by myself.

Closer to the front and back doors.

That wasn't going to happen.

"Or in Lily's room," I threw out.

Rip stood up, tall, so freaking tall, and I had to tip my chin back a little to keep making eye contact with him. He stretched those muscular arms over his head and yawned, "You look like you need a good rest too, baby girl."

I did. I really did.

I also needed to ignore the use of that b-word again.

And I needed to quit being a chicken and sleep wherever.

"Nothing's gonna happen, you know that, yeah?" he asked in his careful voice, making me focus on him.

I nodded.

His breath was deep but true, and he was looking right at me as he asked, "Why don't you sleep in here too?"

Too? On the same bed?

I mean...

I said "Okay" before I stopped myself, or even realized what in the world I'd just jumped into.

What the hell was I doing?

Before I could stop myself, Rip said, "Let's get to bed then."

Just like that.

Well. Hell.

I was so nervous I held my breath as I went to the wall and flipped off the lights, blindly making my way toward the lamp that had survived these assholes coming into my house. The lamp lit the room just enough, showing me that Rip was on the other side of the mattress—the side I didn't sleep on—already pulling the white coverlet back like it was the most natural thing in the world.

I wished.

Or at least I would if I was asking for a side of heartache.

"Is this a good idea?" I couldn't help but ask. Sleeping in

the same bed with my boss just seemed, like it shouldn't happen. At least to me. At least not when that boss was Rip.

"Why wouldn't it be?" he asked right back before slipping under the sheets I had put on earlier.

Huh.

If he thought there wasn't anything that would make this a bad idea...

I could ignore that this was something new. That my heart beat just a little faster at the idea of sleeping beside him. There was no reason this wasn't strictly platonic.

I pulled the covers back and climbed in too. Flicking off the lamp, I snuggled into the covers and felt the mattress beside me moving, saying that Rip was adjusting himself too.

I rolled over onto my side to face where he was and slipped my hands under my cheek.

"Luna?"

I closed my eyes without even trying to. "Hmm?"

"You good?"

"Uh-huh, you?"

"Yeah."

I yawned. "Thanks for coming over. Give me a poke if I'm moving around too much, okay?"

My eyes popped open the second I heard him snicker.

I was so tired, but I still laughed.

I was pretty sure he said something else, but I had zero energy, I couldn't even find it in me to overthink Rip being in the same bed as me or me telling him to give me a poke. I fell asleep instantly.

And I was pretty sure my dreams started up instantly too.

Maybe it was the stress of getting burglarized. Maybe it was my worry and anger over Thea... Maybe it was the fury that speaking to my dad fueled me with. Or my beef with Kyra now too...

But I fell into a dream that starred my dad in it. Again.

Some part of me knew it wasn't real, knew that it wasn't actually happening, but despite all of that, my panic felt real. Too real as it started off with Kyra saying she was hungry while we all sat in my bedroom while we worked on our homework. I made my way into the kitchen from the back of the house, grabbing two boxes of macaroni and cheese from the secret hole I'd cut into the sheetrock in my closet. I could hear my dad and the girls' mom arguing from the living room, and I tried to rush—to somehow make the water boil faster so I could go back to the room—but it hadn't happened.

Something broke in the living room, and I thought *hurry up.*

But I hadn't been fast enough. I was standing there when I heard, *"What the fuck are you doing?"*

I tensed. Shook. Wanted to throw up.

I don't know what I responded with, but I was aware of what was going to happen before it did. I tried to wake up. Tried to force myself to wake up before... before... but I didn't, and the metal was as cool as ever as it hit the base of my neck first, and—

I woke up with a gasp in my dark room. Woke up on my back with my entire body strung tight. Woke up with goose bumps all over my arms and my hands instantly going to my face to rub it.

It was just a dream.

I knew it was. I was fine. I was safe.

Something heavy landed on my stomach a moment before Rip's voice pulled me even further back into the present with a rough, "Luna?"

Crap.

"I'm fine," I whispered, hearing the lie in how my voice wobbled.

The mattress moved as I figured he rolled. "Bad dream?"

It was still so dark, we must have not been asleep too long, but I still felt guilty for waking him up. It was bad enough when it was just me. "Yeah." I took a breath through my nose and rubbed my face again, my fingers trembling just a little but more than enough. "I'm okay. I'm sorry for waking you up."

The warm breath on my upper arm told me he was facing me. "What happened in it?" he asked unexpectedly.

I held my breath, thinking over the details. It only kept the goose bumps on my arm for longer.

"You're not the only one who knows how to keep secrets," his voice rumbled.

I froze, staring blindly into the darkness. I had never told anyone about what happened the day before I left. Not even Lenny. Not Mr. Cooper. Nobody.

I hadn't been in the middle of making macaroni for the girls like in my dream, but...

"Luna," he said my name carefully.

I sniffed and reached back to rub at the nape of my neck, touching the spot that had never felt the same after that day.

"Baby, you cried out," a sugar-sweet voice murmured a moment before what I knew were his fingers reached for my arm, sliding down it until his hand took mine and swallowed it whole. "Tell me what happened. It's not real. You know it's not."

I took a breath through my nose, my nape itching again.

"It was real, Rip," I sniffed, feeling him squeeze my shaking fingers.

"Somebody do something?"

I tried to rub my fingers over his rough ones.

"Somebody hurt you?" the man beside me repeated himself.

Every day for years. Hurt didn't have to be physical, but I didn't tell him that. He could keep secrets, he said, and I believed him. And maybe I shouldn't tell him, maybe I shouldn't say the words out loud and make them more real than they already were just living in my own head but...

But I had to try.

Isn't that what I had tried to do with Lily and Kyra for years? Try to get them to talk about things so they wouldn't bottle them up and explode from pressure later on?

I was such a hypocrite sometimes.

"I had a dream my dad..." Hell. How could I explain this? "He was always an asshole. Always, you know? When he was drunk or mad or because I was breathing too loud if the TV was on or if something had gone wrong and I happened to be nearby..."

The fingers covering mine moved to linked us together. His palm warm, so much warmer than mine, it felt like it gave me strength. Or assurance. Or something. Something too nice and necessary. And not mine at all.

But I kept going. "He caught me stealing money from him. My little sister Kyra had a fever, and when I asked her mom for money, she told me to fuck off. I told him I was just taking it to pay for the doctor, but he wouldn't listen. He thought I was trying to steal his product or something, I don't even know... but he got so mad, so much madder than ever before... and he said all kinds of things, and when I tried to leave the room, he grabbed me by the hair and he... he...."

The soft spot at my nape itched, but I wasn't about to let go of Rip's hand to mess with it. I wasn't. I wasn't.

"He put a gun up to my head and told me that if I ever did it again, he would fucking kill me," I whispered, unable to hold back the shake... and trying to pick at the slice of anger of what that man had put me through, of what he had done to me. "Sometimes, I have dreams about it, but it's really rare. But the back of my head starts to itch, and I feel like I'm back there again..."

The silence between us stretched far and wide, and if it wouldn't have been for how his fingers had jerked in mine as I told him the last part, I would have thought maybe he had fallen asleep.

But I guessed he just didn't know what to say, and I couldn't blame him. I wouldn't know what to say if our roles were reversed either.

I hadn't even been sure I could tell him.

"I went to my grandma's house that day afterward, you know. I told her what happened, and she told me to go. It wasn't the first time she'd mentioned it. She said I would never be safe there, and I made her promise me that she would take care of my sisters as long as she could, and she said she would. And I told her... I told her I'd make sure she got them..." I squeezed his hand. "I couldn't stay there after that, Rip. I couldn't.

"I called the cops the next day while the girls were in school—while I should have been in school too—and told them there were drugs at my house. I told them where to find it and how there were kids living there. And they came... they came and they arrested my dad and their mom. He screamed at me that he was going to fucking kill me...

and I found out later on in the paper that they ended up arresting his brother too." I had known from the moment I'd been little what my dad did. How the cops were always on his case, according to him. They had told me a thousand times that I better keep my trap shut or else.

What I didn't share was how I had warned my sisters I was leaving. How they were going to go live with Grandma for a while. How things were going to be so much better. How I told them I was sorry they couldn't come with me, but I had only been seventeen.

She had never offered to let me live with her for whatever reason she'd had, but she had volunteered for them.

So I did it.

"That was what I didn't want to tell you. How I ratted him out. How he went to jail for three years because of me. Because I don't feel bad for what I did. Not even a little bit. I wish he would have stayed in jail for longer. That's why I went to go get my sisters. Because my grandmother called when she found out he was getting out, and she knew they wouldn't be safe with her, not with him so close. And so, we made it work and I went to go get them..."

I sniffed again, letting the anger fuel me, letting it remind me of what I'd done and would never look back on. "It's okay if you think I'm disloyal or a piece of shit for turning my own dad in, you know."

His fingers jerked while tangled with mine again, and I had no preparation for how he replied. For the strength in his tone, for the assuredness. "I'd never fucking think that about you," he said in that incredibly husky voice, full of... something. Something I wasn't sure of. "You did the right thing. You did the only thing you could have. There's nothing you got to feel bad about. You hear me?"

Did I hear him? Was he serious? I couldn't help how

small my voice sounded, how small I freaking felt. "You still want to be my friend then?"

"Christ," he hissed before making a choking noise. "Goddamn, Luna."

I didn't get a chance to think his words over before the hand holding mine left, and the next thing I knew, a hand snuck between my rib cage and the bed and another went to my hip, and he pulled me toward him. Onto him.

Lucas Ripley pulled me halfway onto his body, or at least that's how it felt when his bicep turned into my pillow and his hip and thigh a part of my mattress.

"You kill me, girl," he murmured in the roughest voice I'd ever heard. "I swear to God, you're a fucking puzzle I thought was all in the box, but every damn day I find a piece or two hidden all over the place."

I had no clue what he meant by that. Maybe Rip was aware of that because I didn't expect him to roll onto his side just a little, just enough so that he could look down at me with that face that I couldn't help but stare at every chance I got. The angles of it were heavy and the room was so dark it made it hard to see little else.

But I saw enough. Felt enough.

It really was too late to think I could love him if I gave myself the chance, I thought, before shoving that idea away as far as possible. I wasn't reckless enough to mess with that thought though. I wouldn't be.

My vision was just good enough to watch him as he propped himself up.

"What is it?" I asked, hearing the nerves in my voice.

He didn't reply though. Rip just loomed there, on a hip and an elbow, looking and looking and looking for so long, I had to lick my lips. For so long I wondered if he thought there was something wrong with me. Until suddenly, he dipped his face down—and I held my breath—and he did the last thing I would have ever expected.

Rip brushed his dry, warm lips over mine. Over the corner of my mouth. Over the length of my lips. Just the quickest, lightest, most feather-like kiss of my life.

And just as quickly as it happened, it was over. He rolled back down to his back, leaving me....

Just like that.

Rip had kissed me. *Me.*

Was it... was it for comfort? Did friends do that? Kiss each other sometimes to make the other person feel better?

Yeah. Yeah, they did, I told myself as I heard him exhale. That's what I was going to keep telling myself. He hadn't slipped in any tongue, that wouldn't have been friendly. *And you wouldn't have said no*, my brain tried to whisper, but I ignored it, for now and forever, to cling onto the one and only thing hanging around in my head that made any sense. My one genuine worry in that moment that had nothing to do with this man maybe-yes-maybe-not kissing me. "You still want to be my friend though?" I asked him.

I'd swear on my life he just scooted closer to me, and I wasn't going to overthink it. I definitely wasn't going to think about what had just happened either. "Luna, if you knew the things I've done..."

"I would still want to be your friend," I told him, breathing in through my nose that Irish Spring scent all over him. I licked my lips again and told myself I was only imagining that they tasted different. "Unless you like... hurt a kid or an animal or a woman."

I could hear the breath he took, feel the tension of his bicep under my arm.

I was lying on Rip's arm. *I was lying on Rip's arm.* After his lips had met mine.

He was comforting me, I told myself. That's all.

"No, I've never done any of that, but other men..." He trailed off, still speaking in that rough voice. "You don't have a single idea the shit I've done, and I don't wanna tell you." I could feel the breath he took because it made the chest I knew from touch that was directly in front of my face expand and expand and expand.

There. There. He was telling me a little. Just a little. "It's okay, you don't have to tell me."

"I don't want to, but you should know, you should know who you wanna be friends with."

"Tell me later," I told him softly, taking in another big gulp of that clean male scent. But I thought. I thought about his words. I thought about all the different backstories I had come up with over the years.

"But can I ask you one thing? One thing that won't change at all regardless of what you say? Because I swear it won't matter, but I've thought about it a lot and I just... I just want to know. We don't have to talk about it anymore afterward. And you can count it as my favor. We'll put it in our box of secrets."

I didn't want to think that his "hmm" sounded worried, but I thought it did.

I squeezed his hand again, letting my fingers linger over the two fingers I knew had an M and a C on them. "Were you in a gang before?"

The arm beneath my head went hard again, and it took seconds for it to relax. Seconds that seemed like minutes as his body finally lost its defensiveness. And I couldn't say I was totally surprised when he said, "Yeah, baby. You can say that."

Well. I couldn't say I was surprised. I wasn't, not even a little bit, but his response tickled at that part of me that had a dozen different questions. I was only going to choose one. "Can I ask you one more thing?"

His "yeah" was a rumble.

"Why'd you do it?"

If the question surprised him, I would never know for sure. What I was aware of was the way he sighed and how I felt it before he answered, "I was mad after my mom died. Real fucking mad. I didn't go out to join... it. I was raised here; I don't think I ever told you that. Few months after Mom passed, I packed up my shit and left. Moved around a lot there for a while. I'd spend a couple days here and there, New Mexico, Colorado, California for about a year, then I headed back. I don't got a whole lot of family, but back then I had an uncle in San Antonio—"

Some part of me startled at the mention of the city I'd grown up in, but I didn't make a peep.

"He was into that life. My mom's brother. I was mad as hell over life, and... they... took me in. It was kinda like having a new family, if your family was fucked up and everybody had lost their minds," he kept explaining in a steady voice. "I spent eighteen years there."

I curled my toes under the blankets, thinking about what he'd just said. "Were you happy?"

The sound that came out of Rip's mouth was a twisted, sad, low laugh. "Nah, baby, you don't really think about shit like that in that life, but sometimes you bury yourself so deep into something you don't know how to get out until you wake up one day and know you can't keep going a minute fucking longer."

His words slipped beneath my ribs and right into my chest. I knew exactly what that was like. Knowing you couldn't keep doing something anymore without losing too much. I rubbed my fingers against Rip's and felt his move right back, not holding mine but just there. There and there and there. Warm and strong and present.

"I got tired of being pissed for almost twenty years. Finally thought of what my mom would've wanted for me and it wasn't that. Wasn't what I wanted for myself as a kid either and being fed up with everything and everybody seemed to be some kinda sign... so I left. That's when I came back."

Rip's knuckles brushed over the fine bones on the back of my hand, and I stared up at the ceiling before I asked the one last question I would let myself wonder over. "Are you glad you came back?"

His chuckle was a puff, and those knuckles moved over me one more time before he said, "Some days, no... but, yeah. Yeah. Coming back was the best thing I ever did."

CHAPTER TWENTY-THREE

IF I HAD THOUGHT THAT MAYBE I WOULD HAVE GOTTEN a break from my Streak of Shit, I would have been mistaken.

Big-time.

Thankfully, as much as I might have hoped things would be different and my luck might have turned around, I hadn't expected for even a second that that would be the case. I knew how my luck worked, and in my life, when it rained... there was a hurricane coming. In this case, the thing with my sister had been the warning it was headed my way—I just hadn't seen it for what it was soon enough. The break-in had gotten me to the eye of the storm, and now I had the other half to live through. So I was expecting not to have the best day, or days, of my life, the morning I woke up holding Rip's hand.

The morning following the evening in which he'd basically admitted that he had been in a gang, or something close to that, based on his words.

But we weren't going to talk about that, not until he was ready. If he ever was.

If anyone knew how hard it was to admit intensely

personal things, it would be me. After all, I had a handful of people in my life that I trusted very, very much, and I had never told them about my dad and the gun. I had never told them about calling the police on him. They just assumed I'd gotten fed up and ran away.

So, I wasn't going to think about it. I wasn't going to bring it up again, and I didn't when he woke up after I rolled out of bed, or when we rode to work together again, and when our lunches overlapped by thirty minutes and he sat next to me, quietly reading through his magazine, his elbow brushing mine often.

The following morning, after he'd spent another night in my bed with me, neither one of us brought up any piece of our admissions... or commented about sharing the mattress again, except this time I had used my pillow instead of his shoulder like I had that first night.

Unfortunately, in the days since the break-in, Jason forgot he was on strike two, or he'd decided he didn't give a crap about his job and had taken being an obnoxious jerk to a totally different level. He'd been even more moody and snarky than before, and I could barely handle him when he simmered with it. He'd started disappearing for long periods of time during the day, and when I asked him about it, he'd claimed having diarrhea as to why he would disappear for twenty minutes at a time every hour.

I had timed it: twenty freaking minutes. That's how on edge he had me that I would time his poops to have as evidence if it ever came down to it. A part of me couldn't help but genuinely hope that, sometime soon, karma would come back and bite him in the ass in the form of him actually getting really terrible diarrhea for being a big, fat liar.

Jerk.

So on that Friday, the last day before he was supposed

to go on vacation for a week, a day I'd been counting down from what felt like the day I'd been born, I wasn't surprised when he showed up in a rotten mood. I could tell just by looking at his face that he was about to unleash a jackpot of bitch faces, sighs, and under-his-breath comments.

That alone had put me on edge.

I wasn't completely surprised when we hadn't even made it to noon before we got into it over him not agitating some paint I'd asked him to prep for me while I'd peeled the tape off a hood that I'd done matching, thick white stripes on—Shelby stripes.

"I was ordering paint for you," he'd tried to claim when I came out of the booth and found the paint sitting in the same spot it'd been in before.

I knew he was full of it instantly. "So you ordered it for me?"

His blank stare confirmed my answer. "They put me on hold and I hung up."

Patience. Patience.

I touched the charm bracelet on my left wrist and asked, "Who put you on hold?"

"Somebody."

"Man or a woman?"

The expression he shot me made me think he thought it was a trick question, but it wasn't. "Man."

"What was his name?"

Jason rolled his eyes and shook his head. "How the hell should I remember what his name was?"

"If he put you on hold, I want to know who did it. We do a lot of business with them, they shouldn't be putting you on hold," I lied. Of course sometimes even Hector put me on hold when I called in an order, but that was beside the point. My gut said he was lying. "What was his name?"

"I don't know," the asshole replied.

"Think about it. Was it Andy? Larry? Hector? Clarence?"

"I don't know. Clarence, I guess? I didn't ask him for his last name and where he lives or what his blood type is, if you're gonna ask that next."

Nobody named Clarence worked at the paint store. Nobody named Andy or Larry worked there either. And as much as I told myself to be patient with him, that patience was wearing out real quick with that tone. This was the wrong period in my life to come at me with this crap.

As much as I wanted to be a good person, and as much as I tried to have people, if not like me, then at least respect me, I recognized the signs when they pointed at a pointless endeavor.

Jason was just that.

"And you just hung up after being on hold?" I asked him slowly, still trying to cling on to being better to him than he was to me by not being rude in return.

The flick of eyebrows he gave me had to be a yes.

This lying *little shit.*

I took a breath through my nose and told myself to be patient, to *let it go.* But it was hard. It was so hard I was honestly tempted to go tell Mr. Cooper about how dishonest he was right in that instant.

But somehow I managed not to. Instead, I figured I would give him another subtle warning, even though I realized it was more than likely going to be in vain. "Jason, I don't like liars, and neither does Mr. Cooper."

Something flashed across his face—annoyance.

He didn't like getting called out, but I didn't like being lied to and played even more.

"Please don't lie to me ever again and definitely don't lie

to him either," I finished, giving him a blank expression that would hopefully hide how frustrated he made me. "I don't need to tell you how Rip feels about liars either."

That had him flushing. "I'm not lying!"

I didn't hold back my own eye roll then. "Look, I'm not arguing with you. All I'm telling you is that you shouldn't lie to anyone here. None of us appreciate it, especially not me."

"I'm not lying!"

I almost told him to lower his voice but managed not to. "You're lying to me right now, and you were lying to me about making a call." He opened his mouth, but I kept right on going. "Don't bother, I know you were. There are only two employees who answer the phone at the store, and none of them are named any of the names I told you."

"You tricked me?"

I shrugged. "Yeah, and I didn't like it, but you made me. I just wanted the truth. I asked you to do something and you didn't. That's not okay, and that's the point. I'm not trying to get you in trouble or get you fired. I don't want you to lose your job, so I'm trying to help you right now by telling you what not to do in the future. Regardless of whether you called or not, you should have done what I asked you to do. I'm not your boss, but I am trying to teach you because they asked me to."

"But I'm not fucking lying!" he shouted.

Patience and kindness, Luna. Patience and kindness.

I swallowed and reminded myself again. *Don't let him get to me.* "All right. If you aren't lying, I'm so sorry for accusing you. So, do you want me to hit the redial button on the phone or do you want to help me carry the hood out of the booth?"

It was his turn to press his lips together. Lying sack of runny crap. What the hell was there to think about? He knew he was lying. I knew he was lying. He was just not going to admit it. Not ever.

When a few seconds passed and he didn't say another word, I said, "Help me carry the hood out, and then you can put the paint to agitate while I go to the bathroom."

In my life, I'd had plenty of people give me looks that might have killed me if they had that kind of power behind them, but the one Jason gave me right then... it was honestly one of the worst. And all it did was piss me off. I wasn't trying to have a contest with him. I really wasn't. If I wanted to get him in trouble, I had more than enough beef with him—and could scrounge up proof—to do just that.

But I didn't.

I just wanted him to do a decent job and treat me with a little bit of respect.

And I wanted him to not act like a prick.

Apparently, that was asking for too much.

If I had been raised by different people, I might have been devastated at the facial expression he gave me, but I'd survived meaner looks from people who actually mattered in my life, so this twerp wasn't going to even get a frown in return.

Not even a blink.

He didn't know who he was messing with.

"Come on," I said, sounding almost as stony and tough as Rip. I didn't give him an option to tell me that he wouldn't follow.

I had learned over the years that if you wanted something, you didn't make it a question. If you made it into a question, sometimes the other person would take it that they had an opportunity to voice an opinion too. You were basically giving them an opening to say no.

The fact was, the last thing I wanted was for this idiot to back talk me more than he already had.

It only took about ten seconds before Jason's nostrils flared and he jerked his chin down in agreement... angrily.

What a sweet, lovely man-child, said no one ever.

Trying to keep my body loose and my mouth closed, I led the way to the booth. I'd already opened the double doors when I'd gone in to take the tape off, so I walked right in and stopped by the hood. Walking slower than a freaking zombie with one leg and intestines hanging out of his belly, Jason went around to the other side and stopped.

He didn't look at me, but it didn't matter.

"On three, let's lift." He still didn't say anything. Okay. "One, two, *three*," I called out, before lifting it. Luckily, he didn't fight with me over that.

I backed out, carrying my part, keeping my attention over my shoulder to make sure I didn't back into anything. In no time, we had set the hood down on top of old five-gallon buckets covered with old rags. For a second, I thought about reminding him of what I'd asked him to do but decided against it. He was a grown man and there was nothing wrong with his memory.

So I went to the bathroom, took my time a little and decided to stop by the floor and tell Rip that the hood was ready for them to come get. Instead, I found one of the builders crouched by a Hummer and told him. By the time I got back to my room, the sound of a paint can being shaken filled it, but Jason wasn't in the room.

Where the hell had he gone?

I had originally planned on letting him paint the engine block that was next on the schedule, but after his attitude, I wasn't sure I wanted to do that.

But....

Kindness and patience. Kindness and *patience*.

I'd wait for him.

And that was what I did. I waited, going through some files, checking my supplies... but when my watch told me it had been half an hour and he still hadn't come back, my irritation went through the freaking roof again. First he was pushing it with twenty minutes? But now thirty?

Patience, Luna, patience.

But patience didn't mean I had to wait around.

I was going to look for this turd and tell him to come paint the block. If he got another attitude with me, well then, maybe it would be time to go tell Mr. Cooper what was going on with him. Maybe I'd even tell Rip depending on how ugly he talked to me. At this point, I was over the fact the only person under twenty-one I could trust was Lily.

Sighing, I headed out of my room and down the hallway, stopping at the men's bathroom to kick it open and call out, "Jason?"

But it wasn't Jason that responded with, "Luna! I'm taking a shit!"

Even being in a little bit of a bad mood wasn't enough to keep me from snickering. "Sorry! I'm looking for Jason, Owen!"

"He walked by me when I was going down the hall," he replied, sounding... strained.

I covered my mouth so he wouldn't hear me laugh at him. "Okay, thanks!" I backed out of there and made my way toward the main floor. Going up to the tips of my toes, I tried to look around to see if I could spot him... but he wasn't anywhere.

Where was he?

I jogged up the stairs and looked in the break room, but

he wasn't in there either. I thought for a second about going to ask Mr. Cooper if he'd seen him but decided against it. From the stairs, I still didn't see him. I had never smelled smoke on him before, but maybe he was outside?

I should just go back to my room and do the work myself. I really should. Or go tell Mr. C first and then do that.

But for some dumb reason, I crossed the main floor, heading toward the door that would lead outside.

"You all right?" Miguel asked, peeking his head out from around the front end of the Malibu he was detailing as I walked by him.

"Have you seen Jason?"

He tipped his chin toward the door. "He was on the phone. He went out that way." Miguel made a thoughtful face. "That was a while ago though. Right after Mr. C took off."

This little shit. "Yeah, it's been over half an hour since I last saw him. Let me go see if he's out there."

My coworker shook his head, and I made a face at him before cutting the rest of the distance toward the door. I saw Rip stop where he was, right by the SS he was working on, and I waved at him. He didn't wave back, but I'd swear his mouth moved and his dimple popped.

Good enough for me.

Three steps later, I shouldered the door open and standing in the doorway, called out, "Jason?"

I could swear I heard voices.

"Jason?" I called out again.

Still, I could hear... something.

I needed to go ahead and tattle. I really did. I let the door shut behind me as I walked across the lot, trying to figure out where the voices were coming from. The lot was filled with employee and customers' cars. I had probably gotten across half the main lot when I spotted Jason's head over the top of his Mitsubishi Eclipse.

"Hey," I called out, stopping in place.

He turned to look at me, and I could see the hesitation on his face before he seemed to nod to himself and start walking toward me.

"What are you doing?" I asked. "I've been waiting for you."

Jason was busy looking at the ground as he approached, and he didn't respond.

I said his name again just as he passed by me.

He still didn't even bother looking over at me.

I stayed where I was and tried again. "Jason."

Still nothing.

What was going on with him?

I turned around to watch him as he walked toward the door I had just come through and opened my mouth to say something—I wasn't even sure what—when I heard the pounding footsteps.

But I wasn't sure what I was thinking. Wasn't sure why I slowed down so much to look over my shoulder to figure out *why* it sounded like someone was running up behind me. But the point was, I didn't turn around. Not fast enough.

I didn't put the pieces together until way too late.

Until I got shoved forward from behind so hard I went flying. Until my hands stretched out to break my fall, them and my forearms scraping the concrete when I landed what had to be ten feet away. It wasn't until *then* that I figured out what the hell was happening.

I wasn't sure why, I wasn't sure I would ever know why, but the first thing out of my mouth was a shouted, "RIP!" at the top of my lungs. I yelled it again the second I could get another mouthful of letters into my body.

But it was the second that name was out of my mouth that I heard the grunted, "Fuckin' bitch" that triggered some part of my brain a second before a hand dug into my hair, my short freaking hair that barely passed my chin when it was wavy, and jerked my head back, giving me a split-second view of a face I recognized.

A face I made a plan for spitting into a second before my cousin backhanded me like the piece of crap he was.

Stars flashed across my eyes just for a moment, just for a second, as that stupid ring he always wore bit into my cheek.

"What the fuck are you doing, Rudy?" a voice I didn't recognize shouted, panicking. "You said we were going to talk to her!"

"I—" my cousin started to say as the sound of a door being opened filtered across the lot. I opened my eyes against the tiny dots filling my vision, every single thing that had gone wrong in my life lately refueling me in that split second... and I swung my leg out, sweeping my cousin just perfectly... just enough that I heard him hit the ground.

I got up as fast as my hands and feet would let me, adrenaline and fucking anger like I had never felt in my life before burning a hole through me.

The bastard was trying to jump me.

My own *fucking* cousin was trying to jump me. Why was that surprising? Why did that make me mad? I wondered as I finally stood, looking down at the man blinking up at the sky on the ground, in a daze, groaning.

"LUNA!" Rip's voice roared from across the lot, the sound of multiple sets of feet hitting pavement telling me he wasn't alone.

But neither was I.

"Fuck!" the man with the voice I didn't recognize hissed, forcing me to look at him just as he turned around and started running toward the lot's gate. The gate that happened to be in the process of closing.

I'd swear on my life that my vision went red.

But the next thing I knew, I reached down and pulled my work boot off—thankful I never tied them too tightly— and I chunked it as hard as I could at the man trying to get away. I watched as my steel-toed boot hit him right between the shoulder blades, heard the "Oh!" escape him as it was his turn to go flying toward the ground, arms stretched in front of him. Heard the "Fuck!" that exploded out of him that told me it wasn't just my boot that hurt him.

And all I could think of was *good*.

Behind me, I heard the footsteps stop, heard the sound of something hard hitting flesh.

But nothing could have prepared me for the sight of Miguel and Rip kicking the crap out of my cousin. My cousin who was on the ground, curled up on his side in a tight ball. Like the coward he was and always had been.

I added another thing on my list of stuff I was never going to feel bad over, and that was standing there watching them kick him. At least until I cut the distance between us and then aimed a hard kick right at his tailbone with my booted foot.

"What the fuck, Rudy!" I shouted at him, reeling back and kicking him in the ass again, seeing out of my peripheral vision that Rip stopped and took a step back, watching me, his handsome, harsh face flushed red, his hands hanging at his sides.

"You okay?" he asked, eyes going down to my forearms

and wrists, taking in what I hadn't even seen were scrapes all across and down them.

I looked at him, breathing so hard, I couldn't catch it, breathing so hard I didn't appreciate Miguel aiming another kick at my cousin's lower half. "He just... ran up behind me and pushed me..." I tried to explain, losing my words between my breathing and just how fucking mad I was.

My cousin was going to jump me in the parking lot of my job.

He'd put his hands on me.

"Stop! God! Fucking stop!" my cousin yelled. "Jesus Christ!"

Miguel looked up at me, foot poised in midair, his normally easygoing features rearranged into genuine freaking anger and disbelief. "Want me to stop?"

"No," I told him without thinking. "What are you doing, Rudy?"

The man only a little older than me stayed in the fetal position as he said, "Fuck you!"

"My wrist is broken, Rudy!" the man I'd thrown my boot at cried.

We all ignored him.

Rip kicked Rudy in the ass that time, way harder than I had.

"Fuck!" my cousin shouted again. "Stop!"

"What are you doing here?" I repeated, totally caught off guard by this entire situation, by the fact that he was here. In Houston. At my job.

How did he find out—

My dad had found my number. How hard would it be to find out my job in that case?

Had my dad put him up to this?

"We told you not to go back to San Antonio!" Rudy had

the nerve to yell in his raggedy but pained voice. "We told you what would happen if you did!" he tried to use as an excuse, but all it did was make me freeze. "Should have gotten you outside your fuckin' place—"

He was here in retaliation for me going back there? For Grandma Genie's funeral? Was he for real?

This terrible sensation of dread hit me right then. *Should have gotten you outside of your fucking place.* Something clicked inside of me, and I looked down at my cousin and wanted to kick him in the balls as hard as I could. I didn't want to believe it, but this was him. Them. None of this should be surprising.

"Rudy, did you break into my house?"

I saw his hand jerk. Saw him flinch.

"Did you break into my house?"

"Am I gonna get kicked again if I answer that?" he had the stupid nerve to ask.

He'd done it. This little asshole, sack of shit had done it. It hadn't been random burglars.

It wouldn't even be the first time I'd overheard about him going into someone's house to rob them. He'd been doing stuff like that since we had been kids.

I was too busy staring at him to look and see who kicked him again, but I knew it happened because he cried out again, "Goddamn it!"

He had been the one to break into my house.

He'd gotten onto private property to jump me. To hurt me. And it wasn't the first time.

If I had thought things had gone red a minute ago, I would have been mistaken, but things definitely went red then. Anger surged through me. So strong, so piercing, I couldn't breathe.

But somehow, some way, it also calmed me to know it had been him.

It calmed me to know I knew exactly what I was going to do.

And so it wasn't so hard to stand there, staring down at him. It wasn't hard to say, "Rudy, my dad never told me not to go back to San Antonio. He told me never to go back home. If you want to play the specifics game, he never said San Antonio."

Because it was true.

Maybe my cousin hadn't come to kill me, but he had come back to wreck my life. To wreck me. To hurt me.

I wasn't okay with that. I was never going to be okay with that.

A Miller never went back on their word, and maybe I was an Allen now, but I had been a Miller first. My cousin reminded me of that. Unfortunately for him.

"Fuck off, you stupid bitch," Rudy kept venting, stupidly.

But I was past it.

"Do you remember what I told you at the funeral?" I asked him, calmly, knowing I wasn't going to get a response. He didn't let me down. So I crouched by him, not close enough to be within striking distance if he was dumb enough to try and get another shot in, but close enough so I could speak more quietly, so he would know I wasn't talking irrationally. Rip had taught me how much more effective that was than yelling.

And just in case he had forgotten, I answered my own question. "You came and you tried to hurt me, and I'll live with that. But I told you at the funeral if you ever put your hands on me again, I was going to break your hand."

His entire body froze, and I heard a noise from Miguel,

but I didn't turn to look at him. I was too focused. I was in this zone I had forgotten how well I was familiar with.

"And you know what that means, don't you?" I asked him again.

"Oh, fuck," I heard Miguel mutter.

But I didn't look away as I asked my boss and my friend, "Will one of you hold him for me?"

Miguel didn't hesitate. He dropped to my cousin and kneeled over his curled legs, pressing his hands down on the arm Rudy had closest to the ground. If he was a little too good at that, I was going to ask him later about it.

Just as I reached for Rudy's hand, another one landed on my shoulder, and Rip's voice was clear as he asked, "Let me do it."

I didn't look at him. Instead I took in my cousin's face, pained and angry and furious—a reminder of a time in my life I never wanted ever again after this. "I can do it," I told Rip.

"I want to," he assured me quietly.

And it was that that had me glancing up at him again. His face was still red, his breathing was still pretty off, and he looked... furious.

For me?

"Go take care of your scrapes. We'll handle this," Rip said in that cool, cool voice, watching me with a face that I had never seen before. One that made the hairs on my arms stand up at the same time it made my chest tight.

There was an emotion behind his eyes that I didn't know what to do with. That I didn't know how to handle.

I nodded at him, knowing I was leaving my cousin to get his hand broken.

And all I could think was that he deserved it. After everything he'd done and had been willing to do, he deserved it.

But I knew there was one more thing I needed to do, and I glanced down at the man on the floor, thrashing by then, and said, "Tell my dad that if I ever see any of you again, if he ever calls me again, I'll do more than call the cops and tell them there are drugs in the house. Tell him that I still remember a whole lot of things from ten years ago, do you understand me?"

"Fuck—" Rudy started to hiss before crying out loud when Rip took his hand.

"Remember what I said," I warned him, taking a step away. It should have bothered me how okay I was about all this. I'd think about that later. Maybe. "I asked you to leave me alone, Rudy. Remember that. I warned you."

"Grab your boot," Rip said quietly. "Then go in, Luna."

I nodded at him, looking at the big man crouched over my cousin, holding his hand in a position I knew well. I heard a moan from somewhere in the lot and I headed toward it, finding my boot just feet away from a man sitting between two cars, holding his forearm and looking at his hand, or wrist, with horror.

I wasn't going to worry about him, I thought as I grabbed my boot. I knew Miguel and Rip could handle their own.

A little too well.

Or just well enough. Huh.

Reaching up to touch my now aching cheek, I couldn't help but shake my head at the figure on the ground as I slid my boot on and headed back the way I had come.

"We got it," Miguel assured me, still covering my cousin as I walked by them. His gaze was thoughtful and somehow mad at the same time.

"Thanks, Miguelito," I said carefully, wondering just for

a second what he was thinking right then. I'd worry about what those thoughts might mean to our friendship later.

I didn't feel bad, I didn't feel even a little bad, I thought as I walked away.

I was only feet away from them when I heard Rip strangely ask, "You remember me?"

CHAPTER TWENTY-FOUR

I HAD JUST FINISHED STRIPPING MY PROTECTIVE SUIT off when the knob to the door of the room jiggled. The knob and door shook once more as whoever was on the other side tried to open it again. I didn't blame them for being confused that the door was locked. It never was.

But the fact was, I hadn't seen Jason in hours. Not since he had walked past me into the building, leaving me out there, alone. Well, not technically alone.

It had taken me maybe ten minutes after washing my hands all the way up to past my elbows to put the pieces together. They didn't make sense. Not exactly at least... but enough.

Someone had let my cousin and the other guy into the lot.

And it didn't take a genius to know there had only been one other person in the lot. One other person who would willingly let someone who didn't like me into it. At least that's what my gut said.

The one and only person who had disappeared. I hadn't had the heart to ask any of the guys who had wandered into the break room what happened or if they knew anything about Jason. By the time I had gotten done and Rip and Miguel hadn't come back, I had gone to the back door and looked outside to find it empty.

What a mess. What a freaking mess.

What was my dad *thinking*? I didn't think anything would surprise me, but he did. After all this time, he still did.

I wasn't going to think about it anymore. It was done. I knew how things were for them. Even if Rip hadn't... hurt Rudy... the point had been made. I would go to the cops again if they made me. But I knew, in my gut, they wouldn't.

"Hold on," I called out as I wiped at my face with a paper towel.

Taking in the face on the other side, I turned the lock and then pulled it wide.

"Luna," Owen peeked his head inside the door.

"Hey." I turned my back to him, needing to sit down so I could pull the rest of the suit off. "What's going on?" I asked just as I made it to my desk and pulled out the rolling chair so I could take a seat.

"Mr. Cooper asked me to tell you to go to his office," my coworker answered, sounding a whole lot more serious than usual.

I pulled the suit off from my feet, glancing up at him to shoot him a smile that made my cheek ache. I had iced and smothered ointment on it afterward, so I knew it hurt less than it would have if I hadn't. I needed a freaking break. A nice, long break, and if things could go right for just a little while, well that would be nice too.

But I wasn't going to hold my breath.

Especially not when one sister still wasn't answering my calls and another one was being weird too.

"Okay, I'll go up there in a second."

Owen hesitated. "You okay?"

I shrugged. "My cheek hurts and the cuts on my hands sting, but I'll be okay."

My longtime friend looked at me in a way that said he believed me, but it didn't make him feel any better. He hadn't been around when I had been upstairs, but the guys at the shop were nosey. They knew something had happened, but I hadn't said exactly what. I'd bet within three minutes, they had come to some conclusion and were just giving me space now.

I appreciated it. There was something really messed up about a family member trying to hurt you, especially when it was your dad who had put it into effect.

But luckily none of that was anything new for me.

And if I got some pleasure at Rudy getting hurt... well, I wasn't going to feel bad. I could feel nice after everything that had happened. It was the least he deserved.

"Luna..."

I couldn't even find it in me to muster up a smile. "Yeah?"

His dark brown eyes slid from one side of the room to the other, and his voice dropped so I could barely hear him as he said, "You want us to deal with it?"

"Deal with what?" I asked him as I stood up.

He was still looking around the room. "With the kid."

I stood there.

He looked at me and let his stare stay. "We looked at the video. He was the one who let them in," he told me solemnly. "You want us to teach him a lesson?"

I don't know what it said about me that I felt more loved by my coworkers than ever before right then in that moment.

You didn't offer to beat up someone unless they meant something to you.

And that's what Owen was in here doing, being the representative. That was what Miguel and Rip had done for me by running out into the lot to help me. *That* was what family did.

And even though I shouldn't have smiled, I did. I probably sounded way more chipper than I should as I answered back, "That's one of the nicest things anyone has ever offered me, Owen, but it's okay."

His eyes narrowed. "Are you sure? Because nobody messes with one of our own."

I had always known I was one of theirs, or they were one of mine, but to hear it...

Well, that took care of the pain more than anything else ever would.

"I'm sure, but thank you. And tell the other guys I said thank you too. I'm touched, honestly," I told him.

"You change your mind, tell us." Owen took another step back and then said, "It doesn't have to be us that do it either, I know people. Miguel knows people."

Miguel had known how to hold Rudy down... but that was something to ask him about later.

All of my coworkers had some shady pasts apparently.

It was nice to know I wasn't the only one. It was so nice that I grinned at Owen even though it stung and said, "I'll tell you if I change my mind, but I'm all right. He isn't going to get to me." More than he already had at least.

"We've all tried calling him, but he's not answering. It looks like he took off right after Rip and Miguel did."

Wait. *Wait.*

Did they watch the cameras... and see what had

happened? Wasn't that literally what he'd said a minute ago? *We looked at the video?*

"Fucker. He better not ever think about trying to come back."

I appreciated what he said, but I was too focused on one thing. "Did you watch the security footage?"

Owen grinned... and he nodded. "All of it."

Well.

Then backed out with that sneaky, and in some way, a strangely pleased, expression on his face.

Well, if I had been worried that they wouldn't like me once they found out I wasn't always Nice Luna, I would have been reassured they were okay with it.

Now, I needed to go talk to Mr. Cooper. He had never asked me to his office before, and I wasn't delusional enough to think this time would be meaningless. He hadn't been around while I had been upstairs. He had left for a long lunch.

I figured he wanted to talk to me about Jason, but...

Why wouldn't he come downstairs then?

I realized now I could have prevented most of this by not sucking everything up. If I would have told Mr. C about how rocky things had been the entire time the younger man had been stuck with me... well, I wouldn't be here, with my busted cheek and torn up forearms. Or if I would have just told Rip straight-out that I couldn't stand the weasel....

It was my fault. The only person I could blame was my own freaking self.

Maybe if I would have genuinely tried to be nicer to him, we could have built a better working relationship.

Then again, probably not.

Rubbing at the spot between my breasts where the fox necklace I'd put on that morning was, I made myself head toward the door and pull it open. I waved at the guys on the main floor and gave them a grim smile when I made it to the main floor. I got a mix of a couple of head tilts, a couple raised hands, and one thumbs-up in response.

But it was Miguel standing in the middle of the room that had me pausing. "You're good," he mouthed with a slow smirk that seemed really pleased.

"Thank you," I mouthed back, getting an even wider grin in response.

I shook my head at him before I turned around and headed back up the stairs.

At the office, I knocked on the door. "It's Luna," I called out, shoving my hands into the pockets of my jeans.

"Come in," Mr. Cooper yelled back.

With my elbow, I moved the handle down and shoved the door open. Sure enough, the man who had raised this business from an auto body repair shop to include a successful restoration business was sitting behind his desk, clicking away on his computer with a concerned expression on his face. He tried to muster up a smile, but it fell off as quickly as it had come on.

"*Little moon*," he breathed, shoving his chair back and getting to his feet... mostly. It was more of a stoop as he looked me over.

"I'm okay, Mr. C. I promise, sit down." I gave him a smile I knew was strained as I took one of the ancient chairs across from his desk. Taking my hands out of my pockets, I pressed my palms together and then stuck them between my thighs. I didn't miss the tight nature to Mr. Cooper's movements as he sat back down in his chair and shoved it forward to settle down. In a gray Polo shirt and black khakis, he was dressed the exact same he always was since Rip had come, and he'd stopped working on the floor.

"They didn't tell me about your face," he murmured quietly, his mannerisms becoming more and more concerned by the second.

"It's just a little cut," I told him, shooting him a small, tight smile that only slightly made my cheek hurt. It was probably about time that I put more ointment on it.

He shook his head, his eyes glued on what I knew was the cut on my cheek. "I'm sorry, honey."

"You don't have anything to be sorry over," I told him, honestly. "It's all on my family, Mr. C. I'm sorry it happened here."

My boss's expression told me he didn't believe me, and the way his shoulders curled and stooped confirmed it. "Rip is on his way. Let's wait for him, okay?" he asked me, still speaking gently.

"Okay," I agreed, flashing him an expression that hopefully said I didn't want him to feel even a little bad about any of this.

It *was* my fault.

And Jason's.

And Rudy's.

And my dad's.

But I could and would take responsibility for my own actions.

"You mind talking about something else until he gets there?" I asked.

Those green-green emerald-colored eyes watched me. "How's the house coming along?" he decided to go with.

I had forgotten I hadn't had a real conversation about my place getting broken into. The only person I'd gotten around to telling was Lily. What I hadn't told her was that I hadn't been staying there alone.

Much less that Rip and I had shared a couch and a bed those same times.

I wasn't surprised he hadn't blabbed about sleeping in my bed to Mr. Cooper either, but I tried my best not to even think about it in the first place. Then again, why would Rip tell him anything about me?

"Okay," I told him, feeling like even more of a liar than usual. "My house got broken into a few days ago. The insurance is going to cover a lot of the things that got messed up. They didn't actually steal anything but my laptop and my tablet." They. My cousin and whoever else had helped him. Maybe the man I had thrown my boot at.

I wished I could throw it again, honestly. At his head.

"Oh, Luna, I'm sorry. They don't know who did it?"

There it went. "The police had said there had been some robberies in the area, but no one I know said they'd heard that." I swallowed, ignoring the ache right in the center of my chest. "My cousin... the guy I had an issue with in the lot... he admitted he was the one who did it." The more I said it, the easier it would get. I hoped. "So it was him."

A hand went up to his head to scrub at the top of it, reminding me of Rip who did the same thing. Mr. Cooper sighed. "I can't believe they would do that."

Then he didn't need to know that it had to have been my dad who sent him. I didn't have the heart to tell him.

The older man shook his head, clearly looking devastated. "I'm sorry, honey. You should have told me sooner."

I didn't want to tell him that I'd called him the night it happened, but he'd had his phone off. "Thanks, Mr. C. It's all right. I'll get it all sorted, but if I need help, I'll let you know for sure."

My longtime boss's face dropped, and I could see the

argument on his face. But he held the words back and said in a tone that made me feel a little bad, "If there's anything Lydia and I can do, tell us. You know we'll help you with anything, little moon. We love you."

I knew they did, of course I knew they did, but I still told him, "I know, and I love you both too." That was maybe the tenth time in all the years we'd known each other that I had said those words. "And I will let you know, I promise. I'm still just trying to wrap my head around it all. These last few weeks have just felt like a really bad dream."

His nod said he understood, and I knew he did. But it didn't wipe the resignation off his face. "Maybe you should look into getting an alarm system?"

Eh. "Yeah." I paused and thought about withholding my conversation with Rip from him, but there was nothing to hide. And even if there was, I didn't want to. "Rip helped me out with it, the day after it happened, that's why he took the day off. To help me. I'm sorry if that caused a problem between you two."

Mr. Cooper blinked, and luckily there were no hard feelings on his face from me keeping this from him but telling Rip about it. His voice was a little high, a little shocked as he basically wheezed, "Our Rip?"

Obviously, I wasn't the only one surprised by this kindness, and it made me feel a little bad and a little defensive. "Yeah." There was nothing to hide, and I didn't want to keep this from him any longer. "He knew I've been scared, and he's stayed with me the last few nights."

I don't even think he meant to ask, "He did?" But the question did come out of his mouth.

All I did back was nod.

I didn't know what to do with the look that came over his face.

So I decided to change the subject. "How's Lydia, by the way?"

I wondered if he was still hung up on Rip helping me out, but he managed to say, distractedly, "She's great. She was asking me about you a few days ago. I think she was planning on inviting you over for lunch or dinner this weekend, if you're free."

"I'm always free for you two," I told him honestly.

"Have you been going on your dates?"

"Kind of," I told him, giving him a little smile.

Ripley had kept me company at the bar I'd been stood up at, I thought to myself. "I've gone on two and got left hanging at another one."

I could tell he was distracted, but he still managed to ask. "Any winners?"

I *almost* snorted. "No. Not even close, but I've only gone on three. I don't want to waste my time, and a lot of these guys don't want anything serious so...." I shrugged. "I'm just being picky and don't want to settle. I just want... the right man." And my heart wanted the wrong one, but I wasn't going to think about that again in the next millennium. Nope.

Mr. Cooper's nod was grave, but his voice was even more serious. "I get it, honey." He sighed. "I was married before Lydia. Did you know that?"

I hadn't up until I had overheard his and Rip's conversation—a conversation I wasn't supposed to have been eavesdropping on. So I lied and shook my head.

He seemed to swallow, to think for a minute before saying, "We had been together since I was twenty-one." His voice was quiet, serious. "We were together for so long, and it seemed like six months. It was a lifetime, but it never felt like it."

Was it silly of me that I felt embarrassed and even a little protective of Lydia? Knowing now that Mr. Cooper had been with someone else for so long?

He kept going, his voice still holding onto its gravity... and something else that might have been bittersweet. The hard bob of his throat confirmed it. "She was... she was the love of my life," he admitted. "Lydia is too in a way, but Bea was my world. It's been twenty-three years, and I don't miss her any less than I did when she first died. Lydia came into my life a lot sooner than I would have dreamed of, a lot sooner than I would have liked, but...." His shrug looked like he had three hundred pounds on his shoulders. "It was meant to be. Lydia came when she came, and I can't say that it wasn't fate that brought us together."

Oh jeez. I blinked. "How soon after?"

He swiped his hand over his head again and looked up at the ceiling. "I met her six months after."

What was I going to do? Judge him? If he had been anyone else, I would have scoffed or thought something terrible, but Mr. Cooper had always been honest with me. He had loved me back when I hadn't loved myself much. I had seen him with Lydia. I knew there was a deep love there.

I was the first person in the world to understand that life wasn't white and black. I hadn't even been able to find one person to love me romantically, much less two. All I knew was that based on the face he was giving me, other people in the past had given him a hard time for moving on, for finding love. After all this man had done for me, I wouldn't be one of them too.

"Can I ask what she passed away from?"

His hesitation made me feel terrible. The breath he

sucked in and then let out made me feel like an asshole. "She was—"

The sound of knuckles hitting the door came a second before the door creaked open and a familiar voice said, "Ready?"

Mr. Cooper's face instantly flushed, and he lowered his voice, "We'll finish this conversation later, okay?"

He didn't want to finish the conversation because of Ripley, did he? I wondered... but nodded anyway. There were some things in this life that you didn't want to talk about. Not ever. And especially not in front of certain people.

I understood that better than most. There were plenty of years that I didn't enjoy talking about.

"Come in, Rip," Mr. Cooper called out a moment later.

Sure enough, the biggest man I had ever seen in my life, swung the door completely open and stepped inside, shutting it behind him. He stood there in a gray shirt that was plastered to his upper body. I glanced back at Mr. Cooper as Ripley took the seat that I had left unoccupied closest to the door. He glanced at me once, grunting out a "Luna" that I replied with, "Hi, Ripley."

"You all right?"

"I'll live. It's not the first time he's jumped me."

Maybe that was the wrong thing to say.

"Well," Mr. Cooper continued on the moment his co-owner seemed to have settled into the seat beside me. "We brought you in here because of what happened earlier."

And, I was right. This was about Jason. Or maybe my cousin coming to my job and starting issues.... But I didn't think Mr. Cooper would blame me for that. Luckily, there hadn't been any customers around to see it, so it wasn't like it would impact business.

Rip leaned forward and took hold of the conversation, his gaze leeching straight on me. "Tell us what's been going on with Jason."

Mr. Cooper jumped in immediately. "From the beginning, Luna. Tell us what's been going on with him when he's with you. You've told me some of it, but I think Rip should hear it from the beginning too."

So this was where we were going. It had nothing to do with Rudy—thankfully. But either they had watched the video or heard that Jason had been the one to let him into the lot, and his disappearing act afterward hadn't helped either. The dummy hadn't thought that through at all. Didn't he know that even if he never came back, employers checked references?

So I told them, "I never said anything, but I knew him before he started working here."

Somehow I missed how Rip's eyes narrowed as they flicked from Mr. Cooper to me and back to the older man again. I didn't like the look that came over Rip's face before he asked, "How?"

Here we went. "He dated my sister two years ago. It was a mess. I didn't like him when she introduced me to him, and I didn't like him six months later when it turned out he got another girl pregnant. I stayed out of it, but when he would come by the apartment and try to see her, if I was home, I would tell him to leave. Anyway, then he applied here—I hadn't even known he was interested in working in this field back then—but I didn't want to bring up personal stuff to either of you. I could live with thinking he was a... you know, not a good person.

"But almost immediately after he started here, he began being really rude and disrespectful. I wasn't exactly the nicest and warmest person to him, but he was really defensive about everything. I didn't like him, and he knew that, but I tried to be professional. Nothing helped though.

"He's messed up a bunch of times since he started coming to help me, and I swear he does it on purpose. He doesn't listen. He's got a bad attitude. Insubordinate. He's petty and lazy," I kept going. "We get into it over everything, even before he came over to my section. Mr. C knows he's done some petty crap, but it was on purpose, I swear. And, Rip, you've heard him on the phone with me, you know he's a weasel.

"Today though, we got into a disagreement and he walked out of the room and didn't come back for half an hour, so that was when I went to look for him. You can ask Owen and some of the other guys, they saw me or asked what I was doing, and I told them. Miguel told me he saw him outside, and that's why I went out there in the first place. I saw him, and he ignored me and walked right by me, and the next thing I knew..." I'd gotten shoved from behind.

"You saw it happen?" Mr. Cooper asked Ripley with a frown.

"I got there after," my younger boss confirmed, his expression tight. "Miguel and I were by the back door when we heard Luna yell, and we went right by him on the way out the door. I was too... distracted to stop and think about what he'd been doing." I didn't miss the way he fisted a big hand.

"You should've gone back in and made sure he didn't leave," Mr. Cooper replied pretty freaking crisply, sounding angrier than I had ever heard him, and that was saying something because I'd eavesdropped on his arguments with Rip before.

My younger boss's mouth slackened, and I knew whatever was about to come out of his mouth was no good.

So I tried to but in. "It's my fault. I should have said something to one of you and told you the truth when he was being a pain over the last few weeks. I should have followed him back into the building when he was making it obvious he was ignoring me—"

Rip cut me off, blatantly ignoring me as he asked Mr. Cooper tightly, "I was busy making sure Luna was all right. What *should've* happened is that you *should've* listened to me when I said you needed to quit trying to make him Luna's apprentice."

Wait. He'd told Mr. C not to stick him with me?

Rip kept right on going. "*I told you* there was something off about the kid. *I told you* she didn't like him working with her."

He'd done that too?

"I told you we should have fired him after his first fuckup, but you said '*Let's give him another chance. He's young. Everyone makes mistakes,*' didn't you?"

"I didn't know it was that bad," the older man claimed in a wobbly voice, his face flushing.

"Me telling you wasn't enough?" Rip returned. "Her telling you wasn't enough?"

Shit, shit, shit. "No, it's my fault. Mr. Cooper, I should have insisted—"

Ripley's hand came up and he waved me off. "No. I told him." He pointed one thick, long finger in Mr. Cooper's direction. "*I told you*, and her fucking cousin could have had a gun on him. He could've had a bat on him, a tire iron. She could've gotten her brains bashed in because you always think you know what's right!"

I could have not been there or within ten miles based on

how intense the stare down they were having with each other was.

And suddenly, I had a feeling that this conversation had just taken a sudden turn to This Has Nothing To Do With Me.

I would have been right.

"I had no idea—"

"You never have an idea," Ripley said, loudly.

"This is nobody's fault but my own," I tried to tell them, trying to make eye contact with one of them, but they were both staring too hard at each other. It was like I wasn't even in the same universe. "It was my cousin. My family. And I don't know if he paid Jason to open the gate and let him in or what, but it's my fault," I tried to say... but they weren't listening. They weren't even close to listening.

"That's unfair, Ripley," the older man said, completely focused on him.

"You think?"

Mr. Cooper swept another hand over his head. "I know it is. I told you I didn't know."

"You don't think that excuse is getting old after all these years?"

"Son, give me a break," Mr. Cooper almost croaked, rubbing his hand over his chest, his face reddish pink.

But the man in the chair decided he wasn't going to give anyone a break, not his business partner, not the man who had been so kind to me for so long. "Don't fucking 'son' me. You always think you know better than anyone else, but you don't."

Okay. All right. I needed to calm this down. "Hey, Rip. Don't put this on Mr. C. It's on me. I should have said something from the beginning—"

They were still ignoring me as their voices got louder.

"I didn't know!" Mr. Cooper shot back as Rip stood up. "It's not fair for you to keep bringing up things from twenty years ago."

How had they known each other twenty years ago?

"Hey, you two, can we agree it's nobody else's fault but Jason's?" I piped up, getting to my feet to hopefully remind them they weren't in here alone.

I was invisible though because nothing changed.

Nothing changed because Rip jabbed his finger in Mr. Cooper's direction and hurled,

"Twenty-two years ago, not twenty, and it could be another forty and I still wouldn't forget what you did to Mom—"

Wait.

Wait.

Mom?

Mom?

Mr. Cooper wheezing had me snapping my eyes toward him just as he reached up and slapped another hand over the center of his chest.

"Mr. Cooper?" I asked, taking a step toward his desk as Ripley's voice seemed to trail off.

Mr. Cooper sucked in another gasp as his fingers curled over the shirt he had on. "I... I..."

"Call 911!"

CHAPTER TWENTY-FIVE

──────────────────────

"I'm going to get some tea or coffee from the cafeteria. Do you want anything?"

I asked as I got to my feet, ignoring the way my knees popped from how long I'd been sitting in the waiting room at the hospital.

At the hospital.

At the hospital after following the ambulance carrying Mr. Cooper.

Mr. Cooper who I was 99 percent sure, had suffered a heart attack.

Two hours in the waiting room had given me enough time to nurse a pounding headache, a knot in my chest that would have felt like a malignant tumor if those felt like something, and knees that cracked as I stood up. After the paramedics had shown up, I had followed behind, wanting to throw up and pray at the same time, but I hadn't prayed for anything in so long, I wasn't sure I knew how to do it anymore.

And behind me, in Mr. Cooper's car, had been Ripley in his truck.

Rip who hadn't said more than a handful of words to me since he'd first shouted for someone to call an ambulance. Who had stood there to the side while the EMTs had loaded Mr. C up. Who hadn't made a move to leave, which was why I had taken his car since mine was at home.

Rip and I had sat there, three chairs apart, in silence the entire time. I wasn't sure what he had been thinking, or what he'd felt. And I sure hadn't known what to say.

I didn't know what to think, if I was going to be honest with myself.

Mom.

Twenty-two years.

All that anger...

It wasn't the time to think about it, but it was hard not to let my mind wander to those words and what they possibly meant.

I wasn't stupid.

I'd had my heart in my throat for the last two hours. My stomach felt off and tight and hot, and I genuinely felt sick with worry over a man I loved and cared for. It didn't help that I had been blowing up Lydia's phone and she hadn't answered. I'd left her voice mails on her cell and their home phone telling her to call me, but she still hadn't.

Was it normal for whatever they were doing to him to take so long? I wondered. I wasn't sure. I had tried looking up things on the internet, but the information was so broad, all it did was make me sicker.

Which was why I knew I needed to get up and move around for a little while, even if it was just a short trip to the cafeteria. Being helpless was one of the crappiest things in the world.

Rip stared straight ahead at the television playing an

episode of *Law and Order* as he answered in a voice I had never heard before. "No."

He had barely moved in the hours we'd been sitting there. Was he worried too? Did he feel guilty for getting into an argument with Mr. Cooper—his maybe-possibly-I-think-Dad—right before? I couldn't blame him if he did.

I felt guilty for not doing more. For not stopping them. For not opening my mouth and complaining about that little jerk when Mr. C had first stuck him with me.

A small part of me, that honestly wasn't so small, felt dumb for not putting the dots together.

Another small part of me felt a little betrayed that, if it was true that they were related, that neither one of them had ever said a word.

Especially not Mr. Cooper, who had been a better father figure to me than my own dad had been. This man that I genuinely loved hadn't even hinted at the fact that the forty-one-year-old man I saw five days a week, if not six days a week, might be his son.

If I thought about it... if I really thought about it... they both had the same tall, broad builds. Wide shoulders, big chests, they were tank-like. Ripley didn't have his eyes, but he did have his chin. And if I hadn't met Mr. Cooper after he'd gone completely gray, they might have the same hair color too. They liked their coffee the same way, had a couple of the same tics....

If they were related, then their hostility toward one another made so much sense it was annoying.

If anyone knew what it was like to be resentful toward a relative, it was me.

And I hadn't known.

I hadn't even had a clue after nine years of knowing the older man.

Maybe it wasn't true. Maybe I had misunderstood, but I seriously, *seriously* doubted it. Why else would Rip use the "mom" word around Mr. Cooper? If they were related by any other means, I bet it would have been brought up by that point. And the years made sense. Hadn't Rip said he was eighteen when his mom had died? Hadn't Mr. C remarried a year later and been with Lydia twenty-two years?

They were related.

They had to be.

And they had kept it a secret.

Secrets, secrets are no fun. Secrets hurt someone.

It wasn't the time to focus on that, I tried to tell myself. It was time to worry about Mr. Cooper. This had nothing to do with me.

Sometimes, it was a lot easier to accept things when you realized that at the end of the day, you were just an innocent casualty in a train wreck that had been caused by something that had slowly rusted and fallen apart over decades.

Going up to my tiptoes to stretch my calves, I took in the grave, withdrawn expression on Ripley's face as he sat in his chair a few feet away from the one I had been in, and asked, "Rip? Do you want anything? I can get you a soda too if you don't want coffee."

He still didn't take his attention away from the television as he said in a gravelly, tight voice, "No."

I wasn't sure if he'd even eaten his lunch. I hadn't felt like eating mine after everything that had happened with my cousin. "Something to eat?" I asked, battling that helpless feeling for the man in the operation room.

"No."

I saw his fingers spread where they were on his thighs, watched the way he flicked his gaze up to me as his lips parted a little, this... annoyed expression coming over his face. I knew that expression. I'd seen my parents make the same one enough times over my life.

Specifically when I would try to talk to them and just ended up bothering them instead. It was their *stupid idiot kid* face. Like they pitied me for caring. For wanting something that they knew I wouldn't get, something I should have known they wouldn't give me, but had been too young to understand.

It was the face they made right before I had a reason to feel regret.

"I don't fucking want anything, Luna, okay?" he said so calmly it was eerie.

I swallowed. I reminded myself that he might be feeling guilty and angry because someone he had a history with was in the hospital, and he felt bad. Someone who might be his father. Maybe.

So I tried to shrug it off. I tried to forgive him for that face that made my stomach clench harder. I tried to tell myself that sometimes people didn't know what they needed or wanted when they were suffering. Nobody was rational when they were upset. Not even me. I had asked this man to break someone's hand for me in retaliation hours ago. Hello, hypocrite.

"Are you sure?" I didn't drop it, because I knew he needed to eat or at least drink something. "I don't think you've eaten anything and—"

That ugly, *ugly* expression didn't go anywhere, that calm, weird, soft voice sticking around his vocal cords. "I already fucking said I don't want anything, *okay?*" he growled.

His dad had a heart attack and you need to be patient

with him, I told myself, told my heart as it hurt and my stomach as it got impossibly tighter.

I kept my gaze on his face, and told him patiently, "I'm just asking, Rip. You don't have to bite my head off. I'm only trying to help. I won't ask again, okay?"

This man who had slept in my bed rolled his eyes. His hands opened and closed on his thighs, and I tried to prepare myself. Tried to tell myself, *kill him with kindness. Choose patience.* And that all fell apart and away as this man I knew but didn't know snarled, "Go back to the shop, Luna. I'm not in the mood to deal with your shit."

Deal with my shit?

Okay. All right. He was dealing with stuff. I had to remember that. *I had to.* He didn't mean what he said. So I kept my voice as friendly and patient as I could muster. "I'm here for Mr. Cooper." Then I tried to give him a little smile. A patient one, so he would know I was just trying to help. If I didn't care about him, I wouldn't give a crap about his calorie or liquid intake. Didn't he know that? "I'm here for you too, Rip. You shouldn't be here alone."

It was his head cocking to the side that put me even more on edge. The tone of his voice didn't help. Not at all.

"I'm not in the mood, do you get me? I don't need you to worry about me right now. What I need is for you to give me some space without worrying about hurting your feelings."

I wanted to flinch, but I didn't. "You don't have to worry about hurting my feelings."

"I always worry about hurting your fucking feelings, Luna. Give me a break," he snapped.

It didn't surprise me that I didn't reel back at his words. Not even if his statement stung me like a burn under hot water. "Since when?" I asked him, hearing the tension in my voice and not liking how he was making me feel.

This man shook his head. "I'm not in the fucking mood."

He wasn't in the mood?

"I'm not in the mood to have you be mean to me when I'm only trying to be your friend," I replied, feeling my face go hot and indignation fill my soul at how he was just trying to get rid of me like we were strangers.

He had slept in my bed the night before. He had made me lunch and dinner. Bought me breakfast.

Friends were there for each other, and that's what I was doing. Trying to watch out for him. Be there for him.

And he was pushing me away, and not in a nice way.

The next few words out of his mouth proved it. "You're trying to be my friend? Be my friend by giving me some space before I say or do something I'll end up regretting later. Give me some space so that later on I don't have to feel bad for making you feel bad."

Maybe I should have let it go, should have walked away and given him the space he wanted, but it had been a long day and I felt riled. Prickled. Hurt already physically and emotionally. I didn't feel like letting him steamroll me.

Especially after everything that had happened lately with the funeral and my sisters and my dad. Maybe if my sister hadn't kicked me out of her place, or these wounds from my dad hadn't been reopened, or if my cousin hadn't just shown up to my work to try and hurt me... Maybe I could have let it go if all those things hadn't existed so recently. If they hadn't rubbed me raw as much as they already had.

Now this? From him of all people?

I didn't like being threatened, especially not today.

"What is that supposed to mean?" I asked him cautiously, fear pooling in my stomach as I tried to think about him having things to say that would intentionally hurt me.

"Drop it."

Drop it? There was something to drop? My heart started beating faster, and that survival instinct told me to let it go. Told me this wasn't worth it. But I couldn't. *I couldn't.* "What's that supposed to mean?" I repeated myself. "What would you say to me that would hurt my feelings?"

The face he made... the face he made warned me. It was the only preface I was going to get before he aimed blue-green eyes at me like they had fire in them.

"Tell me," I kept going even though some part of me knew I didn't want to know.

"*Stop.*"

I couldn't though. *I couldn't.* Not today. Not after this life I'd been living for so long where it seemed like half my loved ones didn't trust me or didn't value me enough. I didn't want to take it from one other person I was so invested in. I didn't want Rip to be on that list. Was that so wrong? "I want to know. I don't want you to tiptoe around me because you think I'm weak or pathetic. I'm not. I'm not either. I want you to *tell* me."

His expression alone might have killed me. "Yeah? That's what you want?" he asked, something about his tone almost cruel. "I've known what you fucking did to your family from the day we went to the funeral, Luna. It's not some fucking secret. I knew. Everyone fucking knew, Jesus Christ."

Don't you let him see you flinch.

But he wasn't stopping. He wasn't freaking done. "You wanna know how I knew? You wanna know the truth? I didn't read about the bust in the paper. I knew about it because that *gang* you asked me if I was in wasn't a *gang*. I was in an MC. A motorcycle club. The Reapers. And we didn't fuck with your family's drugs, but I'd met your uncle. I'd met your dad. I heard all about the girl that got half the family arrested. I knew about you before I met you."

Some rational part of my brain tried to tell the rest of it that what he was saying wasn't a big deal. That it didn't change anything. That it didn't mean anything.

I wasn't embarrassed by it. I didn't feel bad about it.

But...

"Cooper's known the entire time too, so you know. He told me years ago that he'd hired a PI to look into you, and he's always known where you came from and who your family was."

He'd known too. For who knows how long, maybe from the beginning, he had known.

And he'd never said a word.

I could understand keeping his first wife a secret. Maybe, I could even understand him keeping Rip a secret if I really wanted to be logical. But he'd known about my background and never said anything? Not in nine years?

"Is that good enough? Will you go now and give me a fucking break, or do I need to spell it out for you? *Leave me alone.*"

Leave me alone, my sister had projected at me wordlessly countless times.

Leave me alone, my dad had hissed at me countless more.

Leave me alone.

I could have held a whole lot of anger in my heart. When people like Thea or Kyra made me upset, there were a million things I could have thought of to hurt them, but I never would. Because I would never want anyone I loved to hurt because of me. I would go out of my way to make sure that didn't happen.

Yet...

I froze. I blinked, and I swallowed as I said, almost woodenly, attempting to ignore the familiarity of what had come out of his mouth, "I'm only trying to be your friend."

"Does it look like I give a fuck about that right now?"

I had gotten real good at getting crapped on by people. By being taken advantage of.

But not from people who I thought I could trust. Who had made me believe that I could. Yet here I was.

You can't make anyone love you or care about you. I knew that better than anyone.

The hairs on my arms stood up, my back prickled, and I just went... numb as I stood there, looking down at the man I had cared for, for years. The one who had started to make me feel that I wasn't a nuisance, that it was okay to ask him for things. That had made me feel safe. Understood.

And I realized the burn in me was actually a freezer burn.

Leave me alone, Lucas Ripley had just said to me.

I didn't have much pride, but I had enough.

Maybe Rip couldn't put things together enough, but I had left the people who hadn't wanted me around and never looked back. Enough was enough. I was over it—those words, getting shoved aside by all these people I cared about, being made to feel dispensable—that all of *this* felt like acid on my soul.

He wanted me to leave him alone too? He didn't want to be my friend? He wanted to keep things from me like everyone freaking else?

Biting the inside of my cheek, I kept my gaze steady on

him as that freezer burn pain spread through me. I could feel it in the pores of my face, along my mouth, in my eyes.

I should have let it go, I knew. I should have avoided this conversation, but I hadn't. I had walked right into this, and this pain was all my own freaking fault. I had nobody else to blame but myself.

Then again, he could have said just about anything else to me, too, that wouldn't hurt half as bad.

But the funny things was: he hadn't. I was fed up. I was so damn tired I couldn't remember the last time I had felt more exhausted. And all of a sudden, so lonely I couldn't bear it.

This was what I got for hoping. For forgetting.

Everyone deserves love, but there are people that don't want it, no matter how desperately and truly you might give it to them.

I took a step back and then another, giving him one single nod as I said with a calmness he didn't deserve, "You're right, Mr. Ripley. You knew better than me that you could hurt my feelings, but you did it anyway." I bit the inside of my cheek and squeezed the hell out of my soul. "I'm sorry for stepping over the line. I'm sorry for pushing you. I won't ever do it again."

I didn't shed one single tear as I turned around and walked out of the waiting room. I didn't shed a tear as I made it to the cafeteria and got myself coffee. And when I carried it back with me to the same waiting room where I'd left the last person to ever break my heart, I was proud of myself.

Just because he didn't even want my support didn't mean that I was going to run and hide, not when someone I cared about and someone who cared about me right back was undergoing surgery. Lucas Ripley might have kicked me in the chest just now, but he wasn't going to make me forget why I was there.

This was for Mr. Cooper. The man who wouldn't have kicked me out of the room. The one who had been there for me time and time again.

Maybe he had known where I had come from, and that hurt me that he would keep so much from me, but I'd deal with that later. Deal with it when I knew he was fine. I wouldn't hold any bad feelings toward him when I wasn't sure if he was even going to be okay.

Thanks to the clear glass that was used as walls for the room, I could see it was still empty except for the one dark-haired man I was not going to look at.

I kept my chin up high as I took the same seat I'd been in before instead of taking one further away from *my boss*.

Then I sat back, put my eyes on the television screen, and didn't look at Ripley again until thirty minutes later when a doctor came in, asking for relatives of Mr. Cooper's. I eavesdropped long enough in the conversation to hear that he had made it through surgery successfully but would be in intensive care for the time being, which could be hours or days. Until then, only family.

And that was one thing I wasn't. Any of their family.

Maybe I didn't have the best basis for what a family was supposed to be like, but I was fed up with being lied to. Fed up with being kicked aside, over and over and over again. Even I knew that wasn't what *family* was supposed to be like.

Leave me alone.

I was fucking *sick of it*. Sick of those words. Sick of even myself.

I picked up my phone, dialed Lydia's number, and waited for her to answer. When she finally did, apologizing for being with a client, I told her what happened. Then I listened to her wail of shock and her promise to be there as soon as possible.

Only at that point did I get up and leave; as much as my heart might tell me otherwise, I wasn't family.

My family consisted of a dad who had threatened to kill me, a brother who had walked out on us, a cousin who had tried to beat me up, two lying sisters, and the one and only person who loved me as much as I loved her.

I loved myself enough to know what I deserved.

And this... shit... that had just happened, was not one of those things.

There weren't enough donuts or homemade lunches in the world to make this worth it. That was for freaking sure.

CHAPTER TWENTY-SIX

THE NEWS THAT MR. COOPER, OUR BELOVED BOSS, HAD suffered a heart attack had shaken up everyone at the shop. It hadn't been a major one, but it had been severe enough that his doctors had insisted that he take his time coming back. That he *rested*. That he manage his stress levels better.

Lydia had been kind enough to call me soon after I'd left the hospital—in the process asking why I hadn't waited for her—and then kept me up to date on how he was doing. The next day, I went to visit him again just as Grandpa Gus was leaving the hospital.

"You saved me, honey," my boss had whispered when I'd made it over to his bed the day after his heart attack.

I had reached out to take his hand, giving it a gentle squeeze as I smiled down at the lined, still too pale face, trying not to think about what could have happened to him if it *hadn't* been a minor attack. I'd made the mistake of reading that heart disease was the leading cause of deaths in the country. "All I did was give you an aspirin," I told him, trying my best to ignore the sting of pain when I thought about the things he had kept from me for so long.

"You told me to buy a new bottle of aspirin when the last one had expired, do you remember? You insisted I get aspirin, '*just in case, Mr. C,*'" he tried to argue in his weaker-than-usual voice, giving my hand another squeeze.

I had been thinking about him specifically when I'd insisted he buy more aspirin. When he first told me he had high blood pressure, I had done a little research, not that I ever brought that up. But he mattered to me, and I wanted to make sure to take care of him any way I could so that he wouldn't get worse. Because that was what you did when you cared about people. "Well, I'm glad you listened," I told him.

The smile he gave me in return, as he laid in the hospital bed, was weak. "I don't know when I'll get back to the shop."

The first thing I thought of was Ripley.

"You'll hold down the fort for me until then, won't you?" he asked.

Emotion had clogged my throat as I looked down at him, and it was my turn to give his hand a squeeze. "I'd hold down the world for you, if you want me to, Mr. C. Don't worry about the shop. We'll all be fine."

I specifically didn't let myself think about Ripley and what Mr. Cooper being gone would mean for the rest of us.

The day had been hard enough as it was. Tense and awkward and even a little charged weren't good descriptions about how all of us had been. All of us minus Rip, who I hadn't spoken to, made eye contact with or even been in the same room as. Over time, all of my coworkers had filtered into my room to ask about our favorite boss.

Well, besides Jason, who hadn't shown up for work, and who I'd bet never would again. But I didn't give a single crap about that twerp anymore anyway. I could get his address *like that*. But luckily for him, all that seemed unimportant compared to Mr. C's heart attack. And if I had to choose between kicking his butt or my cousin's, I would always choose my cousin. Always.

This man I loved and loved me back, gave me a gentle, warm smile that further put things into perspective for me. *Life was too short to hang yourself up loving someone who would never love you back,* I finally saw that clearly now. "I know you would, Luna," Mr. Cooper told me. Then he sighed, and his eyes narrowed a little and he said, "I'm sorry about Jason. You have no idea—"

Oh, hell. We were back to him. "Don't worry about him or my cousin. It's fine," I tried to assure him, even giving him a smile so he would know I wasn't saying it for the sake of it. "It's not the first time my cousin has tried to jump me, but it'll be the last."

Miguel had made sure to tell me they had made it clear whatever they had done or said had settled things. I hadn't asked for specifics because that had been good enough for me.

Hopefully he would give my message to my dad so he would know too that I wasn't screwing around. I knew enough to get him into trouble still, and if I didn't, I would have no problem digging up what would. Because going that far wasn't out of the realm of possibility if they tried to do something again, and he had to be smart enough to realize that.

"It's not fine, but I am sorry," the older man argued. His eyes slid in the direction of where Lydia was sitting before coming back to me. His throat bobbed softly, and he let out another deep sigh. "There are some things I want to tell you... some things I should have told you before...." He trailed off, the expression he was making almost like he was trying to tell me something.

He was confirming it, wasn't he?

He was trying to tell me that he really was Rip's father and they had kept the secret to themselves.

He hadn't lied. Not technically. He just hadn't... told me or anyone else the truth.

The man who had worked with us for the last three years was his son. A son from the wife he'd had before the one a few feet away from us. A son from the same woman he had told me was, or had been, the love of his life.

And that son happened to be the man who he couldn't talk to for two minutes without getting into an argument with.

The same one who had made it real clear twenty-four hours ago that he held me in the same regard as just about everyone else who had ever really hurt me did.

Man, that didn't feel nice to think about.

"I'll come and see you tomorrow," I promised, giving him a smile of reassurance so he would know that if I had put things together, I was fine with what he had kept from me.

I wasn't. Not totally.

But I wouldn't hold it against him. He had his reasons. He had to. And I would just deal with the small sense of betrayal I felt from this not-a-lie until then.

I wasn't feeling up to adding another person to my list.

"I'll come to your house to see you after you're out of here too," I kept going, barely holding on to that thread inside of me that decided not to be hurt. "I'll have to keep you up to date on the shop gossip, huh?"

Mr. Cooper's gaze searched mine, and after a moment, he tipped his chin down just enough for it to count as him agreeing. But whether or not it had anything to do with him agreeing he needed to hear what was going on at the shop was a different story. We were both well aware of the giant elephant in the room looming over us. *There are some things I want to tell you... some things I should have told you before...*

Because right then—and I had a feeling that it wasn't just going to be in that moment or the next, or the one after that—I knew I wouldn't care enough to get the full story.

My heart honestly just didn't give a crap anymore.

My heart had been broken, stomped on, and moved to dust just yesterday, and like the other times the same thing had happened, I knew I could regrow it. That was my other superpower. I would make myself always come back from the dumps.

Because that was exactly where Rip had left me to wallow.

I had told him once I didn't sulk, at least not for long, and I wasn't about to start for him. It was easier to forget and ignore than it was to hold on to things that hurt.

Before Mr. Cooper or I got a chance to say another word, there had been a knock at the door before it opened a crack and then fully. I knew instantly who was coming in before I actually saw the stained work boots and the white compression shirt that was just long enough to go over the stained blue jeans the new hospital room visitor was wearing.

I knew it was Ripley.

And that was why I slipped my hand out of Mr. Cooper's and bent over to give him a kiss on the cheek. "I should get going. Call me if either one of you need anything. I'm sure my boss won't have a problem with me sneaking out of the shop for a little bit if I have to," I said, trying to sound as chipper as freaking possible.

Mr. Cooper's head was already tilted in the direction of the door when he said, "Thank you, little moon," in the same tone he spoke to me every time Rip was around. With a little less affection. With a little more distance.

I had always thought he just didn't want to make him mad or make him feel like he was playing favorites, but I could see now that it was for other reasons that I wasn't totally sure I understood. To not make him jealous? To not rub in our relationship and how well we got along?

I didn't know, and it honestly wasn't my business to find out. Not anymore. Not ever from the beginning apparently.

"You too, Lydia," I told her before bending over to give her a kiss on the cheek too, watching as her eyes settled on the man I could hear walking into the room.

Her eyes shifted to me, but her smile was as brittle and tired as her nod. "Thank you, honey. I'll give you a call soon."

I nodded and took a step back. "Rest, Mr. C. I'll come check on you tomorrow."

I got a "drive safe" and a "take care" from them just as I turned to walk out, but I couldn't miss the strain in their voices as they said it.

Sure enough, by that time, a figure a head taller than me and a lot wider, stopped right at my side.

I wanted to pretend he wasn't there, but I wouldn't.

It wasn't his fault I had started to believe he genuinely gave a shit about me. I could handle his moods at work. I could handle his secrecy. But making me feel dumb, pushing me away, those things I couldn't.

It was my fault for thinking things had been changing between us. For being desperate and clingy. It was my fault.

Instead, I looked right up at my other boss and said, pretty freaking calmly and coolly, "Hi, Mr. Ripley."

He had already been looking down at me. His face, that mask I never knew what to think of. It was that same mask that I tried to replicate, just for a moment, because that was how long I stood there before saying "Bye" over my shoulder to all three of them.

My chest hurt only a little as I left the hospital, and like so many other things, I squashed it down into an even smaller hurt and threw it away.

I was loved, and I had everything. I wasn't happy *then*, but I would be again.

My chest had only continued hurting just a little every time I saw Rip at the shop.

The very first day, three days after our conversation in the waiting room, I'd had to find him to ask about some vague details on an order. He'd been on the main shop floor, pulling out upholstery inside a 1970-ish Ford Bronco. I had only stood in my room for maybe one minute trying to pump myself up to talk to him the way I envisioned I could and would in my head.

Like he hadn't hurt my feelings.

Like he hadn't been mean and cold and cruel.

I could do it, I had told myself.

I didn't play games, and I wasn't about to start then.

So in that minute, I got myself together and headed over.

"Mr. Ripley?" I called out, a little smug with myself for keeping my voice under control.

He had instantly stopped was he was doing, crouched in place just outside of the SUV.

I didn't wait around to stop right beside him and thrust the invoice between us. "I was about to place an order, but I wanted to confirm what you marked off and scribbled in. There weren't any notes added into the computer. You want the color you wrote, correct?"

Correct. Man, I was good.

Rip watched me silently, passively, for a moment before taking the sheet and looking it over.

I let myself take in his features, even though I shouldn't have. There were bags under his eyes and serious tension at the corners of them as he read his scribbles. I bit the inside of my cheek as he glanced at me, all cool detachment, and said, "It's right."

I didn't give him the smile I usually passed around. I had just nodded at him and, just as quickly, said, "Thank you" before I headed back.

And when he had come into my room a few hours later to take a look at a hood I had done that morning, all I had done was tell him "Hi" and then gone straight back to work taping. Just like he wasn't there. Just like I should have done since he was my boss and I was his employee.

And if anger had ridden through my veins, leaving me hot and tense for a couple of minutes, I ignored it.

I wasn't mad. I wasn't hurt. I was fine.

I was always going to be fine.

And that's what I was from then on.

I went to see Lily one weekend with Lenny. Another weekend, we had game night at Grandpa Gus's place. I did some overtime but not much. I went to the gym, had one okay date that didn't rock my socks off. I chugged along. I made it.

It had been two weeks, and the shop was surviving. I wasn't sure who was doing payroll, but I was an employee, so I wasn't going to worry about it. That's what Rip was for. The only extra thing I had taken upon myself was ordering things for the break room and charging them to the shop's account, but that was it.

Things were all right. Everyone at the shop was doing fine. From what I overheard from the rest of the guys during lunch and in bits and pieces when we'd happen to be in the break room at the same time, or they would come to my room to move something or pick something up, they told me about how much more short-tempered Rip was being, and how annoying it was when he was the only one they could ask questions to.

I didn't say a word. I didn't agree or disagree. I just patted them on the back or would try to make them laugh.

I wasn't going to talk bad about him.

In that time, Mr. Cooper and I still hadn't gotten a chance to talk. I had gone to visit him every other day at his home after he'd been released and brought him food and movies from the Redbox closest to his place, but he hadn't told me much of anything.

It might have been because Lydia had never been far away.

If I had thought months ago that I would have a hard time cutting someone I saw on a regular basis out of my life, I would have been mistaken. I had forgotten how easy it was.

I had a feeling that was mostly because I hadn't been able to get Rip's words out of my head. I had them memorized. Or pretty close to it. *Leave me alone,* he had said to me in that waiting room.

I'd stopped pining for people who didn't treat me as

well as I treated them as a kid. I had promised myself back then that I would never fall for that crap again, and in a life where I had failed myself a dozen times, that one oath had been the only one I managed to uphold.

It was why I had no problem making my coffee and ignoring Rip when I walked downstairs and toward my room.

He wanted coffee? He could get it his own self. He wanted me to leave him alone? Sure thing. I wasn't going to beg anyone for their time, their love, or attention. I definitely wouldn't beg for friendship or company either.

Not anymore.

So when I had a dream about two weeks into Mr. Cooper's recuperation about my dad again—a dream that was an exact replica of the night before I had left San Antonio for good—I was upset and irritated like I couldn't even begin to explain. It didn't help that my nape had itched and burned from the moment I had woken up. Or that it reminded me of having a very similar dream with Rip in the bed with me not long ago. A night when he'd pulled me close....

Even a busy morning at work and the entire *Hairspray* soundtrack hadn't made me able to shake off the restlessness brewing under my skin.

When lunch came and I went upstairs and found the room full, I grabbed my food from the fridge—taco casserole that was dry and just weird— warmed it up, and decided I was going to do myself and my coworkers a favor and go somewhere else where I could be in a bad mood. It wasn't because of Ripley either. He hadn't bothered looking up when I had walked into the room. If that didn't say enough about how things were between us, I didn't know what else could.

So I took my food and ate it on one of the chairs set up

around the back of the shop where the guys took smoke breaks. It was Northside Houston, warm and always humid, but in the shade, with a decent breeze, a lack of bugs, and away from the worst of the street pollution closer to the entrance of the shop, it was... fine.

Honestly, it was kind of relaxing, even if I was just around the corner from where my cousin had backhanded me. But I didn't have a scab or a scar on my face, and I wasn't going to focus on that dipshit. Not when he'd done similar things to me as a kid when I had been walking home from school.

Rudy was nobody. My dad was nobody. And nobodies didn't hurt anyone.

I was fine. I had a job. I was loved.

Mr. Cooper was going to make a full recovery.

Lily was happy, healthy, and making lots of tip money.

Thea and Kyra were both alive, but I only knew that because Lily confirmed it.

My dad hadn't called again.

Jason had never come back to work.

I was safe. I had a roof over my head and food to eat. I had so much. Not everything was perfect—and I hated how resentful I felt toward my sisters—but it was better than most people had it.

That's what I kept telling myself as I sat there, all by myself.

About twenty minutes into my lunch, I shoved the hems of my sweatpants up to just above my knees and stretched my pale legs out in front of me to catch a little bit of sun.

When I had ten minutes left on my break, I packed up my things and headed back inside. I didn't look around to see who was on the main shop floor before going up the stairs, but when I got to the break room and found it empty except for two of the body guys—and Rip—I made sure to smile at both of them.

When I accidentally shifted my gaze over just enough to meet Rip's eyes, I didn't let the smile slip from my face.

I wasn't going to give him my hurt. I was going to treat him the way he wanted me to months ago. Like he was my boss. Like he hadn't dug a space into my life and then decided he didn't want to be a part of it anymore.

Like he hadn't told me those three freaking words.

But when I met his eyes, keeping the smile on my face, those teal-colored eyes bounced all over my face, lingering on the star necklace that had fallen out from where I'd tucked it under my shirt.

It lasted for a second.

Because I looked away and toward the fridge, keeping my gaze on that as I passed by the three men so I could put the rest of my almost-gross casserole away.

"Luna, what'd you eat for lunch?" one of the guys asked as I set my bag back inside.

I closed it with the back of my hand as I said, "Casserole. It tastes like butthole, but if you don't have taste buds, you can have the rest."

They didn't sound that interested, but I filled my water bottle from the filter and left the room only saying "see ya" to the two I was on speaking terms with.

I got back to my room and finished taping the car I was set to start priming that afternoon. I was going over my notes for it, triple checking the paint color on the invoice with the number on the label when the door opened. I didn't look up after I heard the first two steps taken inside. Only one person walked that heavily.

"Do you need me to do something?" I called out before he got too far in.

The footsteps kept coming and so did his voice. "I wanted to double-check something on the SS," Ripley answered immediately.

I didn't pinch my lips together or make a face. I stood up and immediately handed over the clipboard with the notes I was holding. He was already standing beside me. I kept my eyes on the board as he took it, those long fingers flipping to the page I had just been reading.

Then I took a step back and headed into the booth to look around and make sure all the taping was correct, even though I knew it was.

Rip didn't immediately say anything; I managed to make it halfway around the car before he called out from somewhere outside the booth, "I'm done."

I didn't get why he didn't just look up the order on the computer, but I wasn't going to waste my time even wondering.

The petty part of me almost wanted to ignore him, but I didn't. I wasn't going to give him even that. So I called out in return, "Okay."

When I headed back out to the main room and didn't find him there, I was relieved.

I really was.

* * *

THE NEXT DAY, I was in the middle of waiting for our machine to finish agitating the paint I was about to start using on a late model Audi A4 when the door to my room opened. A big figure headed inside, letting the door close behind him.

I knew who it was.

I was going to be the bigger person, so I made myself ask, "What can I do for you?"

Rip waited until he'd taken a few more steps inside the room before saying, "I wanted to check the wheels that were on your list this morning."

When had he looked at my schedule?

But I didn't ask. Instead I made sure to meet his eyes briefly—really briefly. His face was that usual mask of tightness and control, and I sucked it in and spit it right back out, then gestured toward my right where I had moved the wheels an hour ago. Out of my peripheral vision, I watched him move to them, those long legs eating up the room that usually felt massive for me. Then I focused back on the machine, hoping it would hurry up and finish its cycle so I could move on with my next project before lunch.

Rip was quiet, and I purposely moved to give him my back.

The cycle finished before he got done inspecting my work, and I headed toward the booth to transfer the paint.

When I headed back into the main room to put on my protective suit, he was still there, this time looking through one of the paint catalogues I had sitting on the counter. If he looked over at me, I honestly had no idea. I kept my eyes straight forward, on the wall across the room. He didn't say a word to me as I changed into my sneakers first, then stepped into my suit and zipped it up, and he didn't reply as I headed into the booth and called out over my shoulder, "Knock if you need me."

I closed myself in my room, and at some point later, when I glanced over at one of the only windows in the white room, I found Rip standing there, looking in.

I focused back on the panels that needed my attention.

When I took my lunch break later on, I went outside

again. Just like the day before, when I headed back to the break room to drop off my bag and leftovers in the fridge, Rip was sitting there, eating something made with chicken and leafing through a magazine. We made eye contact, and I only broke it when I got too close and had to open the fridge.

Then I took myself back downstairs.

* * *

THE NEXT MORNING, well after nine in the morning, once all the shop guys were there, I made my way to the main floor to ask them to help me move what we called the rotisserie—an engine block was mounted to it—from the main floor into the booth. We had set it up the day before, but it was too heavy for me to move it by myself or with just one other person.

Was it on purpose that I headed straight toward Owen and Ashton to help me roll the rotisserie into the paint room? It sure was. But I kept my head held high and a smile on my face as I moved between the cars parked on the floor and made my way to the two men who were always really nice to me.

"Hey," I said as I came up to them.

Ashton, who was the one standing, immediately tipped his chin up and flashed me a warm smile. "Hey, Luna."

Beneath the car, Owen called out, "Need help with the rotisserie?"

There was a reason why Owen was one of my favorite guys at CCC. "Yes," I answered, stopping right beside Ashton to take a peek at what he was looking at. There was a spot of something dark and liquid-like on the floor beside where Owen was lying, looking up with a wrench in his hand. "Would you guys help me roll it out when you get a chance, please?"

"Five minutes?" Owen asked.

I nodded at him from where I was standing looking down at him. "Thanks. I'll meet you in my room then whenever you're both ready," I told them.

The new guy nodded.

Keeping my gaze locked on the cars on the floor as I made my path back to my room, I could see Rip turning down the same hallway I was heading to, but he ducked into the bathroom instead. Back inside my room, I went through the booth one more time to make sure everything was where it needed to be. Soon enough, I heard the door open and slam closed. Figuring it was them, I headed back out and almost completely stopped walking when I found Rip standing there with his hands on his hips.

"Need help moving something?" he asked as he wiped his hands on a rag, those intense eyes on me.

I couldn't help but slide my gaze toward the door for a split second before aiming them back toward his face and saying, "I already asked the guys for help."

A muscle in his cheek twitched.

I made myself stop looking at it. "They said they'd be about five minutes," I finished, glancing toward the door one more time.

Rip's nose wrinkled for a moment before he shoved his rag into one of the pockets of his coveralls and said carefully, "You didn't ask me."

I blinked. "Ask you?" For permission?

"For help," he clarified, his voice tight.

Oh. "I figured you would tell them to help me." I kept my voice even, calm, controlled. "It's what you always do." Then I couldn't help it as I glanced toward the door one more time. "I didn't want to waste your time when I can ask myself."

His nose wrinkled again right around the time I said the middle sentence, and it didn't go anywhere as I spoke. What I did notice was the way he crossed his arms over his chest, that gaze still locked on mine like he had no intention of moving it elsewhere. He tipped his chin back, giving me a good view of his long and strong neck. "What have I told you about wasting my time?" he asked in that same voice.

The skin along my spine instantly prickled, and I couldn't help but feel this tiny stab of pain right in my heart. Indignation. That would have been the perfect word to describe how I felt right then.

That and betrayal.

And anger.

But mostly indignation.

I didn't let myself get riled up as I said, "I don't want to assume anything, Mr. Ripley."

Okay, maybe the *Mr. Ripley* part was a little petty, but I wasn't going to beat myself up over it.

When I glanced at Ripley's face as I said the words, and watched the way the entire length of his jawline went tight, it didn't make me feel any better. It made me feel like crap. I wasn't trying to make him feel bad. I didn't want that from him.

I didn't want anything from him.

So I got myself back on track. "You have better things to do with your time. You have enough going on right now with Mr. Cooper being gone." His dad. Not just Mr. Cooper. His *dad*.

He didn't say a word. This massive man just stood there, watching me.

I kept going, my voice even... maybe a little monotone. "If there's an issue, I'll let you know, of course."

Rip still didn't respond.

Sliding my gaze toward the door, I willed it to open and Ashton and Owen to be there, ready to help.

But nothing happened. The story of my life.

"I appreciate you checking though, but we can move it on our own, I think," I finished, keeping my voice the same businesslike way I would have used on any other boss I would have, except Mr. Cooper—and Rip if this had been months ago.

But this was what he wanted, and this was what I would give him.

So when he took four long steps toward me, stopping the exact moment the tips of his boots met mine, his hand nudging my chin upward, I held my breath. Because Rip was *right there*. In my space. Forcing me to look at him.

And look at him I did.

I looked at the tattoos peeking out from just above the hem of the slight turtleneck coverage his compression shirt gave him. Took in the tiny dark shapes just above the hem. I took in the very faint stubble across the underside of his chin and over the lower half of his face. I took in that almost thin pink mouth pulled into a line at the angry expression he was shooting my way.

And I took in the way his eyes seemed to be blazing down at me.

Like he either wanted to yell at me or something else.

I didn't know what that "something else" was, but from the line of his jaw, I wasn't sure I wanted to know.

Rip's chin tipped down lower, drawing his face even closer to mine. "Can we be done with this?" he asked, his voice rough and so low I could barely hear him.

I held my breath. "With what?"

That incredibly handsome face stayed remote, but those eyes... "With the Mister Ripley shit. With that tone. With you not wanting to talk to me or ask me for fucking help." That chin dipped, and I'd swear I could feel his breath on my face in tiny puffs. "With you freezing me out."

I wanted to raise my eyebrows, but I didn't. "I don't know what you're talking about," I only partially lied. Because it couldn't be a complete lie when I didn't understand why he would be saying these things to me when he was the one who had asked for them.

"You know exactly what I'm talking about, Luna," Rip replied, his voice still this low hum I almost had to strain my ears to hear.

The tips of his boots edged over mine even more.

It didn't matter. It didn't freaking matter.

"You are Mister Ripley," I said, still wound tight. "I'm talking to you like I would anyone that was my boss, with professionalism, because that's what I should have been showing you from the very beginning."

This hoarse sound escaped his throat, sounding almost like a... grumble? A growl?

"I'm not going to bother you when I can handle things myself."

His boots tapped into mine so roughly, it scooted my own boots back a half inch.

"I'm just treating you the way I always should have," I cut myself off before adding another "Mister Ripley" to the end. Something inside of me said it would be a terrible idea, like baiting a starving lion or something. "You're my boss, and I shouldn't have forgotten that."

I could have sworn his neck swelled bigger and bigger

with each word that came out of my mouth. His face might have gotten redder too.

But when had his face gotten red in the first place?

The hand on my chin drew my face up even higher, until I almost strained with the pressure, with the stretch. Then I could definitely feel his soft breathing on my face. On my mouth. I could feel the heat of his body along the front of mine. A month ago, this would have made my freaking year. A week ago, it would have made me want to swoon.

But now...

Now I forced all that crap down and away. I buried it with a shovel and a half ton of dirt. Gone. Gone, gone, gone.

He had asked for it, and I had given everything I'd been willing to part with for too long.

Only an idiot kept giving after a certain point, and I was no one's fool. No one's punching bag. No one's temporary entertainment.

I had given him more than I had another person ever, and he'd burned that bridge between us once and for all. He had told me the same thing that other people had: *leave me alone.*

"I'm only doing what you asked," I told him slowly, each word drawn out, syllable by syllable. I kept my gaze on his for a heartbeat, and then two, and then drew it back down to his chin as I let myself take a breath through my nose.

Then I took a step back. Then another.

"I appreciate you coming to check and see if I need help, but I don't. Ashton and Owen are coming," I explained to him. "Anything I can handle on my own, I'll do. But thank you, Mr. Ripley."

Mr. Ripley didn't move an inch.

Then he opened that mouth and said, "We need to—"

And I would thank a God I wasn't sure I believed in for the fact that the door opened in that exact same moment and Owen said, "Sorry about that, Luna. Let's move the rotisserie—Oh." He stopped there. He looked from one of us to the other, eyes widening as the new guy came in right behind him.

I smiled at my coworkers and took a step toward them. "I'm ready if you two are."

* * *

DETERMINED as hell to keep my distance from my boss, I grabbed my lunch for the third day in a row and headed to the chairs and table in the parking lot of CCC.

It was another hot day, not that it wasn't a hot day every freaking day in Houston, but under the shade, it wasn't too unbearable. Since there weren't any bugs either, it was about as good as I was going to get. Fresh air. Some open space.

I should have been coming out here years ago.

Which reminded me...

I picked up my phone and dialed the same number I had every day for a week now.

It rang.

Rolling up my pant legs and the sleeves of my T-shirt up to my shoulders, I held the phone between my ear and shoulder, taking in the continued rings. I stretched my legs out to get some sun and slouched in the chair as I pulled my lunch out of my bag. I'd barely opened my container of three-day-old casserole disaster, when the door leading outside opened and a familiar figure in a long-sleeved shirt that clung to every single muscle on his chest and dark jeans made his way over.

I didn't narrow my eyes, but I did watch him a little too carefully.

What did he want now? I wondered as Thea's voice mail picked up.

"Thea, it's Luna again. I hope you're okay and you'll call me back, all right?" I said, trying not to sound mad or sad before ending the call.

Picking up my fork from inside my bag, I stabbed at the mush of rice and ground beef, making sure to focus on it and not the man making his way toward me. I managed to poke my fork through something that looked a little too brown and even got it into my mouth before the big man walked in front of me.

He didn't say a word, and neither did I as he went to the chair on the other side of the table and pulled it forward until it lined up with the one I was in.

I watched him as he set his glass container on the table between us and took a seat.

Just as I was about to ask if there was something I could do for him, I stopped myself. I was on my lunch break. I didn't have to do anything then.

And he had his lunch, same as me.

So...

I just didn't understand why he was out here too all of a sudden.

I kept my curiosity to myself and made sure to look away from him as I chewed my food and brought my phone onto my thigh.

Whatever he was doing out here... it was none of my business.

The light pop of the lid coming off his food filled the air between us, punctuated by the occasional sound of him chewing or taking sips of whatever he was drinking.

Me on the other hand, I sat there and sucked back my can of Sprite and ate my casserole while I started looking up prices for television screens.

When my lunch hour was almost up, when there was sweat at the base of my neck and lower back from the heat, and when the skin on my legs was tight from too much sun, then I got up.

Neither one of us said anything as I walked away.

CHAPTER TWENTY-SEVEN

My lunch break the next day was a repeat of the one before it, and I honestly didn't know what to think of it.

Or even if I should waste my time thinking it over.

I went outside, had all of my food out, my clothes were rolled up the way I liked them, and I had my legs stretched out in the sun when the door opened and out came the same man I had just seen hours ago when he'd come into my room and peeked through the window of the booth while I sprayed. That day, he had on a gray compression shirt and another pair of jeans that were somehow dirty even with the coveralls he wore over them.

Everything on him was covered like usual.

From his neck down over his wrist bones, everything accentuated that big, muscular figure I had checked out every chance I could without getting caught for years.

But this time, it wasn't so hard to look away. It really wasn't hard at all.

I'd had another dream about my dad the previous night, the same one as before that left my head uncomfortable and tight and left me in bed sweaty and out of breath. It had only taken me a couple hours to shake it off. All it did was remind me of why it wasn't hard to look away from Rip right then.

The thing was, I didn't need to use my eyes to know what he was doing.

Rip did the same thing he'd done the day before. He came over and sat beside me, and neither one of us said a word. Not while we ate. Not in the sparse minutes I had after I'd forced down my food. Not while I looked at my phone and scrolled through reviews of couches that were on sale.

When the time came to get back to work, I didn't even do more than glance at him as I collected my stuff and headed back to my room more than half an hour after he'd appeared.

* * *

THE VERY NEXT day went a lot like every other day before it, at least since Mr. Cooper's heart attack.

I showed up to work. Ripley was already there. I pretended not to see him as I headed into my room, and then pretended not to see him some more when I went upstairs to prepare my coffee or when I went back downstairs with it in my hand. Just mine. Not his. Like it was our new thing, because it was. I shouldn't have to go out of my way to be nice to my boss when he didn't want it, and when it wasn't like he was doing me a favor by employing me.

He couldn't fire me without going through Mr. Cooper. Because even if chances were very, very high they were related, I knew that when it came down to it, I had a better relationship with him than Rip did. I had gone to see Mr. C the night before, had dinner with him and Lydia, and stayed to watch a movie. I knew my place in the older man's life.

But just like every other day lately, at some point in the beginning half of the morning, I had a visitor stop by my room.

A six-foot-four-inch visitor who I would bet weighed around two hundred and fifty pounds.

The man I didn't want all up in my space anymore.

"Can I help you with something?" I asked, using the same exact words I had used every other time he'd come in. Calm, cool, professional.

Unlike every other day though, my boss didn't use an excuse about wanting to check something or see something.

He just stood there with his hands on his hips, gritted his teeth, and said, "You done?"

"Yes. I just finished the hood in the booth, and I'm waiting a minute before I get it out of here and start on the panels. Ashton already said he'd help me move it out."

He stared.

I stared back.

Then he let out a deep, deep sigh, cocked his jaw to the side, and grumbled, "You know what I'm talking about. You done for real?"

I used my nicest voice as I asked, "With what?"

Lord, he was staring right at me as he held his hands out to his sides. "With this."

"With what?"

He pressed his lips together. If I looked hard enough, I bet I could see how white they became as he did it, but I didn't. I didn't even look a little bit. "With *this*, Luna," he replied, flipping his hands again.

Looking back on it, I should have chosen a different

approach. But that was the thing with looking back on your actions: life didn't have a rewind button. Unfortunately.

But at least I could look back and remember that I'd held my head up high, kept my voice even, and looked my boss right in the eye as I told him, "I'm treating you the way you wanted me to treat you, Mr. Ripley. With respect. Like you pay my bills. I'm leaving you alone. I'm not annoying you. I'm not forcing myself on you or asking you to do things you wouldn't want to. I don't know what else you want from me."

That intense gaze didn't stray a centimeter. Not for a second. Not for a millisecond. He stared at me like his gaze was made of laser beams and he wanted to burn me to ashes.

And then he tried.

"Would you fucking stop with the Mister Ripley?"

I didn't flinch. Didn't move. I just looked at him like his words didn't affect me at all. "That's your name, sir."

Maybe the "sir" was overdoing it.

"You fucking kidding me right now?" Rip's asked, his voice starting to rise.

All right, it was a little much, I guessed, but that didn't change a single thing. Not about me, not about this situation. "No, I'm not," I answered him calmly. "And I don't understand why you're raising your voice. I'm not doing anything."

Rip's eyes almost, *almost* bulged out of his skull as he leaned forward. "The fuck you're not doing anything. You're talking in circles, doing exactly what you know is gonna bother me."

"I'm not doing anything to bother you. I've done enough to bother you in the past, remember? So I'm stopping. I've stopped. All I'm doing is exactly what you asked."

My boss took a step forward. "Quit talking to me like that."

"Like you're my boss?" I asked slowly, knowing I was baiting him but not sure what else I could say. "Like an employee who didn't lie to the cops for you when they showed up one morning asking where you'd been? When I gave you an alibi because I believed that you were home alone? So I told them I had been with you that night and you let me give you a kiss on the cheek?"

"Goddamn it, Luna," he griped.

I could hear my dad's voice using that tone with me. I could hear him saying those exact same words.

But I was done listening to that tone and that phrase when it was said like that together. I really was. Especially when it was out of Rip's mouth.

"I know you didn't do anything, Rip. That's why when the cops came, I told them you were with me that night. I didn't expect anything from it. What I'm saying now is I know where we stand. I had no problem lying for you, but you started this favor business. And you told me to leave you alone," I spit back at him, trying to sound collected and distant but knowing I was failing. "So that's what I'm doing. I wanted to be your friend. I tried to be your friend. I thought you wanted to be mine too. I wanted you to like me, and I would have wanted you to like me as more than a friend, Rip. You know, I would have wanted that more than anything.

"I knew better, but I still felt that way. But I really would have just taken being your friend if that's all you'd been willing to give me. I was trying not to think of you like that anymore. I think one day, I would have eventually moved on with this stupid infatuation I had with you, all on my own. Probably once I found someone else to like. I'm used to caring about people who don't care for me in return, Mr. Ripley.

"But I've got enough people I love who haven't wanted me around. And I'm not going down that road again. You want to be mean to me and push me away because you were upset or whatever it was with Mr. Cooper? I get it. I can't begin to figure out how confusing your relationship with him is. I get that you're mad he married someone else so soon after your mom. I get it. But I didn't do anything to deserve you kicking me aside. I tried to be there for you, and even if you warned me that you didn't want to hurt me, you still did.

"But I'm done. I know how to listen. I can tell when I'm wasting my time, and I'm not going to waste my time anymore. I'm not going to give and give and give to someone who doesn't want what I have to share. My parents have done it to me, my siblings have done it to me, everyone does it to me when I let them, and you're going to be the last person who makes me feel like a freaking nuisance.

"All I'm doing is what you've asked for. I'm doing what you told me, and I'm totally fine with it. Don't feel guilty. You're doing me a favor. You're speeding along exactly what would have eventually happened.

"I'm not quitting. I'm not going to start doing a bad job, or start deciding I'm not going to stay late if I have to, so you don't have to worry about this affecting my work, all right? I'm just going to mind my own business like I should have been doing from the very beginning, Mr. Ripley, instead of spending my time and energy on something that would never happen," I finished snapping out, the wind rushing from my lungs, my shoulders coming down hard when I hadn't even realized how tight and high they had been in the first place.

God, I was *pissed*.

I was *hurt*. But mostly, I was pissed and exhausted, and some part of me wanted to cry, but I wasn't going to. Not for someone with misguided guilt. Not for someone who wanted me to leave him alone. Not for someone who didn't want me and never would.

We didn't want the same things, and I had been too stubborn and desperate to see that.

I watched him the entire time I spoke. Witnessed the way his fists tightened. Took in the way the tendons at his throat became more pronounced.

But I missed the way his gaze changed.

And chances were, that wouldn't have mattered anyway.

I felt bad for snapping at him. It wasn't totally his fault I was at this point in my life, was it? He'd been just another hammer on my already bent nail. And none of this had been meant to force him to feel something that he wasn't capable of.

"Look," I said, ignoring how hollow and tired I sounded, "I should have treated you like my boss from the beginning. I haven't, but I will from now on. I'm sorry for making it seem like you broke my heart. Sometimes I forget it got broken a long time before I met you. I'm sorry for making it seem like I was pressuring you into keeping me company or being nice to me. I'm sorry for forcing you into doing me all these favors."

I met his gaze, ignoring the weird expression on his face. Ignoring the way his eyes were narrowed. "I've got enough going on without adding more problems. I just... want to pretend this didn't happen. I want things to go back to the way they should have been from the beginning."

From the moment we had met.

Rip blinked at me. He even swallowed too. It was so rough that the collar of his shirt dipped down to expose more of the skull at his throat than usual.

I managed to take a step back before he said my name.

I looked at him.

He tipped his chin up high and kept those blue-green irises on me as he said just about the last thing I ever would have expected from him. **"I** didn't mean to hurt you, baby girl."

Yeah, I was sure he hadn't.

"I didn't," he insisted like he'd read my freaking mind, watching me with those crazy eyes.

Sure.

Sure, he hadn't.

I was so done with this. I just wanted to go back to when things were less complicated. I just wanted to be happy again.

"Well, you did, Mr. Ripley, and it's fine." I slid my tongue over my teeth and took a step back. "I need to get back to what you pay me to do. If you need anything else, let me know. I'll be here for that."

"Oh, honey," Lydia cooed as she waved me into the same house that I had lived in with them for years.

Giving her a hug first, I stepped inside and waited while she shut the door behind us. I didn't need to look around to know exactly what the layout was like. It hadn't changed much in the time since I had moved out. Lydia had a thing for antiques, and most of the furniture was dark and cherry. From what she had told me, a lot of it had been inherited from her family, but some of it she had purchased herself—a few things with me when I had gone with her on my weekends off.

I remembered how nervous I had been for the first few months after moving in. I had kept worrying I would knock over something that had been in her family for generations. I had gone out of my way not to touch anything. The only nice thing I'd had at my dad's house had been the television, and unless I'd been home alone, or stayed really, really quiet, I hadn't really watched it.

If I was going to be honest with myself, even now, I was still nervous about knocking something over at the Cooper's place.

"How are you?" I asked as I toed off my shoes.

She sighed. "I'm all right. Stressed. Worried. Hopeful." She gave me an exhausted smile. "You?"

I shrugged, purposely shoving all thoughts about Ripley and his actions earlier that day into my imaginary trash can. "Okay. Busy at work." I dropped my shoulders and returned her smile. "Do you need help with anything?"

She shook her head, then stopped. "Actually, would you mind staying long enough for me to run out to the store and pick up his prescription? I was going to wait until Allen fell asleep, but if I can avoid driving at night... These eyes aren't what they used to be...."

"You know I don't mind. I was planning on staying anyway." I tilted my head toward the door.

Lydia flashed me a smile that made me wonder what kind of woman Mr. Cooper's first wife had been like that she had been the love of his life and this woman... wasn't.

That was an unfair thought. They always been happy and loving and warm, and Mr. C had always treated her like a queen.

"I won't be long," she promised, already reaching for the keys left in the bowl by the door.

"Take your time," I said as I waited for her to grab her purse too.

It didn't take long for her to leave. I left my purse where hers had been, and then made my way down to the living room down the hall. I'd spent countless nights on the couch next to the recliner that I found Mr. Cooper sitting in. The upper half was slanted back, his feet propped up on the footrest, and he honestly looked really, really good.

"Mr. C," I called out softly when I realized I couldn't see his face to see if he was asleep.

He wasn't.

"Little moon?" His hand went into the air, waving me closer. "Come sit, unless you want something to drink."

I made my way to the couch and sat down. "I'm fine, but do you want something?"

"No, I've got some water over here." He pointed toward a bottle on the side table between his recliner and the couch. "Lydia has got me drowning in it."

I couldn't help but grin at him as I reached to slip my hand into his. "I told you that you needed to be chugging it."

He squeezed my hand. "Still tastes like dirt."

"You know what would taste like dirt?"

Mr. Cooper gave me a funny face.

"No salt on your food." I raised my eyebrows as I slipped my hand out of his. "No bacon."

The older man groaned. "Don't remind me. They told me no caffeine either." He sighed. "I guess it should be good you've been sneaking decaf into the mix for the last few years."

If I hadn't already let go of his hand, I would have right then. "You knew?"

"*Yes*." He chuckled. "Sneaky girl. You remind me so much of someone I used to know."

"Someone good?"

"The best," he said softly before aiming that gaze, which I just realized was so much like Ripley's, at me. "Luna... I'm sorry, honey. I've gotta tell you, it's been eating me up inside."

It was me who swallowed. "You have nothing to be sorry about," I told him because it was the truth.

The older man shook his head, the face that had aged overnight from his heart attack, showing every inch of the ten years it seemed like he'd lost. "No, I do. I really do."

He knew that I knew, or at least assumed that I had an idea or a guess that, he had kept something from me. "I understand that things are complicated sometimes, Mr. C. I'm sure you had your reasons," I said as gently as possible. I had tried my best not to think about him and Rip, I really had.

I saw his hand going up toward his face before I saw the way tears had beaded up in his eyes and made them shiny. "None of them seem that good when I look back on it," he admitted, his closed fist coming to rest over one eye. "I've screwed up a lot over the years, little moon, and I don't have any good excuse why."

"We all screw up a lot," I tried to assure him. It was the truth.

"It seems like I do more than anyone else does."

"That's not true. I'm still alive."

His laugh was watery. His face was still partially covered as he shook his head and sniffed. "Oh, Luna, I really am sorry I never told you the truth. I thought about it a hundred times. Maybe even a thousand. Every time you would bring me my coffee. Every time you tried to break up one of my arguments with Ripley... I thought, *I should tell her*. And I was too ashamed to." He exhaled. "I didn't want one more person being disappointed in me, especially not you. I know it's selfish, but I couldn't bear it if you were."

I had been disappointed in him for not being upfront with me.

I'd been disappointed to think that he hadn't cared about me or valued our relationship enough to tell me that he had a son.

A son I worked with.

I had been a little hurt he'd looked into my background, but thinking on it, I understood. I'd been a seventeen-year-old girl who magically appeared.

But this wasn't all about me, and I was no one to talk about keeping things to myself so that I wouldn't disappoint others. This was about him and whatever was going through his brain. Whatever had gone through his heart in the time before we had met.

I didn't want to lie and tell him that I wasn't disappointed he had kept something this massive a secret, so I told him what I could. I told him my own truths that I had kept. "I never told you that my dad dealt drugs, or that my uncle made them, that my cousins sold them, or that I left the day my dad held a gun to me and told me he wished I had never been born." I started to smile but stopped because... because I didn't have one in me. "I never told you I had an older brother who up and left one day. I didn't want you to know where I had come from so that you wouldn't expect the worst out of me like everyone else had while I'd grown up. I'm sorry I made you find out another way, Mr. C. I should have just told you the truth, but I was too ashamed of it."

He sucked in a breath and shook his head, those eyes

bubbling over until one tear streamed down his weathered cheek. I wasn't surprised when his hand reached over and took mine, his voice a little shaky as he sniffed, "You are the best girl I have ever met, Luna Allen. I couldn't think that. I wouldn't think that. Not ever. The devil could've been your daddy and you would still be the same girl."

It was my turn to sniff, to hold my breath.

"I hope you can forgive me for not being upfront with you all these years, if we're going to talk about holding secrets." The back of my hand came up to my face to wipe across my cheek. "I've screwed up a lot, Mr. C. We all do things that we can't explain or don't want to. There's a bunch of little things I haven't told you lately either."

Mr. Cooper gulped and nodded.

But I figured it was time to at least ask this one thing before I lost my nerve. "Is Rip really your son?"

He nodded, but it felt... I wasn't sure exactly how it felt. It felt like a weight off my chest, but it had only moved to my shoulders. Maybe I had accepted that they'd both had their reasons for keeping it between them, but I was struggling with it. Just a little.

"As you can see, we don't have the best relationship," he chuffed, trying to make it sound like a joke but failing at it.

"Not that this helps, but I don't have that great of a relationship with my parents either." Then I thought about it. "I don't have the greatest relationship with Thea or Kyra right now either, if that makes you feel better, and I don't really want to talk about it yet, if it's all right."

His laugh was another watery sound that didn't sound like a happy thing at all. "But I bet your sisters don't hate you."

He thought Rip hated him. But what could I do? Deny it?

Instead, all I could get out was, "I'm sorry, Mr. C."

"Don't be sorry for me," he replied quickly. "I deserve it."

Hell. "Was his mom your first wife?"

He nodded, his hand coming back up to cover most of his face. "I messed up so much with him... Nothing I do will ever be enough." He paused and made a choking sound that broke my heart a little more. "I can't bring his mother back, but if I could trade our lives, I would. I would do it in a heartbeat," he said in a gutted voice that broke my heart all over again.

I knew what it was like to live with regrets, and from the tone of his voice, this wasn't just a regret. It was so much more.

It was an amputation that no prosthesis in the world could replace.

And the poor man kept talking in that cracked and hurting voice. "I didn't see him for twenty years. The only reason I knew he was alive was because I'd pay a private investigator every year to find him."

I couldn't help but tense up. Not that I was one to talk, but *twenty years?* That was a lifetime.

Sure, I couldn't say anything because I had left my house for almost ten. The only difference was: I knew no one gave a crap about me. Whether I lived, whether I died, whether I had somewhere warm to sleep or food to eat. Nobody I had left behind gave a single shit.

The longing I had seen on Mr. Cooper's face when he looked at Rip suddenly made so much sense.

"By the time you came around the shop, everyone who had known Ripley as a boy had quit or moved on, so I stopped talking about him at the shop when there was no one around to ask for an update. The years... rolled by, one after the other, and before I knew it, I hadn't mentioned him to any of you until he came back," he explained.

I swallowed for him. For the way his voice wobbled as he told me this story.

"He showed up out of the blue one day, Luna, and said he wanted to buy into the shop... I didn't mean to lie. Not talking about him... snowballed out of control until if I did tell you all the truth, it wouldn't seem so innocent anymore."

"I get it," I told him, quietly. Because I did get it. I really did.

His sigh was sorrowful. "I don't know how to get myself out of this mess."

"I haven't told anyone anything," I let him know. "And I wouldn't. Not ever. It's your story and his, not anyone else's. There isn't a reason why anyone else should know either."

The older man choked, rubbing his hand over his face as a couple tears escaped through his fingers. "He doesn't want anyone to know I'm his father. He hasn't in decades; that isn't going to change any time soon. I could die tomorrow, and he would be perfectly fine with it," he choked out, his chest hiccupping with emotion and maybe even a dozen other emotions I would never understand.

"I would care," I told him. "I know I'm not a replacement for him, and I would never try to be, but you're just about the only father figure I've ever had. And I would care a lot if you were gone. I would miss you for the rest of my life."

The hand he had over his face shifted, and he peeked a glassy, red-rimmed eye at me.

So I kept going. "And I think Rip would care too. I was there while we waited for the ambulance, and I was there most of the time while we waited to hear what happened to you. He was worried, Mr. C. I don't know if that will ever mean anything, but if he really hated you, he wouldn't have sat there for hours to hear from your doctor."

"He was probably making sure I really died."

"Or you have a relationship with him that no one will ever understand." I sighed. "Mr. C, I can tell you that if my dad had a heart attack, I would not have waited around at the hospital to hear how he was doing. I wouldn't go visit period. And when the day comes and he passes away, I won't be at his funeral. They could offer me a million dollars to go, and it wouldn't be enough. Maybe Rip isn't your biggest fan, and he doesn't know how to forgive you for whatever it was that he blames you for, but it could be worse between the two of you. If things were that bad, he wouldn't have come back, and he wouldn't be able to look at you every day."

My boss's Adam's apple bobbed as he nodded. His chest went up and back down. He sniffled and followed it up with another choke that made my heart hurt.

I didn't know what happened with his wife. I didn't know what happened with Rip. I didn't know what happened to *them*.

But I cared about Mr. Cooper, and even though I told myself that I wasn't going to care about Rip the same way I had, a part of me still did and would.

I wanted the best for both of them.

I was just the wrong person to say anything about family relationships, and that was the truth.

He sniffed, and his sniff hit me right smack in the chest. "You know how to make an old man feel a little less like the scum of the earth, little moon."

"You could never be the scum of the earth. And I know how to tell you the truth most of the time, and in this case, I didn't have to lie. I saw Rip's face." Then I lowered my voice and added, "And if it makes you feel any better, he doesn't like me much either."

That had him wiping his face with his forearm. "I highly doubt that, honey."

I smirked to myself, but he must have seen it because he kept talking.

"He doesn't, Luna. I don't know Rip—" He sucked in a breath. "—my son as well as I should, but I know you're the last person he would dislike."

Well. "We can agree to disagree, huh?" I asked and stood up. "I'm getting a glass of water. Do you want anything from the kitchen?"

His expression was wobbly as he dropped his other arm and showed me his pink, puffy face that was pulled into a partial smile. "How about a bag of chips?"

"How about some fruit?"

Mr. Cooper groaned as I made my way around the couch and headed toward the kitchen, directly beside the living room.

And it was right then, as I turned, that I almost bit my tongue.

Because standing in the hallway that led from the front door to the living room and kitchen was a person.

Just. Standing there. Quietly. Not moving.

And that someone was Rip who took up most of the width of that hallway.

Rip who was standing there watching me with heavy eyes and a jaw that was tighter than ever.

"Lu, what—" Mr. Cooper started to say before he cut himself off, head turned toward the doorway. "Rip."

Ripley's eyes slid to his... dad... for a moment. His voice

was gruff, and his question was the last thing I would have expected. "You all right?"

Mr. Cooper didn't hesitate nodding. "Yeah."

Yeah? That was it? I mean, I guess I shouldn't expect him to tell him that *no,* he wasn't okay because he'd just been talking about how his own son hated him.

"Any news from the doctor?" Rip asked.

I bit the inside of my cheek and headed into the kitchen. I listened to Rip's low voice and Mr. Cooper's slightly louder one as I pulled a glass out of the cabinet and filled it with water from the fridge.

"I don't want you to die," Rip said, so quietly I could barely hear him.

The answering pause said everything, I thought, and it made me flinch.

"Shit's not ever gonna be the same, but I don't hate you either, old man," he kept going, gruffly. "Can't stand you but I don't hate you. Got it?"

There was a sniff and a "got it" right back.

Well. Okay. All right.

It was just as I pulled a bag of grapes from the fridge that the two men's voices cut off.

By the time I finished rinsing and setting the grapes into a coffee cup, they still hadn't continued speaking, but I figured that was okay. Peeking over the counter that led into the living room, I found Mr. Cooper in the same spot, and Rip was nowhere to be found.

"Here are your grapes." I handed the cup of fruit over to Mr. Cooper.

He wrinkled his nose as he took it. "Thank you?"

I couldn't help but grin at him. "Do you have medication or anything you need to take, Mr. C?"

"No, ma'am," he responded dryly.

Just as I opened my mouth, another voice cut across the air. "Talk to me outside for a minute, baby girl."

I froze there and only moved my eyes over to the man who had reappeared in the same place I had last seen him. I kept my face nice and even. "I'm supposed to stay with Mr. Cooper until Lydia gets back." That was the truth, and it was believable, wasn't it?

"I can be alone for a minute," Mr. Cooper threw in the second I finished my argument.

I closed my mouth.

By the time I had moved my gaze back over to Rip, he had his hand out.

Toward me.

And he'd taken steps closer so that he was within reaching distance.

So that I could take his hand.

He was just trying to make up for being so ugly to me weeks ago. Maybe he'd gotten tired of having to get his own coffee. Maybe he'd overheard what I had told Mr. Cooper. Hadn't I already learned that he was capable of feeling guilt?

"Come with me," he said in that slow, soft voice, fingers still reaching for me.

Hurt tightened my chest, but I stood up anyway. And I took his hand. Maybe I wouldn't have if I hadn't just learned that Rip had issues with Mr. Cooper over his beloved mom who had died, over how he had remarried so soon after her death, but I would never know.

But what I did know from experience was what it was like to take a leap and have no one there to catch you. Or at least break your fall. And that was why I took it.

Because who knew when the last time he had reached out to anyone had been?

Gently, he tugged at my hand and led me toward the front door, closing the door behind us the second we were outside. I watched as he took a step forward, his free hand going up to the top of his head and smoothing down the back of it. He still hadn't let go of my hand.

Crickets chirped in the evening grass on Mr. Cooper's front lawn. I didn't need to look around to know we were surrounded by shrubs and flower bushes. I also didn't need to glance up to know Lucas Ripley was looking down at me when I tried to pull my hand out of his, and his grip tightened instead of loosening.

So I wasn't surprised when he didn't hesitate, his voice strong and sure, as this man said, "Don't be fucking mad at me anymore."

I bit the inside of my cheek and forced myself to look up into that face I had memorized. Dark brown hair shot through with strands of silver, deep-set eyes, broad, flat cheekbones, and that jaw that would have been a work of art if anyone were smart enough to recreate it, faced me. His eyes focused down on me, intent and unflinching.

Leave me alone, he had said.

"I didn't mean all that shit I said, and you know it," he told me, tugging at the hand he hadn't let go of.

I took a deep breath and kept my voice even. "Mr. Ripley—"

He didn't let me get further than that before he snapped, "Cut it out."

"Cut what out?"

That throat of his bobbed as he dipped his chin in close. "You know what, Luna."

I looked at him, keeping my face blank.

"That Mister Ripley bullshit," he finally growled out.

"But that's your name."

He made a noise in his throat.

"You're my boss," I reminded him.

The fingers around mine jerked. "I'm more than your boss."

That had me trying to pull my hand out of his. "No, Rip. That's what you are, and I just happened to forget that."

He cursed. Rip cursed under his breath, his fingers tightening. "No, baby girl, there was nothing for you to forget."

Leave me alone.

I clung on to those words with both my hands and held on tight. He was my boss. Today, tomorrow, the day after that. He didn't want what I had to offer, and I wasn't going to be naïve enough to believe people changed.

Rip had lost his mind for a little while before deciding what it was that he wanted.

And that wasn't me or my friendship or my problems.

He felt guilty and that was it.

I tipped my chin up, reminding myself I had been through worse and been through things more hurtful than words said out of anger. And I told him what he deep down wanted to make sure. "I've already told you I'm not going to quit, if that's what you're worried about." I swallowed and fisted my free hand, keeping my voice calm. "I get offers every few months from other businesses, but I don't think twice about them. I love working at CCC, even if you don't like me—"

This huge man reared back and blinked, his hand getting tight and his voice going hoarse. "Not like you?"

Be strong. You can handle anything, Luna.

I nodded. "We can call it whatever you want. I'm fine

with it, Mr. Ripley. You're not the first person to dislike me or not want me around. It's fine."

He let go of my hand so quickly I didn't have time to react before the man in front of me cut the distance between us so much there was no distance.

That big hand that had been right by my face moved like lightning, his palm cradling the back of my head. Before I could finish my sentence, before I could even suck in a breath, Lucas Ripley dipped his face close to mine. "I don't *dislike* a single fucking bone in your body, Luna."

And cue my mouth shutting and probably my eyes bugging out too.

"You drive me fucking nuts—"

"That's not very nice," I said before I could stop myself.

I didn't miss the way his eyebrows shot up. "Let me finish, yeah?"

I shut my mouth.

"But I miss the fuck out of you, messing with me all the damn time, provoking me way too much, always fucking laughing and smiling and being a pain in my fucking ass." What had to be his little finger grazed the nape of my neck as I stood there. "I said some mean shit to the one person in this fucking world that—"

He stopped, and if it wouldn't have been for his Adam's apple bobbing, I wouldn't have realized he was struggling with his words. Struggling with whatever he was trying to tell me. Confusing the freaking hell out of me.

"You. I would never want to hurt you," he breathed, beaming me with that intense gaze. "Not for nothing. I'm sorry I didn't tell you I knew your family, but I didn't exactly want you to know how or why I did either. You get me?"

Just as I opened my mouth, his hand moved around and his thumb landed over my lips, shutting me up.

"I swear to Jesus Christ if you say something about work or about how you won't fucking quit, I'll close your mouth my own goddamn self in another way," Rip told me.

That had me shutting my mouth.

That had my heart going *whack, whack, whack, what the hell is happening?*

"What?" was all I could crow.

"I don't give a single fuck how many other companies offer you jobs, or how happy you are at the shop. Me and the old man wouldn't let you go anywhere," he said, his gaze intent.

"I just said I don't want to go anywhere in the first place...," I muttered, trying my best to ignore how fast my heart was going because of the way he was looking at me.

At the way he was even just talking to me.

Rip's cheeks twitched, and his voice was even lower as he whispered, "Good." The pinky he had on the back of my neck moved across the skin there lightly, just grazing it. "I don't want you leaving me alone. I was pissed and you were there, and I shouldn't have taken it out on you. I don't want to hurt you. You hear me?"

I did and I didn't.

I was there and, like always, I was an easy target. That was nothing new.

But I knew words held an edge of truth to them always.

I also knew that I had been right in thinking that I had wasted my time mooning over this man who would never be more than my boss. He did feel bad, and that was nice, but that was it. That was all. I had given him the tools he used to hurt me.

And I really was tired of hurting, but that was on me. I just wanted to move past this.

Warm, sweet breath washed over my face as he leaned in even closer to me. Bringing him so close I had to hold my breath. "You forgive me for fucking up?"

Did I?

I only had to pause for a moment before I knew my answer. "Sure."

"Sure?"

I nodded and that got me a slow, wary blink.

"We good?"

I nodded again.

The finger on my neck was light as his eyes moved from one of mine to the other and back again. I could still feel his breath on my face. I could feel his entire palm on the back of my head.

"We over this 'Mr. Ripley' bullshit?"

I didn't say a word in response to that, mostly because I did forgive him—Rip was shades of black and gray and white, and so was his relationship with Mr. C—but that didn't change my own reality. My own truth.

Plus, I didn't want to lie.

I wasn't sure I was done with the "Mr. Ripley" bullshit. It would help me cope. It would remind me of my hard-earned lesson.

And something about *that* had his face clouding over. His eyes narrowing, moving from one of mine to the other like he knew—*knew*—what I was thinking. "I don't dislike you. Not a little, not at all. How many times do I gotta say that to get it through your head?"

My chest ached as I looked up into that handsome, handsome face.

But I remembered.

I would remember what he said for a very, very long time.

"I forgive you, Rip, I really do. I can't imagine the stress you were under, and I appreciate that you feel bad for what you said. You had no idea I couldn't care less that you knew what I did before I told you. But I never thought you would tell me to leave you alone. That you would push me away, and that's what hurt me. Because I grew up being told to leave people alone. I want you to be happy, and I want to be happy too. And none of this lately has been doing that. It just makes me sad. So I think we're better off just keeping things the way they always should have been. Like you're my boss, and I paint your cars for you, and that's it."

CHAPTER TWENTY-EIGHT

THE NEXT MORNING, I DROPPED MY BAGS—FILLED WITH my food, my phone, and all my extra crap I brought with me every day—on the floor right by the door.

Because sitting there at seven in the morning, on top of my desk in a small glass jar, with a white ribbon wrapped around the stem, was a bright orange rose.

Just... sitting there.

Just waiting.

For me?

There was only one person in the building who could have put it there.

There wasn't a doubt in my mind.

He'd upped his game from bringing me donuts to... a flower. A flower that made my throat tighten up even as I told myself that I knew why he'd done it.

Because of the guilt.

The first flower anyone had ever bought me was because of guilt.

I had to let out a deep breath at that.

I had told him—hadn't I told him?—that I wanted to go

back to us being what we should have been from the beginning?

I had told him. And here he was making things complicated, giving my brain ideas that I had to throw in the trash before I thought about them. Here he was just... messing with me. Trying to pull me into a place that I didn't want to be anywhere close to anymore.

I should have let it go, or should have pretended I didn't see it, but...

I didn't do that.

I was tired. And worn out. And just... freaking tired.

Just like I dropped my stuff, I left it there and walked right back out of my room. One foot in front of the other. One step in front of the other. Taking me closer and closer. I barely cleared the hallway into the main part of the building when I spotted Rip standing by the tool chest, rifling through the drawers.

I wasn't sure why my heart started picking up speed, but it did. With each step, it got faster and faster, despite my brain telling it that it needed to calm down. It meant nothing.

It was a nice, but forced and completely unnecessary, gesture.

And I didn't want him to waste his time doing it again.

"Mr. Ripley," I called out, knowing I shouldn't after our conversation yesterday, but also not backing down from the promise I had made myself.

He glanced up immediately, shooting me that laser-like gaze. Today, he had on a navy blue compression shirt, and his coveralls were already on. The thing that caught me off guard was the fact that he didn't look annoyed at me calling him the m-word. What he did look was too calm. Way too easygoing.

Even though I was positive enough he'd left the flower, I was going to punish myself by asking anyway. "Did you leave that rose in my room?"

He straightened from where he'd been slightly bent over the tool chest. His expression stayed that eerie calm one. He answered in the way I knew he would: directly. "Yeah."

Yeah.

My heart went even faster, but I ignored it. It wasn't like this was news. Who the hell else would it have been?

I held my breath. *Leave me alone.* "Thank you, but you didn't have to. I told you yesterday—"

"I didn't forget," he cut me off.

Hell. "But you don't have to feel guilty or try to make anything up to me—"

"I'm not trying to make anything up to you," he butted in again.

That got me to stop talking. Because... why else would he do it? For the hell of it? He suddenly wanted to buy someone a rose, and I just happened to be the only woman he could get one for?

He slammed the drawer closed with his hip. "You liked it?"

Did I like it? Why the hell wasn't my heart slowing down any? "Yes," I told him truthfully. "It's beautiful, but you don't have to—"

"Good," he cut me off for the third time.

Oh, man. "Mr. Ripley—"

"Rip."

We weren't going there. "Please don't buy me anything anymore."

His grunt wasn't what I would ever call convincing.

"There's nothing to feel bad about," I kept going.

He just grunted again, but he kept looking at me, kept that expression on his face too. The one I didn't know what it meant.

"I need to get started on my day, but all I wanted to do was thank you and tell you that you didn't have to," I said.

Ripley's gaze seemed to shift over my face before settling on my ears. He was looking at my heart earrings. I just knew it.

I gave him a tight smile I was well aware he would know was fake, but oh well. Just as I turned around to head back to my room to start my day like I had said, the man called out behind me.

"What time are you leaving today?"

I stopped but didn't turn around to look at him. *Leave me alone.* "The latest I can stay tonight is six. I have plans." And by plans, I meant a date. With a total stranger.

I didn't miss how he didn't explain why he was asking.

But honestly, I went back to my room so fast, I didn't get a chance to wonder why any longer than I had to.

* * *

I KNEW it had been an extra dumb idea to show up to the bar when the second question my date asked was "How old are you?"

He was a decent-looking guy.

My date leaned back in his chair and muttered, "Huh," his expression funny after I told him.

Something about it didn't sit right with me, that or I was just picking up on things I should have let go. "Why?"

"Thought you were younger," the man had the balls to respond with.

I raised my eyebrows, positive I definitely wasn't liking

where this was going, but... I could give him the benefit of the doubt. As much as I had been telling myself I was fine, I hadn't been. Not really. "What? Am I too old?" I tried to joke.

He shrugged.

Shrugged?

Was he for real?

The partial smile I had on my face just fell right off. "How old are you?"

He was still watching me a little too closely as he said, "Thirty-four."

Thirty-four? *Thirty-four* and *I* was too old?

"You look younger than twenty-six though."

"Oh." I hoped I sounded as sarcastic as I felt. "Thanks?" Man, I was grumpy. I wasn't sure I'd ever been so grouchy before.

His eyes slid around the bar for a moment before coming back to me, looking me over like... well, I wasn't sure what, but I didn't like it.

"So," I tried grasping for straws at that point because all I wanted was to go home. All I had to do was text Lenny a message that said RED and she'd call and save me. The second that option filtered through my brain, I reminded myself that I was supposed to be *trying*. I had to *try*. I had to want someone else to buy me flowers, and not because they'd hurt my feelings. "Have you been married before?" I asked him.

The man snickered, his gaze moving around the room again. "For about a minute ten years ago. Dumbest mistake of my life. You?"

I shook my head, not sure how to take his comment about it being a mistake.

"Thank God," he mumbled, making a face as he said it

like there would have been something wrong with me being divorced.

I opened my mouth just as the chair beside mine got dragged backward. My hands stopped, and I looked over, wondering who was taking the chair without asking, when my eyes zeroed in on the knuckles holding onto the back of the seat. I might have been able to recognize his fingers even if letters on knuckles wasn't something everyone had.

Especially not on knuckles connected to dinner plate-sized hands... hands connected to wrists that were covered by a familiar elastic, tight shirt.

I was pretty sure my mouth must have been partially opened as Rip fell down into the seat hard, his legs spreading wide in a V-shape instantly, his attention straight on the man across from... us.

Across from us.

Ah.

What was he doing here?

"Is this over now?" my boss drawled easily, crossing his arms over his chest as he leaned back in the chair, somehow making himself look even bigger by spreading out.

The other man frowned. "You lost?"

"Rip," I started to say, ignoring the man I was supposed to be on a date with, if you could even call it a date since he'd made me pay for my Sprite. "What are you doing here?"

The other man glanced at me. "Who the fuck is this?"

I ignored him again, but Rip wasn't paying any attention to me. He was staring at my date with a deceptively lazy expression. But there wasn't a single thing easygoing about his next words. "Time for you to go."

Time for him to go?

The other man made another face before focusing on me and asking, angrily, "You got a boyfriend?"

Me? A boyfriend?

"I'm none of your business," Rip kept talking. "You can go home now."

I wasn't sure why I reached over, but I did, and touched my boss's forearm, earning his attention. "What are you doing here?" I just about hissed at him.

Those blue-green eyes slid toward me, still lazily, and his cheek moved just enough to tell me that might have been considered a smile. "Ending this bullshit-ass date you're on," he stated, confusing me even more.

"Who the fuck do you think you're talking to?" the man asked with a scowl.

His words triggered Rip, because his gaze swept over to the side and he gave the guy a blank look I was pretty familiar with. "You."

"Me?"

"She's not interested," Rip claimed calmly.

The guy decided to include me in the conversation again by swiveling his gaze toward me. "Is he for real?"

I decided to ignore him and tapped my fingers on the bigger man's forearm. "What are you doing here?"

That cheeky expression fell off, and he just... stared at me. All of him just... focused. Too focused. On me.

"Are you his fucking girl?" the other guy demanded, his pitch going higher.

His girl? Rip's girl?

My "no" came out at the same time Rip said, "What do you think?"

What do you think?

Was this man, who I hadn't spoken to in two weeks up until yesterday, implying that I was *his girl*?

"No," I told Rip, tapping his forearm again through the material of his compression shirt. "What are you talking about?"

"She is?"

Rip's expression didn't falter for a second, but it was the man he had his attention on. "Did I stutter?"

"Are you fucking serious?" the man spat, shoving his chair back before giving me an angry look. "You know what? I don't have time to deal with this kind of shit. You can fuck off, and she can—"

Rip got to his feet so fast, it was a blur. "You like having all those teeth in your mouth? Or you good with going home, missing a few of them?"

"Fuck—" the other man started.

"Trust me when I tell you that you don't want to finish that sentence," Rip spit slowly. "I've broken fuckboys like you for fun, and now you're giving me a reason to. You don't wanna go there. Trust me."

He'd broken—

Oh shit.

"Fuck you and—" the other guy started to say.

I pushed my chair back instantly, my hand going around the inside of Ripley's elbow, giving it a tug.

He didn't move, but I knew he'd felt me when his eyes shifted over to look at me with this crazy expression on his face. That hit me straight in the heart.

"You know, I think it's time I left." I squeezed Rip. "We left."

The guy snarled as he took a step back, paused for a moment, and then took another, like one hadn't put enough distance between the two men. "I don't know what the hell is going on here, but I'm done. You need to tell your man it's you looking to fuck around."

I could have argued with him or explained that Ripley's wasn't my man. He wasn't anyone's man. Much less mine.

But...

I didn't really care that much, especially not when he'd made me feel old and was overall just kind of a prick and a reminder why I had no business finding a date on an app used for mostly hooking up.

Because the only person I could blame for tonight was myself. I had set this date up. I had downloaded the app two nights ago and had agreed to go out with the first person who had invited me. Because I had told myself I was trying to move on.

The jerk skirted around the table, and at the last minute, raised his middle finger at us before basically tucking his tail in and speed walking out of the bar.

"What are you doing?" I hissed at Rip the second the other guy was out of view.

Rip stood there and looked at me, his expression back to blank. "He was a fucking tool, Luna."

Okay, he had been a tool, but... "If he was or not, what are you doing here?" I asked him, shoving my chair even further back and pretending like I didn't see the other bar-goers nearby standing there, looking over at us. I was done. I was going home.

"I came to make sure you were all right."

I was not going to blow his comment out of proportion. I wasn't, and because I wasn't, I was able to keep myself nice and calm as I asked, "Why wouldn't I be?"

Rip ignored my words but watched as I grabbed my phone and keys and stuck them into my pockets. "Where's your car?"

I took a step back. "I didn't drive."

He took a step forward, making his way around the table as he said, "Good. I'll give you a ride home."

Nope, I still wasn't going to overthink his comment or his offer. I had no idea what kind of game he was playing—or even when he'd decided he wanted to start playing games, especially by referring to me as *his girl* all of a sudden—but it wasn't my problem. I wasn't going to get all sucked up into him being nice to me *now,* then, later on, decide he didn't want to have anything to do with me afterward. I couldn't handle it. I wouldn't.

"Thank you for the offer, but I don't need a ride. I'll just get a car—"

A hand landed on the small of my back a second before Rip started steering me toward the door, oblivious to the way I was looking up at him like I had no clue who the hell he was.

Because I didn't.

I didn't know who this man pushing me through the bar was, showing up and ruining an already crappy date, implying I was his *girl*, being all nice and protective and jealous and—

I wasn't doing this. I wasn't putting myself in this position. I already knew I was weak where Rip was concerned, and that's why I had to shut this down the instant we were outside.

"You eat already?" he asked just as he led me through the door, the bouncer giving me a curious expression since he'd been seeing me so often lately.

"No." I tried to slow my steps, but that hand on my back just kept me right on marching through the parking lot. "Rip, I really don't need a ride. Look, I'm just going to get a—"

"You in the mood for a burger?" he asked just as I

spotted his truck parked maybe fifteen feet away under the lights of the lot.

I looked up at him over my shoulder and told my gut to *back off*. "I'm trying to talk to you. Could you listen, please?"

That had him stopping, his hand sweeping up my spine to stop at my shoulder, and I'd swear he didn't just look down at me, but his body seemed to curl into mine as his eyebrows went up and he said, "I always listen to you."

I wasn't ready for that comment—not right then and, more than likely, not for the rest of my life, especially not when the person saying those words was this man.

The hand on my shoulder trekked even further up, cupping the nape of my neck in a warm, strong grip. "You want to waste money taking a taxi and you're trying to get out of eating with me, am I right?" he asked softly.

Hell.

Hell, hell, hell.

What I knew without a doubt had to be a finger came up to the top of my ear, curling around the shell so lightly it almost tickled. "You told me you forgave me," he accused me in that same tissue-paper voice.

I could do this. I could handle it. "I do forgive you, Rip. I get that people say things they regret later on."

His expression got cloudy. "I do regret what I said, but you're missing the part where I told you I didn't mean it. I said I was sorry I didn't tell you from the beginning I knew about your family."

He did mean it. Everything had some kind of root of truth beneath it. Everything.

And even if this didn't.... that didn't change the fact that I didn't want to go through something like this again. Not ever. Not with him.

That light little touch moved over the shell of my ear again, making that tingle start at the base of my spine. Warm breath washed over my forehead as he curled into me even more. "Whatever the hell you might think, you're the last person I would ever want to hurt. Why are you fighting this?" he asked, sweeping his finger again over my ear and dragging it across the studs at my earlobe.

I could be strong. I could be brave. I could do this. "I'm not... fighting it. I'm just being real. I don't want you to waste your time—"

"You're never a waste of my time."

Where was this coming from? "Rip—"

This mountain of a man took his other hand off my back and settled it on my throat, managing to cup it between his hands before I realized what he was doing. Lucas Ripley dipped his face even closer to mine... so close I tried to move backward so I could get a good look at him, but he didn't let that happen. He brought his mouth, his face, his eyes, some of the things I liked the most about him, inches from me. His mouth a lunge away...

What the hell was I doing thinking about that? Jeez.

"You haven't listened to a single fucking thing I've said, have you? Seen a single thing I've done? You the only person who hasn't put shit together?"

I breathed in through my nose and heard it rattle right out of me.

"I don't know how to give you flowery words and shit like that, Luna. I don't know how to tell you what you want or need to hear. It's been a long fucking time since I've given a fuck about anybody. Do you understand that?"

I could do this. I could—

"I don't like the idea of you sitting next to some random asshole who wants to get in your pants."

And that wasn't at all what I was expecting him to say.

"What?" I didn't mean to whisper.

His finger came up, and the pad of his thumb dragged across my cheekbone. "Don't like the idea of you going on a date with somebody." The pad moved back the way it had come, and he said low, "Can't fucking stand it. Just when I thought I couldn't get more pissed..."

He...

He...

Was... jealous?

"I get that I fucked up, and I'm sorry. I didn't want you to know about me being a Reaper. Wasn't sure I ever wanted you to know about me being in a club like that. You said you grew up in San Antonio. The club had a bad rep there, but I got out of it. I'm sorry I didn't fucking tell you that night in your bed when you said something, but like you said, that shit's on me. But I want it back anyway."

Like an idiot, I asked, "What do you want back?"

"I want my goddamn Luna back," he breathed, stealing the air from my lungs. "I don't want you to leave me alone. I want you bugging my ass for random shit again. I wanna see your fucking face first thing in the morning, even if you don't bring me my coffee anymore. I wanna make you something to eat so you don't end up with Salmonella from that shit you try to cook," he said in this strangely calm voice that seemed like the opposite of what someone using a jackhammer on my entire existence would have been.

And he told me carefully, too carefully, "Two fucking weeks and I want it back. You gave me these pieces of you I know you haven't given to anybody else, and they're mine. You can't take 'em back. I need them more than you do, you hear me?"

I took a breath in through my nose, ignoring that thing

bubbling and living under and inside of me. But as I stood there, watching him, the distrust running so fiercely through me as my brain called out *liar, liar, freaking liar*, something big and hard formed in my chest. This knot. This... prediction. I wasn't sure what it was going to be of, but it was going to be something... something I wasn't positive I was ready to handle after all.

The hands on my throat slid down to cup my shoulders, and it was his turn to let out a deep breath. "I know I fucked up, and I can tell you're not gonna make this easy on me, and I get it. But I want you to eat a burger with me in the meantime, yeah? Get some ice cream with me. You promised the day of the wreck. Remember?"

Of course I remembered. How could I forget?

Rip took a step back, and I still didn't say anything.

He took another step and, still, nothing.

Then another and another, until he stopped right before the door and gave me an intent look as he said, "Let's go eat a fucking burger and some ice cream, baby girl. There's nothing for you to be scared of. You can trust me."

I wasn't sure about all of that. I wasn't even sure about part of it, especially the part of my head that needed to make rational decisions.

But I had never been one to hold grudges. That wasn't what this had been about in the first place.

And... I wanted to believe him. I wanted to believe him so bad it burned my throat and everything else south of the border. I wanted to trust myself even though I wasn't sure I could.

But this need in me to try, to believe, burned the brightest flame in my chest. In all of me, really.

Trust him?

"I got you," he said with so much conviction there was no way to ignore it.

When we went to go eat a burger and two ice cream cones a few minutes later, I wasn't sure how I felt.

What I did know was him telling me to trust him was on repeat in my head the rest of the night.

CHAPTER TWENTY-NINE

The following morning, I didn't drop my stuff on the floor when I went into my room and found another flower sitting on my desk. This time, it was a purple rose—a pale lavender that was almost white but just barely not—with a lacy white ribbon tied around it. It was beautiful. Honestly, just freaking beautiful.

But was it there because of guilt?

Or was it because of the things he'd said last night? The things I hadn't been able to stop thinking about since we'd sat across from each other eating burgers and splitting an order of fries. The things he'd said that lit up a part of me that was scary. That gave me too much hope.

He wanted his Luna back.

His.

In what way though?

And why did I want that more than anything even though I'd told myself before I had fallen asleep all alone in my bed last night that it was dangerous and stupid and way too risky... because it was. It really was all of those things.

Don't be dumb, I tried to tell myself as I put my bag into the right drawer, still looking at the rose. It was perfect. There wasn't a single blemish on any petal. The tips had a slightly darker shade of purple on them.

It was just as beautiful as the one from yesterday, sitting there alone in its jar.

My hand felt unsteady as I picked it up, took a whiff of it, tried my best to ignore the way my heart started speeding up, and then set it in the jar beside the orange one.

It was just a flower. The second of my life. Bought out of guilt or just because Rip had lost his mind and gone delusional, imagining things that he had no business sharing with me.

But...

You know what? If he wanted to keep buying me flowers, fine. I was still going to tell him he didn't need to, because he didn't.

With my lunch bag in hand, I knew exactly what I needed to do as I headed toward the main floor to have a conversation before starting the coffee so I could move on with my day.

Rip was looking through a manual beside an old Corvette I hadn't seen before. He glanced over the second my footsteps started to get louder. He had the same face he'd had on the day before when I'd asked him about the orange flower. Calm, patient, serious.

"Mr. Ripley—"

He smiled.

He full-out, outright smiled. Dimple and everything.

At me.

"You mean Rip."

I was going to ignore it. I held my head up, took a breath through my nose, and said as professionally as possible, "I told you, you don't have to buy me anything if you feel bad—"

His eyebrows went up just slightly as he beamed that beautiful closed-mouth smile at me. "Told you I'm not doing it because I feel bad."

Then why, Rip? Why are you doing it?

"You said nobody's ever given you flowers before," he went on, still too calm, still smiling.

I shut my freaking mouth.

"You like it?"

Say no. Say no. Be a bish and say no.

The problem was, I wasn't used to being one. At least not a real one.

So I told him the freaking truth. "It's beautiful."

His smile wavered. "Good."

And before I could open my mouth to remind him again he didn't need to do the flowers or the donuts or going to bars where I had dates, he jerked his chin to the side, toward the wall of tool chests and said, "Made your coffee. Not sure if I got it right, but I think I did."

He'd made my coffee?

What in the *hell* was happening? It genuinely felt like I'd gotten hit on the back of the head and was having delusions or something. It felt like... I didn't know what it felt like. But not real.

Not even like a freaking fantasy. Not even close.

All I could do was stand there. Stand there feeling like this man had punched me as hard as he could in the solar plexus. Then as if that wasn't enough, he'd kicked my legs out from under me.

Before he could say anything else, before I could remember how to speak or think about what I could or should say, his cell phone started to ring. His hand was pulling it out of his pocket when he said, his smile melting into a smaller, gentler one, "Used some of the decaf you have hidden too, in case you're worried about your hands."

And then he answered his call. Like I wasn't there standing like a dum-dum as I figured out why he was taking this so far that he made *me* my coffee. I'd watched him. When he was lazy, he didn't even make his own coffee the way he liked it.

But he'd made mine.

On the same day he'd brought me a purple flower that reminded me of my house.

The night after he'd kicked my date to the curb and taken me to eat burgers, fries, and an ice cream cone, while I'd mostly stared at him the whole time, thinking.

Sure enough, when I picked up my coffee mug as he spoke to what I figured was one of the companies CCC ordered parts from, I took a sip and... it tasted exactly how I made mine.

Exactly.

And like the chicken I was now, I headed back to my room before he got off the phone.

I needed to think. Well, I needed to do more than think, but....

I hadn't told Lenny about the rose the day before because I hadn't seen a point, but when I made it back to my room with my coffee burning a hole straight into my heart, I had to pull my phone out and type a message.

Me: He brought me a purple rose and made me coffee.

There was possibly a thirty-second delay before she responded.

Lenny: Who?

Me: Rip

Lenny: O.O

Lenny: Why?

I hadn't gotten a chance to tell her about anything that happened yesterday, and I sure hadn't told her about him knowing about my family. All she knew was that he'd been a jerk at the hospital and we hadn't been on speaking terms since.

Me: He bought me an orange rose yesterday and left it in my office too. So I went to tell him he didn't have to make it up to me or anything… and he said that he wasn't trying to make it up to me.

Lenny: And???

Me: You know how I had that date yesterday? He showed up at the bar and ran the guy off. Then he said he wanted his Luna and how he wanted to see my face first thing every morning, and then we went to eat burgers.

Me: I thought he was full of crap and just stringing me along so I wouldn't get pissed off and quit, but now he's making me coffee and bringing me roses and asking me if I like them, and telling me he listens to everything I say… and I don't know what I'm doing.

Me: No one's ever bought me flowers before, and he remembered that.

Me: What do I do?

Lenny: And why are you asking me what you should do? I don't know.

Lenny: He kind of deserves for you to tell

him to fuck off, but I'm on my period and want to kill half the guys at the gym.

Lenny: I do have to say that's pretty sweet though.

Lenny: The only men that have ever made me coffee are Grandpa Gus and Peter. Food for thought.

Me: You're useless.

Me: I'll think about it.

Lenny: Sorry

Me: I didn't tell you he's been coming by my room every day for no reason.

Lenny: Now you're just rubbing it in.

Lenny: Tell me what happens. I need to live through you since it's the only romance in my life.

Me: I don't think it's romance. I think he just feels bad.

Lenny: Bish, I've grown up with guys. Even if they feel bad about something, most of the time, they won't even say they're sorry. They'll just act normal and hope you forget. They're not going to get you flowers and make you coffee and say things like that to you. Not even if they want to get in your pants. Just saying.

Me: You just said you don't know what I'm supposed to do.

Lenny: I don't, but I know men and I know assholes, and neither one is going to be buying you flowers for no reason. Or telling you shit like they want you back.

Lenny: Want me to ask Grandpa Gus and see what he thinks? He's been a man for seventy-two years now. Even if he doesn't know, he'll make something up.

I wasn't crazy about her asking Grandpa Gus what I should do, but who else did I have to give me advice? Mr. Cooper? Miguel?

I rubbed my palm over my forehead and sighed as I replied.

Me: Okay. Ask him.

Lenny: You're welcome.

Me: Thanks. Gotta get to work now.

Lenny: Some of us have already been at work...

Lenny: Kisses

I sighed again and set my phone into my back pocket as my eyes went back to the two flowers sitting in the jar, just... taunting me.

* * *

Lenny had texted me last night and said that Grandpa Gus had told her that she was right: Rip wouldn't have said that kind of thing unless he meant it, and that Len was right again. He wouldn't be buying me flowers if he felt guilty either.

But...

What if that wasn't the case?

What if he changed his mind?

* * *

A WEEK WENT by and the flowers kept showing up on my desk every morning. Different shades of pink, red, orange, yellow, lilac, purple... All of them short-stemmed and without thorns, waiting for me.

And if that wasn't enough, my cup of coffee was there every morning too. Sitting beside the coffee maker one day, beside the little jar of flowers on another day, and on three other occasions on whatever tool chest was right beside him. And when I'd go to get it, he would shoot me a smile and ask if I liked the flower he'd left.

I wasn't even going to think about how every afternoon there was a container in the refrigerator with my name on it.

Much less how I ate it instead of the lunch I brought myself, which wasn't a tenth as good as what he made.

If none of that was enough, when I got to work one random morning, I found that my Ball jar had been replaced. In its place was a pretty globe-shaped vase with an icy blue and white lace ribbon wrapped around the fluted end. Pretty, it was so freaking pretty, I had almost been scared to touch it.

Rip didn't go easy. It was like he set a bar he needed to go above and beyond.

He started coming over to my room for no reason. He came in every morning around ten without fault, and in the afternoon too, and would look at me through the window if I was in the booth, or just fart around looking at things he'd seen a dozen times in my room.

But he watched me, even when I purposely avoided looking at him.

He watched me, and he was patient.

He kept that warm smile, or pretty close to it, on his face every time I looked at him, like he was purposely giving me time and space to... I wasn't sure what.

I really wasn't sure.

Every time I called him "Mr. Ripley," he corrected me and then moved on with our conversation, even if it was mostly me responding in one-word answers and trying to be professional.

One week turned into two, and the next thing I knew, there were two vases on my desk, filled with the most beautiful, perfect roses. When one started to wilt, he took it out before I'd even gotten to work, but a new one was always sitting on my desk like he wanted me to see it and appreciate it.

Lenny: He's trying. You've gotta give it to him.

Me: He doesn't need to be trying. I don't want him to try.

Lenny: Liar.

Lenny: You love it, and that's okay.

Me: That's what scares me. I'm tired of loving people who decide they're done with me.

Lenny: You only miss all the shots you don't take in life, Lu, you know that.

He was trying.

And Lenny did have a point.

But...

But.

* * *

I WAS GOING to blame sleeping like shit the night before on why I finally lost it the next morning.

I could blame the letter I'd found in the mail the night before on why I hadn't been able to sleep. The letter I had read and reread a dozen times. Knowing I would end up reading it a dozen more. I had slept with it on the nightstand.

Dear Luna,

I want to tell you that I'm sorry, but that feels like a cop-out now. But I am sorry. I'm so, so sorry for everything. I've wanted to call you, but I don't think I can handle hearing you being all decent after what a bitch I've been lately.

I didn't mean for you to find out about Dad the way you did, okay? He called me right after he got out of jail and kept calling me every once in a while for years after that, and I never answered, until one day I finally did. I was having a bad day, and I answered intending to tell him off... I yelled at him, I asked him why he'd been such an asshole my entire life. I spent at least ten minutes screaming at him, and he took it all. He apologized, Luna. He told me how sorry he was, how unhappy he'd been and how much he regretted how things had worked out. He said he was sober and was trying to make amends for the things he'd done.

If it makes you feel better, I hung up on him that first day after all that. He called again a few days later, and I was a bitch then too. But he kept on calling, and I kept answering.

I know that's not an excuse or really even an explanation, but that's how it happened. Please don't get more mad than you already are, but he isn't so bad. He's changed a lot. He asks about everyone. (Yes, including you.) (But mostly me, Kyra, and Lily, but I'm sure you already know that. I just don't want to lie to you anymore.)

I've asked him not to call you again so you know. I know you won't ever forgive him, and I get it, but I guess I was just worried you would make me choose between you or him. Kyra and I both thought the same thing. If it makes you feel any better, my boyfriend thinks I'm an idiot and says I deserve you shutting me out of your life now. But I hope you don't. I hope one day you can forgive me.

If you're still reading this, you should know how bad I still feel about the night you came over. I'm sorry doesn't cut it, but I am. I'm sorry for so many things I don't know where to start.

The other thing is… look… I haven't known how to tell you this, and I still don't, but… I'm not selling drugs or anything like that. Don't freak out. I started stripping, okay? I didn't tell anyone. I barely told Kyra a year ago. I couldn't keep it a secret any longer. I make enough money to pay for most of my school expenses, and I only have to work a few hours a day. My roommate is a stripper too. I'm just doing it until I graduate.

I dated this older guy for a while, and he was the reason why I got the apartment I was at. We split up and things got weird, and... to make a long story short, it was him who got into my apartment that night. He was jealous over my new boyfriend, but I got a restraining order now and I'm moving out when my lease is over in January.

You always do the right thing, and I didn't want you to get mad at me. By the time I knew I had to say something, it had been too long and I don't know how to fix any of this anymore. Lies always spiral out of control, even if you don't mean for them to, huh?

I love you, Luna. I'm sorry for fucking up so much and lying to you and just being a shitty sister, but I want you to know everything.

Please don't be mad.

Love,

Thea

P.S. You should know Rudy went to your house and job on his own. Dad didn't send him there. He said that Rudy overheard me telling him about getting broken into and got the idea to try and get away with it. Dad had asked me to check with you that one day to make sure you were okay. He had a feeling Rudy would try to do something. I should have warned you, but now I have to live with that too if it makes you feel any better. I'm really glad you're okay. Lily told me all about it. Not that it means much, but I'm sorry.

. . .

THAT's what I'd gotten.

So I was going to blame my sister's kind of passive-aggressive note on why I slept like shit.

I was still mad. Me. Who was rarely ever mad. But how could she think I would give a single crap about her stripping? I wouldn't care what she did.

Why couldn't she just call me? Why couldn't she just tell me? I wasn't scary. I understood, I guess to a certain point, but it still just felt like BS.

What I was, was mad.

And that was what I was going to blame as the reason why I lost it.

Then again, maybe it was finding Ripley bent over the engine of a Corvette he was restoring and getting a great view of his butt that might have been the icing on the cake.

Maybe it was the six red roses cut short and sitting in a glass bowl-like vase that were the icing on the cake. They were beautiful. But they were too beautiful. And when I really took in the vase and saw that it was spotless, without a single fingerprint on the glass, and imagined Rip carrying something super delicate in his hands and then wiping it down with maybe his shirt or a rag before leaving it there for me to find it....

I lost it.

It was that simple.

I barely remembered dropping my bag and things on the floor and heading back out to the main floor to find the man who had left my gift there.

"Rip!" I called out, knowing exactly where he was.

There was no lapse in response. "Yeah?" he responded from the furthest end of the floor, still looking at something inside the Corvette.

My coffee was sitting in a mug with the poster of the Rocky Horror Picture Show on it.

That hadn't existed in this building before. Had he bought it... for me?

I sucked in a breath, eyeing it until I was right beside him before I forced myself to look over and say, "Rip," I started, not even realizing I'd forgotten the "mister" part, "you can stop now with the flowers, all right?"

He didn't look up as he asked in that congenial, soft voice, "You didn't like 'em?"

"It isn't about whether I like them or not—"

He still didn't glance over as he cut me off. "You liked them then?"

"You know I do. They're beautiful—"

"You don't like them in your room anymore?"

I blinked. "No, I like them there—"

"So...?" he asked, still busy doing whatever it was he was doing.

I didn't glance at his butt.

I didn't.

"So then, you don't have to keep buying them, okay? I told you already, I'm over what happened, if that's why you're doing it."

Now that had him straightening, his head just barely missing the hood of the Corvette.

"You can stop. I get that you're trying to make it up to me, but you've done enough. It's just messing with my head and confusing me, and I would rather you stop now than stop a month from now or six months from now or a year from now when you decide you don't want to do it anymore, okay?"

That had him turning around slowly to meet me. He waited until he was fully facing me, that giant body tuned into mine, as he said, "I'm not trying to make anything up to you. I told *you* that already." He set down the wrench in his hand and took a deep breath, watching me closely. "I'm getting you flowers because I want to. Because you said nobody has ever given them to you, and I'm not about to let anyone else do it. This isn't some boss shit, baby. This doesn't have shit to do with Cooper's. This is Luna and Rip. This is me trying to get you to give me a chance. Understand me?"

Oh hell. He was being serious. Luna and Rip.

He was trying to... what? Win me over? I wasn't being delusional. Just stubborn. And scared.

You only miss the shots you don't take, Lenny had texted me. Was that what I was doing? Not wanting to take a shot because I didn't want to miss? Was it so bad to want to protect myself from getting hurt?

I wasn't sure, but some part of me must have been because I asked, "You're not?"

His smile grew slowly. "No, baby, I'm sure as hell not."

"Why?" I asked him as slowly as his smile had grown.

"Because."

My heart was beating fast. When did it start beating so fast? Damn it. "You don't get to just decide all of a sudden you want me to... to..." What was I going to say? Have a crush on him? I had no experience on how to talk to people, men specifically, without sounding worse than a teenager. "You don't get to decide all of a sudden that you want me to like you—"

"This isn't me wanting you to *like me*. That's not what I want. That's the smallest part of what I want, Luna."

For some stupid reason, I took a step back and bumped into the car right beside the Corvette. "What do you want then?"

Rip took a step forward, and then his hand came up toward my face. The backs of his fingers grazed my cheek... and they stayed there, just touching my skin, just barely. "I want what I should've been taking from you from the moment you started being sugar sweet to me. From the first time you went out of your way to make me feel good... made me feel better than anyone has for the first time in a long fucking time."

He licked his lips, and I watched every second of it as his hand stayed exactly where it was. On my cheek.

His fingers trailed down my jaw and lingered on the side of my neck. "You calm me. You know that? You do to me what all that jewelry you wear does for you. Just looking at you makes me feel better. And not just fucking better but *better*. Different. Like you look right through me and my bullshit and you know what's in there better than I do."

I stood there with my mouth open, not knowing what to say.

"Lady at the flower store said orange means admiration."

My brain and nervous system decided all I was going to be capable of doing right then was blinking and, even then, that seemed almost like too much for me to handle.

Because... *excuse me?*

"Pink's happiness... gratitude... appreciation. Those purples are desire... love at first sight... Yellow is affection. Red is love. I owe you a couple of white ones, but I was going to wait a while more because I know I fucked up." He dropped his hand. "But I'm not going anywhere. Not today. Not tomorrow. I thought you were the most beautiful fucking girl I'd ever seen when you walked into that tiny-ass office three years ago being all cocky and shit. And I think about that girl every single night as I go to bed, Luna. I know I've walked away from some shit in my life, but the last thing I want... last thing I could handle is going through you not talking to me anymore. You spoiled me, Luna, and I know I've been a real piece of shit a lot. I know you deserve better than somebody like me. I've told myself that a thousand times but it hasn't changed a single thing. I fucking miss you, and my greedy ass needs you around."

CHAPTER THIRTY

"WHAT'S THAT TROUBLED LOOK ON YOUR FACE FOR, little moon?" Mr. Cooper asked later that day.

Sitting across from him at his dinner table, I took a second to finish chewing the lightly seasoned chicken breast that Lydia had made that night. The same piece of chicken breast that I had more than likely been chewing for the last two minutes while I'd been busy thinking about the first part of the day. Specifically, the part of the day that involved my interactions with Ripley.

The part where he told me he wanted me in his life in a way that had nothing to do with work.

That entire conversation that had left my heart pounding, my brain confused, and my entire existence uprooted.

That was what I'd been thinking about all day. Even right then, while I ate with the Coopers and spent time with them... until my date in two hours.

My date.

What the hell was I *doing?*

"Problems at work? Ripley said Jason never came back,"

Mr. Cooper kept picking, his face genuinely concerned, which pulled at my heart.

Finally swallowing the chicken, I shook my head, not sure what I should say. *Sir, your estranged son of twenty years that was in a motorcycle club says he needs me. I love him, but I'm scared he'll change his mind and won't care about me someday, or he'll tell me to leave him alone again.*

That wasn't going to happen.

"Yeah, he never came back. He probably knew the guys would kick his butt if he did," I told him with a smile that was mostly genuine, at least beneath the confusion screwing up the rest of me into Gordian knots.

That had Mr. Cooper grinning. "Doesn't surprise me. I'm too old to be fighting with boys young enough to be my grandchildren, but I have to say, I would've put a world of hurt on that boy if I were ten years younger. Gus"—he was referring to Lenny's grandpa—"called me after he found out what happened and tried to talk me into doing something about it."

The smile I gave him that time was totally genuine. I could already imagine Grandpa Gus's crazy self wanting to do something about it. He hadn't gotten the memo he was in his seventies.

"What is it then, honey?" Lydia asked from her spot across the dining room table from me.

It comforted me. They comforted me. Living with them had been the first time ever I'd sat around a dining room table to eat. We had done it every night after work unless we all went out to eat, or they went out and I stayed at the house. It had been one of my favorite things about living with them. The sense of family.

It had made me want that for my own someday.

They deserved more than me keeping things from them,

even if those things revolved around a man who they both had strained relationships with. But I guess life was just one big complication any way you looked at it.

Life wasn't easy or black and white.

And I really did need to tell them the truth.

Because if Rip wasn't lying....

"It's...," I started to say before lowering my fork and knife to the plate. "It's Rip."

Both of them blinked and stayed very, very still.

"Did he finally decide to get his head out of his ass?" Mr. Cooper asked with a wary smile after a moment.

"What?"

He repeated himself. "Did he finally get his head out of his ass and tell you to save those dates for him?"

My mouth gaped open, and I was really, really glad that I had set down the knife and fork. Out of the corner of my eye, I could see the cautious little smile on Lydia's face as she bent toward her food and started cutting her chicken while Mr. Cooper and I made eye contact.

"I knew you didn't see it, little moon. I knew it from the first moment that I saw that look in Ripley's eyes. Didn't I tell you, Lydia, honey?" he asked his wife.

Lydia nodded as she chewed her food and then held a hand up to cover her mouth as she agreed. "You did, and I saw it with my own two eyes too."

"What did you tell her?" I asked slowly, trying to process what he was implying.

He cocked his head to the side. "That you didn't know."

"Didn't know what?"

His smile was bittersweet. "That he took one look at you and knew."

"Mr. Cooper, you know I'm not that great with puzzles and contexts clues. What did he know looking at me?"

"The same thing I knew when I looked at Lydia." His smile changed from a bittersweet one to a soft one, and I could see in his eyes that he thought about another woman he had known once. "My daddy was the same way. His daddy was the same way. Us Coopers, we just know. The only difference is, Ripley got his stubbornness from his mom's side of the family. I didn't fight it."

"You think Ripley... likes me?" I asked.

The older man cocked his head to the other side and went about cutting a piece of his chicken as he answered, "I don't *think*. I know. I've seen it on his face a thousand times, Luna. Especially when he was being hard on you. I've tried telling him a few times that he should do something about it, but God knows when he sets his mind to something, there's no convincing him to change it unless he decides to. And I know that takes an act of God. Just like his mom. He's got that Ripley blood in him."

He still didn't look back up at me as he continued going. "I don't know him that well anymore, but I still see the boy he used to be in bits and pieces of him. He's got the thickest skin I've ever seen, but I know those bones are still made out of love like they were... before."

Before his mom's accident? Before he'd left Houston and done all those things he didn't want to talk about?

"Luna, honey," Lydia spoke up. "Our relationships with Ripley are what they are. I couldn't hold it against him, but I wish he would forgive us after so long. I never had kids, but I was close to my mama and daddy, and if my daddy would have married some strange woman a year after my mama died, I can't say I would have behaved any better than he did. I knew what I was doing coming into Allen and Ripley's life back then. I've gotta live with knowing that because I loved someone, his son packed up his things and left him for twenty years," she paused. "We both have to live with that."

It all made sense all of a sudden. Rip's reaction to Lydia. And as much as I would want to think that if I had a healthy relationship with my dad that I would want him to be happy... well, I wasn't sure what I would think if or when he got remarried.

I tried to think of how Lenny would have reacted to Grandpa Gus getting married again, and really, it wasn't a pretty scene when I imagined it.

A large hand drifted over my forearm and settled there, and even though I knew it was Mr. Cooper's, I still glanced at his face. "He's a difficult man. Trust me. Nobody knows that better than me. But he pushes the people that love him, pushes them like he's trying to make sure they won't go anywhere. Rip is the total opposite of you. God knows I love him and I will until the day I die, but I love you too. And you both deserve to be happy. He thinks the world of you, and I can't help but think God brought you into our lives for a reason."

I stared at this man, feeling the fear in my chest, and I asked him, "But he loved you and he left you for twenty years, Mr. C. That's not... what I want."

His smile was slow and honestly heartbreaking. "Luna, he threatened to quit on me a hundred times in the first year he came back."

I blinked.

"He hasn't stuck around because of me, honey."

* * *

WHY WAS I EVEN HERE? I asked myself as I put my car into park and then turned off the ignition.

Why was I? I should have cancelled the dumb date. I was wasting my time, gas, and money, and doing the same for whatever poor fool was meeting me here.

Because I didn't want to meet this guy that my sister Kyra had set up for me over a month ago.

I didn't want to meet any of the guys that I had. The more I thought about it, the more I accepted it.

This whole thing was a mess I didn't know how to handle or what to think of.

Mr. Cooper had been adamant as I'd left, that regardless of what had happened between him and his son, that Rip did care about me. And *Rip had been Lucas Ripley Cooper at one point. He was still in there.*

But why he'd waited until now, I would never know.

Or maybe I would.

Did I want to though?

That was a stupid question. Of course I did. I wanted to know everything.

I wanted it to be true.

I wanted it to be true, but I also knew what it was like to hope and dream for things and not have them happen.

I was being a chicken. I was being a giant chicken, wasn't I? I gave Thea hell for not telling me the truth, because it seemed so easy for me, and here I was, doing the same thing as her.

With my phone on my lap, I sent Lenny a text.

Me: Do you think I'm being a coward with this Rip thing? Tell me the truth.

Not even a minute went by before I got a response.

Lenny: Yes

Lenny: I didn't make a chickenshit my best friend.

I ignored the guilt and nerves floating around in my stomach as I sat there, reading Lenny's message over and over again.

There was no reason for my stomach to hurt.

Luna, Luna, Luna, my conscience seemed to whisper in disappointment. *You're lying to yourself now.*

I was. I really was. I was being a coward. A chickenshit. A freaking scaredy cat.

And I was sitting in my car, about to go on a date I wanted no part of.

But...

I couldn't find it in me to just be a no-show. Getting stood up wasn't nice, and neither was telling some innocent person *sorry, bud, I'm in love with someone else*. But I could live with the latter a lot easier than the first. That was for sure. It was the least I could do. If I could have cancelled without calling Kyra, I would have, but I hadn't had it in me to do it. The text messages we had sent each other to set up the date had been awkward and painful enough.

In and out. I'd get this over with as quickly as possible. Then I could go home and figure out exactly what I would tell Rip. *I love you* and *please don't hurt me* didn't sound good enough.

It was with that decision in mind that I got out of my car and slammed it shut behind me. I flashed my license at the bouncer as a formality, because we both knew he'd seen it before. Then I headed into the bar where I had met the other guys I had gone on dates with, dates that hadn't gone anywhere.

For a reason.

Who was I kidding? Of course it had been for a reason. Because none of them were built like wrestlers, with a dry sense of humor and a bland look better than any scowl.

Inside, I looked around the half-filled room for a guy with long black hair…

I didn't need to glance at my phone to know I was a few minutes early. Maybe he was running late? If he was, how long was an acceptable amount of time to wait before I left? Three minutes? Five?

Spotting a table closer to the back, I beelined for it, still looking around at the crowd to make sure the man that Kyra had sent me a picture of back then wasn't sitting in some dark corner where I couldn't find him. He was thirty-two and worked on an oil rig. That's why we'd had to wait a month to meet. I glanced at my phone again as I took a seat.

Sitting back in the chair, I kept looking around the room, hoping he'd magically appear so I could tell him to his face thank you but no thank you.

The door opened just as that thought had entered my brain. Coming in, already looking around, was a man too blonde to be the one I was meeting up with. He was tall, lean, and… not Rip.

He was not Rip.

He was too young. Too slim.

But mostly, he wasn't the man who ran his hands through my hair when I was upset and listened.

The guy was everything that would have been exactly my type four years ago.

Before a six-foot-four man with a chest twice the size of this guy's, with forearms that rippled with muscle, a thick neck, and a lower body that should have inspired sculpture makers into recreating it, strolled into my life.

Screw it. I was going to hide in the bathroom.

The thought had barely occurred to me when a man sitting at the bar turned in his stool and stood up.

I realized I knew that body. That head shape. I knew that height.

And as the familiar body turned and started heading in the direction of where I was sitting, I stayed there. The lights hid a lot of the nicest bits of him, but I knew who it was. I would always know who he was.

And he had a pissed-off look on his face.

What the hell was he doing here? How did he know...

He didn't say a word as he pulled out the seat opposite of the one I was in and slid into it. In the dark, I couldn't see those amazing teal-colored eyes, but I could tell where they were focused. I could see the slant of his eyebrows.

Yep. He was definitely pissed.

And honestly, I had definitely never been less pissed.

Never.

He was here. *Here.*

"What are you doing?" I asked him, feeling the tension in my stomach unraveling slowly.

He planted his elbows on the table between us and crossed his arms as he answered, "You know what I'm here for."

I held my breath, and then I lied... hope and love blooming inside of me so quickly I couldn't help but want to mess with this man. "No, I don't."

His voice was a low, low growl of, "Yeah, you do."

"You're making sure I don't get kidnapped again?" I deadpanned as seriously as possible. Why did this feel like the easiest thing in the world now? Messing with him? Giving him crap? "Or are you stalking me now?"

He blinked. Then he took a deep breath... and his cheek went up a millimeter in the blink of an eye. "Not funny, Luna."

I couldn't help the smile that instantly came over my

face as I spoke again, not letting this go, not planning on ever letting this go. "I don't need a babysitter, if that's what you're worried about."

That cheek went up another millimeter. "You're right there, baby girl. You don't need a babysitter. 'Specially not when the dumbass you're meeting up with didn't look old enough for you."

I processed his words... but then processed them right back out and focused only on the important part. "When did you see him?"

He smiled at me. "Before you showed up."

I didn't need to glance around the bar to make sure the man still wasn't hanging around. I knew he wasn't. How he even knew who to look for was beyond me, but it didn't matter. Not even a little bit. I also had a feeling I knew exactly what had happened, but I needed to make sure. I tipped my head closer to him. "Where did he go?"

He shrugged a rounded shoulder. "Somewhere not here."

Uh.

"I told him to get the fuck out," he kept going unapologetically. "Told him you weren't going to be meeting him tonight or any other night, and he might as well go hit up someone else's girl because he wasn't getting mine."

My heart shouldn't have started racing at him referring to me as his. It shouldn't. I knew that. I definitely shouldn't have gotten goose bumps all over my arms and back.

But that was exactly what happened.

I let the thrill go through me before I decided that messing with him was too much fun. Messing with him would always be too much fun. "Rip, you had no right to do that—"

"I had every right to."

He could say those words to me every day for the rest of my life and they wouldn't get old.

He proved it when he leaned forward and slid me the most heated look I might ever see in my life. "Yeah, I did, Luna. You wanna go out to eat? I'll take you. You wanna go out and get a Sprite? Tell me. You want to watch a fucking movie? I'll take you to the goddamn movies. If you want to go to beat the shit out of your cousin again, *I'll fucking take you*. You want to meet someone to be your best friend and your fucking partner? I'm right fucking here, baby girl."

Oh hell.

Oh freaking hell.

"How many times I gotta tell you I just like being around you?" he asked, his voice lowering as his gaze roamed over what was my stupefied face. Because what other face could I have when the man I'd liked for years was running off my dates and sitting here telling me he'd take me on any dates I wanted to go on?

None. There was no other face.

"I can do this same thing a hundred times, Luna, this running off your dates thing, but it's never gonna happen. I'll tell you right now, I'm not going to have a problem telling them off. I've got into a lot of fucking fights in my life, and I'm starting to think it was all to get me ready for you," he threatened.

I sucked in a breath and just sat there, looking at him, feeling overjoyed and terrified equally. Wanting this more than I wanted anything, but still...

"What if you change your mind? I'll have to find another job because I won't be able to look at you. I can barely look at you now," I admitted to him, this low-level feeling that might have been terror, but was more than likely adrenaline, running through my veins steadily.

This beautiful man gave me the most earnest expression I had ever seen. "Luna, why the hell would I do something that stupid?"

I fisted my hand. "You don't—you've never even had a girlfriend."

"So? Want me to lie and tell you I've had a couple dozen? Or you good with knowing it'll only be you?"

Well.

Hell.

"You're too young. You're too sweet. You're too good for me. But I'm done standing around trying to suck up all the goodness you make me feel without you even knowing, Luna. You are my girl. Just you. Nobody else ever has or will be."

I sucked in a breath and lifted my face to look at his. "I am?"

He nodded, his expression something different than any other I'd ever seen before.

"Really?"

"Really," he agreed, his smile soft and almost shy.

I bit my bottom lip and couldn't help but wring my hands as he centered on me so intensely it made me want to hold my breath. *You only miss all the shots you don't take,* Lenny had said. I had always told myself that nothing and no one scared me because I had seen the worst in people.

But I had also seen the best, hadn't I?

"You know everything that matters, Luna. Only thing you don't is what happened with the cops that day you lied for me. I was with Gio, and he fucked up his sister's boyfriend because he hit her. I didn't do shit, but I was there. His family did the same for him. That's why they came. They needed somebody to try and blame, but I swear I didn't do shit."

There it was, and it was exactly the kind of thing I might have expected if I'd thought about it. "I know, Rip. I don't know how I knew, but I did."

Those eyes penetrated mine as he said, so carefully, "You wanna know something else, all you gotta do is ask, and I'll tell you. I've already warned you about the rest and you're still here."

He made it seem so easy. Could it be that easy?

"Rip?" I asked him carefully, my apprehension disappearing by the second.

"Yeah?"

I swallowed and made myself look him in those blue-green eyes. "Do you like me, or is it more than that?"

He took a deep breath before responding. "Get out of here with me and I'll tell you."

* * *

THE RIDE back to his place didn't take long at all considering the unending traffic even in the evening.

Rip had offered to drive us over to his home, but I hadn't wanted to leave my car in the bar's lot, so I followed behind, watching the road as we turned onto a sleepy street in north Houston with spaced-out single-story homes and driveways filled with cars.

When Rip turned his truck into an open graveled lot, with a new-ish rectangular home settled right smack in the middle of it, I knew this was where he lived. I parked my car behind his truck, watching as he got out and headed over, pulling mine open too before I really made much of an effort to beat him.

Rip gave me that one-cheek smile with a dimple in it as he took my hand and led me out, slamming the door shut.

"You made it seem like you lived in a dump," I accused him.

"It's no pretty purple house," he tried to explain as he fiddled with his keys.

I took in the extended sides and length of his home. "Rip, I bet this thing cost almost as much as my house."

He shrugged, giving my hand a squeeze as he slipped a key into the lock and turned it. "It's still no pretty purple house."

He was obviously never going to agree, even though I was right.

But in that moment, I couldn't find it in me to argue with him over it. That was because... because... connected to the same keychain his house key was on, something dangled from it. Something that looked like an ice cream cone charm. An ice cream cone charm that I'd had on a necklace. A necklace that I had put on him after the car accident.

He'd kept it? He'd put it on his keychain?

I was a goner. I was such a goner that no one was ever going to find me again. Ever. It took everything in me to keep my mouth closed. To save the moment for later, since there seemed like there might be a later between us. I hoped.

He shoved the door open, leading me up the metal steps as he fiddled with a light switch on the wall closest to him.

Light blazed on inside the trailer just as he pulled me in, closing a screen door and a heavier one as I took in the inside of his home.

I hadn't been wrong when I told him his place had to be as expensive as mine. It was *nice*. Patterned tan and rich brown colors were used as the upholstery of two big, comfortable recliners to the right of the entrance. To the side was a table that could sit four. His kitchen, to the left, was way nicer than mine. The appliances were new and shiny, and there was a four-burner stove with an oven and a microwave. He had a nice kitchen island with storage beneath it. If my eyes didn't deceive me, there were a handful of old-looking cookbooks under there, too. I wondered if they had been his mom's and couldn't help but hope he'd tell me someday. He even had a nice fifty-some-thing-inch television on the wall beside a door that had to lead somewhere. The bedrooms? Bathroom? I didn't know.

And it was clean.

Really clean.

"Are you always this clean?" I croaked, still soaking it all up.

His laugh was warm and rich and so natural, I had no defense for it. It slid underneath my ribs and settled right over my heart. "Not messy, but I might've been taking extra care the last few weeks in case you came over."

I sucked in a breath and looked up at him standing right beside me, watching me even then. "Not for every girl you bring over?" I made myself ask.

He shook his head and fully turned to face me, his hand coming up and sliding across my throat, palming it. Those teal-colored eyes didn't stray from mine for even a second as he breathed, "I told you I bought this after I moved here."

"I know." Did my voice *have* to sound so small? "It's none of my business if you have—"

"Nuh-uh," he said, still shaking his head.

I blinked. "But that was three years ago."

He raised an eyebrow.

"But you didn't even like me."

"Oh, I liked you just fine, baby. I've always liked you just fine."

Yep, I was a goner. "But you were mean to me."

His smile was slow. "I was tough on you, not mean, and that shit ate me up for hours and days after."

It had? "You could have always been sweet."

"I thought I was too old for you. Thought I'd done too many shitty things in my life to have you in it, Luna," he explained softly. "I didn't want to care about you, and I fought that shit as long as I could."

"Because of the bad things you think you've done?"

His face softened. "Because of the bad things I know I've done," he confirmed, and that too snuck under my ribs.

I knew all about the guilt that came with doing things that you weren't proud of. Necessary evils. Unnecessary ones too.

I took a step closer to him, my breasts brushing just across his chest. I felt his hand slip around my back to land on the small of it, pulling me in even more. "But what if I would've started dating someone?"

Rip tipped his head closer to mine, bringing his mouth just inches from me. "I would've made sure there hadn't been a second date, baby girl. I know you went on seven of them until this bullshit recently. I know you went to dinner on three, to the movies on two, a baseball game on one, and Mickey's on another. I listened. I know. I was there the night you got your place broken into. I just wanted to make sure you were all right."

That was true. That was all true. "How'd you know that?"

I'd swear I could already feel his lips on mine. "I listen, I told you."

"What else have you heard?"

"Everything." His head moved, his mouth brushing my throat so lightly it was the best tickle of my life.

And just as soon as he brushed his pink lips over me, he pulled back.

"What's wrong?" I asked him, trying to smile so he would know I was happy... and I hoped he was too.

One of those big hands went up to the top of his head and he scrubbed it back and forth across the top, still watching me with these eyes that said a dozen different emotions. The only one I could focus on was that uncertain one though.

"What is it?" I asked him, still holding on to my smile. At least until it hit me. Maybe... "We don't have to do anything you don't want to do."

He blinked those long eyelashes, and I couldn't miss the way his eyes just kind of sort of squinted at me. "Baby girl, that's not it at all."

"What is it?"

But he still looked off. His hand came up and moved across his chest, from one massively rounded pec to the other and then going up to the base of his throat, where his fingers curled into the material of his compression shirt and he peeled it away from his neck maybe an inch. "I should tell you something first."

Oh, no. "There's something wrong with your...?" I dipped my eyes toward the lower half of his body.

That got me a blink. "Excuse me?"

All right, maybe that wasn't it. "You have three nipples? Because that wouldn't be a big deal. I've got stretch marks if you—Why are you looking at me like that?"

Because he was looking at me weird. He really was. "I couldn't give less of a fuck about you having some marks, and I don't have three nipples."

I wasn't surprised that my hands were steady as I set

them on his hips, feeling the warmth of his body through his shirt. "What is it then?"

His hand tugged at his shirt again, drawing my gaze down to the inch of tattooed skin I could see... and *then* it finally settled in my brain.

Ohhh.

"You have a girl's name tattooed on you?"

That had him rolling his eyes. "Let me tell you, yeah?"

I widened my eyes, watching as he gave his shirt another tug at the collar.

"I've got some tattoos..."

"I know. I've seen some of them."

He shot me a look as he scrubbed at his head again. "Luna, I gotta tell you before I show you, all right?"

I nodded.

"I told you what I did with about twenty years of my life."

I nodded because he had. How could I forget he'd been in a freaking motorcycle gang... club... whatever it was called?

"I got a lot of tattoos from those days, and I haven't gotten around to covering them up," he said in a quiet voice, and something just *pulled* at my heart. It just yanked it tight and crazy.

I loved this man. I loved him, I loved him, I loved him.

"Rip, I don't care about your tattoos from back then," I told him gently. "Unless you have another girl's name on you somewhere, but you don't, right?"

His face instantly softened so much I couldn't help but smile. "Quit with the dumbass questions, yeah? And no, I don't fucking have somebody's name on me."

"Okay then." I tipped my chin up. "You have gang tattoos. Thank you for telling me."

"They're not *gang* tattoos."

"Club tattoos, whatever you want to call it." I raised my eyebrows and wiggled my fingers in the sliver of space between our bodies. "Show me the goods."

His laugh took the edge off his word. "Luna—"

"I'm being serious," I told him carefully. "I don't care." I held my hand out for him and opened and closed it to get him to come closer to me. "None of us are who we used to be, and luckily for you, I think you're the hottest man on the entire planet, and that's with me only seeing you fully clothed." I smiled. "Show me."

Rip watched me with those heavy eyes, and the breath he took in and then out was deep and rough.

I recognized the uncertain expression that made the lines at his eyes deepen, and it made my heart clench up again.

I loved this man. I had loved this man for a long time, but I had never loved him more than I did right in that moment as he stood there, with dread in his eyes. Because he was worried what I would think.

"Come here," I said again, smiling.

The tiny little breath he took in through his nose just made me love him even more.

So I gestured him toward me again. "I don't think I ever told you about how many times I stole things from the grocery store or from people's wallets."

This huge man blinked. "You?" he asked, but it sounded more like he didn't believe me.

And that only made me smile wider as I nodded. "Yeah, me. If it was small enough for me to hide it in my hoodie pocket, I was taking it. I was hungry, and I didn't want to spend my money when I started to run out," I explained, not struggling at all to remember what that Luna had felt when I'd gotten to the last of my money.

"I stole all kinds of things before that too. Usually candy from the convenience store since no one ever took me to the store or anything like that. And when I could take money from my parents, I'd go back and give the owner money. I'm pretty sure that old man knew exactly what I was doing, but he never called me out on it or called the police on me."

Ripley took a step forward as his fingers dropped away from the collar of his shirt. "They never got you candy?"

I shook my head. "I used to make my own birthday cakes." I shrugged. "After I stole the cake mixes from the grocery store. My dad loved milk and eggs, so there was always some at the house. He'd always give me money for that." I blinked. "He'd ask for his receipt and make sure I brought every penny back."

This man took another step closer to me. "February thirteenth, yeah?"

He was asking me for my birthday, and the fact that he even knew what day my birthday was.... "Yeah."

He took another step forward. "I've got you from now on."

"For birthday cakes?" I asked, hoping that I didn't sound as... hopeful as I was sure I did.

"Yeah." He took another step. "I'll make you that red velvet cake you like."

"Okay." I smiled. "Now let me see what you've got since you know you're not the only one who's done some shady things."

He took another step closer, another step that got him to stop directly in front of me, his fingers coming up to nudge me under the chin. "You are a shady shit under there, aren't you?"

"When I've needed to."

His finger traced along the line of my jaw up to my ear, and his voice was low as he said, "Yeah, I noticed when you had me break your cousin's hand. I'm not gonna lie, Luna, I was ready to kill his ass, but I was too busy thinking about how you kicking his ass and throwing that fucking shoe like a ninja star was the greatest thing I've ever seen."

Reaching forward, I pressed my fingertips against the band along the top of his jeans where the belt loops went. "You still like me even after that?"

His smile was gentle. "You could steal the Mona Lisa, and I know you'd do it for a good reason. I don't think there's anything you could do that I wouldn't be all about, baby girl."

I laughed, and that just made him smile wider and drag his finger the opposite direction of my jaw, his thumb just lightly brushing the skin under my throat.

"You are the goodest, sweetest thing I have ever had in my life, and I don't want you to go screaming the other way, you understand me? One day I'll tell you about everything," he said softly.

I just stared up at him, and if he would have taken a picture, I'm sure my mouth would have been partially open, and if there could have been big, pink hearts behind my head, they would have been there.

I couldn't even find it in me a little bit to be embarrassed as I wrapped my arms around his waist. "I've wanted to do this a hundred times."

"What?" he asked quietly.

"Hug you."

It took a moment, but the second his palms landed on the top of my head, I pressed my cheek against him. One of those big palms cupped the back of my head while the other landed right between my shoulder blades, and his voice was hoarse as he whispered, "Baby girl."

"You are the sweetest thing I've ever had in my life," I told him.

Something that sounded like a laugh that had gone through a meat grinder trickled out of his mouth.

"You are. Don't argue with me."

That meat grinder laugh came out of his mouth again, and I hugged him so tight, it was easy to ignore that my forearm was pressed right up against his butt cheeks.

"I'm not saying any of it either to get you to show me your tattoos."

"I know."

"Can I see them now though?"

His laugh was lighter, but I felt him moving, felt his fingers leave me before sensing him pulling his shirt over his head. He just barely moved away from me.

I squeezed him one more time before I finally lifted my face and instantly spotted the almost olive skin at his waist...

Covered by thick lines and shapes in faded black ink.

I held my breath as I dragged my eyes over the ink on him, beneath his belly button letters spelled out ENFORCER, big and shaped in half a circle. Above the word, on top of his ribs were two skulls with wings on them. The lines were thin and detailed. And everything above that were these massive tribal lines that spread out across his pectorals, his shoulders, biceps, going up over his throat....

They weren't pretty.

They weren't pretty at all.

Without saying a word, Rip turned in front of me, showing me his back.

And that's where the oversized skeleton holding an

umbrella within an imperfect circle was. The word REAPERS MC 1978 were tattooed directly before it, the lettering uneven and tilted up higher on one side than the other. Wrapped around all that were the same giant tribal curves and lines.

I reached up to trail my fingers over the smooth skin pulled tight over his muscles.

And I heard him let out a deep breath.

Dragging my fingers up higher, over the dip of his spine and higher up over where the notches of his spine were underneath him, I said, "I'm a little disappointed there isn't a Chinese symbol for strength."

The laugh that exploded out of him only made me laugh too.

"Your skin is really soft too, do you moisturize?"

He kept on laughing. "No. They aren't something I want to last. Not anymore."

"So what you're trying to say is that your skin is just naturally soft?"

His "mm-hmm" was low.

I dragged the pads of my fingers up higher along the curve of where his spine went, leading up to his shoulders. Ink crisscrossed his spine, and it didn't take a genius to know that it must have hurt like hell to have that tattooed.

"I have a tattoo."

His head tilted up and his eyes focused on mine. "You do?"

"Yup."

"Where?"

"On my ribs. I wanted it on my hip, but the artist talked me out of it."

"It small?"

I shook my head, and that only earned me another blink. A slow one.

"What is it?"

"It's a fox."

"A fox?"

I nodded, reaching down to grab the bottom of my shirt, pulling it up over my head in one movement. I was wearing a decent bra, nothing that sexy, but it was cute and turquoise. I lifted my right arm and pivoted just enough for him to see my side clearly.

But it only took a quick glance to notice he wasn't looking at my ribs. He was looking at all of me. At my breasts held up high by my bra, at the soft slope of my stomach, at the band of my jeans high on my hips.

"Look," I told him, showing him the fox head that spanned from just below the band of my bra to just lower than my bottom rib.

And I watched his eyes finally move there, his nostrils flaring.

"Pretty, huh?" I asked, knowing it was. Delicate black lines outlined the fox's head and ears, a little girly but fierce. Beautiful and feminine and strong. "I got it when I was nineteen."

A warm hand landed on my hip, just short of the bottom of the fox's head. "Why a fox?"

"Because," I barely got out as his fingers stroked my skin. "People think they have to be lions or lambs, but I've always just wanted to be something in between." I bit my lip and lifted a shoulder. "Something that still has sharp teeth, just in case."

He hummed low in his throat as he dragged his fingers up my rib cage, just over the fox's face. "Just one?"

"For now, I almost passed out with that one. I cried,

don't tell anyone," I answered, squeaking when his fingers moved over the front of my stomach, one finger dipping lightly into my belly button. "I should probably tell you something else right now too."

"Hmm?" he asked, all husky and sexy as he dragged that same finger straight up my stomach.

"I've got a piercing too."

Rip's head dipped down until his mouth landed on my shoulder, his lips warm and dry as they trailed up my throat, pecking one kiss after another on the way up. The hand he had on my stomach trailed back around to my spine, and I felt him tugging at my bra as his lips latched onto this spot right where my neck met my shoulder, sucking it lightly, forcing me up to the tips of my toes while I squeaked again.

"It's only one too," I warned him. "I wanted to do both, but it hurt so much, I chickened out."

His grumble floated over my skin as he moved his mouth a little more across my shoulder, dragging his tongue too, before he sucked a spot there, his hand still messing with the clasp on my bra. I loved him struggling with it, how much I would never mind helping him out by reaching behind myself to undo it, feeling it loosen and slip lower the instant it happened.

And that was when I told him. "It's one of my nipples."

He sucked in a breath so loud that the hairs on my arms stood straight up. The hand he'd had on my bra fell away a moment before both his hands landed on my hips and his head *dove*. Dove straight for the nipple with a small bar through it. The piercing that had hurt like a freaking son of a bitch for months.

But all of a sudden, the memory of the pain didn't feel as sharp as it had.

Not when Rip's lips sucked my nipple into his mouth, his

warm tongue flicking the piercing back and forth before he opened his mouth a little wider and took more of my breast in. His "goddamn" went straight to my bones just as his hands moved from my hips to the front of my jeans, undoing the button there and dragging the zipper down just as I managed to get my own hands on his shoulders to hold me up.

Arching my back, I sucked a breath in and let him shove my jeans as far as they could, which was only a few inches lower since they were so tight. And when I went to my tippy toes again, trying to get him to pay attention to my other breast or be greedy and have him take more of the current one into his mouth, Rip crouched and pulled my jeans down roughly the rest of the way. Impatient, jerky, and *so hot*. How was this man so freaking hot?

"Rip," I groaned as his hands went back to my hips and yanked my underwear down to my feet in the same quick movement that stung my skin from the fabric scraping it. By the time I took another breath, my pants, underwear, socks, and shoes were all over the carpet.

"I know, baby," the sexiest man in the world grumbled as he stood straight up again and yanked me so close to him we were pressed together.

Those huge hands went to my butt, and he started walking us backward. His mouth shifted from one nipple to the other, sucking, flicking, suckling even more, these hungry, rough noises bubbling out of Rip's throat as we kept moving, and moving...

Then he dropped back into one of the recliners by the door, and with me totally naked, he pulled me onto his lap, making me straddle his hips. His mouth trailed up, pecking kisses along my chest, up and up, over my neck before he kissed me.

And kissed me. Warm, closed-mouth pecks that drove me nuts and had me finding his lips. Had me slipping my tongue against his, brushing over it. Wet, wet kisses that had me grinding my totally naked body against his half-naked one. If it wouldn't have been for the soft ripple and the brush of his hands low against my stomach, or how he arched his hips for a moment, I wouldn't have known he'd undone his jeans.

At least not until something blunt, and hot, and so freaking hard and thick nudged me right below the belly button.

Prodding.

Brushing.

Kissing.

Lowering my hands to my lap, I wrapped them around the hard, hard dick that bobbed between us. *And holy crap.* Rip was warm, softer than soft at the same time, but mostly he was thick and long and dripping over my fingers and himself.

"Fuck," he hissed low and broken into my skin.

With my hands stacked one on top of the other, ending right below a wide, mushroom-tipped head I couldn't get myself to look down at when Rip had his head tipped back and that mouth of his parted. I squeezed him, loving how big he was. How good he felt. How handsome he looked breathing deeply. So I gripped him a little tighter and moved my hands up an inch and back down, toward the root.

And that was when he opened his eyes, aiming those blue-green irises right at me with a suck of an inward breath. I knew, I knew right then, what he wanted. Knew what I wanted. What my body didn't want to wait another second for either if the wetness between my legs meant anything.

I looked at that face with its harsh bones and hollow cheeks and moved my hands, and him, until the damp, damp head of his dick found the place we both wanted and... I lifted my hips, like this with him was the most natural thing in the world, and slowly, slowly, slowly dropped my body back down, gasping as one inch after another slow inch eased inside of me. *Holy crap.* Lifting my hips again, I dropped down even lower, taking every long inch inside, our kisses never ending. Over and over, I took that thick, long shaft in me, sucking in a breath when I could manage until I bottomed out on what had to be nine solid, hard, so-freaking-hard, inches.

"Jesus fucking Christ," he hissed right as my butt met his warm balls.

I sucked in a breath, squirming just enough on top of him that both of us panted.

I rode him slow, grinding down on that broad base, up and down, his wiry hair just the perfect brush against my clit as his hands rested on my hips, guiding me as I took him over and over again. In and out. In and out. Kissing him. Him kissing me. Dragging his mouth across my neck. Licking one nipple, then the other. Sucking the right one deep into his warm mouth both before taking the other one and doing the same exact thing to it. Rip licked and sucked and suckled little nooks and crannies I had no idea could feel so good...

"Fuck," he groaned, arching his hips, pushing as if I wasn't already fully seated on him. But he was as rooted as he could go. He twitched hard inside of me as he curled his hips again, making our bodies press even tighter together.

I circled my hips, faster, rougher, taking every single

thing he had to give me, over and over again until I came, squeezing down around him on a cry that even I could barely hear.

And when he sucked in a breath and with his hands and body tight on mine, Rip shoved me down all the way on him a moment later, stuffing me so deep my muscles fluttered over him, his grunts were hoarse in my ears and on my mouth as he came inside me. That massive body shuddered, his dick pulsing slowly and steadily. I took it all. Every single little bit of it.

I draped myself over him afterward, my arms over his neck, our sweaty chests pressed against each other as we both struggled for breath. Those huge arms wrapping around me, holding me close, was the greatest and most welcome surprise of my life. There was nowhere else I wanted to be other than right freaking there. Nowhere. Not for a million dollars.

I pressed my nose against his throat, taking in that sweet scent of his: clean, fresh deodorant and warm skin.

His palms moved over my back, on either side of my spine. Sweeping me up and down and up and down. "You good?"

I smiled. How could I not smile? "I don't think I've ever been better, Rip."

His chuckle was soft against my ear. "Can't say I don't feel the same."

"Oh, yeah?" I asked, soaking up the heat of him. The love of him. The feel of him.

"Yeah," was his reply as his hands did that trek over my spine again, almost like he loved the feel of me too.

I hoped he did.

We sat there for a while, him in me, softening, but his

arms as solid as ever. And I loved it. I loved it so much I had no words for how much.

"I'm sorry, baby. Sorry I haven't been there for you lately, sorry I was such a fucking ass there for a while, but you gotta know I won't do that again," Rip told me, sounding so grave. "I couldn't even if I tried, you know that?"

I didn't let myself tense up, and even though I didn't really want to ask, didn't want to be the kind of person who needed reassurances... I was that person. I might always be that person, but I hoped I wouldn't. But I still asked, "Why?"

And handsome, amazing Rip didn't hesitate for a single second as he said, "'Cause I love you, Luna. Because I love the shit out of you, girl, and those two weeks when you were acting like you were done with me were some of the worst days of my life."

That had me sitting up so I could look at him. Look at him I did. At that serious face. At those intense eyes. At the earnestness coming straight out of him like a beam. I could be honest, I could admit I whispered, "You love me?"

Not *yeah*. Not *uh-huh*. Nothing watered down or broken up. He gave me the four greatest words I would ever hear. "I love you, girl." A confirmation. A promise. A Band-Aid that shouldn't have been a Band-Aid but was.

Because I knew Rip wouldn't say those words if he didn't mean them. Maybe he'd said some things weeks ago he hadn't meant, but I understood why they had come out the way they had. I definitely knew he wouldn't take them back for no reason.

In that moment, I knew he meant those three words from the bottom of that rough, complicated heart.

"I love you too," I told him, freaking going for it because

why not? People smarter than me would say that the world wasn't for chickenshits, and I didn't want to be a chickenshit.

The corners of that mouth tipped up and his smile was gentle but bright and sweet. "I know you do, baby." One of those hands went up my spine again as he leaned forward a little, not breaking eye contact for even a second. "I know you do. And I know you've had a lot of people not do right by you, and I know things with your sister aren't that great—"

"She sent me a letter," I cut him off. "I've been wanting to tell you."

He didn't say anything, but I could tell he wanted me to tell him the rest by the way his eyebrows went flat.

"She said that she was sorry. That she didn't know how to tell me about talking to my dad—"

His snort wasn't even close to being a surprise. I couldn't say I blamed him.

"Supposedly an ex-boyfriend was the one who broke into her apartment, and she's been acting weird because she didn't want to tell me she was a stripper. That's how she's been paying for her apartment," I finished with a blink. "I think I was worried there for a moment she was selling drugs, so..."

Rip's face was carefully blank as he asked, "How you feeling about it?"

I leaned forward and kissed his cheek, earning an expression that was somewhere between a smile and a smirk that went straight into my soul. Was this how easy it was going to be? Was that how it was supposed to be? Rip just letting me kiss him whenever I wanted? I was all for it. I really was. "It makes me sad she didn't feel like she could tell me. I'm not going to lie. It hurts me a lot that she's talking to my dad of all people and has been for years. I don't get it, Rip, you know? I mean, I guess I kind of do but not really at the same time. He wasn't anywhere near as mean to them, just to me, but even then, I don't get how she could even bother wanting to *try*. Her and Kyra. He was horrible. He didn't give a single crap about her or any of them when they lived with him, and I'm not exaggerating that. If it was her he'd been mean to, I would never be able to forgive him. Not ever."

That big, warm hand went to my throat. "You don't get it because you're not them." His thumb swept over my cheek. "I'm talking about your sisters. You wouldn't do that, Luna. I don't get why they would either."

"She also said my dad didn't send my cousin over to the house, that he did it on his own," I told him. "I haven't tried calling her again since then. I don't know what I'm going to do. I love her, but I'm mad."

"You'll do the right thing."

"I hope so."

His smile was soft. "You will, baby. You always do. I don't know anybody with a heart half as good as yours."

"Aww, there's plenty of people—"

"No, there's not." Rip kissed the side of my mouth, then the opposite side, the short bristles on his cheeks kissing mine. "There really isn't. You got that little fox on you, but you're a wolf, baby. A fucking miracle. I don't know how you came out the way you did, but you teach me something about forgiveness and love every single day. And here I thought for most of my life, until I met you, that I stopped learning things a long time ago."

Me?

That laugh was soft. "Yeah, you. Only you."

I swallowed, I gulped, and I raised my eyebrows at him

because I didn't know what to say. Had no idea what to think. He must have known that because he kept on going.

"I don't know what the fuck to tell you to do about your sisters, but I know you'll figure it out. I sure as hell don't know what to tell you about your dad, but if you wanna know what I think, I say let's go burn down that house you lived in with him. If you just wanna move on with your life though, I'd get behind that.

"What I know is that I'll tell you right now I'll never let anybody treat you like fucking shit or make you feel like they don't want you around. Not me, not even your family. I wasn't fucking around when I said I love you, and I know there's a lot of shit I need to tell you, but we'll figure it out." His thumb rubbed over my cheek again, and those blue-green eyes that sucked me up and wouldn't spit me back out were locked on my face as he said, "If you want."

If I wanted.

Oh, man.

I bit the inside of my cheek. "And if I don't?" I asked him even though we both knew that wasn't going to be the case.

"Then I got more work to do to talk you into it," he replied softly.

The funny thing about life is that there's a lot you don't get to choose. You don't get to choose whom you're related to. You don't get to choose your hair color, your height, or what natural talents you are given. You don't get to choose where you are born, or who or what the world will see when they look at you.

But the best part of life is that in the end, none of that matters. You get to choose who you become. Who you love. You can change your hair color and, to an extent, you can even change your eye color and height. You can learn to be great at something.

There's a whole lot you don't get a choice in, but there's a whole lot more you do.

And I knew right then what I would choose. What I would always choose.

The best decisions of my life had been those I'd jumped into terrified even though some part of me knew they were necessary.

In that moment, and for the rest of my life, I knew that nothing would ever be as necessary as this man in front of me, who would sabotage my dates and make me food because he knew I couldn't cook and mostly because he saw me for who I wanted to be. For who I tried to be even when I did things that weren't very nice. This man, Lucas Ripley, who was just as much of a taped together puzzle as I was.

Or as we all freaking were, I guess.

So I told him the only answer I would ever let myself live with.

I looked into those blue-green eyes and told him the truth. "I want to. I really want to."

EPILOGUE

It was the dream that woke me.

That dream that had me waking up with a gasp.

It wasn't real, I told myself as I blinked up at the darkened ceiling. It had been at least two or three months since the last time I'd dreamt about my dad and that house and the *stupid-ass* and the *idiot* that had my subconscious jerking awake to get out of it. It wasn't real. *It wasn't real.*

I was fine, I was safe, and I was loved.

I wasn't seventeen years old, and I was fine.

But I didn't have to roll over to know that it was after midnight now, so technically I was thirty-one now. Thirty-freaking-one. And it was *that* knowledge that had me smiling in my bedroom, that had my heart rate slowing back down, and that had the goose bumps I'd woken up with, retreating.

Of course I'd had a dream about my dad after one of the best nights of my life. That was how this stuff worked. Those dumb memories were spread out more and more as time went on, but they were still there in the those dark, little corners I didn't go visit that often.

Reaching over to the other side of the bed, I found it empty but still warm, the covers thrown over partially on top of me. I glanced toward the bathroom to find the door closed and the light off, and I knew exactly where Rip was. I knew exactly what he was doing.

And that, even more than the reminder of my night before, calmed me down that last little bit.

Swinging my legs over the side of the bed, I rolled up to sit on the edge, grabbing my half-full glass of water and chugging the rest of it down before standing up. The house was *quiet*, which honestly surprised me because according to my cell phone screen it was three in the morning. Rip and I had made it to midnight before we'd gone to our room to shower—together—and then gone to bed, leaving everyone else up and farting around the house.

Everyone else. That had me smiling even more and getting to my feet, still holding my empty glass.

Opening the door as quietly as I could, I listened down the hall but still couldn't hear a peep.

And I already knew well enough not to screw up a bad thing, so I headed toward the living room as quietly as possible. It was then that I heard the noises. The freaking snores coming from it. Before we'd gone to bed, I'd told everyone that hadn't gone home where the air mattresses were in case they wanted to stay over. Apparently, someone had.

I came up to the living room to find the seventy-five-inch television that Rip had insisted on buying two years ago on but muted, I had to stop there and look at the two air mattresses that had been blown up. On one was Lily and her boyfriend of the last two years, this really nice guy named Abner. On the other mattress was Kyra and her boyfriend, a guy I didn't like anywhere near as much. They were fully clothed without a single blanket or pillow anywhere around, but totally passed out, one of the guys and Kyra snoring like chainsaws.

On the couch was the greatest surprise of my day, Thea.

To be fair, Thea and Kyra, both, coming to my birthday party in the first place had surprised the hell out of me.

Lily wasn't surprising at all. In the year since she had finished her undergrad, she had gotten a job back in Houston but moved into her own place, even though she spent the night at our house more often than at her condo. Rip and I had assured her she could move back, but she had insisted she was fine on her own.

But Thea and Kyra? Some days I wanted to think that things between us were the same as they had been *before*, but they weren't. I could accept that now. I could get through my life knowing that I loved the hell out of my sisters and that they loved me back, but that everything that had happened almost five years ago had changed those little ties between us.

It didn't help that I could see it in their faces every time we talked. The hesitation. The worry that I would ask them something they didn't want to answer. The worry that they would say something I didn't want to hear.

Even though there was only one topic I didn't want to hear and it started and ended with a "D."

But I wasn't going to think about that person tonight or tomorrow or any other night. The dream I'd just had had been enough. Plus, it was my freaking birthday now, and I'd had a great night, and nothing was going to get to me at this point. No, siree.

So I kept on creeping through the house, heading into the kitchen that we had never gotten around to opening because the wall there was structurally important, and I didn't want to spend money redoing especially when I bought all my appliances and gotten granite countertops for the price it would have cost to put in a supporting beam. All thanks to the money Grandma Genie had left me in her will.

The door closed behind me quietly as I flicked on the lights and headed for the cake I'd put in the fridge hours ago.

The pretty, two-layer white frosting cake with blue glitter on it that Rip had made me that was halfway gone now.

Pulling it out, I sliced off a nice, big slice and set it on a plate, pulling out a fork before setting the cake back into the fridge.

I had barely sat down at one of the stools under the brand-new island we'd gotten installed two years ago when the door swung open again and a big, familiar body was there.

I smiled.

"Whatcha doing, baby?" the giant hunk of a man I could look at every minute for the rest of my life, asked, as he stood there in a tight, white undershirt that clung to every inch of that solid upper body. The cut-off navy blue sleeping pants he was wearing right then hadn't been on his body before we'd gone to bed.

"Getting a piece of this awesome cake," I answered him, sliding the plate toward him an inch and raising my eyebrows. "Come split it with me."

Rip smiled that freaking smile that went straight to my heart before he came over, pulling out the stool beside mine with one hand while the other one slid through my hair to cup the back of my neck. I'd been letting it grow out lately, and the cotton candy pink and blue strands just barely grazed my shoulders now. I wasn't even a little surprised when he leaned over and kissed my neck before scooting the stool even closer to me, one thigh straddling the back of mine while the other one grazed the knee closest to him.

"I wake you up?"

I slid the fork through the tip of the cake as I answered him. "Not even a little bit. I had a bad dream and figured I might as well come down here and get a slice while you finished up." We both knew I still struggled going back to sleep on nights like these, but usually I woke him up when I did or stretched out on the bed until I could press up against him to relax so that I could fall asleep again. He never minded, and honestly, our best conversations were always in moments like those, when we could tell each other things that weren't so easy or pretty.

His answer was a grumble as I held the fork up to his mouth and he took a bite.

"Thank you for everything," I told him as I slipped the fork out of his mouth, looking at those pink lips for a second longer than I needed to, before dipping the tines back through the cake and scooping more into my own mouth.

Man, it was delicious.

A big, warm hand landed on the middle of my back and gave it a circle. "You have a good time tonight?" he asked quietly.

I nodded at him and smiled before swallowing.

All of our coworkers and their girlfriends or wives had come, some of their kids, had too. Mr. Cooper and Lydia. My sisters and their boyfriends. Lenny and her gang. And even two of Rip's friends and their ladies.

Rip and Lydia had made all the food. He'd made the

cake. Lily had bought the snacks. Lenny and Mr. Cooper the drinks.

All to celebrate my birthday. In the house that I had bought, and that over the years, Rip and I had fixed up even more. A house that was under both of our names now. A house that we had made even more of a home together. A place where our little baby daughter woke up in the middle of the night and her daddy got up to feed her or change her diaper or just snuggle her like it was the greatest honor.

He never woke me up to help, but half the time, the monitor told me what was going on anyway. Most of those nights, especially if he left the little device in the room, I just lay in bed and listened to him talk to her, patiently, with so much love it felt like I'd burst. It wasn't hard at all for me to accept he was such a great dad.

I mean, before things had gone to hell, Mr. C had been a great father to him. Rip had told me stories here and there of the things they had done while his mom had still been alive. He'd had a great role model.

Things between him and Mr. Cooper weren't *great*, but they weren't bad either. It might have helped that after Mr. C's heart attack, he had taken to working half the hours he had before, only doing scheduling. They had even hired another mechanic too, to help out Rip since he had to take over more of what Mr. Cooper did.

They hardly argued anymore. They didn't agree half the time, but they didn't fight. I doubted I would ever see them hug or talk about anything that wasn't work or family-related, but it was something. I'd even seen Rip pat Lydia on the back twice.

If that wasn't something I didn't know what was.

So right then, I leaned over and kissed him right on the mouth. "Every year is the best birthday ever."

Rip didn't smile as I pulled away from him, but he watched me with those eyes, and I wondered what he was thinking. But when his hand slipped underneath the back of my black tank top, those fingers I knew like the back of my hand, giving my bare skin another rub, I stopped thinking about everything else. The cloud of bad birthdays before hovering in the dark corner of my head, the dream, my sisters in the other room, how lucky I was, just... *everything*.

At least, I stopped thinking about everything for the ten seconds he waited to say in that quiet, quiet voice, "I'm gonna give you your birthday present now."

That had me raising my eyebrows again. "Right here where anyone can walk in?"

He had a grin on his face as he rolled his eyes and shoved the stool back, getting to his bare feet and circling around the island toward the cabinets above the refrigerator. He opened them easily, pulling out a shoebox-sized thing wrapped in white paper with blue ribbon.

I didn't need to ask to know he'd wrapped it himself. He always did and he never half-assed it. Not ever.

He closed it and turned around to head back toward me, a funny expression on that handsome face. "What? You'd never look up there. It's only pots and pans."

Years and countless cooking lessons with Rip later, and I still hadn't gotten much better at it.

He didn't take a seat again as he set the box down right beside what was left of the cake we were sharing.

I smiled up at him as I undid the ribbon and tore open the wrapping paper as quietly as possible. It wasn't a shoebox but just a regular gift box with a lid on top. "I'm going to be pretty excited if you got me a new respirator," I told him as I lifted it and set it aside.

If I thought it was weird that he didn't chuckle, I didn't think much of it, because the pictures in the box stole every thought out of my head.

I knew I was lucky. I knew that life had worked out in a way that I never would have even dared imagining. I knew that I had so much love in me, I would fight to the death for it.

I was fully aware that I wouldn't change a single thing that had ever happened in my life because it had all gotten me *here*. With this man. With this life. With these people that I loved and loved me back.

But as I looked down at the stack of pictures in that box, I wasn't sure whether to be excited or just a little devastated.

Because I had never seen the face looking back up at me. Not once.

But I knew whom it belonged to. Somehow. Some way. I knew.

The woman couldn't have been any older than eighteen. She was sitting in a pose with a purple gown and cap on, holding a fake diploma in one hand, her expression tight but smiling. Light olive-skinned. Medium-haired. She didn't have the Miller green eyes, but why would she?

"Know who it is?" Rip asked quietly, setting his hand back on my spine.

I gulped and barely managed to get out, "My mom, right?"

That big hand went up and down before he confirmed, "Yeah, baby. It's your mom."

I pulled the top picture off and stared down at the next one. It was another graduation picture with a different background, with her sitting in a different position, still smiling tightly at the camera like she would rather be anywhere else.

It was my mom. *My mom.*

"Took me three years to find this. She was on the drill team for a year. Supposedly she was really good at art, but she didn't like school much," he spoke quietly. "You two look a lot alike, I think."

I flipped to another picture to find the same woman sitting in a drill team uniform, that same expression on her face.

It was my mom.

"She left home right after graduation and no one knew where she went," Rip kept talking. "No one knew she passed away. They didn't know about you or your brother. I thought for sure they were making it up, but they weren't, Luna, baby. I could tell they weren't. They had no idea about you..."

I had to swallow. Press my lips together. Blink because my eyes started burning all of a sudden, and I didn't know what to do. Flicking my gaze up, my hand went to his—to that hand I held every chance I had—, and I asked him before I could think twice about it. "Who is they?"

Lucas Ripley leaned down and brushed his mouth over mine, then pulled back, his free hand going to my cheek. "Your mom's family, baby. If you want to meet them, you've got a grandma and an aunt staying at a hotel, right now, a couple miles away that would really love to see you tomorrow."

"Are you serious?"

"Yeah." His thumb brushed my cheek again. "You all right with that?" he asked softly, with tenderness in that rough voice. "You okay with making the family just a little bigger by meeting them?"

You'd have figured he would have gotten used to my hugs over the years, but he hadn't. He still sighed into my neck like it was something new, and wrapped his arms around me as tight as ever when I threw my arms around him suddenly. Squeezing him tightly. Squeezing him like he meant the world to me and had made my life ten times better by just existing. By just being the person that he was.

I was seriously the luckiest person in the world.

ACKNOWLEDGMENTS

A book is never written without a lot of love and patience from a whole lot of people.

First and foremost, to the greatest readers in the entire universe—I can't thank you enough for your love and support. Every email, message, post and review means the world to me. You guys never cease to amaze me. Seriously. You really are the best readers ever.

To the best reading group, my Slow Burners, thank you for your patience and love. To my pre-readers/friends for putting up with me and the wrecks I call drafts that I send you. Ryn, my friend, I can't thank you enough for not just being an amazing person, but for also helping me out so much with this blurb. (Forgive me for being a stubborn-ass with it.) Kilian, I'm so glad I've got you on my side.

An enormous thank you to Letitia Hasser at RBA Designs for designing the best covers ever and for putting up with me changing my mind all the time. Jeff at Indie Formatting Services, thank you for your excellent formatting and always being so nice. To Virginia and Kim at Hot Tree Editing, thank you for helping me so much with Luna and Rip's story. To Ellie at My Brother's Editor. Kemi Faderin, Lauren Abramo, and Jane Dystel at Dystel, Goderich & Bourret for their support and helping me reach audiences I had no idea were a possibility.

To Eva-4-Evah. This book wouldn't have been the same without you. I'm so grateful to have you in my life. I'm going to summarize how much you helped me with Luna by using two words: banana hammock.

A great big thank you to the greatest family I could ever ask for: Mom, Dad, Ale, Raul, Eddie, Isaac, Kaitlyn, Nana, my Letchford family, and the rest of my Zapata/Navarro family.

Last but never least, Chris, Prince Dorian, and my little prince, Kaiser. Every book is for you three.

ABOUT THE AUTHOR

Mariana Zapata lives in a small town in Colorado with her husband and two oversized children—her beloved Great Danes, Dorian and Kaiser. When she's not writing, she's reading, spending time outside, forcing kisses on her boys, harassing her family, or pretending to write.

Facebook: www.facebook.com/marianazapatawrites

Website: www.marianazapata.com

Instagram: www.instagram.com/marianazapata

Twitter: www.twitter.com/marianazapata_

Mailing List (New Release Information Only): http://marianazapata.us5.list-manage.com/subscribe?u=2a6bcf387be0a19aa73aff297&id=1bf284400f

Printed in Great Britain
by Amazon